# Tiger Ragtime

## CATRIN COLLIER

An Orion paperback

First published in Great Britain in 2006
by Orion
This paperback edition published in 2008
by Orion Books Ltd,
Orion House, 5 Upper Saint Martin's Lane
London, WC2H 9EA
An Hachette Livre UK company

A CIP catalogue record for this book
is available from the British Library.

Typeset by Deltatype Ltd, Birkenhead, Merseyside

Printed and bound in the UK by Mackays, Chatham ME5 8TD

The Orion Publishing Group's policy is to use papers
that are natural, renewable and recyclable products and
made from wood grown in sustainable forests. The logging
and manufacturing processes are expected to conform to
the environmental regulations of the country of origin.

www.orionbooks.co.uk

Harry broke into a cold sweat. 'You hurt David or any member of my family—'

'Did I say I was going to hurt him – or Edyth Slater?' Aled pushed his chair back from the table and rose slowly to his feet. 'She's your sister, Harry, not mine. And, with her husband gone, "footloose and fancy free" as the saying goes.'

'Aled, please—'

'Watch your back, Harry Evans,' Aled cut in ruthlessly. 'Watch it everywhere you go, David Ellis and Edyth Slater are just the beginning.'

'We're brothers . . . '

'That, Harry Evans, is something I will never forget.' Aled returned his gold cigar case and lighter to his pocket and left the room.

Catrin Collier was born and brought up in Pontypridd. After barmaiding and waitressing her way through college, and teaching English and drama at various comprehensive schools, she worked as a social worker and business and management consultant before becoming a full-time writer in 1994. She lives with her husband, two cats and whichever of her children chooses to visit.

Visit her website at www.catrincollier.co.uk.

## By Catrin Collier

### HISTORICAL

Hearts of Gold
One Blue Moon
A Silver Lining
All That Glitters
Such Sweet Sorrow
Past Remembering
Broken Rainbows
Spoils of War
Swansea Girls
Swansea Summer
Homecoming
Beggars & Choosers
Winners & Losers
Sinners & Shadows
Finders & Keepers
Tiger Bay Blues
Tiger Ragtime

### CRIME (as Katherine John)

Without Trace
Midnight Murders
Murder of a Dead Man
By Any Other Name
The Corpse's Tale (Quick Read)
The Amber Knight

### MODERN FICTION (as Caro French)

The Farcreek Trilogy

For my granddaughter, Nicky Belle Anderson,
born the second of May 2006

May she lead a happy and charmed life

# ACKNOWLEDGEMENTS

I would like to thank everyone who helped me research this book and so generously gave of their time and expertise:

All the dedicated staff of the Butetown History and Arts Centre in Tiger Bay who are doing so much to preserve the spirit of the old Tiger Bay and chronicle the truly multicultural community that existed there before so many of its fine buildings were demolished in the 1960s.

Rhondda Cynon Taff's exceptional library service, especially Mrs Lindsay Morris, for her ongoing help and support. Hywel Matthews and Catherine Morgan, the archivists at Pontypridd, and Nick Kelland, the archivist at Treorchy library.

The staff of Pontypridd Museum, Brian Davies, David Gwyer and Ann Cleary, for allowing me to dip into their extensive collection of old photographs and for doing such a wonderful job of preserving the history of Pontypridd.

Absolutely everyone at Orion, especially my editor Yvette Goulden for her encouragement and constructive criticism, Emma Noble, my miracle-working publicist, Juliet Ewers, Sara O'Keeffe, Jenny Page and all the editorial, sales and marketing teams.

And all the booksellers and readers who make writing such a privileged occupation.

And while I wish to acknowledge all the assistance I received, I wish to state that any errors in *Tiger Ragtime* are entirely mine.

Catrin Collier
May 2006

# CHAPTER ONE

Judy Hamilton gazed critically at her reflection in the mirror on her dressing table. Dressed in a borrowed, floor-length gold satin frock, with every visible inch of skin on her face, hands and arms covered with gold greasepaint and her black hair hidden beneath a crocheted gold elastic cap threaded with glass beads, she positively shimmered. She turned sideways and checked her profile. The idea for the costume had been her friend and employer Edyth Slater's. But they had expended so much time and effort in putting together her outfit, and those of all the other members of the Bute Street Blues Band, it would be a waste to wear them just this once. They would certainly turn a few heads if they played their next engagement in one of the dockland pubs dressed like this – even without the greasepaint.

'Why is it you look like a glittering angel while I resemble a tarnished brass effigy on a cathedral tombstone?'

Judy turned her head. Edyth was standing in the open doorway. 'You look nothing of the sort.'

'Gold greasepaint highlights dark skin and makes it glow, but it's rusted mine. I only hope there will be other people in the carnival who look just as peculiar.' Edyth went to the hall table and picked up one of the wickerwork baskets she and Judy had painted gold and filled with paper cornets containing tiny macaroons and coconut biscuits.

'You don't look peculiar – well, no more peculiar than I do,' Judy qualified. 'I wonder what mess my uncles and the others in the band have made with the sticks of greasepaint. I told them how to apply it, but I don't think any of them were listening.' She left her bedroom and scooped up the second basket. 'Ready?'

'As I'll ever be.' Edyth opened the door that led down the stairs into her baker's shop. 'Does everyone feel as idiotic as this when they dress up for a carnival?'

'You've never dressed up for a carnival before?' Judy questioned in astonishment.

'I've been to fancy-dress parties, but a carnival is different. It's public for a start. And it doesn't help that my brother Harry has threatened to bring his entire family down to watch the procession. Thank goodness my parents have taken the rest of the tribe to North Wales on holiday; if they hadn't, I'd have the entire Evans clan laughing at me.'

'Half the fun is being laughed at by your friends and relations. I don't know about carnivals anywhere else, but they're always special in Bute Street. When I was little I used to look forward to them as much as Christmas. Although sometimes I think we had more fun preparing for them, than taking part in the actual parade.'

'I must admit I enjoyed helping to make the costumes and watching the children practise their marching in the park. And listening to you rehearse in the bath,' Edyth teased.

'I wasn't that loud, was I?'

'For the first time in my life I know all the words to more than one song.' Edyth ran down the stairs. She would have tripped over her skirt when she reached the bottom if she hadn't steadied herself on the newel post.

'Careful,' Judy cried.

'I was born clumsy and clumsy I'll always be.'

'The carnival party after the procession is the best.' Judy followed Edyth into the shop. 'It starts as soon as the floats have been judged in Loudon Square, and goes

on until the early hours. Everyone stays until the end –
even the priests, the nuns, the vicars, the children, the old
people . . . '

'Sounds like every Saturday night in the Bay since I
moved here from Pontypridd.' Edyth walked into the
back storeroom. The door to the yard was wedged open
and all seven members of the Bute Street Blues Band were
loading a drum kit into Edyth's baker's cart, which was
unrecognisable beneath layers of gold paper ornamented
with all the glued-on gold and silver shiny tobacco and
sweet wrappings they had managed to scavenge for the
last three months.

'Careful! Break that drum skin and I'll break your
neck,' the band's drummer shouted at Judy's uncle, Tony
King. 'You just knocked it against the cart—'

'He didn't, it just looks like he did from where you're
standing,' Micah Holsten, part-time saxophonist, full-
time pastor of the Norwegian Church and acknowledged
leader of the band, interrupted in an effort to calm the
situation.

'There'll be no room for a mouse, let alone us on the
back of that cart. The drum kit fills it,' Tony grumbled
when they finally managed to heave it into place.

'We'll have to perch on the sides and play our
instruments over the edge.' Micah gave Edyth an apologetic glance. 'I know it's your float, but if we are going to
get all the band and our instruments on the back, you'll
have to sit up front.'

'It's the only place for the non-musical.' Edyth handed
her basket to her driver, Jamie. Sitting alongside him was
her baker, Moody. Only sixteen, the West Indian had
been trained to bake bread, cakes and biscuits by the Jew
who had opened Goldman's bakery and sold it to Edyth
before returning to Poland. At Mordecai Goldman's
suggestion, Edyth had kept Moody on as chief baker and
she hadn't regretted the decision. Not only an expert
baker, Moody had also shown a remarkable aptitude for

passing on his skills and was training two of Judy's cousins as apprentices.

Jamie set Edyth's basket on the bench seat next to him. He was keeping the horses on a tight rein although they looked more likely to fall asleep than bolt.

Micah glanced into Judy's basket. 'What's in the cornets?'

'Macaroons and coconut biscuits.' Judy saw him frown and realised she'd said more than she should have.

'After only six months in business you can afford to give away the stock?' Micah looked keenly at Edyth.

'It's only a few biscuits and the Goldman name is on the paper cornets. It's good advertising,' Edyth replied defensively. 'And don't you all look handsome.'

'Don't change the subject.'

'I'm not,' Edyth countered. It didn't help that Micah was right. She knew she couldn't afford to give away stock.

'The carnival is only once a year, Micah,' Judy's oldest uncle, Jed, reminded.

'So is Easter, and Edyth gave away biscuits to all the Sunday Schools in the Bay then. Next it will be Christmas. No doubt you'll want to give every resident a stocking filled with mince pies?' he mocked.

'Is that what Mr Goldman used to do before I bought the business?' Edyth chose to deliberately misunderstand Micah.

'You know perfectly well he didn't.'

Micah sounded more like an angry husband than an irritated friend. Sensing Edyth's embarrassment, Judy attempted a diversion. 'Jamie, stop touching your face. You're smearing greasepaint over the reins and your costume.'

'It will wipe off the reins and my costume is gold, same as the paint,' Jamie retorted truculently.

'It is not the same at all, because your suit is cloth and stage make-up leaves a horrid stain.'

4

'You should know,' Jamie grumbled. 'You're used to dressing up like a clown, I'm not.'

'Come on, Jamie, less of your moaning – grin and bear it,' his father, Jed, broke in sternly.

'You're used to people laughing at you when you play in the band,' Jamie snapped mutinously.

'I trust they don't laugh.' Micah rubbed his fingertips together to check they were dry before picking up his saxophone case.

'They will when they see you in that get-up.' Jamie glared at Judy. Technically she was his cousin, but as he was fourteen, she nineteen, and they had been brought up in the same street, they were more like brother and sister.

'That is enough, Jamie.' Jed didn't raise his voice but Jamie fell silent. He knew when he had pushed his father's tolerance to the limit.

'All right if we leave our instrument cases in your storeroom, Edyth?' Micah asked.

'Of course.'

Jed pulled his pocket watch from his gold satin waistcoat and opened it. 'It's time we joined the other floats at the assembly point in Church Street.'

Micah watched Edyth close the storeroom door after they had all deposited their cases. 'Lock it,' he advised.

'But I never lock the shop,' she protested.

'The carnival attracts all sorts from miles around,' Jed warned, 'including pickpockets and burglars. No one will be leaving the door to an empty house open on the Bay today.'

'I don't suppose you've locked the front door either.' Micah opened the door again, looked behind it and shook his head disapprovingly. 'You've left all your keys on the hook?'

'It's where they're kept.' Edyth knew she'd been foolish. Common sense should have told her that the carnival would attract an influx of strangers, including a criminal element.

'I'll make sure every outside door is locked and the front ones bolted. Leave a couple of inches for me on the cart, boys. I know I'm thin, but I need more room than you've allowed,' Micah called back, before disappearing inside.

Edyth was handing up the last of the musical instruments to the band squashed on the cart, when Micah returned. He drew Edyth into the doorway.

'Tuck these away safely.' He closed her fingers around her keys. After glancing at the cart to make sure no one was watching them, Micah sneaked a kiss.

Judy glimpsed them embracing and turned her back. Edyth and Micah's affair was the worst kept secret on the Bay. But Edyth had married a man who had deserted her less than two months after their wedding.

For the last six months Edyth had worked almost every hour in the day and most of those in the night to make her bakery a success, and in Judy's opinion her friend was entitled to all the happiness she could get. Even if a few – a very few – straight-laced people said that it was scandalous for the pastor of the Norwegian Church to carry on with a woman who was still, on paper at least, married.

Aled James climbed on deck of the merchant ship heading into Cardiff Docks, leaned against the bulkhead and gazed at his approaching homeland. The red-brick, French Gothic façade of the Pier Head building that dominated the shoreline loomed inexorably closer and he closed his eyes and breathed in half-forgotten scents. The July air was warm, balmy, perfumed with the tang of salt, fish and smoke from the funnels of the surrounding vessels and laced with half-forgotten sounds.

The thud of coal barges knocking into one another as they were hauled down the canal to the waiting ships; the metallic slam of coal trams being fastened on to hoists followed by an avalanche clatter as their loads were tipped into holds; the sharp cries of gulls almost but not quite drowned out by the incessant sound of the ships' hooters. But most evocative of all was the Welsh lilt in the warning shouts and cries of the dockers loading and unloading cargoes. It was music to his ears after fifteen years in America.

'Glad to be home, boss?'

Aled opened his eyes and continued to stare ahead as Freddie Leary stood beside him. 'Yes,' he answered briefly.

'Family coming to meet you, boss?'

Aled turned to the six feet four, red-headed, square-built Irishman he had 'employed' for the past five years. 'I have no family left who would want to own me, Freddie.'

'That's sad, boss. I know what it is to be an orphan. Not that I've any shortage of family with nine brothers and eight sisters.'

'With eighteen of you fighting for food and space it's little wonder you left Ireland,' Aled observed dryly.

'I would never have left, if the Catholic Brothers who took me and my brothers into the institution hadn't pushed me out of the old country. They sent my older brothers to farms but put me on a ship bound for Australia. I was nine years old but they said I was big and fit enough to earn my own bread. They even told me that I was the lucky Leary, off to see the world instead of a field in County Cork. Not that I saw much of the world until I jumped ship two years later in New York, and then America wasn't what I thought it was going to be.'

'What did you think it was going to be, Freddie?' Aled asked curiously. Freddie's heavily muscled bulk was enough to inspire fear in the most hardened thug, which was why he'd paid him, and paid him well, for the last few years. But he doubted that Freddie'd had an original thought in his life.

'Land of opportunity where every man is equal,'

Freddie recited as if he were a child repeating a lesson he had learned by rote but failed to understand.

'That's just a story the Yanks tell children before they're old enough to see through fairy tales, Freddie.' Aled resumed his study of the docks.

'I've seen the captain, boss.' Aled's second 'employee', Aiden Collins, a Cuban–Irish Negro from Havana who was shorter and slighter than Freddie Leary, but somehow managed to look even more menacing, joined them. 'He's arranged for one of the boats to be lowered at the stern of the ship before we dock. He said our papers might not pass muster with immigration.'

'They bloody well should, the money the boss paid for them and our passage,' Freddie swore. 'We could have crossed the Atlantic in style on a cruise ship ten times over for what that captain charged. You want me to sort him for you, boss?'

'No, Freddie. I paid the going rate. A cruise ship would have wanted to see our passports and put our real names on the passenger list.' Aled pulled his seaman's cap down low over his face. He was dressed in a dark sweater and slacks like the other sailors on board, although he, Freddie and Aiden hadn't done a stroke of work on the voyage. 'You told them to send our luggage on to the Windsor Hotel?' Aled checked with Aiden.

'Yes, boss.'

Aled watched dockers, women as well as men, unload potatoes from a low-lying, Irish-registered vessel on the quayside. They slung the sacks they'd filled on to their backs, staggered down the gang plank and dumped them on wooden pallets on the dockside. It brought back memories of the days he'd fought older and heavier boys for a few hours' paid casual work after his mother had succumbed to her fatal illness.

He could still recall the pain of the rope burns on his shoulders, knew how impossible it was to stand upright at the end of ten hours of back-breaking work – how it felt to be too tired to eat or even sleep.

He'd believed the offer of a job on board ship with regular meals to be heaven-sent after his mother had died. Disillusionment had set in when he'd received his first whipping before the ship had even left Welsh waters. He'd come a long way in fifteen years but he had never forgotten the skinny, ragged urchin he'd been. Or the people who had turned their backs on him and his mother and allowed them both to starve, and her to die in squalor.

He'd learned a lot in America: how to survive in a slum, how to rise from the bottom of the social pecking order to the top, how to make money – and use the power it bestowed. He'd also learned the value of fear and, most important of all, how to stay one step ahead of the law. If he hadn't left America when he had, he, Freddie and Aiden might well have ended up in Alcatraz. Fortunately for all three of them, he'd amassed enough money to pay their passage and settle anywhere in the world.

Only one reason had drawn him back to Wales – revenge. Unlike fifteen years ago, he now had enough money to buy whatever he needed to destroy the people who had tried to destroy him – and succeeded in destroying his mother.

The crowds lining the pavements in Bute Street heard the carnival procession long before the first of the floats rounded the corner and came into view. Two palomino horses, their golden manes and tails braided with red and black ribbons, pulled an open cart. A broomstick-suspended banner above the driver's seat spelled out 'GOLDMAN'S BAKERY: THE MIDAS TOUCH' in shimmering gold foil letters on a black background.

'As usual our Edyth's being over optimistic. I've seen her shop's accounts.' Edyth's brother, Harry Evans, slipped his arm around his wife Mary's shoulders to protect her from the people who were jostling forward in hope of gaining a better view.

'The bakery is making money, isn't it?' Mary asked in concern.

'Edyth only bought it six months ago; it's early days,' Harry answered evasively. Like his parents, sisters and brother, Harry had assumed that Edyth would return to their parents' house in Pontypridd when her husband had abandoned her in Cardiff's Butetown after only a few weeks of married life. Instead, she had astounded them all by emptying her bank account of her childhood savings and negotiating an overdraft with a bank which had enabled her to buy the bakery in Bute Street. She had kept the name 'Goldman' because everyone in the area was familiar with it. And playing on the 'Gold' part of the name, she had taken down the canvas back and sides of her delivery cart and transformed it into a glittering tableau.

Edyth, Moody and Jamie were crammed side by side on the seat behind the horses. The boys were dressed in floor-length gold cloaks that matched Edyth's frock, and all three wore foil crowns studded with wine-gum 'jewels' and gold make-up. Moody and Edyth were holding gold baskets and tossing paper cornets from them to the children lining the pavements.

Behind them, in the body of the cart, the Bute Street Blues Band, dressed in gold rayon suits, gold make-up and shiny gold boaters, with the exception of Judy who was dressed in an identical frock to Edyth's, were belting out a rousing rendition of 'On the Sunny Side of the Street'. Judy's voice rose, husky and true, above those of the children who marched on either side of the cart, dressed in green, their small faces framed by yellow crêpe paper 'sunflower' petals.

Mary's brother David lifted Harry and Mary's toddler

daughter on to his shoulders, held her hands to steady her and stared mesmerised at Edyth.

'I hope that gold paint comes off easily,' Mary observed practically.

'If it doesn't they'll all be looking odd for a while.' Harry glanced at David before waving to Edyth to attract her attention.

'Isn't that the band that played at your sister's wedding, Harry?' Mary asked when the float drew alongside them.

'Yes, there are Judy and Micah Holsten.' Harry shouted a greeting, but his voice was lost in the music and the buzzing of a jazz band of young girls, led by two drum majorettes that followed the cart.

'Look, Ruthie darling, Auntie Edyth's seen you.' Harry caught his daughter's hand.

'Sweets for the sweet.' Edyth tossed half a dozen cornets towards her niece but all six were scooped up by young boys before either Harry or David could catch one.

'I'll keep one for you, Ruth,' Edyth called out as the cart passed.

Harry cupped his hands around his mouth. 'See you in Loudon Square, sis.'

Edyth nodded to show him she'd understood. Micah leaned over the side of the cart and played a few bars of the saxophone just for Ruth, before the procession moved on.

It wasn't until the jazz band had been supplanted by another float that David realised Ruth was imitating the noise the 'sunflowers' had made by blowing into their paper 'trumpets'.

'Bit noisier than the farm, isn't it, Ruthie?' he murmured absently, staring at Edyth's back.

The crowd shifted, clearing a space around them. Harry handed their six-month-old son to Mary, lifted his daughter from David's shoulders and set her on his own.

'Sweeps.' Ruth struggled to free her hands from her father's but Harry kept a firm grip on both of them.

'If what they say about it being lucky to have a sweep cross your path is true, we'll have more than our fair share of good fortune today, Ruth,' said Mary with a smile.

A coal cart pulled by a pair of black shire horses had been transformed into a Victorian chimney sweeps' tableau. Small boys in ragged, coal-blackened trousers and shirts, holding flat-topped brushes and wearing top hats fashioned from black crêpe paper and cardboard were clustered around a chimney, which, judging from its cracked and sorry state, had been scavenged from a scrap yard. Two lines of adolescent girls in grass skirts and flower-decked blouses danced alongside the cart, shaking home-made maracas made from tins filled with stones.

'That costume looks a bit draughty even for summer,' Harry commented, when a gust of wind sent the strands dancing, revealing the bathing costumes the girls were wearing underneath.

'Trust you to notice.' There was no jealousy in Mary's comment, only fond amusement. She glanced at her younger brothers and sister. All three were running after Edyth's cart. 'Where are they off to?'

'Loudon Square,' Harry guessed. 'First there gets the best spot in the park close to the bands and the pickings of anything that's left in the way of treats that were thrown from the floats.'

'Will they be all right?'

'They will, Mary', David said, 'but I'll go with them just to be sure. You stay here and watch the rest of the parade.' He had an ulterior motive for volunteering to look out for the youngers. As Harry had said, the first ones into the small park in the centre of Loudon Square would get the best position. But it wasn't the view David was interested in.

He had fallen hopelessly in love with Edyth the first

time he had met her. Drunk and devastated after she had married, he had jumped off a bridge into the river Taff. His attempt at suicide had left him with fractured bones, but they had pained him less than his broken heart. His physical injuries had healed, but it had taken the news that Edyth's husband had deserted her and she was seeking to annul her marriage to heal his shattered spirits.

His two younger brothers were already swallowed up by the throng flowing into Loudon Square. Undeterred, David called out to his younger sister, Martha, and ran after her.

The crowd heading into Loudon Square from Christina Street forced the taxi driver to slam on his brakes.

'Why have we stopped?' Aled demanded from the back.

'Because of these idiots.' The driver slid his window open. 'Don't you dare put your hand on that bonnet, nipper,' he shouted at a child about to steady himself on the cab.

The child stuck his tongue out before running to his mother. Once his hand was firmly locked in hers, he turned and stuck it out a second time. The driver glanced into his rear-view mirror and eyed his passengers. All three were dressed in unseasonably thick black woollen sailors' jackets and black peaked caps, but he knew they weren't seamen. Their hands were too clean and soft and there was something menacing about them. Even if the two he'd marked as 'bruisers' hadn't addressed the tall, slim, fair-haired man with piercing blue eyes as 'Boss' he would have guessed from their deference that he was in charge.

The tallest and largest of the three had the height, build and battered facial features of a heavyweight boxer. But the slighter man who was perched on the drop-down seat facing his two companions had dead eyes, which he found even more disturbing.

He glanced back out of the windscreen. Just as he was about to move off, the blond man opened the door. The driver cursed and thrust his foot on the brakes a second time.

'You trying to kill yourself . . . sir?' he added, only just stopping himself from calling the man something less polite.

'I need fresh air.' Aled stepped outside. 'You remember the name of the hotel, Freddie?'

'The Windsor?' the bruiser who'd sat alongside him mumbled through badly fitting false teeth.

'The street?' he checked.

'Stuart Street.'

'Put my luggage in the bedroom of my suite when it arrives and make sure your rooms are on the same floor. I'll be along shortly.'

'You don't want one of us to come with you, boss?' Aiden asked.

'No.' The reply was finite.

'But, boss . . . '

'Nothing's going to happen to me at a carnival. Don't worry – your meal ticket is safe, Aiden. Don't forget to tip the driver.' Aled pulled his sailor's cap down to cover most of his face and walked away.

The taxi driver watched Aled stroll into the square and filed away a mental description. The police occasionally asked him if he'd seen any 'suspicious characters' and had twice tipped him five bob when he'd been able to give them what they wanted. He had a funny feeling that the coppers might be asking questions about these three men sooner rather than later, and over the years he had learned to respect his instincts.

He'd marked the two bruisers down as hired thugs, but the blond man looked more dangerous. Despite his workmen's clothes he had the air of authority that came with money – and lots of it. He couldn't even hazard a guess why someone like him would want to stay in

Butetown, but he sensed that it wouldn't be for any good reason.

'This will be the first time David's seen Edyth since he left hospital. Do you think he really has got over her?' Mary asked Harry anxiously.

Harry wished he could reassure his wife, but he knew Mary would see through any platitudes. 'I don't know the answer to that question any more than you do, darling.' He stepped forward so Ruth could see a Noah's ark float crammed with 'bird' toddlers dressed in capes covered with chicken feathers. They were surrounded by older children in animal costume who were having difficulty keeping the younger ones away from the edge of the cart. 'Yes, Ruthie, monkeys.'

'And teddy bears,' she cried in delight.

'I've never heard mention of Noah rounding up a pair of teddy bears, but as they're here now, he must have.'

Mary knew Harry was talking to Ruth so he wouldn't have to discuss David's obsession with Edyth, but she refused to drop the subject. 'What if David is still in love with Edyth?'

'If he is, he is. There is nothing we can do about it.' Harry didn't want to consider what his headstrong brother-in-law might do, should Edyth reject him a second time.

'Harry.' Mary touched his arm.

'All we can do is be there to help David pick up the pieces should Edyth break his heart a second time, darling.'

'You do know that Edyth has never encouraged him.' Much as Mary loved her brother, she wasn't blind to his faults and she had grown to love and regard all of Harry's family as her own; especially Edyth, who hadn't allowed the disaster of her marriage to sour her, or affect her ability to turn any family gathering, no matter how small, into a party.

'I know,' Harry mused thoughtfully. 'That's why I find his fixation with her so difficult to understand.'

Aled James stood behind a lamp-post across the street from Harry Evans and his family and watched them. He hadn't seen Harry for twenty-three years, but he had recognised him as soon as he'd caught sight of him through the taxi window because Harry was a mirror image of himself. They could have been twins. Same height, same slim upright figure, same shade of pale blond hair and blue eyes.

The only difference between him and Harry had been in their upbringing – and their fortune. His mother had told him before she died that although Harry had been born a bastard the same as him, their father, Mansel James's family had left every penny the family owned to Harry, simply because, unlike her, Harry's mother was middle class. The injustice of the James's family's decision had burned within him every day since.

He looked from the attractive, beautifully dressed dark-haired woman clinging to Harry's arm to the smiling baby Harry was carrying, and the toddler holding Harry's wife's hand. If things had been different – would that have been him? Wealthy, secure and happily married . . .

'Hello, sailor, looking for a good time?'

Aled eyed the woman who had propositioned him. He had been about to tell her to push off but to his amazement he recognised her too. She had dyed her hair red, but even without the standard prostitute's trademark he would have guessed her profession from her skimpy organza frock and obvious lack of underclothes. The frock was transparent and, considering her age, which he knew to be around the late thirties, the body beneath it wasn't in bad shape.

'I'm always looking for a good time, Anna. I'd have

thought you'd have remembered that much about me. Although it has been a long time.'

She stared at him. 'How long?'

'Fifteen years.'

She continued to look blankly at him. 'I've a good memory, but I haven't met that many Yanks, and none who look like you.'

'I didn't always have an American accent. And when we last saw one another I was a young lad. You were my mother's apprentice.'

'Apprentice,' she repeated indignantly. 'I was never apprenticed to a trade in my life . . . '

'Try the one you're in now, Anna.'

'You've mixed me up with someone else.' She went to move on. He grabbed her elbow. She froze.

'I'll scream if you don't let me go.'

'As if anyone will take any notice of a woman screaming in Bute Street. Come on, Anna, I'll buy you dinner in the Windsor. We'll wash it down with champagne and vintage cognac while we chat about old times. And afterwards you can bring me up to date with what's been happening in the Bay since I left.'

'The Windsor?' Her eyes rounded.

'The Windsor,' he repeated.

She snorted. 'They wouldn't allow me in through their front door.'

'They wouldn't dare object to a woman I choose to entertain in my suite. I'll be paying too much for the privilege of living in it.' He decided he'd teased her long enough. 'I bet you never thought when Maisie's boy Aled sailed out of Cardiff Docks fifteen years ago that he'd be back with enough money in his pocket to move into the Windsor and entertain you in style.'

'Aled Cooper!' she exclaimed. 'You're little Aled Cooper!'

'Aled James now, Anna. I use my father's name.'

'I never met him.'

'Neither did I,' he said dryly.

'You were so small and skinny, you looked half starved. And you were always bloody angry about something or other. You used to come back to the house covered in bruises after fighting boys twice your size . . . '

'I'm older and wiser, Anna. I pay people to fight my battles for me now. Dinner tonight, eight o'clock? Ask for me at the desk, I'll tell them I'm expecting you.'

'It's carnival night.'

'So?'

'I'm hoping to make at least a fiver. I run my own house now, and own it, outright. I have the deeds to prove it,' she said proudly.

'How many girls?'

'Six. And even if I say so myself, they're bloody good. The cream of the docks' crop. You must pay us a visit one night. We cater for all tastes, and I'll see you all right. On the house, for old times' sake. Your mother, God rest her soul, was good to me whenever she had a few bob and I didn't.'

'Which wasn't often.' Aled glanced across the road. Harry Evans and his family were walking towards Loudon Square. The festivities would be going on for hours yet. 'Far be it from me to stop a working girl from working. How about I buy you a drink now, in the Jug and Platter in West Bute Street?'

'Your mother's favourite pub.'

'It used to be,' he agreed.

'And you'll still buy me dinner if I come round to the Windsor tomorrow?'

'The best the house can provide.'

She shook her head. 'Who would have thought it? Little Aled Cooper.'

'James,' he reminded her shortly. 'Cooper is dead and buried.'

There was something in the tone of his voice that

carried a warning. 'James it is. And to think I tried to pick you up.'

He offered her his arm. 'Is your tipple still gin and it?'

'Fancy you remembering that.' She smiled.

It hadn't been difficult – gin and it had been his mother's favourite tipple too.

# CHAPTER TWO

It took David half an hour to fight his way through to Loudon Square. He wasn't only hampered by the crowds. His sister insisted on stopping and staring at the costumes of the revellers every few minutes, and by the time they reached the park in the centre of the square the parade had ended and the floats had drawn up and ringed the perimeter. Families had spread out blankets and coats and were camped on every available inch of space inside the railings, making it difficult to walk between them.

David spotted Edyth as soon as he approached the park. She was still sitting next to her driver on her baker's cart, shaking her head at a crowd of young children who had gathered around it, hands outstretched in hope of scavenging a cornet.

'I'm sorry. I've given out all the biscuits. But if you come with your mother to pick up your bread on Monday morning, I'll see if I can find you something.' To emphasise her words she tipped her basket upside down and hoped that Moody had kept the cornets she had set aside for Ruth safe.

David started towards her, but hesitated when he realised he didn't know what to say to her or how he'd react if she mentioned his stay in hospital. In the event he needn't have worried, she called out to him the moment she saw him.

'David, how lovely to see you. I would kiss your cheek if you weren't so smart and clean. The last thing I want to do is smear your clothes with make-up.'

'I wouldn't mind.' His cheeks burned as he spoke.

'Mary would, and she does your laundry.' Edyth looked around. 'Where are Harry, Mary and the others?'

'Somewhere behind me. I came on ahead to look after my sister and brothers ... ' His voice tailed. He'd volunteered to look after them but he didn't have a clue where any of them were.

'There they are.' She pointed to a spot inside the park. 'I can see them sitting in front of the Bute Street Blues Band. The musicians couldn't wait to get off the float. It was so cramped back there they could hardly breathe let alone play. Isn't Judy a great singer?'

'She is.' He dutifully glanced at Judy, who was leading the band's audience in a chorus of 'Tiger Rag'. 'Can I help you down?' He held out his arms.

'In a moment.' Edyth turned to her driver. 'Jamie, they'll be announcing the winning floats any minute. As soon as they have, you can take the cart back to the shop and put the horses in the stable. Once they are bedded down, you're free until you have to harness the cart at six o'clock on Monday morning.'

'Can I wash off this muck and put on ordinary clothes?'

He looked so miserable she laughed. 'Something tells me you didn't enjoy being part of the carnival.'

'I didn't.' He had the grace to smile.

'Sorry, but it would be bad form if you drove off before the judges announced the winners. It would look like we were throwing a tantrum because we didn't expect to win.'

'You're bound to get first prize. You were easily the best float in the parade,' David gushed.

'Thank you, but I know we weren't. The Noah's ark was.' Edyth smiled at her driver. 'Five more minutes at the most. And thank you. Considering the amount of noise, you did a great job of managing the team.'

'Stan and Olly are bomb proof.' Jamie flicked the reins

lightly over the horses that had been named after Laurel and Hardy.

A hush descended over the crowd. Edyth shaded her eyes against the sunlight and saw the Catholic priest, Father Reilly, climb on to a small platform that had been lashed together from odd bits of wood. Someone handed him a megaphone.

'The standard of the floats this year was remarkably high. Well done, all those who participated in the carnival. We judges had a difficult decision to make and I know we're not going to please everyone but here goes,' he shouted.

The priest was hemmed in by leaders of the various communities who had made their home in the Bay. Edyth recognised representatives from the Welsh Methodist and Baptist chapels, Hindu temple, Muslim mosque, Buddhist temple, Jewish synagogue and Greek Orthodox Church as well as the Reverend Alan Spicer, who had succeeded her husband Peter to the post of parish vicar of the Anglican Church in Wales. He saw Edyth watching and nodded to her. She nodded curtly back.

Both the Reverend and his wife had been overtly friendly towards her, insisting that their housekeeper bought all their bread, biscuits and cakes at her baker's. But Edyth's experience with Peter was too recent and raw for her to accept sympathy. And it didn't help that whenever the Reverend or Mrs Spicer singled her out, she felt that they were only doing so out of pity and their idea of Christian charity.

Father Reilly raised his voice. 'Third prize goes to the boxing club's sweeps' float.'

A resounding cheer shattered the hush. Edyth applauded along with everyone else when the battered and retired boxer who ran the make-shift gym where the boys trained pushed the youngest member of his club towards the priest.

The boy took the cup and, in response to a shout of,

'Hold it up, so everyone can see it,' waved it above his head, which led to an escalation of the cheering. It was several minutes before the priest could continue.

'Second, Goldman's Midas Touch.'

Micah stepped past David, edged up to the cart and pitched his voice below the cheers. 'They didn't dare not give you a cup, lest you cut down on the giveaways at Christmas and Easter.'

Edyth chose to ignore him. She nudged Jamie. 'Go and get it.'

Jamie stared at her in astonishment. 'Me, Mrs Slater!'

'You drove us, didn't you?'

Trying to look as though he wasn't enjoying the attention, Jamie handed the reins over to Edyth, clambered down from the cart and went to accept the cup. When he raised it above his head, the applause and cheering was even louder than it had been for the boxing club.

Edyth leaned towards Micah. 'See what you get for giveaways.'

'Cheers, cups and giveaways don't fill the till, pay the wages or buy the flour,' he muttered.

'And the winner of this year's carnival is . . . ' Silence reigned over the park once more. 'Christina Street's, Noah's ark.'

The din that greeted the announcement was deafening. Micah made his way back to the band so they could play the winning floats out of the square. Edyth held out her hand and hauled Jamie back on to the cart.

'Drive around twice with the other winning floats before you go back to the shop.'

Jamie took the reins from her. He held them in one hand and set the cup on his head with the other. 'Is there anything else you want me to do besides take care of the horses, Mrs Slater?' he shouted above the noise as she prepared to jump down.

'No, but thank you for asking. And don't attempt to

put the top and back on the cart. Wait until Moody and the boys can help you on Monday morning.'

Micah and the rest of the band struck up 'I'm Sitting on Top of the World'. David held out his arms to Edyth but she jumped clear of him, barely touching his fingers. 'The greasepaint,' she said by way of explanation.

The breath caught in David's throat and blood rushed to his cheeks. He felt more of a country bumpkin than ever when he was around Edyth and he knew it showed. 'Jamie called you Mrs Slater. I thought you and Peter were divorced.'

'Our marriage is being annulled but it isn't yet. I'm waiting for him to sign and send me the papers.'

'So you still use your married name?'

'I moved to the Bay as Peter's wife. He may have left me but we're still legally married. I can't pretend otherwise,' she replied crisply.

'He must have been mad,' he blurted.

'More like I was mad to marry him in the first place,' she dismissed. 'But it's a lovely day. Do we have to talk about Peter?'

'Of course not.' He dared to look into her eyes. She smiled and he stared down at his boots.

She saw his embarrassment and tried to ease it. 'I know I should wait for you to ask, David, but do you want to dance?'

'I'd love to.' He offered her his arm. After glancing at her hand to make sure the greasepaint was dry, she took it just as the last cart disappeared up Bute Street and the band stopped playing.

The vibrant echoes of Caribbean steel drums filled the air. Scores of youngsters, boys and girls, ran into the only clear area in the centre of the park, the pitch the judges had occupied. They began to leap and gyrate to the throbbing beat with an abandon David wished he could emulate. But the long weeks he had spent in hospital recuperating had stiffened his joints and sapped his self-confidence. He doubted that he could manage a waltz with his former skill, let alone his favourite Charleston. And, if this was a dance, it was wilder than anything Harry's sisters had taught him.

A slim, attractive girl with skin the colour of dark chocolate looped a blue silk scarf around Moody's neck and roped him towards her. Reaching for his gold boater she placed it on her own head, and stood, legs apart, body pulsating, blowing him kisses.

'Is that your baker?' David asked Edyth.

'It is,' she confirmed. 'I never knew he could dance like that.'

'I've never seen anything like it.'

'That makes two of us,' Edyth concurred. 'Shall we sit – or rather stand – this one out?'

Wary of losing her in the crowd, David covered the hand Edyth had hooked into his elbow with his own. But he couldn't stop staring at the girl with the silk scarf. She was dressed modestly in a high-necked, calf-length, button-through cotton frock, yet her movements and the expression in her eyes exuded a sensuality that sent a peculiar thrill – half excitement, half fear – down his spine.

He had been to dozens of dances since Mary had married Harry, but had seen no one move like that girl. Edyth and her four sisters were considered good dancers but their steps were refined in comparison to the coloured girl's. It was the difference between the Valetta and the Indian war dances he had seen in the cowboy films Harry had taken the family to see in Pontardawe.

He noticed that the girl's movements were gradually being adopted by the people around her, including, to his astonishment, members of the Bute Street Blues Band. Even Micah, who was the pastor of a church. But unlike the chapel minister in the Swansea Valley, Micah obviously had no qualms about making a spectacle of himself.

David stepped alongside Edyth, leaned against the

railings and continued to watch the dancers. The drumming proved intoxicating. The raw sexuality of the girl's movements both embarrassed and fascinated him, engendering feelings he would have found impossible to articulate.

Despite his misgivings, he found himself tapping his feet and swaying to the rhythm, all the while beset by the oddest feeling that the dancers were simply creations of, and extensions of, the music. When it ceased they would disappear, fading into nothingness like the early-morning mist above the reservoir in the valley below his farm.

The drumming slowed to a languorous conclusion. The beats grew fewer and softer until he couldn't be certain the musicians were even hitting the skins. The dancers slowed and wiped the perspiration from their faces with coloured handkerchiefs. Micah left his partner and fell back alongside them.

'Do you think it will take over from the tango?' he asked.

'Possibly, but I can't see me adding it to my repertoire,' Edyth replied.

'Coward.' He turned to David. 'Enjoying the carnival?'

David nodded. The beat picked up again, as first one drummer then another and another began pounding their instruments.

'I saw your feet tapping. Come on.' Judy grabbed David's hand and pulled him into the circle of dancers. David tried to protest but his voice was drowned by the music, and when he tried to retreat back to the railings, Judy grasped both his hands in hers so he couldn't escape.

He glanced around self-consciously. There were onlookers but they appeared to be more interested in chatting to one another than watching the dancers and the people around them were too engrossed in their own enjoyment to care about anyone else. Taking his cue from Judy he tried to follow her steps, and moments later he was waving his arms and leaping with the rest of them, stiffness forgotten, hypnotised by the drumming that seemed to be keyed to his heartbeat.

The drummers quickened the pace, hitting their instruments louder and louder until they reached a fast-paced crescendo that ended abruptly. Silence reigned, so sudden and absolute it seemed incongruously deafening. David stepped away from Judy and staggered.

'I'm sorry, I should have remembered you'd been ill,' Judy apologised.

'I'm fine now.' David only realised he'd snapped when Judy flinched.

'You're a good dancer,' she complimented. 'But I knew that the first time I saw you do the Charleston with Edyth at her sister's wedding last year.'

'Of course, you were in the band,' he commented absently, looking around for Edyth. She was still standing talking to Micah. 'Shall we join the others?'

'If you like, although the Green Swing Band will be playing more conventional dance music in a moment.'

'Harry and Mary are here somewhere. And I promised to keep an eye on my younger brothers and sister . . . '

Judy recognised an excuse when she heard one but she had only been trying to be kind to David. She knew from a few things she'd overheard Edyth say to her brother Harry that David's 'accident' hadn't been entirely straightforward. And from the way David was watching Edyth it was obvious he had a crush on her. 'Let's ask Edyth and Mr Holsten if they've seen them. If they haven't, I'll help you to look for them.'

'Gin and it.' Aled set the third refill he'd bought Anna in front of her.

'And the last this afternoon, or I'll be sozzled.'

'Anna Hughes, lose her head for gin?' he questioned sceptically. 'I don't believe it. Remember that bottle we shared the night before I left.' He pulled his chair close to hers and sipped his cognac.

'We needed it after burying your mother that afternoon. Call me sentimental, but I put up a grave marker – nothing fancy, just a wooden cross with her name and date of death. I wasn't sure of her date of birth.'

'If ever I knew it, I can't remember it.'

She sat back and studied him. 'Whatever you've been doing for the past fifteen years has agreed with you. You're looking well.'

'Thank you. I could say the same of you.'

'So, what have you been doing?' she asked directly when he didn't volunteer any information.

'Growing up, seeing the world, learning a few tricks,' he replied casually.

'Where?'

'Here, there and everywhere.'

'America by the sound of you.'

'For some of the time.'

'You're not going to give me any straight answers, are you?' She took a packet of small cigars from her handbag and opened it.

'Have one of mine, they're Cuban.' He slipped his hand inside his coat and pulled out a solid-gold cigar case. He pressed the catch and it flew open to reveal a neat row of slim black cigars.

She took one. 'Nice case.'

'Nothing but the best.' There was no trace of irony in his voice.

She rolled the cigar between her finger and thumb and sniffed it appreciatively. 'So, at the risk of being ignored again, how long are you staying in Tiger Bay?'

'That depends on whether or not I find the right business opportunity.'

'Such as?'

'I'm thinking of opening a nightclub.'

'That costs money.'

28

'Really?' He smiled. 'I hadn't thought of that.'

'You always were a joker, Aled.'

'How many clubs are there down here?'

'A few.'

'How many can hold between two and three hundred people, put on musical shows with chorus girls, singers and entertainment and offer gambling? Roulette wheels, blackjack, poker . . . '

She burst out laughing. 'It is a long time since you've been in the Bay. I can think of half a dozen cellars and small private bars where you can get a drink out of hours. The biggest casinos around here are still the open-air ones on the street corners, which the police blow the whistle on when the mood takes them. Some of the local bands play in the pubs and clubs, but dancing girls.' She shook her head and smiled. 'Where do you think you've landed, Aled, Paris?'

'Paris night life was probably dull before the Moulin Rouge opened. The right club could put Tiger Bay on the map, provided it was run by the right man. Where do you and your girls pick up most of your customers?'

She drew on her cigar. 'Same place your mother did when she was on the game: the street and the pubs that let us in. Although the bloody landlords take a cut. They demand a bob for every man they see us walking out of their door. They keep a book and it's pay up or get out the next time we try to work there. Friday and Saturday nights are our busiest. We all have our regulars but things aren't what they were twenty or even ten years ago. Trade is bad, but enough crache have business that takes them in and out of the banks, shipping offices and coal exchange in Bute Street – and afterwards to my house for a little relaxation, to bring in a trickle of customers. And there are always the sailors – like yourself.'

He knew she'd thrown out the last remark in the hope that he'd tell her more about what he'd been doing. 'Any good buildings for sale, lease or rent in Bute Street?'

'One or two.' She eyed him suspiciously. 'What trade you aiming for in this club of yours, if it ever opens its doors?'

'The idle and not-so-idle rich who like to drink out of hours and who don't mind paying a premium for plush surroundings. Customers who want to be entertained by professional musical shows. Men who enjoy ogling pretty girls. The gamblers who enjoy a flutter on the horses, dogs and roulette wheel. Plus serious card players in search of a straight game with high stakes.'

'The first thing I learned when I moved to Tiger Bay is that there's no such thing as a straight card game.'

'I'll invite you to play with me and my boys some time, Anna.' Aled flicked the ash from his cigar into the tray on the table.

'Your boys? You're married.'

It was his turn to laugh. 'The ones I employ. They enjoy a game of strip poker.'

'That will cost them if they want my girls to play.'

'Do you do the negotiating for the girls who live in your house?'

'If they ask me, but I don't take a cut. I charge a flat rate of three pounds a week to cover all costs.'

'What about special parties?'

'It's been a couple of years since I organised one of those. All the businessmen around here have cut back on entertaining.'

'But you're still in the market to run them?'

'If someone offered me enough. You asking?' she questioned bluntly.

'I might be able to put some business your and your girls' way?'

'The last thing I or my girls need is a pimp to cream off more of our hard-earned cash the way the pub landlords do.'

'I wasn't talking about pimping. High class has high overheads. And, to go back to your question about the trade I'm aiming for, it's men of means who like to watch pretty girls dancing and singing while they enjoy a drink and a flutter. Some of them might be happy to pay – and pay handsomely – to be entertained in private afterwards.'

'And you'd want a finder's fee.'

'No.'

'Then you'd allow us to use this club of yours – if you open it – as a free pick-up point?'

'No, I want to run a clean place, publicly that is. The kind of place a man could take his sweet aged mother to, if the mood took him. Privately is different, but I'll talk to you again, if and when I find the right place. But I warn you now, if you and your girls ever want to visit you'll have to look top drawer, Anna.'

'You cheeky sod,' she said indignantly. 'You suggesting I look anything less?'

'Not me, Anna. I know who paid the rent on my mother's room the week she died. And I haven't forgotten that gold sovereign you gave me when I sailed out. You told me to hang on to it because I could cash it anywhere in the world if I needed to.'

'And did you?'

He felt in his pocket and laid the coin on the table. 'I've pawned it once or twice but I marked it so I could always redeem it.'

'Sentimental sod underneath that hard-baked crust, aren't you?' Anna said fondly.

'I've never had much to be sentimental about.'

A slim young girl, who looked barely out of childhood, walked into the bar and made a beeline for their table. She had a prominent nose, strong dark features, olive skin, black hair, and was dressed in an even lower-cut, skimpier, more transparent frock than Anna's. 'Lend us a tanner for a drink, will you, Anna?' She turned a pocket inside out in the skirt of her dress. 'It'll save me a walk back to the house. A bloody pickpocket's just nicked my purse.'

'Was there a lot in it?' Anna asked.

'A bob. I've more sense than to bring out more on carnival day.' She saw Aled eyeing her and gave him a practised professional smile.

Anna looked from Aled to the girl. 'Gertie, this is Mr James, an old friend of mine. Aled, meet Gertie, my youngest. She's been living in my house for six months but she's a quick learner.'

'How quick?' Aled continued to study the girl.

'How long have you been at sea?' Anna asked.

'Long enough,' Aled answered. 'Put your purse away, Anna, I'll buy Gertie a drink. In fact, how about I buy a bottle and we go back to your room, Gertie?'

'It'll cost you,' she retorted boldly.

'How much?' Aled grinned in amusement.

Gertie flashed a quick glance at Anna who gave an almost imperceptible nod. 'Two bob, and a bob for the barman,' she said boldly.

'For the rest of the afternoon?'

'If you want to stay that long,' Gertie answered carelessly.

Aled put his hand in his pocket and pulled out two half crowns. 'A bob for the barman, the rest is for the brandy, make sure it's the best French and I'll expect change.'

'Can't I keep it?' Gertie pouted.

'We'll finish negotiating after you've delivered the goods, Gertie, not before,' Aled said firmly.

'I'll be as quick as I can.' Gertie left the table and went to the bar.

'You'll find her accommodating enough.' Anna produced a small printed card. 'My telephone number.'

'You're ahead of the times.' Aled took it and stowed it into his top pocket.

'Second telephone to go into a private address on the Bay, after the doctor and before the vicarage. Call in any time, and don't think I've forgotten about that dinner you promised me in the Windsor. I'll hold you to it.'

'Tomorrow night, eight o'clock?'

'I'll be there.' She left the table.

Aled watched her walk to the door. A middle-aged man staggered in before she opened it. Anna smiled at him. He returned her smile. She took his arm. They left the bar together.

Aled finished his drink and waited for Gertie. He didn't doubt for one minute that Anna would have her fiver by the end of the night.

'I've been looking for you everywhere, Harry.' David tapped Aled on the shoulder as he stepped out of the pub into West Bute Street. 'Where are the others? I lost sight of them an hour ago.'

Aled stared silently at David.

'Harry—'

'My name is not Harry, young man,' Aled interrupted coolly.

'Stop messing around . . . ' David faltered. The man he was talking to was blond and blue-eyed and a mirror image of Harry, but he was also dressed in plain dark working clothes, something he'd never seen Harry wear. And he was with a girl who was showing more flesh than he'd ever seen a girl display off a picture postcard.

Aled pointed across the road. 'I believe that is the man you are looking for.'

David turned and saw Harry standing next to Mary. 'You . . . Harry . . . you're exactly alike . . . ' David stammered.

'There does appear to be a similarity.' Aled offered Gertie his arm. 'There is a young girl singing with a band in the park I'd like to take a closer look at before we get down to business, Gertie.'

'I like a bit of music.' Gertie tucked the bottle of brandy she was carrying under her arm.

'Good afternoon.' Aled lifted his cap to David and sauntered away.

It was then David realised that there were differences between Harry and the man he'd spoken to after all. Apart from the harsh American accent, there was ice in the man's eyes. Harry's were warm and friendly; this man looked as though he were evaluating everything and everyone around him with a view to auctioning them off, just like the dealers in Brecon's Cattle Market.

'I tell you, Harry, he could have been you,' David insisted. They were helping themselves to a selection of the sandwiches and home-baked cakes and biscuits that the women of the Bay had set out on kitchen tables that they'd carried into the streets. The smaller children were picnicking on the blankets laid on the ground in the park. Groups of adults were perched on window sills in the side streets off the square or standing in groups eating and gossiping with plates and cups in hand. The younger housewives were ferrying jugs of home-made lemonade and trays of tea out of their houses and the older women were keeping an eagle eye on the tables, swooping down the moment a plate was emptied and replacing it with a full one.

'They say everyone has a double somewhere.' The maxim rolled easily off Harry's tongue but he glanced at Mary to check she was out of earshot. There were some things he'd never told her about his past, simply because he preferred not to think about them. He'd been five years old when his mother, Sali, had married his stepfather. Lloyd Evans had never made him feel less than his son by birth and both his parents had tried to answer his questions about his real father. He knew Mansel James had planned to marry his mother but had been murdered before she had known she was pregnant. And, after being shown photographs of Mansel, he also knew that he looked exactly like him.

Since he had taken an interest in the businesses he had inherited from Mansel's family, which were being held in trust for him until his thirtieth birthday, he had discovered that he wasn't Mansel's only illegitimate child. The trustees had paid out considerable sums of money over the years to settle more than a dozen claims from different women. And the family solicitor had warned him there were rumours that Mansel had fathered even more children whose mothers either hadn't thought to approach the trust or had been paid off by Mansel before his death.

He hadn't discussed the existence of his half-brothers and sisters with either of his parents, but the facts were undeniable. His real father had been a philanderer who hadn't been averse to using his wealth and position to seduce young girls. He had found the fact difficult to come to terms with.

'Same colour hair, same colour eyes, I went right up to him and called him Harry,' David continued.

'That must have been a surprise for the poor man.' Harry bit into a fruit tart.

'At first I really thought it was you, but then—'

'You took a second look and saw he wasn't me?' Harry interrupted, hoping to put an end to the conversation.

'I knew he wasn't you because of his clothes. He was dressed like a sailor. He also had an American accent.'

'I'll have to see this man for myself.'

'David told me about him but I've never seen anyone who looks like you in Tiger Bay, Mr Evans.' Judy handed Harry a cup of tea. 'And I know everyone who lives here, except the foreign seamen who only stay for a short while between sailings.' Conscious that she'd done little to help serve the food, Judy took the empty tray from her aunt. 'I'll fill this up for you if you like, Auntie May.'

'Thank you, Judy, but you'll have to do it in Doris's. We've run out of cups.' May ran after her two-year-old son who had left the blanket to follow the older children who were climbing the park railings.

'I didn't realise how hungry I was until I started eating.' David helped himself to another sandwich.

'Here, try one of these, they're delicious, I have no idea who made the pastry but it's as light as air.' Knowing his brother-in-law had a sweet tooth, Harry dropped a strawberry tart on David's plate.

'Moody made them,' Judy said.

'Edyth's baker Moody?' Harry asked.

'He made the pasties as well. You should try one of them.' Judy carried the tray across the road to Doris's house.

David bit into the tart. 'You're right, Harry, this pastry is light.'

'Lighter than mine?' Mary looked over David's shoulder to see what he was eating.

'Almost as light,' David amended tactfully. 'Mary, you should have seen this man I met earlier. He could have been Harry's twin.'

'Really?' She took one of the tarts from the table, broke off a piece of the pastry crust and examined it.

'Where are the children?' Harry asked Mary.

'With my sister. They're watching the sack race.'

The Christina Street Musicians struck up a swing number and David looked around for Edyth. He saw her standing in front of a table where another of Judy's aunts was dispensing home-made blackberry wine. 'Here,' he thrust his plate at Harry, 'take this for me, will you?'

Mary watched him run up to Edyth, grab her hand and drag her towards the other dancers.

'He's as keen on her as he ever was,' she murmured disconsolately.

Harry set his own and David's plates on the table and slipped his arm around Mary's waist. 'We'll have him back on the farm tonight, darling. A couple of days and he'll be the old David again, immersed in his cows, lambs and chickens.'

'I'm not so sure, Harry.' She bit her lower lip to stop it from trembling. 'He hasn't been the same since he came out of hospital. His heart doesn't seem to be in the farm any more.'

'As your sister is looking after the children, let's dance.'

'You're trying to distract me to stop me from worrying about David.'

'Yes,' Harry answered truthfully.

'It won't work.'

'I know it won't. But at least we'll have fun while we worry.' He slipped his fingers beneath her chin, lifted her face to his and kissed her lightly on the lips. 'Come on, we can't let the single people have all the fun.'

Half an hour later, when the Bute Street Blues Band had taken over from the Christina Street Musicians, Harry saw a man standing alone on the edge of the crowd: a man who resembled him in every way, a man he knew. He was certain of it.

He had a sudden flash of half forgotten memory. Two small boys playing in colliery slag. One boy bigger and heavier than the other had used his superior strength to beat the younger boy. And that younger boy had been him.

Judy was singing 'West End Blues' and the man was watching every move she made. Harry shuddered, suddenly and inexplicably afraid – not for himself but for Judy. He caught Mary's hand and led her away from the dancers. The man saw him, nodded and strolled off. But by the time Harry reached the corner of Loudon Square there was no sign of him.

'Are you sure I can't persuade you and Mary to stay the night, Harry?' Edyth coaxed. The sun had sunk low over the rooftops of the imposing Victorian houses in the square but the advent of evening hadn't interrupted the music or dancing, only brought out hoarded bottles of whisky and brandy that the men were dispensing to make the tea their wives were still pouring 'Irish' and 'French'.

'It's tempting, sis, but we have to get back to the farm.' Harry took the sleeping baby from Mary.

'I've a light supper all ready in my larder. And although it will be a bit of a squash I can put you all up,' Edyth offered.

'It's good of you, Edie, but we'll stay another time. Ruth is exhausted. If we're lucky she'll bypass the grumpy stage and go to sleep on the train. David and Mary have the farm and dairy to run and I have work waiting in my office at home.' Harry peered at his wrist watch. 'As it is, it's going to take us at least two hours and probably longer to get home.' He kissed his sister's cheek. 'But thank you for the invitation.'

'I've found a taxi. It's waiting for us on the corner.' David joined them.

'See you soon, Mary.' Edyth hugged her sister-in-law, dropped a finger kiss on the forehead of the baby sleeping in Harry's arms, then she kissed Ruth and Mary's sister, Martha. Harry's two young brother-in-laws had disappeared, but they always did when the women started kissing.

'David, see you soon.' Edyth held out her hand, then, on impulse, kissed his cheek.

'You will,' he answered with conviction.

Edyth walked with them to the taxi. Harry embraced her again before taking the front seat. David helped his sisters, brothers and the children into the back before climbing in and lifting Martha on to his knees.

'I'm too big to sit on your lap,' she complained irritably.

'Then you'll have to run behind,' he joked.

'Everyone in?' Harry pushed the window open, looked behind him and checked. 'Good. Bye, Edie; bye, Judy.'

Edyth and Judy linked arms and stood side by side, waving them off and blowing kisses. David looked back until the driver turned the corner into Bute Street.

David shifted Martha on to one knee, sat back and stared out of the window at the ornate three- and four-storey buildings that housed banks, hotels and enormous well-stocked shops, so different from the corner shops in the small Swansea Valley villages that he was used to.

Then he saw them – and wondered why he hadn't spotted them on the taxi drive into the Bay – THE CHINESE SEAMAN'S HOME – JOHN CORY SAILORS' AND SOLDIERS' REST – THE SEA-MAN'S INSTITUTE – lodging house after lodging house.

He'd been a fool. Instead of waiting for Edyth to notice him, he should have followed her to Tiger Bay. There was no way she would ever live on the farm, not with her baker's shop to run. But if he moved here and took a job as a seaman . . .

He knew nothing about ships but sailing couldn't be any more difficult than farming – could it? And in between sailings he'd be able to spend whole days ashore. Days in which he could see Edyth. Maybe she'd even allow him to help out in her bakery. And once they spent time together he knew she would fall in love with him. He just knew it.

# CHAPTER THREE

'I wasn't sure what to expect from the carnival but it was fun. I enjoyed it – and so did Harry, Mary and the children. It was good to see them, if only for a few hours.' Edyth picked up the last of the plates on the scrub-down table she had covered with a sheet because she didn't have a large enough tablecloth, and carried them to the sink. Having invited all the members of the Bute Street Blues Band and their families, as well as her own, to supper, she had laid it out in the enormous kitchen of her shop.

'You miss your family?' Micah took the sheet from the table, folded it and hung it on the back of a chair.

'Of course, but not enough to give up the bakery and go back to Pontypridd.' She smiled when she saw Judy standing over the sink with her eyes closed.

Micah touched Judy's arm. 'Bed, miss, now. You're falling asleep on your feet like a horse.'

'I was just blinking,' she mumbled.

'So I saw.' He took her by the shoulders and propelled her out of the kitchen, through the shop to the foot of the stairs. 'It's quite simple. You hold on to the hand rail, lift one leg, then the other and walk straight ahead. Don't forget to wash off that greasepaint or you'll be scrubbing your sheets for a week.'

Too tired to respond to Micah's sarcasm, Judy did as he ordered.

He returned to the kitchen. Edyth had lifted the last of the plates from the washing-up water and left them to drain on the zinc draining board.

'I've put the leftover food in the pantry. Everything else can wait until morning. Drink?' she asked.

'I've consumed more tea today than there's water in the West and East dock combined.'

'I said drink, not tea.' She took the last flagon of beer from a cupboard and set it on the table next to him before pouring herself a small sherry from the bottle she'd opened for her guests. 'This is cosy.' She sat next to him at the table.

'It could be cosy every night if you allowed me to talk to your father,' he reproached.

'To tell him what?'

'That I love you and intend to marry you as soon as you're free.'

'I'm a married woman and my own person. You don't need my father's permission, only mine.'

'Aside from courtesy, you may be married but you're not twenty-one and, in Peter's absence, that makes your father your guardian.'

'I suppose it does, but as my present marriage isn't annulled, and won't be until Peter signs and returns those papers, which, given that he's on the other side of the world, could take months, any talk of remarrying is premature.'

'But Peter will be returning them any day now and when he does—'

'Micah, I've been thinking,' she interrupted.

He flicked opened the beer, poured some into a glass, replaced the rubber-ringed top and closed it again. 'I don't like the sound of that.'

'What, me thinking? My brain doesn't make a noise.'

'Don't joke, not now, Edyth, please.' He removed his glasses and stared at her.

She knew he was acutely short-sighted, but even unfocused his deep blue eyes seemed to bore into hers, reading her thoughts as they formed. 'If we married, you'd expect me to move into the Norwegian mission with you, wouldn't you?'

'Married people do generally live together,' he agreed.

'Now who's not being serious?' A note of irritation crept into her voice.

'What point are you trying to make?'

'My bakery . . . '

'If that's all you're worried about, you could still run it,' he said with relief. 'Judy will be only too happy to carry on living here.'

'It's not Judy's bakery, it's mine. I'm up every morning at four—' she glanced at the clock on the wall. The hands pointed to ten minutes to four and music was still echoing from the direction of Loudon Square, '—every weekday morning, that is,' she qualified. 'That means I go to bed most nights at nine.'

'I know,' he murmured pointedly.

Not wanting to get sidetracked into a discussion as to what happened on the nights Micah stayed over when Judy was babysitting for one of her uncles, or away for an audition, she said, 'How much sleep do you think I would get in the mission with the sailors whose ships are only in for a couple of days sitting up all night, talking, singing, drinking coffee and eating waffles?'

'Lots if you put cotton wool in your ears. But it's not sleep you're worried about, is it?'

'No.' She poured more sherry into her glass, not because she wanted to fill it but because she couldn't bring herself to look at him. 'I was never sure what I wanted to do with my life, and, truth be told, I still don't know. But I enjoy running the bakery. It's mine, I own it. Granted by the grace of my bank manager, and the interest I pay on my business account, but I employ people who rely on me to pay them wages at the end of the week. I don't want to give that up to run a house or a mission and look after a husband.'

'Marriage doesn't have to be like that,' he countered.

'It was with Peter and maybe it wouldn't be like that with you at first. But in time it would.'

'I'm looking after myself perfectly well now.'

'No, you're not. And please, let me finish,' she begged before he had a chance to say another word. 'Your sister does your laundry and mending; the ladies on the mission committee clean your room when they sweep out and dust the church and the public areas. Whoever's manning the waffle iron makes your breakfast, the ladies' committee your lunch and Moody cooks supper for you most nights when he leaves here.'

'That's hardly surprising. He lives with my sister and he is her brother-in-law.'

'Micah, all I'm trying to say is that your sister and the other women like looking after you and the seamen who call into the mission. It's only natural. Most of them have husbands or fathers who are sailors and they miss them. You told me the first time you took me to your church that they like to help out because it pleases them to think that someone is doing the same for their men in whichever port in the world their ships are berthed. But it doesn't alter the fact that I have a business to run. How could I manage the bakery if I was always worrying about whether or not you had clean underclothes and socks and what I was going to cook you for tea?'

'My sister—'

'And all the other ladies would stop doing your cleaning, cooking and washing if we were married,' she declared. 'They would expect me to take over – and quite rightly so.'

He looked her in the eye. 'So you don't want to marry me, not now, or ever. Is that what you're saying?'

'No.' The long day had finally caught up with her and she felt exhausted. Too drained to think, let alone argue.

'Then when will you marry me?'

'You know I can't answer that until Peter sends me the annulment papers.'

'And if you receive them tomorrow?' he pressed.

'That's not likely to happen,' she said irritably.

'But if you do?'

'I don't know, Micah,' she snapped. 'Do we have to talk about this now?'

'This is one subject you never want to discuss.'

'You know I love you,' she pleaded earnestly. 'Isn't that enough?'

'It's a lot, Edyth, but it would be a whole lot more if I could live openly with you.'

'Why can't you be happy with things the way they are?'

'How can I be, when we have to sneak around and pretend that we are just friends? Don't you know how terrified I am every time we make love in case I make you pregnant?'

'What if you did? I'm married,' she retorted unthinkingly.

'Peter left you months ago.'

'The people who matter most – my friends and family – wouldn't care.'

'I think your parents would. And so would I. And so might some of your customers. Is it so unreasonable of me to want my child to bear my name and not Peter's? I also happen to believe that every child has a right to be brought up in a loving secure home by a mother and a father who live together. As you were,' he reminded her strongly.

'So do I, Micah, but it's my life we're talking about.' She was furious with him for even thinking that she would consider otherwise. 'As for the people around here, where else would they buy their bread? There isn't another decent baker in the Bay.'

'You're changing the subject again, Edyth, as you always do when I try to talk to you about us.' Micah finished his beer, rose from his chair and pushed it back under the table.

44

Edyth had known Micah less than a year but she could tell when he was angry. Unlike most people he became quieter, more softly spoken, something she found difficult to adjust to after the emotional explosions of her four sisters while they were growing up together in Pontypridd.

'Shall I see you tomorrow, on the *Escape*?' she asked in an effort to appease him. They had met every Sunday afternoon on his boat since they had begun their affair. They also frequently stole a few hours during the late afternoons and early evenings in the week.

'It's where I practise my saxophone after services every Sunday,' he said shortly.

'We'll talk then.'

He picked up his saxophone case.

'Micah . . . '

'There could still be strangers lurking around the Bay. Best lock up behind me.' He stepped outside and closed the door behind him without giving her his customary goodnight kiss.

She thrust the bolt home and leaned against the wall. She really was too tired to think. But as she climbed the stairs she wondered why it was so difficult for a married woman to run a business or work outside the home. Her mother had managed it. But then she had worked in Harry's business and she'd had their dedicated and loving housekeeper to run the house and look after the family in her absence.

Even if she found the money to employ a housekeeper to carry out her domestic and family chores – and at the moment she hadn't a halfpenny to spare – where, in this modern day and age, would she find a woman willing to sacrifice her own life to that of an employer's?

David Ellis had never slept in a room with the curtains drawn. Not even when he had shared a bedroom with his younger brother. Since birth he had followed the farmers' dictate of rising with the sun and if not exactly going to bed when it set, sitting up no more than an hour or two after dark, especially during the long winter nights. More would have been considered a waste of coal and candles and although his family no longer had to practise the stringent economies they had been forced to adhere to before his sister had married Harry, old habits died hard.

Despite his late night after the carnival, David left his bed the moment the first cold grey fingers of light highlighted the summits of the eastern hills that towered over the reservoir below the farmhouse. He stood at the window in his pyjama trousers, staring at the view that was so familiar to him he had long since taken it for granted. The Ellis Estate's eighteenth-century farmhouse and outbuildings had been built in a square that enclosed the farmyard. Situated just below the crest of a hill so the top could shelter it from the worst of the winter snowstorms that swept the Brecon Beacons, the house was as large and substantial as any manor in Wales.

For six months of the year it was a cold, bleak and cruel place. But in spring and summer it was easy to forget the deep snowdrifts and heavy frosts that blocked the road and killed the weaker animals. Below him, sheep he had watched grow from frisky gambolling lambs to stolid maturity cropped the grassy slopes that tumbled down to the valley floor. Rabbits popped in and out of burrows and half a dozen wild ducks swam peacefully among the reeds at the water's edge of the reservoir that flooded the valley floor. A pair of kites circled lazily on the same level as his window. It was a quiet, peaceful scene – too peaceful for a man who loved a woman who lived more than sixty miles away.

He strode purposefully from the window and lifted the suitcase Harry and Mary had bought him last Christmas from the cupboard next to the fireplace. Opening it out on the bed, he emptied a drawer in his chest and packed his cotton summer underclothes. Then he stood back and surveyed his wardrobe. He'd need his three good linen shirts, spare collars, ties, socks, sock suspenders, braces, sports coat and thick cotton and woollen trousers, but he wouldn't need the overalls he wore around the farm. Sweaters – would it be hot or cold on board ship? Deciding it could be either, depending on the destination, he folded three of the thickest ones Mary had knitted him on top of his shirts then threw in the wooden box that contained his bone collar studs, silver tiepins and cuff links.

Boots? He packed his newest pair before dressing in the only suit that fitted him. A grey pinstripe he'd had tailored to replace the navy blue one he'd bought for Harry and Mary's wedding and outgrown less than a year later.

He pushed his 'best' gold cuff links that Harry's parents and sisters had given him for his last birthday into his shirt cuffs, fastened his tie with the matching pin and took a last look around his bedroom. Books? He flicked through the selection on top of the cupboard. He hadn't learned to read and write until he was fifteen and since then he'd developed a taste for adventure stories. But he'd read his small library three times over.

There would be bookshops and libraries in Cardiff. He smiled at the thought. He'd never wanted to dot ornaments around his bedroom like his sister Martha. But there were a few things he couldn't leave behind. One was his fountain pen, which he'd bought with the first money Harry had insisted he receive as 'wages' for running the farm, another was a framed photograph taken at Harry and Mary's wedding.

He had carved the frame himself and Harry had bought the glass for it. It was a formal, posed group photograph. Harry and Mary stood centre stage flanked by groomsmen, bridesmaids and all of Harry's immediate family. And, to Harry's right, he stood frozen in time next to Edyth.

'You look smart,' Mary commented when David joined her and Harry in the kitchen for breakfast. 'You've decided to go to chapel with us this morning.'

'No.' David took his customary chair at the table and helped himself to two slices of bread.

'There's a girl in the valley you're out to impress?' Even as Harry said it, he knew it was a forlorn hope.

'No.' David looked around. 'Where are the others?'

'They finished breakfast half an hour ago. They've taken Ruth into the barn to look for eggs.' Harry folded the copy of the *South Wales Echo* that he had bought at the station the day before and set it aside. 'What was all that banging in your room earlier?'

'Nothing.' David spread butter on his bread.

'Two eggs or three?' Mary asked from the stove, where she was frying laver bread, bacon and sausages.

David decided that as he had a long journey ahead of him and an uncertain reception the other end he may as well start with a good meal inside him. 'Four.'

'All that dancing yesterday has given you an appetite.' Harry left his chair when the baby started crying. 'He can't possibly be hungry after you've just fed him, Mary, so I'll see to him.' He lifted Will from his day cot in the corner next to the range, laid him against his shoulder and rubbed his tiny back. The baby responded with an enormous burp and a watery smile.

'Well done, young man,' Harry smiled. 'I'm getting good at this fathering lark.'

'If you're not going to chapel, Davy, where are you going?' Mary transferred four slices of bacon, three sausages and a large portion of fried laver bread mixed with oatmeal on to a plate and carried it over to her brother.

'Cardiff.' David reached for the salt cellar.

'It's Sunday service on the trains. You may have trouble getting back tonight,' Harry warned.

'I'm not coming back. Can I have a lift to the station

48

with you when you take the others to chapel, please, Harry?'

A dense silence fell over the kitchen. 'What do you mean, you're not coming back?' Mary's voice wavered with suppressed emotion as she carried the eggs, still in the pan, over to David.

'I'm leaving the farm.'

Mary stared at her brother. When she saw the expression on his face she almost dropped the frying pan. 'You can't be thinking of living in Cardiff.'

'Why not?' David challenged.

'We have some talking to do. You'd better sit down, Mary,' Harry advised.

Mary lifted the eggs on to David's plate and returned the frying pan to the range. After setting it on one of the covered hot plates she joined Harry and David at the table.

David sensed them both looking at him, but he began to eat his breakfast although it was sticking in his throat.

Unable to bear the tension a moment longer, Harry braved the question uppermost in his mind. 'What do you intend to do in Cardiff?'

'Go to sea.'

'You don't know the first thing about sailing a ship,' Mary pointed out harshly.

'Neither did any sailor until he went to sea. All those ships in the docks must need crew.'

'They do – qualified crew.' Harry sensed the baby growing limp in his arms. He glanced at him, saw he was asleep and returned him to his day cot.

'How hard can it be to sail a ship?' David reached for the butter. 'All right, sailing a ship is skilled work but there's bound to be all sorts of menial jobs that I can do on board while I learn. Don't sailors scrub decks—'

'And peel potatoes, empty slop buckets, shovel coal into boilers—'

'There you are then, Mary,' David broke in triumphantly. 'That doesn't sound too different from farm work.'

'Why Cardiff?' Mary knew the answer but she had to ask the question because she wasn't sure David would admit to wanting to be close to Edyth.

'Because it's a port. From there I can see the world.'

'And the farm?' Her voice cracked and both Harry and David knew she was close to tears. 'Who do you think is going to run the farm while you are off seeing the world?'

'You and Mr Jones manage the farm perfectly well now, whether I'm here or not.'

'But Mr Jones works for us, David. He doesn't own the Ellis Estate. His heart isn't in the place.'

David finally gave up on his breakfast and pushed the uneaten food to the side of his plate. He dropped his knife and fork on top and left the table. 'Neither is mine, Mary.' He opened the door that led into the farmyard. 'I'll find the others and tell them that I'm leaving.'

Mary left her chair and went after him but Harry grabbed her skirt and held her fast until David had closed the outside door.

'Let him go, darling.'

'David can't leave. The farm is his. The Ellises have fought for hundreds of years to keep it in the family. His name – David Ellis – is carved over the door . . . '

'Your ancestor's name is carved over the door,' Harry reminded her. 'The Ellis Estate was his dream, not David's. David's young, he's not sure what he wants from life yet. Please don't be angry with him for rejecting someone else's dream.'

'What was the point of all that work, all that sacrifice? My parents and grandparents worked day and night to build the farm so David could inherit it and now,' she choked back a sob, 'it's all been for nothing.'

He pulled her down on to his lap. 'It's not been for nothing. The farm belongs to you and your brothers and sister. And in four years' time, when I reach thirty and my trust is dissolved, you will own it outright. And if David doesn't want it then, perhaps Luke or Matthew will when they're old enough.'

'But it's always been the eldest son who inherits. I must make David understand . . . '

Harry locked his hands around her waist when she tried to climb off him. 'You can't tell him anything that he doesn't already know.'

'But . . . '

He wiped the tears from her eyes with his handkerchief. 'If you want David to remain part of this family, let him go, Mary.'

'It's hard.'

'My mother always said that letting go is the worst thing about having children. She didn't want me to go to boarding school, neither did I, but the decision was made for us by the trustees of my estate. And if she hadn't gone along with it, she and I might have lost what little influence we have with the board. And there's Edyth. My father and mother predicted that her marriage to Peter would end in disaster but if they hadn't given her permission to marry him, there's no saying what Edyth might have done. Run away to Gretna Green or done something even more stupid. Let David go with good grace, darling,' he reiterated, 'and he might – just might – come back to us and the farm.'

She looked up at him through tear-filled eyes. 'Do you think he will?' she asked tremulously, needing reassurance.

'I don't know. But what I do know is that if we try to keep him here against his will, he'll end up hating us and the farm, so we may as well let him go with our blessing.'

'You know he's only leaving because of Edyth?'

'Yes.'

'I don't think she loves him.'

Harry had watched Edyth and David at the carnival

51

and as Edyth had treated David no differently from him or anyone else in the family, he was forced to agree with his wife. 'I don't think she does either.'

'Then where will that leave David? He'll be stuck in Cardiff, trying to get a job on board ship when he knows nothing about them. And all three of Judy's uncles were complaining yesterday that they couldn't get berths out of Tiger Bay and they're registered as able seamen. David hasn't even got ship's papers. He won't be an ordinary seaman; he'll be nothing – a dogsbody.'

'Judy's uncles have families to support. They'll want higher wages than David.'

'You know Tiger Bay's reputation. David could get beaten up there – murdered even.'

'Darling, Edyth's surviving there and she hasn't been beaten up or murdered.' Harry pulled her head down on his shoulder. 'Edyth may not love David but he's family. She has friends there, good friends. If we ask them, they'll look out for David and see that he doesn't come to any harm.'

'You think so?' She sat up and looked at him.

'I know so.' He spoke with more conviction than he felt. 'After David's left, I'll telephone Edyth and ask her to talk to Micah Holsten and Judy's uncles. They have steady heads and influence in the community. And I'd better make sure that David has enough money to keep himself for a few weeks until he finds work. He'll also need to take his bankbook with him. But for now we'll go outside and tell David that we wish him well and we'll drive him to the station. And no matter what, he'll always have a home here with us, whenever he wants one.'

Aled James stood before the cheval mirror in the luxuriously furnished bedroom of his Windsor Hotel suite and adjusted his shirt cuff to the recommended half inch that should be worn below a suit jacket to show off his solid-gold diamond-studded cuff links. He might have sailed into Tiger Bay as a sailor but he had no intention of being mistaken for one now he had arrived. He had given his seaman's clothes to Freddie that morning and told him to dispose of them.

Clothes were important to him, as were his shoes. All handmade, and not just in London. It was possible to buy anything in New York provided you had the money to pay for it and the last suit he'd had tailored had come from the workshops of a renowned Jewish gentlemen's outfitters in Warsaw. Three pairs of his shoes bore the label of a Berlin cobbler who'd made the Kaiser's footwear until he'd abdicated. His shirts and underwear came from Bond Street, his silk ties from Paris.

He opened his cigar case and removed one he'd already cut. He lit it with his solid-gold cigarette lighter. Like the case, the lighter was Dunhill, his watch, Patek Philippe and Co, Geneva. Only the best for him. He might have felt pleased with himself and what he'd accomplished in America – if thoughts of Harry Evans hadn't kept intruding into his mind.

They brought a sharp unpalatable reminder of the filthy, barefoot urchin he'd been. His skin marked by ringworm and bruises, his body crawling with fleas and lice, as he and Harry had played in the sea of colliery waste around Bush Houses in Clydach Vale. It hadn't been much of a place, but then his mother had never been much of a housekeeper – or, come to that, much of a mother. He'd loved her but he had never been blind to her faults, and hindsight had thrown every one of them into sharp relief.

He buttoned his beige silk waistcoat, adjusted the knot on his paisley silk tie and checked his cream linen suit for creases. The maid had done an excellent job of pressing it and he made a mental note to tip her more generously next time he asked her to look after his clothes. He had lived in hotel suites since the day he had begun to make serious money. It saved him the bother of having to buy a place and staff it, and it was easy to entertain business associates at short notice. Provided the hotel was high class, he had learned that money could buy him whatever he wanted – at any time of the day or night.

There was a knock at the outside door and he shouted, 'It's open.'

Freddie showed a thin man with a pencil moustache into the sitting room. Aled left the bedroom and joined them.

'Mr Arnold, the estate agent, to see you, boss.'

'Mr Arnold.' Aled gave the man a broad, empty smile. 'Would you like a drink?'

'Coffee, please,' Geoff Arnold replied cautiously.

'Freddie, telephone down for coffee for two. You have brought your portfolio of properties for sale and rent, Mr Arnold?'

'I have, Mr James.'

'Sit down. We may be able to do business.'


Edyth hadn't attended church since she'd bought the bakery. When the Reverend Spicer had visited her to reproach her on her absence, she'd used the excuse of lack of time due to the pressing needs of her business. But lack of time hadn't stopped her from taking Sunday-afternoon walks. Micah's boat, the *Escape*, was berthed among a flotilla of other small boats in a secluded dock, well away from the large vessels that towered over the quaysides.

Micah had inherited the boat from a friend. It hadn't sailed in years and since Micah had sold the engine and sails, it was no longer even capable of moving. But it made an ideal retreat from the crowded and noisy Norwegian mission. He went there whenever he wanted to read or compose music and practise his saxophone. And, in the last few months, it had become Edyth's sanctuary from the world too.

Not quite knowing what to expect after the words they had exchanged the night before, Edyth's steps slowed as she approached the plank walkway that stretched across the dock to allow access to the boats. She could hear Micah playing 'Ain't Misbehavin', recognising the tune from a record her eldest sister Bella and her husband Toby had brought back from their honeymoon in New York. She waited until he finished before tapping on the cabin door.

Micah opened it and looked at her in surprise. 'Why the knock?'

'Because I wasn't sure you wanted to see me after what you said last night.'

'I was angry, wasn't I?' He stood back to allow her to walk in.

'Does the past tense mean that you aren't any more?'

'I've decided to postpone the argument until you are free. Then I'll start it up again.'

'I warn you now, Micah, I won't become an appendage to your mission.'

He set his saxophone down carefully in its velvet-bedded case. 'I said I'll postpone the argument.' He took off his glasses. Folding them, he set them beside the case before wrapping his arms around her and kissing her.

Relieved, she leaned against him. 'I do love you.'

'I know.' He glanced down at the table separating the two bench seats that could be converted into a bed. 'Tired?'

'Exhausted.'

'Judy?'

'I left her eating a late breakfast. She intends to spend the rest of the day with her uncles and their families. What about the mission?'

'A visiting ship's chaplain asked if he could take evening service. I told him that I'd sacrifice the pleasure of conducting it just this once.'

She smiled. 'A whole afternoon and evening.'

'I would say, "Let's see if we can stay awake because that way, we'll make it last longer", but I've a feeling we'll be asleep five minutes after we stretch out on the bed.'

'Five minutes?' She lifted her eyebrows.

'Maybe ten.' He folded the table away.

'Ten minutes can be a long time. I can barely keep my eyes open now, let alone after you've had your wicked way with me.' She watched him bolt the door. 'We're all right, aren't we, Micah?' she asked seriously.

'For the time being.'

Trying not to think further than that afternoon, she pulled the cushions from the bench seat and tossed them on to the floor.

He stepped over them, gathered her into his arms and unbuttoned the back of her dress. Sliding it over her shoulders, he allowed it and her petticoat to drop to the floor. 'Did I ever tell you that you're beautiful?'

'Always when you take your glasses off and can't see.' She drew back, unbuttoned his waistcoat, helped him out of it and pulled down his braces.

'I can see everything I want to.' He slipped the straps of her bust shaper over her shoulders. When her breasts were exposed he kissed each nipple in turn.

'We should make the bed properly.' She was still unbuttoning his shirt when he pressed her down on to the cushions.

'Why?' He kissed the soft skin at the base of her ear.

'Because we'll be uncomfortable later.'

'And then we'll wake up and do this all over again.' Unbuckling his belt and unbuttoning his flies, he kicked his trousers off and pulled down her French knickers. 'I like you just the way you are now – naked. You do realise once we're married I won't allow you to dress. And then we'll have a lifetime of Sunday afternoons.'

He entered her and for once, she allowed his forecast of their future together to go unchallenged.

*

Judy was washing her breakfast things when the telephone rang in the ante room off the kitchen, where Edyth did her accounts and kept her invoices. She picked it up and recited the telephone number.

'Judy?'

'Hello, Mr Evans,' she said, relieved that it wasn't a customer demanding extra baked goods or cancelling an order. She enjoyed working for Edyth but hated making decisions that might cost the business money if she got them wrong.

'Is Edyth there?'

'No, she went out an hour ago.'

'Is she likely to be back soon?'

'Not until this evening, she's gone to visit a friend,' she answered evasively.

'Damn! Sorry, Judy, I didn't mean to swear. Can you get a message to her?'

'If it's urgent, Mr Evans, I can try.' She knew exactly where Edyth was because every gossip in the Bay had seen her visit Micah Holsten's boat on Sunday afternoons, but the last thing she wanted to do was disturb them.

'My brother-in-law David – what am I saying, of course you know David – you were dancing with him yesterday. Well, he left the farm this morning for Cardiff. His train is due in at four o'clock. He's taken it into his head to become a sailor.'

'Now? When there's a slump in trade and all the shipping companies are laying off seamen?'

'You don't have to tell me it's a crazy idea. But there's no point in trying to talk David out of it. Once he makes up his mind to do something, he does it, no matter what the consequences. He's going to have to find out how impossible it will be for him to become a sailor the hard way. He doesn't know anyone in the Bay except you and Edyth and although he's practically family, he's not related to Edyth by blood so I don't think he should move in with you two,' he said flatly. 'But I don't want him wandering around the doss houses on the docks. He's lived on the farm all his life, he's not used to people, especially ones who will take advantage of a young boy's naïvety.'

'I understand, Mr Evans. Helga Brown – Pastor Holsten's sister – takes in lodgers. She lives in the same street as my uncles.'

'That sounds perfect. Do you think she'll have a room to spare?'

'I don't know about a room, Mr Evans – they come expensive on the Bay. But she'll probably have a bed.'

'If she has, reserve it for David, please. He has enough money to keep himself for a few weeks. When it runs out I hope he'll have enough sense to come home. If Micah's sister can't put him up, try and find him respectable lodgings somewhere else. And tell Edyth I'd be grateful if she'd meet the train and see him to Micah's sister's house. Ask her to telephone me as soon as she can. Mary's worried sick about him.'

'I will, Mr Evans, and if Edyth can't meet the train I will.'

'Thank you, Judy, you're a gem. I must go and pick up Mary and the others from chapel now. Look after yourself and Edie for me.'

'I will, Mr Evans. Goodbye.' Judy replaced the receiver and walked back into the kitchen.

David Ellis was coming to the Bay to live – and, he thought, work. With the situation as it was at the moment an unskilled man would be lucky to get a berth on a coal ship to Ireland in return for his food. Judy only hoped David had enough sense not to advertise the fact that he was carrying sufficient money to pay for a few weeks' lodging. If he didn't, he'd soon attract the attention of some of the more desperate seamen in the doss houses.

She'd have to persuade him to hand over the bulk of

his money to Helga Brown in advance to pay for his board and lodgings. She tried not to think what might happen if he chose not to listen to her. She didn't know David well, but the fact that he'd insisted on coming to the Bay in the face of Harry and Mary's opposition was testimony to his stubbornness and lack of common sense.

Her heart beat faster as an image came to mind of Harry Evans, handsome, debonair, well to do and respectable, unlike some of the rougher characters who lived on the Bay. And he was devoted to his wife and children. She didn't love Harry – how could she when he was a married man? – but she hoped that there would be a man a little like him in her future. One who would love and cosset her and take care of her and their children the way Harry did Mary.

She sighed. It was more likely she'd continue to be surrounded by immature headstrong idiot boys like David Ellis, who needed looking after because they were just as stupid and troublesome as her cousins and their friends. Boys who had about as much romance in their soul as the dull-eyed codfish that lay on Tommy the fishmonger's cart.

Irritated by the thought, she threw the dishcloth back into the washing-up water and carried on washing her dishes.

# CHAPTER FOUR

'It's an excellent location, Mr James. And, as you see, the building is in good condition.'

'Externally,' Aled qualified. He stepped back on the pavement and glanced up at the imposing, Victorian-built three-storey building in Bute Street while Geoff Arnold unlocked the front door. He noted that the roof was in good repair, as were all the windows and the three doors that faced the street. He also noticed that the woodwork had been freshly painted and the ornamental brickwork around the windows and doors newly pointed.

'It used to be a hotel, but,' Geoff hesitated before adding, 'times are hard.'

'The bank repossessed it?' Aled guessed from the recent renovations.

'Not many visitors to the docks can afford hotel prices now that trade has slumped and those who can tend to stay at the Windsor since they reduced their room rate. As for ordinary sailors – they can no longer be sure how long they'll have to stay in the port, so they're reluctant to even pay for a bed in a doss house.' Geoff opened the door.

Aled walked ahead of him into an imposing hall that housed an enormous, elegant curved staircase, two sets of double and two single doors. 'This is a waste of space.'

'The last owner had the reception desk here.' Geoff opened the double doors on their right and they walked into a large, empty room that had been stripped back to the bare walls and floorboards. 'This was the residents' sitting room.'

Aled saw a door in the back wall. 'Where does that lead?'

'Offices and lavatories.' Geoff opened the door. Aled looked up and down a narrow corridor. There were two doors marked LADIES and GENTLEMEN and another marked OFFICE. 'What else is on this floor?'

'There's a smaller room to the left of the hall that was used as a bar.'

Aled walked back through the hall, opened the second set of double doors and looked inside. A bar ran the width of the back wall, but like the sitting room there was neither flooring nor furniture. He returned to the hall. 'Where do those two doors lead?'

'One to the servants' back staircase, the other to the stairs down to the cellar.'

Aled ran up the grand staircase. Three corridors opened off a wide galleried landing.

'There are fifteen double bedrooms, two bathrooms and three lavatories on this floor,' Geoff Arnold said, panting breathlessly as he caught up with him.

'You're very familiar with this place.'

'I enforced the repossession order for the bank and arranged the auction of fixtures and fittings.'

'And bought the building at a knockdown price?' Aled guessed shrewdly.

'I paid off the remaining mortgage. The bank directors were happy.'

'I bet they were. Where's the staircase to the next floor?'

Geoff opened one of the doors. Aled walked up a plain narrow staircase to the top floor. 'Were these servants' quarters?'

'The family's living accommodation.' Geoff opened the doors in turn. 'Sitting room, drawing room, dining room, four bedrooms, bathroom, kitchen and study. And, as you see, all well proportioned. There are four attic rooms, which were used to house the maids.'

Aled stood and looked around thoughtfully. 'The asking price?'

'Fifteen hundred pounds, freehold. I think you'll agree it is very reasonable for a place of this size.'

'It would have been two years ago.'

'The slump can't last, Mr James.'

'No, it can't, Mr Arnold. I've just comes from the United States and I've seen first hand what's happened there since the Wall Street crash in 'twenty-nine. It can only be a matter of time before we hit a full economic depression here. In my opinion it's going to get a great deal worse before it gets better. It will be years before this place is worth fifteen hundred pounds again. I'll give you eight hundred pounds for it. Cash.'

'That's ridiculous . . . '

'Cash,' Aled repeated. Growing up in abject poverty had made him cautious with his money. He had placed the bulk of his fortune in gilt-edged banker's drafts because they were portable, independent of the commodities markets and easy to realise in any country in the world. 'You or the bank – and, from the way you operate, I guess the bank before you bought it from the directors – have had time to repair and repaint this place since it was repossessed, which means buyers aren't queuing up. If you accept my offer, there'll be a hundred pounds extra in it for you in cash, if the contracts are signed within a week.' Geoff Arnold reddened and for all of Arnold's mixture of sycophantic fawning and arrogance Aled wondered if he'd insulted him.

'Nine hundred pounds is less than I hoped for, but you're right, it has been on the market for some time,' Geoff agreed.

Aled looked at him carefully. 'I'm sure we've met . . . '

'And I'm sure we haven't, Mr James. I've never done business with an American before.'

Aled didn't enlighten him but he made a mental note to ask Anna about Geoff Arnold when he saw her that evening. He walked to the window. 'I'll need a builder, a good one who can work quickly. Can you recommend one?'

'But the building is in excellent condition,' Geoff Arnold protested.

'It's not suitable for what I want.'

'You don't intend to reopen it as a hotel?'

'You just told me the last owner went bankrupt.'

'He did.'

'In which case, wouldn't it be rather foolish of me to repeat his mistake?'

'If you intend to change the use of the building you'll need the council's permission,' Geoff warned.

'I didn't expect things to be that different this side of the Atlantic,' Aled said with a ghost of a smile.

'May I ask what you intend to do with the place, Mr James?' Geoff ventured.

'Open a nightclub.'

'I don't know what it's like in America, but you'll not only need to get the council's permission, you'll also need a licence—'

'That won't be a problem, Mr Arnold.' Aled wondered how much it would cost to 'buy' Geoff Arnold. It had cost him two thousand dollars to buy a New York estate agent. But it had been a worthwhile investment. He had made a fortune from the agent's tip-offs about property people had been anxious to offload when they suddenly and unexpectedly found themselves on the verge of bankruptcy.

Geoff Arnold watched Aled stride across the floor to the head of the staircase. 'George Powell is just about the best builder around here.'

'Where do I find him?'

'Loudon Square.' Geoff Arnold took a notepad from his pocket and scribbled a note. 'This is his address and telephone number.'

'Thank you, Mr Arnold.' Aled pocketed the piece of paper. 'I'll engage a solicitor tomorrow.'

'May I suggest my own?'

'You can suggest him, but I won't engage him to act for me until I've met him and checked out his credentials.' Aled looked around the first floor. 'The sooner the contracts are exchanged and the alterations made, the sooner The Ragtime can open her doors.'

'The Ragtime, Mr James?'

'It was the name of my club in Harlem in New York. It did well enough for me to want to keep the name.' Aled opened his cigar case and offered it to Geoff. 'On second thoughts, Tiger Ragtime might be better in honour of the Bay. What do you think?'

'I think both names sound well.'

Aled made his way down to the ground floor and opened the doors to the largest room again. 'You'll be here six weeks from now, Mr Arnold, enjoying a drink and watching a first-class variety show. Wind up the paperwork within a week and I'll throw in twenty pounds' worth of chips with your invitation.'

'Chips?' The estate agent looked at him blankly.

'Gambling chips, Mr Arnold. What do you favour, roulette, blackjack – poker?'

'I've never gambled in my life.'

'And you call yourself a businessman.' Aled smiled coldly. 'If buying up repossessed properties isn't a gamble, I don't know what is.'

'The properties are investments.'

'Which might not pay off, Mr Arnold.'

'This one certainly didn't,' the estate agent agreed.

'I doubt there's a businessman alive who hasn't lost money on a venture at least once in his lifetime.'

'The council take a dim view of organised gambling, Mr James,' Geoff Arnold warned. 'They'll never grant you a licence to open a casino. Not in Tiger Bay.'

'We'll see.' Aled slapped him across the back. 'Telephone me at the Windsor tomorrow to let me know about those contracts.'

'I will, Mr James.'

'I'll expect your call before midday.' Aled angled his panama to the side of his head and stepped out into the warm sunshine that flooded Bute Street. His first day back in his home country had gone well. Very well indeed.

Judy stood on the platform of Cardiff station clutching her platform ticket and anxiously watching the passengers stream off the incoming train from Swansea. She was terrified she'd miss David and he'd head down to the docks, book into one of the rougher doss houses and get into trouble. If that happened she felt that not only would Harry Evans have every right to be angry with her, but also Edyth for taking on too much responsibility rather than disturb her and Micah.

All the beds in Micah's sister's house were occupied by seamen who had been forced to stay longer than they'd intended in Cardiff because they couldn't get a berth out. But she'd persuaded Helga to borrow the old army surplus cot she'd slept on when she'd stayed with her Uncle Jed before she'd moved in with Edyth, and put it in Moody's room.

Helga hadn't been difficult to win over, but Moody had. He hadn't wanted to share his room with anyone, much less a farm boy who thought he could get a job on board ship without any seafaring experience. It was obvious to Moody that David wasn't likely to get a berth soon, if at all. It had taken all of Judy's wiles, and a promise that she would clean the kitchen in the baker's for Moody three times a week while David remained in his room, to win him over.

David saw Judy before she saw him. He dropped his

suitcase at his feet and stood in front of her. 'What are you doing here?' he demanded suspiciously.

'I came to meet the train. Mr Evans telephoned the bakery to say that you were coming down to the Bay.'

'I might have known Harry would interfere,' he said angrily.

'He was concerned that you might not find anywhere to stay tonight.'

'That's stupid. With all those doss houses on the docks—'

'All those full doss houses,' she interrupted, her temper rising at the thought of the trouble she'd taken to find him decent lodgings. 'Haven't you heard that trade's slumped and hardly any ships are sailing? Berths out of the Bay, even for experienced sailors, are like gold.'

'Did Edyth send you to meet me?' He looked over her shoulder as though he expected to see Edyth standing behind her.

'No, she doesn't know you're here. She's out for the day, visiting friends. I managed to find you a bed in a lodging house run by Micah Holsten's sister. She didn't have any to spare, but I borrowed my Uncle Jed's camp bed and persuaded Moody to let you share his room.'

'I'd really have trouble booking in somewhere?' he asked, slightly mollified, when he realised that Judy must have gone to some trouble on his account.

'There are scores of seamen trapped here who'd be only too happy to sail out on any voyage that will provide them with meals and get them to another port where they might find a job that will pay wages.'

'In that case, I suppose I'd better thank you.' He picked up his suitcase.

'Don't put yourself out,' she retorted caustically.

'Sorry.' He lifted his cap and wiped his forehead with his handkerchief. 'The train was unbearably hot and a woman in my carriage wouldn't let me open the window because she didn't want to sit in a draught.'

Judy glanced at his case. 'That looks heavy. Do you want me to find a taxi?'

David thought of the ten pounds that Harry had pressed on him and insisted he take as well as his bank book. As Harry and Mary saw to the finances on the farm he didn't know much about costs or prices, beyond animal feed and what livestock fetched at market, but he did know that he couldn't afford to be extravagant until he found a job. 'Is Mr Holsten's sister's house far?'

'Half an hour's walk, but we could take a tram part of the way.'

'Then we'll do that.' He picked up his case again. 'When did you say Edyth would be home?'

'I didn't,' she replied shortly. 'Are you serious about wanting to work on a ship?'

'Very.' He had to walk quickly to keep up with her as she ran down the steps that led from the platform to the tunnel that opened into the street.

'As soon as you've met Mrs Brown and paid her for your board and lodging, I'll take you across the road to meet my Uncle Jed. He's worked on and off ships for over thirty years.'

'He'll find me something?' David asked excitedly.

'If he could find work, he'd find it for himself and his two brothers first. They've been living on next to nothing for months,' she retorted bluntly.

Anna Hughes sank down on the plush sofa in the sitting room of Aled's hotel suite before taking the glass of champagne Aiden handed her.

'A little bird told me that you've put in an offer for the old Sea Breeze,' she said to Aled who was sitting, telephone at his elbow, in the chair opposite her.

'If that was the name of the hotel before it closed. I see the little gossip birds are flying around Tiger Bay as fast, nosy and garrulous as ever.' Aled shook his head when Aiden held up the bottle of champagne. 'I'll have a brandy. After you've poured it, tell the hotel staff to serve us dinner here in an hour. I won't need you or Freddie again until tomorrow morning. You can do what you like, as long as you don't stir up trouble with the natives.'

'Thanks, boss.'

'Here.' Anna handed Aiden a card. 'If you two boys are out for a good time, tell my girls to give you one. But we don't give discounts, not even to friends of old friends.'

'Thank you, ma'am.' Aiden mixed Aled's brandy and soda the way he liked it, with a splash of soda to nine-tenths brandy, handed it to Aled on a tray and left.

'Good boys you have there,' Anna complimented after Aiden had closed the door.

'Almost as good as your girls,' Aled replied.

'I heard that you enjoyed yourself at my house yesterday.'

'You talked to Gertie?'

'She's hoping you'll become a regular.'

'No chance, but I might send for her sometime if I'm bored.'

'Why not visit?'

'You've a nice place, Anna, discreet, well staffed, comfortable, but I feel more at home in my own territory.'

'In other words, you wanted to see my set-up for yourself.'

'And your girls,' he replied frankly. 'One or two of them are a bit rough, Colleen for instance. She has a mouth on her like a colliery siren, but given less obvious clothes, better make-up and perfume instead of scent, the others might clean up well enough.'

'Thank you for the compliment,' Anna retorted sarcastically. 'What did you expect? Greta Garbo?'

'That wasn't a criticism, so you can smooth your ruffled feathers. Some men like a girl with a mouth like a colliery siren.'

'Each to their own – that's what your mother always used to say.'

'Among other things.'

'It's all over Bute Street that you intend to open a club in the old hotel,' Anna fished blatantly.

'If everything goes to plan. The ground floor is large enough to take a small stage – or will be, once the rooms and hall have been knocked into one. The casino will go on a mezzanine on the first floor so the gamblers can watch the show in between losing their money, and that brings me to the top floor.'

'Before we go that high, you seem very sure of getting planning permission,' Anna commented.

'I am, and that's where you come in, Anna.'

'Me?' She looked at him in surprise. 'I'm strictly a small-time business woman. I don't know anything about nightclubs.'

'Don't put yourself down. You run a successful bordello—'

'A what?'

'Sorry, American word.'

'You've been there so long, you look like a movie star, you talk like a movie star and the way you're splashing your money around you behave like one. When can I expect to see you in the pictures, Aled?'

'Never. I like to keep my face out of the limelight. And, in my black heart, I'll always be Welsh,' he joked. 'You run a brothel . . . '

'I prefer house, and me and my girls are doing very nicely, thank you. We don't need any business partners. I made twelve quid last night.'

He whistled. 'You must have rolled a couple of drunks to get that much, Anna.'

'Just one with peculiar tastes,' she replied honestly.

'I have no intention of muscling in on your house, but the fact that you're still operating means you know the right people.'

'What if I do?' she challenged.

'I'll pay well for introductions.'

'Most of our clients are small time. Clerks, councillors—'

'Clerks and councillors who work for the big boys. They'll know which politicians I can pay to jump into my pocket and those who'll turn a blind eye. They'll also know who I should avoid. The sooner I get my club up and running the sooner I'll start turning profits. And these people I need to be introduced to – they may like the odd private party.'

'Introductions and the odd private party – that's all you want?' she asked cautiously.

'For the moment. There may be more later.'

'I'll not work for you or any man. I'm good to my girls and they're good to me. I answer to no one except myself and I'm not about to change that for all the tea in China, Aled.'

'I'm not going to offer you a job – just commission you to run the odd special party in the upstairs rooms in the club for selected guests.'

'I'll charge you full rate.'

'I wouldn't expect you to do otherwise.'

'Now that's cleared up, I can relax.' She held out her glass. He reached for the bottle Aiden had left in the ice bucket and refilled it.

'I also need information,' he added. 'There was a very pretty young coloured girl singing with one of the jazz bands at the carnival. They were dressed in gold, even the musicians.'

'That would be the Bute Street Blues Band?' Anna eyed him carefully. 'Don't tell me you've fallen in love.'

'I'm looking for a singer for the club. I thought I'd seen the best in America but that girl was better.'

'She's also respectable. And all the men in the band look out for her. The Chinese drummer has a fearful temper, as does the Arab who plays the trumpet. The

70

white man is pastor of the Norwegian Church and you can't get any more respectable than that. And the three tall West Indian Negroes are her uncles and they watch her like a hawk.'

'What else do you know about her?' he probed.

'Her name's Judy Hamilton, although I've heard she sometimes uses King nowadays, which was her mother's maiden name. Her father's a drunk and a sailor. I think she's only seen him twice in her life, and the last time he robbed her of everything she owned. She's nice as well as respectable. I've sold her a couple of evening frocks over the years. Her share of the money the band pulls in playing the pubs and clubs around the Bay doesn't amount to much. But saying that, she hasn't bought much off me lately. She moved in with Edyth Slater who took over Goldman's bakery just before last Christmas; works for her too when she isn't playing with the band. And, if it's a band you're after, you could do worse than the Bute Street Blues. But they're not professional and I doubt they'd work for you full time. Steve Chan – the drummer – runs his father's laundry; as I said, Micah Holsten – the saxophone player – is pastor of the Norwegian Church, and Abdul and the others spend as much time at sea as they can, which isn't much at the moment but you'd have to pay them well to make them give up the day job.'

'I'm more interested in the girl than the band. Musicians are ten a penny, get the right musical director and he'll knock even mediocre players into shape.' Aled went to the drinks table and mixed himself another brandy and soda.

'Just how interested are you in the girl?' Anna probed.

'Very, but only on a professional basis. I use the Gerties of this world to provide me with company whenever I need it. It's less messy that way.'

'You always were a cold fish, Aled. Even as a boy.'

He returned to his chair. 'When it comes to ice in the blood, I had good teachers,' he said quietly.

'This club of yours, if you need any young girls, I might be able to help. I know people in the valley who are on the lookout for ones with potential. They charge ten pounds an introduction but—'

'I'll do my own recruiting,' he broke in. 'I'll employ hostesses and cigarette girls but I've no intention of setting up in competition with you. I'll have enough sweeteners to pay without bribing the coppers to look the other way every time a tart tries to pick up a customer. If my chorus girls want to make a bit on the side, that's between them and the punters. I don't mind them socialising, anything more will have to be off the premises. The real money is in gambling. The bar should bring in a bit but I'll be lucky if the shows break even.'

'You're a pessimist.'

'I'm a realist. This won't be the first club I've owned.'

'So, what will go on upstairs?' she questioned curiously.

He walked to the window and looked down on Stuart Street two floors below. 'As I said, the occasional strictly invitation-only private party for privileged customers.'

'And nothing else?'

'No, so you can stop feeling under the pillow for things that aren't there, Anna.'

'You're not looking to put my house out of business?'

He turned and smiled at her. 'You always were suspicious, Anna.'

'Can you blame me?'

'We're after different markets, you and I. Keep your sailors and clerks. I'm after the big money. And the parties will be occasional. Very occasional.' He returned to the drinks table and refilled her glass. 'You said you were semi-retired apart from carnival and holidays.'

'And my regulars. I am.'

'I'll pay you twenty quid a time to hostess them.'

'What.' She dropped her glass. 'Bugger it!' She jumped up and tried to dry the stain she had made on the plush upholstery with her handkerchief.

'Leave it. I'll call housekeeping, they'll see to it.'

'You did say twenty quid?'

'To look after the customers, deal with any difficult clients and make sure there's no trouble.'

'In my experience if a customer is hell bent on making trouble no one can stop him.'

'You've met Aiden and Freddie.'

'They can't be everywhere. You'll need them in the casino.'

'How many unemployed Freddies and Aidens are there on the Bay who'd be prepared to work for me for a tenner a week?'

'For a snotty-nosed kid who sailed out of here with nothing more than the clothes on his back, you've some big ideas, Aled.'

'Here's to bigger ones, Anna.' He touched her glass to his. 'One more thing, what do you know about Geoff Arnold?'

'He used to be a bank clerk, but like you he had big ideas. He scraped together enough money to buy a house in Loudon Square that he let out in rooms, then another and another. Apparently he owns a dozen or more now. He left the bank years ago and set himself up as an estate agent in an office in Bute Street. But he lives somewhere posh, Rhiwbina way I think. Butetown wasn't grand enough for his wives and daughters once he'd made a bit of money.'

'I'm sure I've seen him before,' Aled mused.

'You have. He used to be one of your mother's regulars.'

'So that's why I didn't like him.'

'He used to give her five bob on the nail every Friday. It was half the rent on her room. She couldn't afford to turn it down.'

'That's our dinner,' he said in relief at a knock on the door. He had several years' worth of memories of his mother and none he wanted to revisit.

'I hope you've ordered the most expensive dinner on the menu,' she joked.

'What else would I order for you, Anna?' he said seriously.

David was surprised by how ordinary Jed King's house was. He'd expected something more exotic given the King family's West Indian blood. Also, he didn't have that much to compare Jed's house to.

Although he'd delivered his family's farm produce to shops in the Swansea Valley before Harry had married his sister, he hadn't visited many private houses aside from the few farmhouses around them and they had all been similar to his own. The comparative luxury of Harry's parents' home in Pontypridd with its thick carpets, soft upholstered furniture, bathrooms, indoor toilets, running hot and cold water and electric lighting in every room had come as a culture shock before Harry had introduced similar luxuries into the farmhouse.

Jed's back kitchen was a quarter of the size of the one at the farm. The range that dominated one wall was doll-like in comparison to the massive one Mary used. But although the furniture was on a smaller scale than the pieces he was used to, they served the same purpose.

There was a Welsh dresser filled with everyday blue and white china. Two easy chairs were set either side of the range, and a scrub-down table flanked by benches, which took up less room than chairs, filled the centre of the kitchen. Waist-high cupboards had been built into the alcoves either side of the chimney breast. A marble-topped iron stand stood below the window that overlooked the yard. On it was an enamel water jug and basin.

There were a few ornaments. A framed embroidered

picture of a country cottage hung on one wall, a mirror on another and neat rows of books had been arranged on top of the alcove cupboards. A green pressed-glass vase filled with the large white flowers Mary called dog daisies stood in the centre of the table. A bewildering number of chattering children sat on the benches, the older ones reading, the younger ones drawing pictures in charcoal on brown paper bags.

Given the King family's dark skin, David was amazed to hear all of them speaking English with pronounced Welsh accents. There were no 'foreigners' living in the Swansea Valley or on the hills between the valley and Brecon town. And, unlike the Ellises, most of the people also spoke Welsh as a first language. The occasional English person he had met while visiting the cattle markets in Brecon and Pontardawe had seemed positively alien. As a result, he found the variety of races, languages, skin colours and music in Tiger Bay over-whelming.

Harry had brought recordings of Negro jazz music home that David had admired and listened to, time and again. And, as he could neither read music nor play an instrument, he believed that all musicians, even Judy who he knew reasonably well, possessed some kind of magical quality. To him, musicians existed in some world other than the mundane one he inhabited. Yet Jed seemed to live no different a life in his kitchen to the one he'd lived with Harry, Mary, his sister and brothers in his farm-house. Apart from maybe the food. There was an appetising smell of unusual cooking in the air, which he put down to mysterious rare ingredients.

'Sit down, David.' Jed pointed to the easy chair opposite his own.

'Thank you.' David took it while Judy and her aunt gathered the children and herded them next door to Tony King's house.

75

'Judy tells me you want to go to sea.' Jed pulled an empty pipe from his pocket and stared thoughtfully at it.

'I do,' David confirmed.

'Why?'

The question took David by surprise. He hadn't expected anyone to query his motives. 'Because I want to see more of the world than I can from my farmhouse windows.'

'And you think you'll see more of the world on board ship?'

'Of course,' David answered. 'I've always wanted to travel out of Wales, and visit different countries.'

'Go to sea and ninety-nine days out of a hundred you're not likely to see more than the water that surrounds the ship.'

'But ships land—'

'In ports,' Jed broke in. 'They discharge their cargoes and take on new ones. And during that time you'll be expected to help with the ship's maintenance that can't be done at sea, as well as supervise the stowing of the cargo. You'll be lucky if you're given a couple of hours to go ashore to get drunk in a dockside pub. Unless, of course, you decide to leave the ship and look for a berth out of wherever you are, on another vessel. In which case you'd better pray you strike lucky before your money runs out. Not all ports have seamen's missions or doss houses that dole out meals to the destitute.'

'I see.' David cleared his throat.

'Not what you expected?' Jed asked.

'Judy told me that shipping trade was down.'

'I don't know about down, it's practically non-existent. And it's hard to get a berth since they made us all register. You'll actually be better off than me, because white British sailors get first chance of any jobs that are going, coloured British sailors second, although they've made everyone with coloured blood register as an alien irrespective of where they were born, and foreigners last.'

'That's hardly fair—'

Jed interrupted him. 'Go to sea, boy, and you'll find out that fair isn't a word that's understood any better on board ship than it is on land.' He replaced his pipe in his shirt pocket. 'Still want to go to sea?'

'Yes,' David replied stoutly, too proud to back down.

'Come here at five o'clock tomorrow morning. That too early for you?'

'We get up earlier on the farm.'

'I'll take you to Penniless Point. If any ships' masters are looking for crew, they'll go to the Corys building first. But I warn you, the only work that's been on offer for the last six months is with the Irish shipping lines. Take coal out, bring potatoes in, which amounts to four or five days work at most, and without experience all you'll get is your food and not much of that. But you'll earn your ticket.'

'That's what I want.'

'You won't be classed higher than cabin boy, not without experience. And the Irish Sea can be rough, even in summer. Ever been seasick?'

'No,' David retorted swiftly.

'Ever been to sea?'

'Once.'

'Where?'

'On a ship from Swansea, around the Gower.'

Jed laughed. 'A pleasure cruise.' He shook his head. 'You'll be letting yourself in for a bit more than pleasure on board a ship bound for Ireland, boy. But first you have to find someone who's prepared to take you. And if you do, you'll find out what going to sea means for yourself.'

'That's all I want, Mr King,' David said soberly.

Jed laughed. 'You've guts, boy, I'll give you that much. But I'm not sure how far someone can travel on guts alone.'

# CHAPTER FIVE

'Do you have to go now, right this minute?' Micah lay back on the make-shift bed in the cabin of the *Escape* and watched Edyth hook the welts of her stockings on to her suspender belt.

'It's six o'clock. By the time I get back to the shop, make tea for Judy and me – and you, if you'd like to stay – and clear up the last of the carnival debris it will be bedtime.'

'I suppose that's a hint for me to move.' Micah rolled over and leaned on his elbow.

'Only if you want to walk me back to Bute Street.'

'I wish I could stay the night with you in your bed—'

'Stop right there.' Edyth took her comb and lipstick from her handbag. 'You promised earlier that you wouldn't bring up that subject again until I was free.'

'Sometimes I think you don't want Peter to send those annulment papers.'

'You promised.'

'I did, didn't I?' He reluctantly sat up. 'Will you be able to get away early any night this week?'

She threw his vest and shirt to him. 'Most nights, I should think. I've nothing special on. But Judy has an audition tomorrow.'

'That's strange; she hasn't mentioned it to me – or her uncles, that I know about. Is it in London?' he asked hopefully.

'The New Theatre.'

'That explains why she hasn't said anything. She's had

six call–backs for auditions there in the last three months and none have resulted in an engagement.'

'Let's hope this one will be different. Although I'm worried. I know it's selfish of me to want to keep Judy working in the bakery when she's so talented, but frankly I wouldn't have been able to manage without her the last six months. I dread the thought of trying to replace her.'

'The selfish works both ways. If you hadn't offered Judy a job and a place to live she would have had to move away to London where there are live-in service jobs even for coloured girls.' He finished buttoning his shirt and picked up his sock suspenders. 'As for replacing her, you'll have plenty of girls to choose from.'

'But they won't be Judy.'

'If she's in the New Theatre, she can carry on living with you, so you'll still see her, unless you need her room for someone else.'

'With four bedrooms above the shop, she's more than welcome to stay.' She watched him pull on his trousers and clip on his braces. 'Come on, slowcoach, I thought it was women who were supposed to spend a long time dressing.'

'Nagging me before we're even married,' he teased.

'I'll ignore that remark.'

'If Judy does get that job in the New Theatre there's no guarantee it will last more than a couple of weeks.' He picked up the rest of his clothes. 'Then she'll be back to auditions again.'

'I know.'

'If it's a temporary worker you need, you could do worse than ask one of her uncles to cover for her. I know all three are finding it hard to make ends meet at the moment.'

'I can't afford to pay anyone more than I'm paying Judy now,' she warned.

'A pittance is better than nothing. And the way this

slump is beginning to bite, you could pay people in bread.'

She looked him in the eye. 'Has Moody told you that I've had to cut back on production?'

'He didn't have to.' He finished lacing his shoes and rose to his feet. 'I walk around the Bay. I see the women shopping, and the men hanging around street corners. And I've not heard the sound of any spare coins jangling lately.' He lifted the cushions back to the sides of the boat and heaved the table between them. 'How much have you had to cut back?'

'Ten per cent on bread, forty on cakes and biscuits.'

'Can the bakery survive a lower turnover?' He flicked a comb through his hair, and dropped his boater on his head.

'Just about.'

'You are managing?' he asked seriously.

'For now. It's not just me; all the shopkeepers in Bute Street are complaining that trade's down.'

He slipped his arms around her shoulders. 'You will tell me if you need help?'

'What would you do?' she asked. 'Order all the Norwegian sailors who visit your mission to buy their bread from me when you deliver your Sunday sermon?'

'I have a little money saved . . . '

'I don't know much about accounting but I do know that you'll lose money if you try to prop up a business that has more going out than coming in. Things aren't that bad, Micah – yet,' she qualified. 'Hopefully the ships will start sailing again soon and then trade is bound to pick up.'

He decided not to tell her that all the shipping agents and bankers he had spoken to in the past few weeks were predicting the opposite. 'What time is Judy's audition tomorrow?'

'Four o'clock. Want to come round for tea about five?'

'As she's only in the New Theatre, I'd prefer a picnic

here. Less likelihood of being disturbed. Then I'll walk you home and Judy can tell us whether or not she's been successful.'

'In that case I'll make a special supper for the three of us and we can offer Judy our congratulations or sympathies, whichever is appropriate.'

'Sounds perfect. I'll even call in and walk you down here.' He dropped a kiss on her forehead before opening the door of the cabin.

'So you're going to Penniless Point with Uncle Jed tomorrow?' Judy said to David when he escorted her back to Edyth's bakery. She had wanted to walk back alone, but over protective as always, her uncle had insisted that someone take her and as David was anxious to see Edyth, he was the obvious choice.

'He seems to think I'll get a job.'

'Not a paying one.' She reinforced Jed's warning.

'My keep would be a start and I can work up from there.'

'Like my uncles?' She couldn't resist reminding him that they were out of work.

'It's different for them.'

'Because they're coloured.'

'Jed told me about having to register as aliens although they were born on the Bay. But I didn't mean that,' he said swiftly. 'They have families to support; I have only myself to look after so I don't need as much money.' He stopped in front of the baker's shop.

'We use the back door when the shop's not open.' Judy led the way around to the yard. Edyth and Micah were standing, locked in one another's arms, oblivious to everything outside of one another.

David cried out.

Judy turned and saw a look of pure anguish on his face before he raced back down the alley into Bute Street.

When Edyth heard David cry out, she turned and saw him and Judy standing at the entrance to the yard. She pushed Micah away and tried to follow David when he ran off but Micah held her fast. She fought to free herself.

'Let me go,' she shouted.

'If anyone should go after him, it should be me.'

'You don't understand,' Edyth continued to struggle.

'Your brother telephoned after you left, Edyth,' Judy explained. 'He asked me to pick David up at the station. He wants to be a sailor.' After the way David had snapped at her since he'd arrived, Judy wasn't sure whether to go after him or not.

'David doesn't want to be a sailor.' Edyth finally wrenched free from Micah's grip. 'He's in the Bay because of me.'

'He's staying with Helga.' Judy dashed after Edyth when she darted into the street but Micah was quicker. He reached Bute Street before Judy. Edyth was standing on the pavement looking up and down the road. A tram hurtled around the corner and passed a procession of white–garbed Sunday school children from the Catholic Church. A donkey cart loaded with fresh fish meandered slowly up from the direction of the docks. Several groups of people stood gossiping but there was no sign of David.

Micah touched Edyth's arm. 'Did you hear? Judy said David's lodging with my sister.'

'Do you think he'd head back to Helga's?' Edyth's eyes were dark with concern.

He frowned. 'Is there something you're not telling me about you and David?'

'There is no me and David,' she countered touchily. 'Not as far as I'm concerned.'

'But David thinks otherwise?' he guessed.

'I have to find him, Micah,' she insisted. 'After seeing us together like that, he could do something stupid.'

'Aren't you being rather melodramatic?'

'I wish I was.' Finally giving up on David, she faced

Micah. 'The night I married Peter, David tried to kill himself by jumping off the Old Bridge in Pontypridd. He almost succeeded.'

'I thought he was trying to rescue a dog.'

'That was a story Harry and my father concocted with a police constable, so David wouldn't be charged with attempted suicide,' she explained. 'If he'd been found guilty he could have been sent to gaol.'

'Did you know that David was in love with you when you married Peter?'

'I didn't encourage him, if that's what you mean. I didn't even know he liked me until I read the note he left before he jumped off the bridge. For pity's sake, he's Mary's brother, Harry's brother-in-law. That practically makes him my brother too. We – my sisters and me, that is – thought of him as just that. We used to tease him the way we tease Harry.' She glanced up and down the street again. 'I won't be able to live with myself if David does something stupid again.'

'Go to Helga's house with Judy and wait for David there,' Micah ordered abruptly.

'Where are you going?' Edyth shouted after him as he ran down the street.

'The dock,' he called back.

'Pastor Holsten's right. David will probably go back to his sister's house.' Judy took Edyth's arm.

'Damn! Damn! Damn! And Vladivostok!'

As damn was the strongest swear word Judy had heard Edyth use, and Vladivostock Edyth's substitute for a more conventional curse, Judy realised how upset she was. 'Don't worry, we'll find David. He was so full of himself and sure of finding a berth out of the Bay, I can't see him hurting himself.'

'You heard what I said to Micah?' Edyth looked at her friend.

'I heard, but I'll keep it to myself.'

'I know you will. I only hope you're right about David not hurting himself.'

Judy linked her arm into Edyth's. 'I bet we'll find him sitting at the table in Helga's back kitchen, drinking tea and eating pickled herrings, Norwegian cheese and rye bread with her other lodgers. And listening to their tall stories about life at sea.'

Gertie was generally happy with life and especially happy with the money she was making. Even after she paid Anna three pounds to cover rent, food and household expenses, she still made five times as much as she could have expected to earn if she had gone into service. But being the youngest and newest resident in Anna's house did have its drawbacks. She was always the one sent on errands, especially on Sunday afternoons, when most of her 'regulars' were with their wives, children, extended family and friends.

Anna and Colleen had regular bachelor clients who visited them at that time, but she and the rest of the girls weren't so lucky. Unless a ship came in, and not many had berthed on a Sunday even when the docks had been busy, they generally spent the day visiting their families – if they were allowed to step over the threshold of the family home – or reading or playing cards with Anna and Colleen's children.

Still in her dressing gown at mid-afternoon, Gertie was lying on her bed immersed in a Mills and Boon romance she had borrowed from Boots' lending library, when one of the children discovered they had run out of sugar. Despite the fact that she didn't want tea, Gertie found herself unanimously 'volunteered' to go to the shop. Annoyed at having to dress, she opened her wardrobe and, remembering that it was Sunday, chose a relatively sober outfit.

Hot, bothered and put out at being picked on by the others, she left Abdul's corner shop with a pound of sugar and a chocolate bar she had bought on impulse. Abdul's was one of the few shops open in the Bay on a Sunday because he was a Muslim who ignored both the Christian calendar and the Sunday opening laws. She was heading back to the house when a good-looking young man hurtled around the corner ahead of her. Never one to let an opportunity slip by, she shouted, 'Want a good time?'

David halted and looked back at her. He recognised Gertie as the girl he had seen with the man who resembled Harry. Only this time, she was wearing a dress that wasn't transparent, although the hemline was just as short and the neckline as low.

Harry had warned him about the 'good-time girls' on the docks and told him to steer clear of them because all they wanted from men was money, and they were prone to work with roughnecks who would beat up and rob an unsuspecting customer for as little as sixpence. Even worse, they carried horrible diseases. But this girl was young, had a good figure, and although her features were too strong to be considered pretty, she looked too clean to be carrying a disease.

Having gained David's attention, Gertie gave him her toothy professional smile. 'My house is just around the corner. Five bob will buy you an hour of paradise.'

'I haven't got five bob.' It was the truth. Judy had insisted that David pay Helga a week's lodging in advance, which had come to seventeen shillings and sixpence and she had then made him lock his nine remaining pounds together with his bank book into his suitcase, which had left him with a few coins that amounted to a little over half a crown.

'How much have you got?' Gertie asked.

Used to haggling with the livestock buyers in Brecon cattle market, David answered, 'A shilling.'

'I never go below two bob.'

He fingered the coins in his pocket. 'What would I get for my two bob?'

Gertie lifted the hem of her dress a few inches. Her Sunday best was more subdued than the clothes she wore during the week, but David caught a glimpse of white thigh above the silk welts of her best pair of white stockings, bright green, diamanté-studded garters and vivid green silk French knickers. His cheeks burned at the glimpse of flesh.

'All right, two bob,' he said recklessly.

'Show us the colour of your money.' She held out her hand.

He shook his head. 'You could run off with it.'

'Two bob when we get to my room. And if you haven't got it, I'll call the others and they'll throw you out.'

'What others?' He recalled Harry's warning about loose women's violent and thieving accomplices.

'You'll see,' she murmured mysteriously.

'I don't want a fight. I'm going to sea,' he added superfluously.

'No one's going to roll you, lover boy.'

'Roll me?' He looked at her in confusion.

'You really are wet behind the ears, aren't you?'

David almost walked away at the taunt, but she lifted her skirt even higher. The even greater expanse of bare thigh below the green French knickers decided him. He followed her around three corners and along a street to an ordinary-looking terraced house.

She opened the door, and shouted, 'Come and get the sugar.'

'Why should we?' answered a bored voice.

'Because I've found myself a lover boy.'

What seemed like dozens of scantily dressed girls flooded into the narrow passage and stared at David. Embarrassed, he retreated towards the door, but Gertie grabbed hold of his hand and held him tight.

One of the girls brushed her hand over David's cheek.

'Very pretty, Gertie. Did you find him in the babies' class in Sunday school?'

'No, next to the sugar sack in Abdul's. Catch.' Gertie tossed the brown paper bag at her.

'Careful,' the girl cried out. 'Good job Abdul twists the top good and hard or we'd be clearing up sugar for a month.'

'Come on, lover boy, up the wooden hill to paradise.' Much to the other girls' amusement and David's mortification, Gertie grabbed his tie and led him up the stairs, making him feel like one of the lambs he dragged into the slaughtering shed every spring.

Micah didn't stop running until he reached the south end of Bute Street. The road ended at the dockside and he walked past the Pier Head to where the larger vessels were berthed, on the premise that David might have decided to ask some of the captains for work. But there were few people around. He was just about to give up when he felt a tap on his shoulder. He whirled around and his face fell.

'Not glad to see an old friend, Micah.'

'Very, Lars.' Micah took the hand the old sea captain offered him and shook it firmly. 'But I was looking for someone else.'

'A girl, judging by the disappointment on your face.'

'You're wrong, it's a boy.'

'Young boys have a habit of turning up, especially when you don't want them to,' Lars said wryly.

'This one ran away and he's particularly stupid.'

'And you think he'll turn up here?'

'I was hoping he would, but if he's going to,' Micah looked around again, 'he's not here yet.'

'Is he likely to go anywhere else?'

'Helga's house, possibly, he's lodging with her.'

'I have a bottle of aquavit in my cabin on the *Vidda*. We could crack it open?'

Micah hesitated, Lars Nordheim had been a good friend of Micah's parents, and had helped him when he'd needed it most, just after their deaths. The thought of sitting in Lars' comfortable cabin and drinking a glass of aquavit or two or three – and knowing Lars' hospitality eating a bowl of Norwegian fish soup to soak up the alcohol – was very tempting. But the anxiety on Edyth's face when David had run off haunted him.

'Send a message to Helga to tell her you're on board the *Vidda*. Ask her to let you know if the boy turns up there. In the meantime, we can sit on the wheel deck and look out for him. You won't get a better vantage point on the dock,' he added persuasively.

'No, I won't.' A thought occurred to Micah. 'When are you sailing?'

'Dawn tide in the morning. It's a short stopover this trip, otherwise you would have found me in your sister's house. So don't say you'll come back tomorrow.'

'I wasn't going to, Lars.' Micah laid his arm around the old man's shoulders. 'Can I ask you a favour?'

'Does it involve money?'

'Mine, possibly, if you need it.'

'Ask away.'


'Welcome to cloud nine, my bedroom and soon to be your paradise.' Gertie walked into the room, kicked off her shoes and faced David. 'Before you close the door I want to see your entrance ticket.'

'My what?' Mouth dry, heart thumping with anticipation – and fear – David stared at her dumbly.

'Your money? Two shillings, remember.'

He pushed his hand into his pocket and fingered the coins. Discarding the large heavy pennies, he pulled out a shilling, two small silver threepenny pieces and a sixpence. He held them out to her. She looked at them, took them from him and dropped them into a slot on a piggy bank on the mantelpiece.

'I'm Gertie.'

'David,' he muttered, summoning the courage to look around. The bedroom was untidy but not dissimilar to his younger sister Martha's, apart from the clutter of lipsticks, face creams, pots of rouge and scent bottles on the dressing table, and clothes scattered on and around the only chair.

The wallpaper was printed with pink roses against a background of leafy greenery, the linoleum was green and the bed was covered by a rumpled cream cotton cover that looked as though someone had been lying on it. Every inch of the mantelpiece and chest of drawers was crowded with china animals, mainly dogs and cats, and there were two vases, one on the window sill and one perched amongst the clutter of make-up on the dressing table. Both held bouquets of dusty purple and blue wax flowers.

Gertie took a book from the bed, dropped it to the floor and went to a marble washstand. To David's astonishment she continued to meet his steady gaze, while unbuttoning her frock. It dropped in a puddle at her feet and she stood before him dressed only in her stockings, garters and French knickers.

'My regulars tell me I'm quite an eyeful and have a very nice pair of gentlemen's comforters.' She thrust out her chest, and fingered her nipples. 'Do you like them?'

'They're very nice,' he mumbled, embarrassed at being asked and even more embarrassed because he couldn't stop staring at them.

'A "very nice" is hardly poetry, but I suppose it'll have to do.' She walked to the washstand and poured water from a china jug patterned with cornflowers into a similarly patterned bowl and shook some coloured crystals into it. He peered over her shoulder and watched the water turn purple. 'You can wash in this.'

'Wash?' he looked at her blankly.

'Wash,' she repeated.

He plunged his hands into the bowl and she burst out laughing.

'You've never visited a pro before, have you?'

'Lots of times,' he blustered.

'Really?' she mocked. 'Do you even know what to do?'

'Of course I do.' He meant to look at her face but his gaze kept slipping lower.

She moved close to him. 'There has to be a first time for everyone and I think it's nice of you to trust me to see you all right.'

He jumped back when he realised she was unbuttoning his fly. She slipped her hand inside his trousers and clamped it over the front of his underpants. 'Now that is *very* welcoming.'

'Gertie . . . '

'That's why you came, isn't it? Time to get you undressed, washed and on the bed so this,' she pinched him lightly, 'can start having fun. Nice suit you're wearing.' She unbuckled his belt and unclipped his braces. 'Is it your best?'

'My only, and I'll undress myself.' He grabbed his trousers as they slipped down.

'It's your two bob.' She pulled down the waistband of her French knickers and wriggled out of them. He froze, mesmerised by the sight of the first naked woman he had seen.

'Wash?' she reminded him after his clothes had joined hers on the floor. 'Or do you want me to do it for you?' Without waiting for him to reply, she soaped her hand and washed his private parts, but before she had time to reach for a towel he pushed her on to the bed. Unable to contain himself a moment longer he rolled on top of her and thrust himself into her. She cried out.

It took every ounce of willpower David had to pull away from her. 'I'm sorry. Did I hurt you?'

'Yes. You're clumsy but I suppose that can be cured by practice – yours not mine.'

He looked down at her. 'Your legs, your arms, you're covered in bruises. I'm so sorry . . . '

'The ones you've given me haven't had time to come out yet.'

'Then . . . '

'You're not my only clumsy customer. Come on.' She opened her arms, but he held back.

'They look painful.'

'Just slightly.' She wrapped her arms around his neck and he bent his head to kiss her lips. She turned her head aside. 'House rule, no kissing on the mouth but you can kiss anywhere else.' She moved sideways and leaned over him, lifting her breasts to his eye level.

'Gertie . . . '

'Ask me how a nice girl like me got into a business like this and I'll give *you* a few bruises.'

Terrified of hurting her a second time, he lifted her on top of him and thrust himself into her, as gently as his passion would allow. 'I was only going to say, this is bloody great,' he cried as he moved inside her.

'It might be for you, but I'm telling you, nicely mind, you do need a lot of practice. I'll clear a spot for you in my diary tomorrow and the day after. A couple of weeks of hard work on my part and I'll make every girl you do this with in future grateful that you picked me to teach you the basics.'

Micah was finishing his third glass of aquavit when he saw David leaning on the railings on the dockside. He made his excuses to Lars, shook hands with him and left the ship. He joined David, but although he was convinced that David had seen him, the boy continued to stare down at the dirty, grey-green water, flecked with coal-speckled foam.

Micah searched his mind for something to say. He loved Edyth and was certain she loved him – but that didn't stop him from feeling unaccountably guilty for causing David pain.

'What do you want?' David asked eventually, in a more civilised tone than Micah had expected.

'It's a free world and a nice evening, I came out for a walk in the hope that I would find you,' Micah said quietly.

'Why?'

'I thought we should talk.'

'I have nothing to say to you.' David was angry, and not just with Edyth. He hadn't given her a thought when he had been with Gertie. But he hadn't been able to stay in Gertie's room for as long as he'd wanted. Half a dozen theology students had turned up unexpectedly and he'd been unceremoniously bundled out at five minutes' notice. Gertie had told him he had no right to feel slighted because he'd had more than his two bob's worth. He sensed that he had, and he hadn't argued with her because she'd offered him another half hour at her special Monday-morning price of one shilling, but only on condition he left quietly.

He'd hoped to stay with Gertie long enough to make Edyth and Micah worry and feel guilty about what they'd done to him. The problem was he wasn't sure why he wanted Edyth to worry about him when she clearly didn't love him. For the first time he realised just how futile his feelings for Edyth were. And his experience with Gertie had complicated the situation. She'd introduced him to a whole new world of sensuality and sexual excitement that he couldn't wait to sample again.

'Please, David, you have to talk to someone.' Micah's plea broke in on David's thoughts.

He finally looked at Micah. 'Even if I wanted to talk, and I don't, you're the last person I'd talk to.'

If looks could kill, Micah knew he would have been six foot under. 'I'll buy you a drink if you'd like one.'

'It's Sunday.'

'All the pubs and hotels on the Bay serve travellers. We could be travellers. Please, David, give me a chance to explain my relationship with Edyth.'

'I've eyes in my head. What I saw you doing to Edyth doesn't need explaining.'

'Edyth's upset—'

'And you both probably had a bloody good laugh at my expense,' David interrupted furiously.

'If you think that, you don't know Edyth – or me – very well.'

'I've known Edyth for a damned sight longer and better than you. As for you,' David added contemptuously, 'I don't want to know you. You're supposed to be some sort of vicar and you were kissing a married woman.'

'A woman whose marriage was a short-lived disaster. I've asked Edyth to marry me as soon as she's free,' Micah confided.

'I hope she had the sense to tell you to go to hell.' Even as David said it he knew he wasn't making any sense. Micah hadn't been forcing himself on Edyth. From what little he'd seen, she'd been kissing Micah as passionately as he'd been kissing her.

'At the moment she's not free to give me an answer.' Deciding that a change of subject might be tactful, Micah said, 'Judy told me you want to be a sailor.'

'What if I do?'

'I can help you.'

'I don't need your help.'

'Please, David, you're a member of Edyth's family—'

'I thought Judy's uncles were your friends,' David interrupted.

'They are,' Micah confirmed, mystified by David's train of thought.

'They need jobs on ships, so why don't you help them?'

'Because I only know Norwegian ships' captains who ferry timber out of Scandinavia and carry coal back, which doesn't pay well. Most of them are having a hard time employing their existing crews, but see that ship over there?' Micah pointed to the *Vidda*.

'I've eyes in my head,' David snapped.

The captain is a friend of mine and if you're prepared to work for your keep and a seaman's ticket, he'll take you on as an unpaid apprentice ordinary seaman. He's sailing out on the dawn tide tomorrow.'

'Tomorrow!' All David could think about was Gertie's offer.

'You don't have to go if you don't want to, but it will be a chance for you to sample life at sea and see something of the Norwegian coast.'

'You just want to send me as far from Edyth as possible.'

'I don't want that at all, David.' Micah looked back up Bute Street. Couples and families were walking out in their Sunday best, on their way either to or from church, chapel, or visiting friends and neighbours. He wished he and Edyth were among them. 'When Edyth saw you run off like that, she was worried about you.'

'If she was so worried why didn't she come and find me herself?' David questioned.

'Judy told us that you were staying at my sister's boarding house. Edyth went to look for you there. She said she'd wait until you turned up.'

'You've just given me reason to stay out all night.'

Deciding another change of subject was politic, Micah said, 'It wouldn't cost you anything to talk to the captain.'

David moved away. 'I don't want anything from you.'

'You wouldn't be taking anything from me. The captain said he'd take you on, not me.'

'You persuaded him,' David pointed out logically.

'I asked him if he would consider the idea, but I won't even go with you when you talk to him if you don't want me to.'

'You won't?'

'I have to get back to the mission.' Micah wanted to find a boy who would take a note to Helga's house to let Edyth know that he'd found David, safe, sound and still angry with both of them.

'Why are you so eager to help me?'

'Because Edyth likes you and regards you as her friend,' Micah replied honestly.

'And you don't want to send me away from her?'

'Not unless you want to go. I want what you want for yourself, David.'

'And you'll let me talk to the captain by myself?' David moved away from the rail.

'When you get to know me better you'll find out that I always keep my word,' Micah reiterated wearily.

'That's the ship?' David pointed to the *Vidda*.

'It is, ask for Captain Nordheim and tell him that you're the boy I talked to him about.'

'I will.' David walked away without giving Micah a backward glance.

# CHAPTER SIX

'What does it say?' Judy asked when Edyth read Micah's note, which had been hand delivered to Helga's house.

'That David's safe and talking to a Norwegian ship captain who might give him a berth.' Edyth folded the sheet of paper and slipped it into her pocket. She had kept every note, no matter how trivial and mundane, that Micah had sent her. As a result she had a biscuit tin full of keepsakes, ticket stubs from films, concerts and plays they had seen together, as well as the notes. She had even pressed some of the flowers he had given her and pasted them into a book.

'The sea is the best place for David,' Judy commented, uncharacteristically sarcastic for her.

'You two didn't get on too well?' Edyth guessed.

'He thinks he knows it all.'

'That's only the front he shows the world. He's always been unsure of himself away from his farm,' Edyth said, remembering how tongue-tied and nervous David had been the first time Harry had brought him to their parents' house.

'Then he should go back there.'

'Harry and Mary would probably agree with you. But perhaps David left there to assert his independence. As the oldest boy he regarded himself as head of his orphaned family until Harry married Mary. And if my brother has one fault, it's a tendency to try to make people's decisions for them – always from the best possible motives. But I've sensed David's resentment, especially when Harry talks about making a home

96

elsewhere for himself and Mary in a few years, and handing the farm over to David.'

'But it is David's farm, isn't it?' Judy asked.

'The Ellises have managed it for generations and they will own it in a few years,' Edyth said vaguely, not wanting to go into the intricacies of Harry's inheritance, 'but I don't think either Harry or Mary have thought to ask David how he feels about taking full responsibility for running it.' Edyth checked the time. 'You should go back to the shop, Judy.'

'Not without you.'

'You know what sailors are once they start talking. It could be hours before David returns here. There's ham, cheese and fruit cake in the pantry, make yourself some supper and go to bed. It's hard enough to get up at four in the morning during the week and doubly hard after a lie-in on Sunday. After a late night I'm never fit for much, which means I'll probably be relying on you more than usual tomorrow.'

'You relying on me? That will be a first.' Judy smiled and left the table.

'Thanks, Judy.'

'Ask one of your uncles to walk you back,' Helga advised her.

'The shop's only ten minutes away and it's not even seven o'clock yet.'

'And the docks are full of unemployed sailors, who manage to get drunk at all hours of the day and night no matter how little money they have.' Helga lifted the vase of flowers from the centre of her kitchen table and set it on the window sill.

'Helga's right.' Edyth helped Helga spread the patchwork quilt she was making on the table. 'Besides, don't your uncles go down to the mission most evenings? It will only take them a few minutes longer to walk you past the shop.'

'You're a pair of fusspots,' Judy said fondly, before kissing Helga's cheek. 'Bye, Helga, thanks for the tea.'

'Thank you for helping me to clear up after my lodgers. And good luck with the audition tomorrow.'

'You told her?' Judy asked Edyth.

'And Micah,' Edyth confessed. 'Sorry, I didn't know it was supposed to be a secret.'

'It's not,' Judy said. 'It's just that I'm tired of being on the receiving end of sympathy when I get "thanks for coming but no thanks".'

'Tomorrow will be different,' Helga assured her.

'How do you know?' Judy picked up her cardigan from the back of a chair.

'I inherited my grandmother's second sight.'

'I wish I could believe you.' Judy opened the door.

'It's true, you'll get the job,' Helga lifted her work box on to the table alongside the quilt, 'but only if you believe in yourself.'

'That sounds more Irish than Norwegian to me.'

'Can I help it if my native culture's been affected by living in this melting pot?' Helga picked up her needle book.

'Did your grandmother really have second sight?' Edyth asked, after Judy had left and she and Helga were sitting at opposite ends of the table, stitching patches on to the quilt.

'So everyone in my family and our home village believed. Hasn't Micah told you the family legends?'

'No.' Until that moment, Edyth had assumed that Helga was unaware of her relationship with Micah. Suddenly she wasn't so sure.

'Micah never knew her; he was only a few months old when we left Norway for Gdansk when my father was asked to manage the Norwegian Mission Church there. But our parents talked about her all the time. She must have been a strong woman. She was only ten when her father was lost at sea. Three years later her mother died after falling from a hayrick on to a pitch fork, yet she kept the family farm going and brought up her six younger brothers and sisters.'

'A strong woman indeed.' Edyth knew that Micah's parents had died young, which was why he'd followed Helga and her husband to the home they'd made for themselves and Moody in Cardiff. But she knew nothing else about his family and hoped that Helga would tell her more.

'I was very small, only three or four years old, when I last saw her, but I remember her as very tall, slim and upright – like Micah – and her hair was even whiter than ours. The last thing she said to me was that Micah and I were going to have long and happy lives and that I would have four children and Micah three. Mine have been a long time coming, but Micah's even longer.'

There was a tone in Helga's voice that alerted Edyth. 'Helga, you're . . . '

'Three months, but don't tell Micah. He frets over me like a mother hen with a single chick whenever Alex is away as it is. He'll be ten times worse once he knows he's going to become an uncle.'

Alexander Brown, Helga's West Indian, ship's engineer husband, had sailed out on a vessel bound for Australia six weeks before and wasn't expected back for months.

'It will be hard for you, keeping house for your lodgers while you're pregnant.'

'Moody helps, and not just with the housework. You've no idea how glad we both are that you kept him on when you bought Goldman's. A steady job these days is worth more than gold – no pun intended.'

'Moody's a brilliant baker. I'm lucky to have him.' Hoping that worsening trade wouldn't force her to close the bakery, Edyth crossed her fingers superstitiously under cover of the quilt.

'I'm sure my grandmother knew when she waved us off from the dock at Oslo that she would never see any of us again. I remember looking at the tears in her eyes and thinking they were more than just goodbye tears. She was dead from lung disease within a year.'

'I'm sorry. I know how you feel. I was very close to my grandfather. He died four years ago.'

'I was only a child and children accept loss more easily when it's at a distance. We hadn't seen her in months. I had new friends, a new dog; a new place to live, a new city to explore, which was much grander than our home village.' Helga stabbed her needle into a patch, and ceased stitching. 'It was much worse when my parents died, especially for Micah. I had left Gdansk the year before to come here with Alex. But friends wrote and begged me to go to Micah after it happened because they were worried about his sanity. It was a terrible time for both of us but more so for him because he was with them.'

'How did they die?' As soon as the words were out of her mouth Edyth realised she was prying. 'I'm sorry; you don't have to tell me if you don't want to.'

'Micah has never talked to you about our parents?'

Edyth shook her head.

'Which means he still hasn't come to terms with their deaths. There was an epidemic of diphtheria in Gdansk. There was a shortage of beds in the local hospital so my parents threw open the doors of the mission and took in the overflow. They worked day and night with the local doctors and nurses for a week before they caught the disease. Micah did all he could, but they died within four hours of one another. My father went first, my mother died without even knowing he was dead.'

'"Micah did all he could"?' Edyth repeated in bewilderment. 'But what about the doctors?'

'He's never told you that either? Micah was only six months away from qualifying as a doctor when our parents died.'

'I had no idea.' Edyth reflected how little she knew

about Micah's life before they had met. 'So that's why the police send for him whenever someone gets injured in a street fight.'

'Oh, he's happy enough to patch up cuts and bruises and even strap up a simple broken bone on a drunk, but despite all my nagging he refuses to go back and finish his studies. I tried arguing with him when I went to Gdansk to help him arrange our parents' funeral and I've carried on arguing with him ever since he arrived here, but,' she picked up her needle again, 'you know how stubborn he can be.'

'Yes, I do,' Edyth said thoughtfully.

'So, are you going to marry my little brother when Peter sends you those papers?' Helga asked.

'Not immediately,' Edyth replied.

'I can't say I blame you. You're what – eighteen?'

'Nineteen.'

'I didn't marry Alex until I was twenty-five and even then I'm not sure I knew my own mind. You've made a good and independent life for yourself, Edyth. I told Micah you'd be foolish to give that up to wash his socks.'

'You've discussed me with Micah?' Edyth was more surprised than annoyed.

'He asked my advice. He wanted me to tell him how he could persuade you to marry him. I told him that the only person he should discuss marriage with is you. I'm on your side.'

'Thank you, Helga,' Edyth said gratefully.

'I've never had a sister, so I'm looking forward to having you as a sister-in-law.' She parried Edyth's quizzical look. 'I did say I had second sight.'

Unsure whether Helga was serious or not, Edyth moved the conversation on. 'If you need any help here or with the baby . . . '

'I'll call on Micah and Moody first and you next. Family is everything.' The front door opened and closed.

Helga glanced at the clock. It was a few minutes before eight. 'I expected David to be later.'

Edyth braced herself. She hadn't read out the last line of Micah's note to Helga and Judy, the one in which he'd said that David was still angry with him – and her.

David walked into the kitchen, flushed and excited. 'Mrs Brown, I'm sailing to Norway and I'll be leaving before dawn—' He saw Edyth sitting at the table and fell silent.

'You have a berth on a ship?' Helga asked.

'On a Norwegian ship that's taking coal to Norway, and returning with wood for pit props.'

'Then I'd better make sandwiches for your supper, and a few extra that you can take with you. If you're sailing at dawn, the ship's breakfast will be late. Do you want to leave any of your things here?'

'I only have the one suitcase,' David reminded her.

'Sailors don't carry suitcases, they take canvas kitbags. My husband has a spare one upstairs. I'll get it for you.' Helga tactfully left the room.

Edyth waited a few moments. When it became clear that David wasn't going to acknowledge her presence, she began, 'What you saw earlier in the yard—'

'Forget it,' he broke in.

'I can't, not after what you did when I married Peter.' All the emotions David had kept pent up for the past year finally erupted. 'You must have known how I felt about you. I loved you. Do you know what that means? How serious I was about you?'

Encouraged by the 'was', she murmured, 'You never told me.'

'What did you think I was doing at all those parties at your parents' house? I only danced with you, no one else. Only you.'

'There's a difference between dancing with someone and being in love with them.' Edyth recalled her visits to Harry and Mary on the farm where David had lived all his life. The wilderness around it, how isolated it was and she realised how lonely David must have been when he'd been growing up, with only his immediate family for company. It was little wonder that he had set so much store by the casual friendship she had offered.

'I could understand you not wanting to go back to live with your parents when Peter left you. I could even understand you wanting to run your own business,' he reproached, 'but to start carrying on with another vicar before your marriage to the first one is over—'

'I've made a lot of mistakes,' she acknowledged, not wanting to hear any more. 'And I'm sorry for hurting you. But it's the last thing I intended to do. If I could turn the clock back I would.'

'To do what?' He folded his arms across his chest and stood before her, silent and self-contained.

'To take the time to get to get know Peter properly. If I had, I never would have married him. Also, to explain to you that I couldn't help falling in love with Peter any more than I could help falling in love with Micah.'

'So you do love the vicar.'

'He's a pastor, David, and yes, I do love him.'

'And you're going to marry him?'

'Perhaps, in time. But I won't be able to answer that question until my marriage to Peter is annulled.'

'Where does that leave me?' he demanded, reminding Edyth of the self-centred demands her small brother Glyn used to make when he was a toddler.

'Your sister is married to my brother, we're family, David, and hopefully we'll remain close – and friends.'

'And if I want more?'

'I can't offer you any more than friendship. I've never lied to you and I'm not about to start now. But I'll always wish you well and think of you as my third brother.'

He fell silent again when he heard Helga walk down the stairs.

'You'll come and see me when you return from Norway?' Edyth pressed.

'That depends on whether or not I return to Cardiff. I could go anywhere in the world,' he said airily.

'In which case, I hope you'll write to me.'

'There's no point in my doing that, is there?' he challenged.

Helga opened the door and handed David a white canvas kitbag. 'Leave anything you don't want to take with you in your suitcase and lock it. I'll put it in the box-room along with the things I'm keeping for my other lodgers.'

'Thank you.' He took the bag from her.

Edyth held out her hand to him. 'Good luck.'

He ignored it. 'I have to pack.'

'And I'd better go home. I have to get up early.'

'You're not walking back to Bute Street on your own,' Helga remonstrated.

'I'll be fine, Helga. I'm almost regarded as a resident of the Bay now. Besides it's not late.'

Sensing the atmosphere between them, Helga said, 'David, why don't you walk Edyth home?'

'I don't have time.'

'I really would rather go back alone, Helga. Good luck, David.' Edyth almost ran from the house. She walked quickly down the road. A cold shiver ran down her spine when she heard footsteps behind her. Too frightened to turn around to see who was following her, she quickened her pace but the faster she walked, the faster they resounded.

'There wasn't much point in my waiting for you if you're going to run away from me.'

She weakened in relief. 'Micah.'

He drew alongside her, opened his arms and she went to him. 'Did David give you a rough time?'

'It could have been worse. Did you speak to him?'

'I tried but gave up. I've arranged passage to Norway and back on a freighter for him with a captain I know.'

'He told us he was sailing tomorrow but he didn't give you credit for organising it.'

'Perhaps a couple of weeks in the North Sea will cool David's temper.'

'Time will tell.'

'Can I walk you home?'

'I'd be cross with you if you didn't.'

He offered her his arm and she hooked her hand into the crook of his elbow.

'David will be all right,' he assured her.

'How do you know?' she asked, her suspicions roused.

'Because I know Lars Nordheim. He's the captain of the *Vidda* – the ship David's sailing out on – and he looks after his crew like a father.'

'You paid him to take David on board, didn't you?'

'I did not,' he countered indignantly.

'I can see your fingers crossed behind your back.'

'They are not. And you really can stop worrying.' He smiled wryly. 'But I'm not promising that David will go to sea again after this voyage. Norwegian sailors can be a rough lot. On the other hand, he may develop a taste for aquavit in which case we can expect him to turn up back here an honorary Scandinavian and a confirmed drunkard.'

'As if that's likely.'

'At least I managed to bring a smile to your face.'

'Thanks, Micah, but I've a feeling we're not out the woods yet as far as David is concerned.'

'Everyone has to grow up,' he said quietly, 'let's hope that David manages it soon.'

Judy wandered through the following day in a daze. She rose at four, helped to clean the shop and set out the bread, rolls, cakes and biscuits as soon as her nephews carried them in, hot and steaming from the kitchen where Moody was working flat out.

She bagged bread rolls, boxed cream cakes, smiled at customers, took their money, gave them their goods and counted change from the till, all the while barely hearing a word anyone said to her beyond their actual order.

She was totally preoccupied with the rehearsal outfits she had laid out on her bed. Should she wear the white short skirt and sleeveless top with her white tap shoes? Or should she opt for her red outfit with its pleated skirt? Or would her yellow ballet tutu be better? And all the while she considered her clothes, she mentally rehearsed the Pagan Love Song she'd been asked to practise for the call-back . . .

*Come with me where moonbeams light Tahitian* – no, not Tahitian, for Tahitian substitute Indian. She couldn't afford to get that wrong! If she did they might think she couldn't remember lines – *Indian skies and the starlit waters linger in your eyes. Native hills are calling, to them we belong and we'll cheer each other with the pagan love song—'*

'Judy?'

She looked blankly at Edyth.

'I've been trying to talk to you for the last two minutes. Go and get ready for your audition.'

Judy glanced at the clock. 'But it's not for another two hours.'

'The shop's quiet and we've almost sold out of goods. If it's too early to go to the audition, practise in your room.'

'You sure?' Judy was already untying her apron.

'I'm sure. Edyth suppressed a smile, lest Judy think she was laughing at her.

Moody stuck his head around the door. 'I suppose now that David's sailed out and no longer sharing my room, you'll forget about the promise you made to clean the kitchen three times a week for me.'

'David only slept in your room for a couple of hours,' Judy reminded him.

'The camp bed's still there and he'll come back.'

Judy only just managed to contain her exasperation. 'I'll clean it for you tomorrow. Once and once only. When David comes back we'll renegotiate.'

'I didn't know you promised to do Moody's work in exchange for David sharing his room,' Edyth remonstrated.

Moody winked at her. 'This is between Judy and me, Mrs Slater.'

Judy hung her apron on the hook on the back of the kitchen door. 'I have to get this job, if I don't . . . '

'You'll get the next,' Edyth consoled when Judy didn't finish her sentence.

'There won't be a next one. I'll give up auditioning.'

'You can't do that,' Edyth protested.

'Yes, I can,' Judy said seriously. 'I discussed it with my aunts yesterday. You've no idea what it's like to put yourself up time and again only to be knocked down and told you're not suitable for this or that role when you know – absolutely know – that you can play it ten times better than the girl who was given it.'

Edyth knew Judy was referring to her colour. She had been called back to dozens of auditions only to be turned down at the final call as 'unsuitable', a bitter pill to swallow, especially when it was accompanied by the rider that Judy's lack of success was not down to lack of ability. 'You're talented, you're happiest on-stage. And I know, even if you don't, that one day your name will be up in lights over a theatre door.'

'Now you have second sight?' Judy referred to Helga's assertion.

'It must be catching,' Edyth replied. 'Go on, off with you and good luck.'

'Break a leg,' Moody shouted from the kitchen doorway.

'Sorry, I forgot, break a leg,' Edyth corrected herself.

'Thank you. If wishes counted more than hopes, this girl would already be in a chorus.' Judy ran up the stairs.

'I hope she does get something soon.' Moody pushed his baker's hat to the back of his head. 'Given the number of hours she spends training her voice and practising her dance steps, she deserves it. But her aunts have been on at her for weeks to give up auditioning and settle for the work the Bute Street Band gets around here.'

'Why would they do that?' Edyth asked in surprise.

'It stands to reason: if Judy does get a job in a long-running show in the New Theatre or touring, she won't be able to sing with the band. And as she's their main attraction, the Bute Street Blues won't get many – if any – bookings without her. There's no way they'll be able to replace her, that's for sure. Judy's just about the best jazz and blues singer on the Bay.'

'She is the best,' Edyth agreed. The thought hadn't occurred to her before Moody mentioned it, but she suddenly realised that if Judy did get a job in the New Theatre it would mean the end of the band as she and everyone else on the Bay knew it. Although every player was a consummate musician, Judy's voice was their main asset. Moody was right, the Bute Street Blues wouldn't get many bookings in the pubs and clubs without her. And, it also explained the attitude of Judy's aunts. The money her uncles made from playing with the band wasn't for extras. They relied on it for essentials.

She didn't envy Judy her choice: stay with the band and remain an amateur, or aim high and hit her uncles' pockets at a time when they could least afford it.

Judy stood in front of her bedroom mirror in her underclothes and held up one rehearsal outfit after another. Five feet six inches tall, which was two to three inches above the ideal height for a chorus girl, and slim built, she had inherited her Welsh grandmother's thick straight dark hair, a lighter tint of her West Indian grandfather's rich coffee-coloured skin, and her Scottish father's green eyes. The white outfit was the one that contrasted most with her skin. The red and yellow toned it down a little but whichever she wore there was no escaping the fact that she was coloured. And she knew, although no one in the New Theatre had ever had the courage to tell her outright, that the main reason she had never been chosen for the chorus of any of the Cardiff shows was not so much her height, because exceptions had been made for other girls, but because she had West Indian blood.

Deciding she was what she was, she opted for the white outfit. She slipped it on and covered it with a calf-length, loose cotton black button-through dress. Packing both her tap and ballet shoes into her vanity case in case they asked her to dance more than one routine, she threw in her hairbrush, scent and lipstick and sheet music.

Then, unable to resist the temptation, she retrieved the music and, tapping time with her foot, sang through the lyrics, remembering to substitute Indian for Tahitian, although she couldn't imagine why they wanted to make the change. She went through it again – and again – experimenting with the phrasing and the pitch, all the while conscious of her heart thundering and the metallic taste of excitement in her mouth.

She had been to dozens of auditions; this one was no different to any other, for all of Helga's predictions of success. She glanced at the alarm clock on her bedside table. It was time to go if she was going to catch a tram and avoid a long hot walk up Bute Street into town.

She snapped her case shut, picked it up, glanced at her reflection in the mirror one last time and took a deep breath.

She was nineteen years old, she could sing, she could dance, she could act, and if she didn't get into the chorus this time, it certainly wouldn't be for the want of trying. It was time to give it her very best.

Aled was in the Gentlemen's Only bar of the Windsor, talking to George Powell, the builder Geoff Arnold had recommended, when a short, stocky, swarthy man approached their table.

'Mr Aled James?'

'Who's asking?' Aled glanced at the bar where Aiden and Freddie were sipping pints of beer. They both rose to their feet and instinctively clenched their fists.

'Stan Peterson, theatrical impresario, at your service.' He held out his hand. After a moment's hesitation Aled shook it. Aiden and Freddie subsided back on to their chairs.

'I put on shows in the New Theatre, the Empire, the Hippodrome – what am I saying? – not only in Cardiff but all over South Wales. I produce and book the best of the best,' he boasted. 'The manager happened to mention you've bought a hotel in Bute Street that you're turning into a theatre.'

'A nightclub, not a theatre, Mr Peterson, and considering I only closed the deal on the property this morning, news travels fast.'

'A club? But you'll be looking to entertain your members with musical shows and acts?' the impresario asked hopefully.

'Musical shows, no,' Aled said flatly. 'Acts, possibly, depending on what and how good they are.'

'Then I'm your man.' Stan brightened.

Aled caught the waiter's eye and he rushed over. 'We're drinking brandy, but you can name your own poison, Mr Peterson.'

'Brandy's good for me, Mr James.'

'Bring the bottle and a soda siphon,' Aled ordered the waiter.

'When do you envisage your club opening, Mr James?'

'I was just discussing that with Mr Powell. He's my builder.'

'I'll pull out all the stops, Mr James, but I won't make any guarantees. Six weeks is tight to have all the major structural alterations you want finished, as well as the interior decorating.' George Powell pocketed the rough notes and sketches he'd been making.

'There'll be a generous bonus in it for you if you meet the target.'

'Speed and quality mean extra men, they cost.'

'You have to put out money to make it, Mr Powell.' Aled sat back when the waiter reappeared with the brandy. 'Are you producing a show in Cardiff at the moment, Mr Peterson?'

'I am.' The impresario looked at his watch. 'Final auditions for the chorus and minor roles begin in one hour. We cast the major roles in London last week and every one of them is a headliner.'

'Chorus girls or boys?' Aled asked, suddenly interested.

'Both. We employ a first-class choreographer. She knows how to pick them and coach them to deliver the goods and—' he gave Aled and George Powell a sly wink, 'excite the audience,' he leered, 'if you get my drift.'

'We get it, Mr Peterson,' Aled replied flatly.

George Powell finished his brandy. 'If I'm going to finish this building by the end of next month I need to go and hire some men.'

'The best, Mr Powell,' Aled reminded him. 'If I am going to pay top dollar I want top tradesmen working on the place.'

'You'll get them, Mr James. My foremen have been with me for years. They can tell a fine craftsman from an odd-job man.'

'I look forward to seeing the results.'

'Give us a week to move in supports and knock out the walls and it will begin to take shape.'

'I'll be there to superintend the interior decoration, Mr Powell.'

'As you're paying the piper you can call the tune, Mr James.' George Powell reached for his hat, nodded a brief goodbye and left the bar.

Aled refilled his own and Stan Peterson's glasses. 'I'm not familiar with the theatrical scene in Wales.'

'I gathered that from your accent. It's not often you see an American investing in the old country.'

'I was born here, Mr Peterson. Tell me, are there many talented acts out there looking for bookings?'

'Not as many as you might think from the slump that's hit trade and industry. People will always scrape together enough pennies to buy a seat in the gods, even when they can't afford to put bread on the table or coal on the fire. It's a cheap way of forgetting your troubles for a couple of hours.'

'So most acts are booked up?'

'The good ones make a living,' Stan replied evasively. 'Although I've noticed, when it comes to chorus girls, there tends to be a greater choice of lookers and talent in the provinces – and Wales. It takes a lot of nerve for a young girl to head for London, even when she has a bit put by in the bank, and not many have these days. Most of them play it safe and stay at home with Mam, where they can be sure of a roof over their heads if not much else. And in between skivvying to pay for their dance classes they try their luck whenever the local Hippodrome or Empire are hiring.'

'I'll need a well-rehearsed, glamorous and experienced chorus when we open, no amateurs,' Aled said.

'Put yourself in my hands and you'll get them,' Stan promised glibly. 'How many girls are you thinking of?'

'Given the size of the stage, we can fit in no more than six, but they'll have to be good. Very good indeed.'

'You'll need a resident headliner as well as touring acts

to bring in the class punters. You thinking of male or female?'

'Female and you don't need to trouble yourself there, Mr Peterson. I have one picked out.'

Stan's face fell. 'A male comic then? All the best clubs have a comic these days as well as a headliner.' He nudged Aled's elbow. 'Just this side of clean, eh.'

'Possibly, if I can find one talented enough,' Aled replied unenthusiastically.

'You know what you should do, Mr James? You should come along to the auditions we're holding this afternoon. Our production is going into two weeks' rehearsal next Monday then a four-week run. There won't be a tour. This is a spin-off from a successful West End show. You'll be able to pick your six girls from our twelve-strong chorus. They'll all be looking for work when we close and in my experience chorus girls are prepared to stand on their head, swing around the lampshade three times a night and give out whatever extras it takes, to guarantee them a steady wage.'

'I suppose it's as good a way as any of gauging the standard on offer, Mr Peterson.'

'Please, call me Stan. Now about that comic, I've just the man in mind for you. Successful and on the up, after a change of career from junior lead. He's lost his looks and his figure but a few extra pounds can be an asset in a comic. The audience find it easier to laugh at a fat man. He's in the show I'm producing but he won't be there this afternoon because he's one of the headliners from London I was telling you about, but I happen to know he'll be free after this engagement—'

'One thing at a time, Stan.' Aled corked the brandy and waved the waiter over. 'Chorus girls first.'

# CHAPTER SEVEN

Judy's hopes had been raised only to be dashed at so many auditions, she could sense the atmosphere that accompanied them blindfolded. They had a peculiar smell all of their own: an unwholesome mix of cheap scent, cold sweat, fear, unhealthy anticipation and forlorn hope. And, although she turned up at the stage door over half an hour before the time she'd been given on her call-back sheet, the changing room was already full of girls vying with one another for space in front of the mirrors that lined two of the walls.

She unbuttoned her dress and hung it on a peg, changed into her tap shoes and ran a comb through her hair. There were only half a dozen chairs and they were all occupied by glamorous peroxide blondes who oozed confidence as they applied superfluous layers of lipstick to their red and glossy mouths. Hardly anyone spoke and when a lone pair of high heels clattered down the corridor, Judy sensed that they were all holding their breath.

After a sharp tap, the door was opened by a young woman dressed in a plain black skirt, white blouse and black bow tie, in sharp and demure contrast to the girls who were auditioning. She consulted the clipboard she was holding. 'Girls' chorus, on-stage. Take your numbers.' She held up a pile of numbered cards pierced with safety pins. 'Fasten them to the front of your skirts where they can be clearly seen.'

'On-stage!' one young girl who looked about fourteen

years old gasped. She was so excited Judy thought she was about to pass out.

'On-stage,' the woman repeated, 'and quick about it, we've only got until six o'clock when the stage hands have to prepare for tonight's performance. We've a lot to get through.'

Twenty girls shuffled forward and took it in turns to pick a card, before clacking, taps ringing, down the corridor to the wings. The secretary rushed alongside them.

'Line up facing the auditorium.'

Even Judy, who had performed under footlights many times with the Bute Street Blues Band in various clubs and concert halls, found the harsh glare of the New Theatre's lights intimidating. Some of the younger girls were so terrified they froze.

'Link arms, high kick, step time,' a masculine voice shouted from the black shadows that shrouded the stalls. The orchestra struck up after a false start, the same voice shouted. 'One – two – three – go—'

Judy recalled the dance steps they'd been asked to perform at the previous audition and fell into step, which was more than the girl to her left could do. After five minutes the disembodied voice yelled.

'Stop!'

The orchestra fell silent.

'Numbers nine, eight, three, eleven, thirteen, nineteen and fifteen, thank you, you can go.'

Judy glanced down the line. Twenty girls had auditioned for the chorus and they had kept back thirteen. A chorus was twelve. One more girl in the line-up had to go. She glanced surreptitiously up and down the line. As usual, she was the only coloured girl.

'Two, six and ten, stay back, please, the rest of you wait in the dressing room.'

Judy had to tense her muscles to stop herself from shaking. She was number six. She studied the other two girls. Like her, both were slightly above average height with straight black hair. But unlike her they had dark eyes and clear, white skin.

'Number ten, step forward, two and six to the wings. Number ten, 'Pagan Love Song' after introduction.'

The orchestra struck up, the girl began to sing during the introduction, faltered, turned crimson and fought back tears.

'And again.'

Judy could actually see the girl's knees shaking when she began to sing a second time. Struggling for breath, her voice was reedy and weak.

'One verse only, thank you,' the voice shouted, when the girl sailed into the second verse without orchestral accompaniment. 'Number two.'

Judy stood and watched the second girl belt out the first verse with more vigour and verve than skill. She knew she could do better, but she wasn't at all sure she could manage it in an atmosphere so impersonal, it bordered on hostile.

'Number six.'

She stepped forward, listened to the introduction and tried to imagine herself in one of the pubs, with the Bute Street Blues Band behind her. Staring blindly ahead, she sang every lyric from the heart.

'And thank you. Male chorus next,' the voice shouted.

The woman who had escorted the chorus on to the stage, ushered Judy and the other two girls who'd waited in the wings back down the corridor.

Nine fewer girls in the dressing room had made a difference. Judy even managed to find a chair, so she could sit down to unlace her tap shoes. She was buttoning on her black dress when the secretary shouted outside the door.

'Number six.'

'Here.' One tap shoe on, one off, Judy stepped into the corridor.

'Rehearsals begin one week today. Seven in the morning until two every afternoon for two weeks. Sunday is free. The run will be for four straight weeks after rehearsal. You'll be on half pay, that's three pounds a week for the rehearsal weeks, and six pounds for the run. Twelve performances and two matinées a week. The show will not be going on the road at the end of the run so don't get your hopes up. Here are three copies of the contract, sign all of them, one will be returned to you after you begin rehearsals.' The women saw Judy staring at her. 'Is there something you don't understand?'

'I'm in the chorus?' Judy asked in bewilderment.

'No, you're Tiger Lily. Didn't they tell you? The show is *Peter Pan*.'


Stan Peterson pulled a packet of cigarettes from his top pocket and held them out to Aled.

'I prefer cigars.' Aled opened his case and offered it to Stan.

'Thank you, I believe I will. I'm still not sure about that coloured girl playing Tiger Lily . . . ' he began hesitantly.

'She out sung and out danced the others by a mile,' Aled declared decisively.

'But she's coloured.'

'And in every state in America except the Southern ones that would have been enough for her to get the job. The Americans – the ones who live in the northern states, that is – recognise talent when they see it. No one can sing or dance like those with African blood running through their veins. I only wish I'd found someone as good as her when I was running my club in Harlem.'

'Harlem, New York?' Stan asked, impressed.

'It wasn't Holland,' Aled said dryly.

'She's talented, I'll give you that. But it's a good job the show's based here. Theatrical landladies don't like boarding coloureds on tour.' He flicked through the sheets of names and addresses on his clipboard. 'She must live in Tiger Bay.'

'She does,' Aled confirmed.

'In that case, seeing as how she's local, I may be able to put more work her way in Cardiff. Depending on audience reaction to her in this show and given the right follow-on production, she could be quite a draw.'

'She could be, but not for you.' Aled rose to his feet as twenty young men and boys filed on-stage.

'You think the audience will take exception to her?' Stan asked, concerned that Aled had talked him into making the wrong decision.

'Not at all, they'll go for her all right.' Aled, flicked the ash from his cigar into a tray on the back of the seat in front of him. 'Just as I did the first time I saw her singing in the Bute Street Carnival. Who do you think my headliner is going to be, Stan?'

Too excited to wait for a tram, Judy ran out of the theatre, through the town, under the railway bridge and down the length of Bute Street. When she reached the baker's three-quarters of an hour later, too breathless to speak, she found Edyth pouring coffee for her Uncle Jed and Micah. Moody was cutting up an expensive fruit cake that hadn't sold, an increasingly common occurrence.

'Where's the fire?' Micah enquired mildly when she lurched into the shop.

'You're been picked for the chorus?' Edyth guessed excitedly. She tried to recall how much sherry had been left in the bottom of the bottle after the carnival supper and whether it would be enough for all five of them to have a celebratory mouthful.

Judy mouthed a silent, 'No,' and clasped a stitch in her side.

'Never mind, Judy, darling.' Jed slipped his arm

around her shoulders ready to console her, as he'd done on so many other occasions.

'I'm Tiger Lily.'

'You're what?' Moody looked blankly at her.

'Tiger Lily in *Peter Pan*,' Edyth cried, quicker to grasp what Judy was trying to say than the rest of them.

Judy nodded. 'Tiger Lily,' she squeaked. 'I start rehearsing next week and I'm going to be paid three pounds a week for two rehearsal weeks and six pounds a week for a four-week run ... six pounds ... ' For the first time since she had run out of the New Theatre she thought of her job with Edyth and the bookings Micah had made for the band. 'I can't take it, can I?' she said slowly. 'I won't be able to keep my job here or play with the band ... '

'Of course you must take it,' Edyth countered briskly. 'We have it all worked out.' Edyth eyed Jed, daring him to say otherwise. 'You'll carry on living here.'

'But you pay me a pound a week plus my keep—'

'And I'll be mean enough to charge you ten shillings a week for your keep while you work in the theatre.' Edyth interrupted. 'I'll pay your aunts one pound ten shillings a week to cover for you while you're there. They look after one another's children now, so they'll be able to manage the job between them.' Given Jed's news, which was almost as exciting as Judy's, Edyth couldn't take the advice Micah had given her and offer the job to Judy's uncles.

Realising what Edyth was doing, Jed nodded agreement. 'They'll all be glad to get away from the kids for a few hours. And you're not the only one with news,' he added proudly. 'Tony, Ron and me have all found jobs too. It's only a short-term contract but the pay is good, we'll be working for George Powell. He's renovating the old Sea Breeze and he was looking for carpenters. As Tony is an experienced ship's carpenter he was first on his list and Ron and I have labouring jobs. So this couldn't have come at a better time all round, love. We'll be too busy to rehearse with the band.'

'And we only have five bookings for the next five weeks. I'll give the pubs the option of taking the Bute Street Blues without you or finding a band to replace us.' Micah took the coffee Edyth offered him.

'So, I can take the job?' Scarcely daring to believe it, Judy looked from Edyth to her uncle.

'You most certainly can.' Edyth went into the back room and lifted the bottle of sherry and a tray of small glasses from the cupboard. She carried them into the shop. 'Here's to Judy's success.' She divided the sherry that was left in the bottle between five glasses.

'It is only a temporary job,' Judy said cautiously.

'But it's an actual *part*,' Micah reminded her. 'And every part is a showcase. Someone important is bound to hear how good you are and come and see you perform. There's no knowing where this could take you.'

'The sky's the limit, or should I say your name in lights in the West End is the limit, not to mention radio and films. You've taken your biggest step, Judy, you're finally out of the chorus.' Edyth handed out the glasses.

'Not that I was ever in a chorus, only auditions for one.'

'You aimed too low, love,' Jed said fondly.

'Here's to Judy Hamilton, the next West End headliner,' Micah toasted.

'Judy King – not Hamilton – and Cardiff's a far cry from the West End,' Judy said practically.

'You'll get there.' Micah touched his glass to Judy's.

'It's just as well I have four bedrooms. One will be yours permanently, no matter how far you travel, it will be waiting for you whenever you want it, I promise you,' Edyth assured her. 'I simply can't wait to see your name on the bill. Tiger Lily played by Miss Judy King.'

'We'll all have to come and see you,' Jed said quickly.

'On opening night,' Judy smiled, just beginning to believe her good fortune was real.

'And we'll cheer and stamp like mad whenever you come on-stage,' Moody teased.

Seeing how close Judy was to tears, Jed caught her hand. 'This is just the beginning, love. And if anyone deserves success after all the work you've put in, you do.'

'Be warned, young man, some people never find their sea legs. You might be one of them.'

David opened one eye and glared at Terje, the ship's engineer, who had taken it upon himself to instruct the 'apprentice cabin boy' in the minutiae of life at sea. The tall Norwegian wavered before him. David closed his eyes but not quickly enough to avoid seeing the clothes swinging from side to side on the hooks on the back of the cabin door. Keeping his eyes closed, he leaned over the side of the bunk and pushed his face into the foul-smelling bucket on the floor. He heaved and retched, wishing there was something left in his stomach to bring up, so the agonising cramps would cease, if only for an few seconds.

Before he had climbed aboard the *Vidda* the worse pain David had suffered was during the weeks he'd spent in hospital after he had jumped off the bridge in Pontypridd. But then, his injuries had been so severe he'd been sedated. The doctors and nurses had been careful not to allow him to experience more pain than he could bear.

Caught in the rough North Sea winds, the *Vidda* tossed and turned constantly, churning him around until he felt like a rag caught in the dolly Mary used to agitate their clothes in the wash tubs on the farm. He had never felt so sick or so incapable of standing or sitting upright, let alone doing anything more energetic. All he could think of and wish for was oblivion, an oblivion that escaped him when he was beset by a constant urge to retch up his non-existent stomach contents. It didn't help that he was sharing a cabin with what seemed like dozens of Norwegian giants who persisted in munching cheese, ham and raw onions within sight, sound and smell of him – and slapping him soundly across the shoulders in a supposedly friendly gesture every time they passed his bunk.

Even the captain had visited him and given orders that the ship's cook was to feed him thick pea soup, toast and black coffee – all of which had been duly forced down him only to reappear minutes later.

'I knew a man from Trondheim who went to sea when he was thirteen. It was a long voyage, to South Africa.' The oldest sailor on board whittled a piece of extraneous wood from the prow of a ship that he was carving for his grandson. 'When they landed, he was so weak from seasickness he had to be carried down the gangplank. The doctor in Cape Town thought he wouldn't survive.'

'Did he?' Terje asked the question David couldn't because his head was in the bucket again.

'Oh, he survived, all right.' The old mariner scraped another piece of wood on to the floor, and scuffed it into the pile at his feet. 'But he may as well have died as far as his family was concerned. He couldn't face getting back on a ship again, so he stayed where he was. Last I heard he was working in a South African gold mine.'

'There's no way I'm staying in Norway,' David protested feebly.

'It's a nice clean country, the women are beautiful, the food's good and the aquavit has a bite. You'll get used to it,' Terje consoled mercilessly.

'I want to go home.'

'You sure you're prepared to go through all this again?' the old man laughed.

'It can't last for ever,' David muttered, before hanging his head back in the bucket again.

'Stop teasing the boy.' Terje wiped David's forehead

with a damp cloth that stank of fish. 'Another few days and you'll have land beneath your feet again, lad, although the way you are now, it may take you a month or two to feel it.'

Edyth sat at her dressing table and screwed a pair of gold and pearl earrings into her ears. She was wearing one of her favourite frocks, a rust-coloured silk that brought out the tawny gold highlights in her brown hair and eyes. She fastened a string of pearls around her neck, ran a comb through her hair and sprayed her throat, wrists and behind her ears with a blue glass and silver perfume atomiser that she had filled with Lily of the Valley scent.

She applied a final coat of scarlet lipstick to her mouth and decided she was as glamorous as she could make herself, given the shadows beneath her eyes and the limited time at her disposal.

She glanced back at her wardrobe in the mirror. The door was open, revealing a row of calico-shrouded evening gowns she had bought before her marriage. When she'd lived at home with her parents, every weekend, and even the occasional weekday evening, had brought a private party or public dance. Now it seemed like another girl had worn those frocks. Since she had taken over the bakery she'd had little time for dressing up and even less inclination for going out in the evenings when she had to rise so early six days a week.

'Edyth?'

She shouted, 'I'm upstairs, Micah?'

'I hope you're ready.'

'I am.' She picked up the fringed silk stole that matched her frock and ran down into the shop. Micah was in the kitchen with Judy's uncles, their wives and children and Helga and Moody.

Jed looked around. 'Six uncles and aunts, nineteen cousins and four friends, and that's without all the friends and neighbours who are making their own way to the New Theatre. Judy is going to have a fine Bute Street audience.' He ran his finger around the inside of the starched collar of his dress shirt in a futile attempt to loosen it.

'You look pretty, Mrs Slater,' Moody said diffidently.

'Thank you, Moody,' Edyth replied, tactfully ignoring the boy's blushes.

'Watch out, Helga, he's beginning to notice women,' Micah warned.

'It's when you stop noticing them that the problems start. Then you know old age is setting in,' Tony grumbled.

'I look forward to the day your head stops turning every time you pass a pretty girl,' Tony's wife rejoined sharply.

Sensing one of the Kings' legendary domestic arguments brewing, Micah intervened. 'Ladies, your carriage awaits.'

Edyth glanced through the open door into the yard. 'You hired a charabanc?'

'It would have cost a fortune to get taxis for all of us, and you could hardly walk up Bute Street in your finery. Besides,' Micah lowered his voice, 'Old Bill could do with the work. Hardly anyone has the money to hire a charabanc these days.'

'Do we?' she whispered.

'Don't tell anyone I sold the church's silver.'

As the Norwegian Church had never owned any plates other the wooden ones, carved and donated by sailors, Edyth laughed.

Micah helped Edyth into the back, Judy's aunts and cousins followed, and the men arranged themselves in seats behind the driver. 'Old Bill,' a First World War veteran who had bought the charabanc for ten hard-saved shillings at a recent auction, drove slowly out of the yard. It looked as though everyone in Tiger Bay who wasn't going to see Judy in the New Theatre that night had turned out to see her family off. When they drove towards the town, the crowd applauded.

'They can't cheer Judy so they're cheering us,' Micah observed.

'It's a pity she had to spend all day rehearsing, she would have loved this.' Jed lifted his two youngest daughters on to his knees to they could wave back.

'I can bask in reflected glory. It's the first time a King has made it into a real theatre,' Tony returned the waves as though he were royalty.

Edyth opened her evening purse and checked the tickets Judy had picked up for her. Judy had booked three boxes for her uncles and their families but despite an invitation from Jed to join the Kings, Edyth had insisted on paying for front-row stalls for herself, Micah, Helga and Moody. At best a box held six adults, any more would be a tight squeeze and she didn't want to spoil the Kings' night by crowding them.

Old Bill drew up outside the theatre and Edyth was amazed by the size of the crowd milling through the doors.

'I can't believe all these people are here this early on a Monday evening.'

'I'd be surprised if they weren't.' Jed opened the door and lifted the younger children on to the pavement. 'Tickets for Monday's first house are traditionally given to pub landlords and shopkeepers for displaying show bills in their windows.'

'Then none of these people have paid.' Edyth took the hand Jed offered her.

'Don't look so downhearted, they can still applaud,' Tony said cheerfully.

'Who wants sweets?' Micah asked the children.

'No spoiling them,' Judy's Aunt May admonished when the younger ones shouted 'me, please' in unison.

'What's a godfather for, if not to spoil his god-children?' Micah demanded.

'I didn't know that you were the King children's godfather,' Edyth commented as she followed him to the sweet counter inside the theatre.

'Not to all of them, only six, or is it seven? I keep forgetting, but as I can barely tell them apart and they're all related, I feel I can't treat any of them differently to the others.'

'But you're a Lutheran Minister and the Kings are Catholic.'

'And I thought you understood the Bay by now.' He handed her what seemed like dozens of tuppenny paper cornets. 'Here, share these out while I pay for them.'

She turned and the smile froze on her face. Jed, Tony and Ron King and a few of their neighbours from Bute Street were arguing with a man in evening dress. He was flanked by two other men, also in evening dress, but as their height, build and demeanour was intimidating, Edyth suspected they were the theatre management's brawn. She joined them in time to hear Jed say, 'Our niece is in the production, she paid for these boxes—'

'And I've told you, sir, there's been a mistake.' The manager was polite but firm. 'These boxes were booked before your niece procured the tickets.'

'What about these stalls?' Edyth passed him the four tickets from her evening bag.

He glanced at them before handing them back to her. 'These are fine, madam.'

'They were booked at the same time as the boxes by Miss Judy King.'

'As I keep saying to this gentleman, there's been a mistake . . .'

Angry shouts resounded from the foyer. Edyth and Jed turned and saw an usherette refuse to allow a group of young boys from the Bay up the stairs.

Micah took in the situation at a glance. He joined them and confronted the manager. 'You're refusing entry to people from Butetown.'

'Not at all, sir. It's company policy to only allow people into the theatre who have valid tickets.'

'And you're telling me that none of these people have valid tickets? Abdul?' Micah called to the trumpet player from the Bute Street Blues Band who had been stopped along with the others. 'Can I see your ticket?'

Abdul handed it over.

'This has today's date and a time that's . . . ' Micah looked at his wristwatch, 'twenty minutes away. What's the problem?'

'There appears to have been an error on our part, sir. Double bookings have been made and double tickets issued for the same seats, we will be happy to reimburse people for any expense they have incurred.'

'Including the taxi fares here and back to their homes?' Micah demanded in a loud voice.

'Regrettably not extra expense, sir. Only the cost of the tickets.'

'And replacement tickets?'

'That might be difficult, sir. Bookings have been heavy.'

'For the whole month's run?' Micah enquired sceptically.

'Peter Pan *is* a popular play.' The manager succeeded in maintaining a poker face. 'If there are no double bookings, you are going to have an empty theatre,' Micah warned, 'and I will be inside to check just how empty it is.'

'I assure you, sir—'

'Why don't you come straight out with it and tell us that you don't serve coloured people, like most of the other cinemas and restaurants in the centre of Cardiff?' Jed challenged.

'I don't make policy,' the manager said tartly.

'But you implement it,' Tony snapped.

'I—'

'These tickets have been sold,' Micah said fiercely, 'either you honour them or—'

'Are you threatening me?' The manager drew himself up to his full height, which was several inches short of Micah's and Jed's.

'I'm informing you that I will report you for selling tickets under false pretences. Taking money and not delivering the goods is fraud,' Micah said coldly.

'And you are?' the manager asked.

'Pastor Micah Holsten of the Norwegian Church.'

'Steve,' Jed stopped the Chinese boy as he left the foyer, 'where are you going?'

'They won't allow us in – any of us.' Steve Chan glared at the manager.

Micah pulled a notebook from his pocket and held a pencil over it. 'Is it the official policy of the management of the New Theatre to operate a colour bar, or have you decided to implement it on your own authority?'

The manager stared at him for a moment then began to stutter. 'I . . . I . . . '

'Is it or isn't it?' Micah persisted.

Aled James climbed out of a taxi, glanced in their direction, strode over and asked, 'Is there a problem here?'

Having been introduced to Aled by Stan Peterson, the manager looked to Aled for support. 'Mr James, sir, I am explaining to Pastor Holsten that we have inadvertently made some double bookings.'

'Apparently only in the seats reserved by coloured people.' Micah stared at Aled. He had only met Edyth's brother a few times, but he found the resemblance between the two men startling.

'Stan?' Aled called to his companion, who was paying the taxi driver. 'Come over here.'

Edyth gazed at Aled in astonishment. If it hadn't been for his American accent and a few extra lines around his mouth and eyes, she would have believed he was Harry.

'What's happening?' Stan looked warily at the angry people congregating in the foyer and outside the door of the theatre.

'It would appear that the New Theatre has a policy of not allowing coloured people into the audience,' Micah said flatly. 'Miss Judy King booked three boxes for her family. Various friends and neighbours have also booked tickets and, amazingly, all the seats appear to be no longer available.'

Stan Peterson drew the manager aside for a hurried whispered conversation. The manager returned. 'If Miss King's party will follow me, I will take them to their boxes by the most direct route.'

'Through the stage door?' Tony queried cynically.

'It *is* the most direct route, sir.'

'Tony, we're here to see Judy in a show, not to make a point,' Jed reminded him.

'And the others?' Micah demanded.

'We weren't going to open the upper circle, sir, but I've just been given contrary instructions by management. Any overflow can be accommodated there.'

'Especially if the people are coloured,' Micah observed.

'Would you rather we didn't open it, sir?' the manager challenged.

Micah didn't answer. He offered Edyth his arm and Helga took Moody's. Micah continued to meet the manager's eye, daring him or one of his silent henchmen to make a comment about Moody. But the only person who spoke was Aled.

'Did I hear you say that you were with Miss Judy King's party? Pastor Holsten, isn't it?'

'It is, and we are,' Micah replied shortly.

'I'd like to invite her, her family and your party to an after-theatre supper in the Windsor.'

'Why?' Micah questioned bluntly.

'I have a business proposition I would like to put to

Miss King and, as I believe her to be under age, her guardians.'

'If Miss King accepts, we will,' Micah answered.

'I'll send an invitation to her backstage and speak to her family during the intermission. Enjoy the show.' Aled tipped his top hat and followed Stan Peterson inside the theatre.

Aled leaned over the balcony of Stan Peterson's box, which was opposite the ones that held the extended King family, and watched Judy lead a column of Indians across the stage in a theatrical version of an Indian war dance. They were singing 'Wigwam Blues' and Judy's voice rose higher and more melodic than the mixed chorus of boys and girls, all of whom were trying, with varying degrees of success, to follow her accomplished and elegant steps.

'My choreographer said she's never worked with anyone as talented or as quick to learn,' Stan murmured.

Despite the fact that there were twenty-five people on-stage, Aled knew exactly who Stan was talking about. 'Is that your way of saying you're glad you took my advice about giving her the role of Tiger Lily?'

'What do you think of her costume?' Stan questioned evasively. 'It was my idea to go for white.'

Aled eyed the mid-thigh-length, figure-hugging, beaded leather tunic. 'It makes her skin glow.'

'Doesn't it? She'll make a terrific Julie La Verne in *Show Boat*. The part could have been written for her,' Stan enthused. 'I'll have a word with my backers as soon as I return to London.'

'Miss King won't be available.'

'Because she'll be headlining in your club?' Stan questioned.

'Precisely.'

'Have you asked her?'

'Not yet.'

'There isn't a singer or actress who'll turn down an

opportunity to work in the West End to stay in the provinces,' Stan declared authoritatively.

'You won't be able to top my offer,' Aled warned.

'From the West End she could go anywhere – radio, films, Hollywood even.'

'And if she doesn't get an offer after she's worked in the West End? You'll put her on tour?' Aled reminded Stan what he had said about provincial landladies refusing to accommodate coloured artistes.

'She could stay in London. There are enough theatres outside of the West End to keep her busy and the landladies in the suburbs are nothing if not cosmopolitan.'

'You mean they only look at the contents of an artiste's wallet, not their skin colour.' Aled shook his head. 'I have two trump cards.'

'And they are?'

'Her relatives. It was obvious from the way that her uncles were talking about her when they arrived at the theatre tonight, that Judy King is a member of a close-knit family.'

'Everyone has to grow up and leave their family,' Stan dismissed. 'What's the second?'

'Tiger Bay,' Aled declared. 'It's one of the few areas on this earth where no one gives a damn about nationality, colour or religion. That was proved in the foyer of this theatre tonight. I've travelled around and I've never seen so many people of different origin stand shoulder to shoulder as I did here this evening. The Bay coupled with her family will be too much for Judy King to give up, especially if a fixed annual income is thrown in, as opposed to an uncertain weekly wage. Sorry, Stan,' Aled didn't look the slightest bit apologetic, 'Judy King is mine.'

'Bet you a tenner she isn't,' Stan wagered.

'Make it fifty and you're on.'

'I'll buy you a glass of champagne out of the proceeds as a consolation prize.'

'That's one drink I'll never see.' Aled looked down at Judy. She'd taken centre stage in preparation to sing her 'Pagan Love Song' solo.

'You're very sure of yourself, aren't you?'

'I only wager on certainties.' Aled glanced at the stalls beneath them. Pastor Holsten was sitting between a coloured boy and the girl he'd seen wearing the same outfit as Judy's at the carnival. When he'd approached her group outside the theatre, she'd stared at him as though she'd seen a ghost, which probably meant she knew Harry Evans. Another couple of hours and he'd find out whether or not his guess was correct – and, if it was, just how friendly she was with his half-brother.

'Judy King's number may have finished, but there's ten minutes to go to the intermission,' Stan protested when Aled left his seat after Judy had taken her third bow.

Aled opened the door at the back of the box. 'I need to make arrangements.'

'What kind of arrangements?' Stan asked suspiciously.

'For refreshments to be delivered to Miss King's party.' Aled walked down the corridor and stairs to the kiosk on the ground floor. Tea, ice cream and biscuits for the King adults, sweets, orange juice and ice cream for the King children, he decided – and he had a telephone call to make. To the Windsor Hotel.

# CHAPTER EIGHT

'Five encores and two standing ovations. I've never seen anything like it in Wales. The savages have finally learned to appreciate true artistry.' The actress who was playing Peter Pan pulled off her cap and shook her hair free after the final curtain had fallen.

'Darling, they were applauding the *star*, not the child dangling on the wire,' Jeremy Dupois, who was playing the dual role of Mr Darling and Captain Hook, drawled nonchalantly.

'And who was that?' the middle-aged actress who had slapped four coats of greasepaint on to her face so she could play the youthful Wendy demanded.

Jeremy adopted a lecturing tone as if he were the professor and she the idiot child. 'There's only ever one *star* in any production, darling, and it's never the ageing junior lead on the slide down.'

'*Peter Pan* is an *ensemble* effort,' 'Wendy' stressed.

'The hell it is,' 'Peter' snapped. 'The play is *Peter Pan*. And *I'm* Peter.'

'I couldn't agree with you more, darling, there's no such thing as an ensemble.' Jeremy smiled sweetly at 'Peter'. 'The audience came to see the name above the title on the posters, not the immature nobody pretending to be a puppet on strings. And in case you haven't looked, there's only one name above *Peter Pan* on the door, and that's Jeremy Dupois.'

'If you're the star, Jeremy *darling*, go and twinkle, preferably elsewhere,' Lennie Lane the roly-poly actor playing Smee bit back smartly.

'Quick with the repartee, aren't you, Lennie? It's a pity you haven't the talent to back up the stroke of miscasting that landed you a supporting role,' Jeremy sniped.

'Make the most of your twinkling, Jeremy, it's waning like a dying Tinkerbell, only in your case Props won't be able to switch you back on,' Lennie retorted.

'Bitchiness won't bring your career back, Lennie, not that you ever had much of one outside of your imagination. And if anyone should be looking at Tinkerbell it should be you, because that's where you'll be in a year or two: manipulating little bells and balls of lights in Props. That's if you manage to stay off the pies and beer and can get in the props box. It would be a tight squeeze now.' Jeremy tossed his head in the air and stalked off as regally as his close fitting Mr Darling costume allowed him to.

'Better a Props than a washed-up old ham,' Lennie called after him. He made a few remarkably realistic pig snorts, followed by even more realistic squealing.

Judy watched and listened in amazement. Lennie Lane had been a leading West End romantic lead before his weight had ballooned to Fatty Arbuckle proportions. He'd also been kind to her in rehearsals. As a result, the venom in his voice took her breath away. She'd seen the odd outburst of spitefulness in auditions, and even come across rivalry that had bordered on acrimonious when the Bute Street Blues Band had played the same event as other bands, like the carnival, but she had never witnessed such open and vitriolic hostility between performers before.

'My pets, my darlings, please.' Hands fluttering, the director walked out from the wings as the fire curtain came down. 'No squabbling and no upsetting Jeremy, I won't allow it. Carry on and I won't take you out for that celebratory dinner I've booked in the Windsor Hotel.'

'Dinner?' It was the first Judy had heard of it.

The director turned scarlet. 'Sorry, pet, principals only. Management can't run to treating everyone.'

'The chorus are going.' Lennie crossed his podgy arms across his chest and eyed the director defiantly.

'Principal players only,' the director repeated. 'Must dash, impresario and backers are waiting to be entertained.'

'Sorry, Judy. I tried, even if I didn't get anywhere,' Lennie apologised.

'We were all angry when we saw the way your family were treated,' Mandy, the head chorus girl, commiserated. Too many performers had watched Judy's relatives being escorted through the backstage corridors to their boxes for management to keep it quiet.

'You're the best performer I've seen on-stage here for a long time, Miss King,' the orchestra leader complimented when he joined them from the pit.

'Thank you,' Judy said sincerely. 'I've certainly had a night I'll never forget.'

'Hurry up, my pets, you have to change quickly, the table's booked for half past ten, if we're one minute late they won't serve us.' The director returned and drew Judy aside. 'You do understand why we couldn't invite you, don't you, darling?'

Judy noticed that he'd waited until most of her fellow performers had returned to their dressing rooms before waylaying her. Deciding that important as her career was, she couldn't allow the slight to her family to pass unnoticed, she said, 'After seeing the way you pulled the curtains halfway around the boxes I reserved for my guests so they couldn't be seen from most of the auditorium, yes, I understand perfectly well.'

'Judy, come quickly.' Mandy beckoned her forward. 'You've never seen anything like our dressing room.'

'Enjoy the rest of your evening, Miss King.' Glad of an opportunity to escape, the director dashed off.

Judy walked down the corridor to the large dressing

room she was sharing with the chorus girls. The door was open, and every flat surface was covered with huge baskets and enormous vases of red and gold roses.

'Some girls are popular,' Judy smiled.

'Some girls, huh,' one of the older chorus girls sniped. 'They're all for you.'

'They can't be.' Stunned, Judy looked from one display to another. She knew her uncles couldn't possibly have afforded to buy such expensive bouquets and she'd pretended she hadn't seen the small basket of violets Edyth had hidden in the stockroom of the shop.

'The florist said they're all from the same man. He spent an absolute fortune. Here's the card.' Mandy handed it to her.

Judy opened the small envelope and read the name at the bottom of the card. 'There must be a mistake. I don't know an Aled James.'

'He obviously knows you.' Mandy sniffed the nearest rose. 'Scented too, and they smell heavenly.'

'Perhaps he's seen you coming in and out of the theatre and admired you from afar,' one of the younger girls said, sighing romantically.

Judy read the message.

*Congratulations on a magnificent debut performance. I would be delighted if you, your family and friends would be my dinner guests at the Windsor Hotel this evening. I have a professional proposition I wish to put to you and your guardians.*

*Aled James*

Mandy looked over Judy's shoulder and read the card. '"A professional proposition." And he's invited your uncles, so he can't be thinking of selling you into slavery. I'm not surprised. After the performance you gave tonight, you deserve to be picked up by a director or producer or at the very least a talent spotter. Ooh!' she gasped. 'Perhaps he's from Binky Beaumont.'

'Or Mr Charles Cochrane,' one of the others said excitedly.

'I bet it's radio.' The youngest chorus girl had aspirations to be heard all over the country. 'Your voice is incredible, the rest of us sound like squawking crows in comparison.'

'Or Hollywood . . . '

'You'll sail across the Atlantic on the *Queen Mary* and make films with Gary Cooper . . . '

'He may buy you out of your contract here . . . '

'It's more likely to be all-singing, all-dancing talkies with Al Jolson than Westerns with Gary Cooper . . . '

'If he's a scout for Binky Beaumont it will be the West End. A musical like *That's a Good Girl* with Noel Coward . . . '

'Or you'll be a Rockette in New York's Radio City . . . '

Judy's head began to spin as much from the noise the girls were making as the ideas they were floating. She struggled out of her tight white leather Tiger Lily outfit, removed the beaded band from around her forehead and ran her fingers through her hair. As all the chairs were taken, she crouched behind one of the girls, peered into the mirror, opened her pot of cold cream, slapped it on her face and wiped off her stage make-up with a couple of balls of cotton wool.

When she'd finished cleaning her face and hands with the cream, she slipped on the plain black satin evening dress and peep-toe sandals she'd packed for the family party her aunts had organised in her Uncle Jed's terraced house. A dab of powder to tone down the shine on her nose, a spot of lipstick on her mouth, a quick comb through to smooth her shingled hair back in place and she was ready.

'You're very plain for the Windsor,' Mandy criticised.

'I'm not sure I'm going. It's up to Uncle Jed whether we accept the invitation or not,' Judy replied cautiously.

'Your dress is fine, but it needs jazzing up. Here.' Mandy opened Judy's hand and pressed something into it.

Judy stared down at a pair of sapphire and gold earrings and a sapphire and gold pendant. 'I can't possibly wear these.'

'Yes, you can, give them back to me tomorrow.' Mandy lowered her voice. 'First rule I learned backstage is never, never look poverty-stricken. Present a high-class image and you'll get whatever you ask for, especially from impresarios – and aristocrats.' She raised her eyebrows. 'My older sister not only snared but married a real live lord. And not a poverty-stricken one either. He has a castle in Scotland, a flat in London and a yacht in the South of France.'

'Honest?' the chorus girls gasped.

'Where do you think I got jewels like these? She gave them to me at Christmas. But we have to call her "your ladyship" whenever she deigns to call on us in our terraced back-to-back in Cwmtwrch. Mind you,' Mandy's mouth twitched suspiciously, and Judy wasn't sure whether she was being serious or not, 'her husband is seventy-two to her twenty-four. Here, let me fasten these for you.' She slipped the chain around Judy's neck and hooked the safety catch while Judy pushed the earrings into her ears. 'You need scent. Try this, it's called "White Linen".' She sprinkled it liberally over Judy's neck, hair and ears.

'Why are you being so kind?' Judy asked.

'Because your family had a rotten deal from management tonight. And because I was just like you when I was your age. Full of hopes and dreams. I only got this job on sufferance. I know, and management knows, I'm too old for this lark. Next show I'll be doing, I'll be backstage looking after the costumes.'

'You're a fantastic dancer . . . '

'And people's memories of me will be kinder if I hang up my tap and ballet shoes now.' Mandy opened the door, pushed Judy out and whispered, 'Good luck.'

'Thank you.' Judy turned and barged into the show's producer. 'I'm so sorry, Mr Peterson . . . '

'Never mind that,' he winced and rubbed his ankle where Judy had kicked him. 'I've been talking to the director. There's been a mistake. Of course you're invited to the cast dinner at the Windsor.'

'I'm afraid Miss King is otherwise engaged, Stan.' Aled strode down the corridor, flanked by Aiden and Freddie. 'Your uncles and friends have accepted my invitation. Regrettably one of your aunts won't be joining us, because she is taking your cousins home.'

'Judy, you have to take at least one bunch with you.' Mandy reappeared with the largest bouquet from the dressing room and handed it to her.

'I knew the colours would suit you.' Aled offered Judy his arm. 'If you'll allow me to escort you to the stage door, Miss King, you can join your party. I am going on ahead to the Windsor to finalise a few details. Enjoy the rest of your evening, Stan.'

'You're welcome to join us as well, Aled,' Stan offered.

'I've made other arrangements.' Aled winked at Stan, tipped his hat to the gawping girls and walked Judy down the corridor before she had time to do more than shout a hurried, 'Goodnight'.


The Windsor Hotel was within half a mile of the house where Judy had been born, but as far as she and her family were concerned it may as well have been on a different continent. It represented another world to the one they inhabited. If work had been plentiful in Tiger Bay, Judy might have aspired to scrub the floors, sweep the stairs, dust the rooms and change the beds within the Windsor's mock-Georgian façade. But she had never dreamed that she'd ever be invited to dine within its cream and gold dining room.

That she knew what went on inside the Windsor was down to her uncles' friendship with the waiters and chambermaids who worked there. From their stories, she had pictured the hotel as a haven of gilded opulence where people with more money than she could imagine lived, and lived well, on mythical foods like lobster, prawns, champagne and smoked salmon. Whenever the off-duty staff mentioned the Windsor, or the wealthy, famous and celebrated clientele they served, it was always in hushed, reverential tones, as if the patrons were as infinitely above and beyond the residents who lived in the backstreets as angels from cockroaches.

Jed helped Judy and the rest of the women from the charabanc but when they approached the entrance, he, Ron, Tony, Judy's two aunts and Moody hung back diffidently, unlike Edyth, Helga and Micah who forged confidently ahead.

The breath caught in Judy's throat when she walked through the doors the porters held open for them. She looked around and instantly felt that the hotel had been designed and furnished to make interlopers – she regarded herself as one – feel inferior.

The carpets were so thick the heels of their shoes sank into them. The attendants who took their coats and spirited them away did so silently, yet managed to convey disapproval at the quality. The walls were clad in marble and studded with mirrors that glittered with the reflected lights of shimmering chandeliers. Amongst so much luxury their images seemed to flit across the glass as fleeting and transient as ghosts.

They were shown into a dining room that on first glance appeared to stretch into infinity. When Judy looked again, she realised that its walls were also mirrored and reflected table upon table set with starched damask linen, gleaming silverware and crystal that sparkled like diamonds. Even the napkins, folded into 'slippers', reminded her of the lessons her grandmother had given her on setting a table for the crache. The young Pearl King had acquired the skill half a century before, while working her way up from kitchen to parlour maid in a grand house in Loudon Square.

Only Micah, Helga and Edyth appeared to be at ease. But Judy recalled that Edyth's father was an MP, albeit a socialist one, and Micah and Helga's father had been a pastor. And as Micah had followed his father into the profession, they were used to moving in 'class' company.

Aled James was waiting for them beside a circular table in prime position in the centre of the room. He was talking to the head waiter who was listening, head bowed and attentive, to his every word. The table had been laid for eleven and a dozen ice buckets were set on stands around the perimeter; half contained bottles of champagne and half mineral water. In the centre was a magnificent floral arrangement of gold and red rosebuds so similar to the one the cloakroom attendant had taken from Judy, it was obvious it had come from the same florists.

Judy suddenly realised that Aled James's invitation hadn't been made on the spur of the moment. The flowers on the table and in the theatre, the booking in the hotel restaurant, the champagne – all suggested that this dinner had been planned for hours, possibly even days.

Aled smiled at her. 'Thank you so much for accepting my invitation, Miss King. I am grateful.'

She nodded, too overwhelmed to speak.

The head waiter clicked his fingers and a platoon of subordinates moved in, smartly and silently pulling out chairs, shaking napkins and placing them on the guests' laps as soon as they were seated. A sheaf of leather menu holders appeared at the place settings.

'Champagne while my guests make their choices.' Aled

watched two of Judy's uncles station themselves protectively either side of her. He didn't attempt to sit close to her. Instead he took the vacant chair on Edyth's left after Micah had taken the one on Edyth's right. As soon as he was seated, Aled raised the glass the wine waiter had filled for him. 'Ladies,' he nodded to Judy, her aunts, Helga and Edyth, 'and gentlemen, the very good health of the new star we saw born on the stage of the New Theatre this evening.'

Edyth drank the toast, and gave Judy, who looked distinctly uncomfortable, a reassuring smile before opening the menu. She was used to the prices in the Park Hotel and New Inn in Pontypridd, neither of which was cheap, but this menu had no prices at all, which she found disconcerting. And, despite Aled James's close physical resemblance to Harry, and his polite, mannered, almost too correct behaviour, she found him disturbing.

If anyone had asked her exactly why Aled James made her feel edgy she couldn't have given any sounder reason other than his American accent didn't ring true, his smile didn't thaw the ice in his eyes, and his manners were too polished for sincerity.

Aled saw her staring at him and broadened his smile. Edyth immediately resumed her study of the menu.

'May I recommend the caviar, lobster mousse or smoked salmon for starters, the fillets of beef or chicken à la king – very appropriate, don't you think – for entrée and the dessert trolley to finish. The chef's creations in that department have to be seen to be believed.' Aled hadn't opened his menu, a fact that wasn't lost on Edyth.

'I've heard that you are reopening the old Sea Breeze as a nightclub, Mr James,' Micah commented.

Edyth had heard Micah asking around the bar for information about Aled James during the intermission. He had also met Harry, and although they hadn't had time to discuss Aled James's likeness to her brother,

Edyth knew the similarity between them hadn't been lost on Micah.

'I am, Pastor—'

'Micah, please, no one except the children call me Pastor outside of the mission,' Micah interrupted.

'My interest in the Sea Breeze is the primary reason I've invited you here.' Aled turned to the head waiter who was hovering behind his chair. 'Max, take our order so we can begin discussing business.'

Edyth and Helga chose the smoked salmon and chicken, Judy and her aunts shyly followed suit, and when Micah ordered the caviar and the beef, Judy's uncles and Moody repeated his order. Aled settled for the lobster mousse and beef.

'As you said, Micah,' Aled signalled to the wine waiter to replenish their water and champagne glasses, 'I am opening the old Sea Breeze as a nightclub and I am looking for a resident singer. I was hoping that Miss King would consider the position.'

'Me, a nightclub singer?' Judy looked at him in astonishment.

'My offer isn't based on your performance this evening, Miss King, although, I haven't seen such a display of talent since I left America. In fact, come to think of it, I didn't see anyone who could bear comparison to you there. I heard you sing at the carnival on the day I arrived back in this country and when I asked around the Bay, everyone who had seen the Bute Street Blues Band spoke highly of you.'

'But I sing with the band . . . '

'The band is hardly up to your standard, Judy. The people around here hire us for local events but it's principally so they can listen to you. You're the only one of us who is talented enough to be classed as a professional, and it's my guess that it's a professional Mr James wants to hire.' Micah realised that Aled James was offering Judy an opportunity that could give her the break into show business she had so desperately been looking for. And in her home territory, where her uncles could continue to look after her.

'Micah is right,' Aled asserted. 'I am looking for someone who can draw in and hold an audience, and tonight you proved you can do just that. Your solo won the loudest applause in the theatre.'

'You're very kind . . . '

'When you get to know me better, you'll realise I am anything but, Miss King,' Aled refuted. 'When it comes to employing artistes for my nightclubs I am swayed by talent and talent alone. And you are exceptionally talented.'

'Thank you.' Judy's cheeks burned at the compliment.

'I am about to hire a full orchestra that will, of course, back you if you take the job. It's my intention to offer both musical entertainment and dancing in the club. If the members of the Bute Street Blues would like to audition for the orchestra, they will receive due consideration.' He looked past Edyth to Micah.

'I know my limitations, besides I have a day job.' Micah saw Aled place his hand close to Edyth's on the tablecloth and he moved his chair nearer to hers.

'The three Mr Kings, perhaps? I'll let you know when we'll be holding auditions for musicians. That way you can keep an eye on your niece.'

'We're all working on the Sea Breeze now, as builders.' Tony had finally found his voice.

'I know.' Aled leaned back in his chair so the waiter could set a plate of smoked salmon and thin-cut brown bread and lemon in front of Edyth.

'And we're sailors by trade,' Ron added, 'not musicians—'

'That's not to say we won't take any work that's offered us,' Jed broke in. 'Jobs are scarce at the moment. I hope you don't mind me coming directly to the point, Mr James, but what exactly are you offering Judy?'

'Five nights' work a week, Tuesday to Saturday, seven until three a.m. A respectable chauffeur escort to and from the club, all stage costumes, the services of a dresser and ten pounds a week salary.'

'Ten pounds?' Judy's eyes rounded in disbelief.

'You'll earn it,' Aled said dryly. 'As for your stage costumes: I warn you I will be very particular about what you'll wear.'

'Skimpy costumes?' Jed asked warily.

'For the chorus girls, certainly, for the star, no. It's Miss King's singing I'm interested in, Mr King, nothing else. If you accept the position, Miss King, I will ask my solicitor to draw up a contract tomorrow. That way, your solicitor,' he looked from Jed to Micah, 'can look it over. I know that Miss King has a cast-iron contract with the New Theatre for the next four weeks. I propose my contract and her wages begin the day after it terminates. And just so we enjoy the rest of this meal, I don't expect you to give me an answer right away, Miss King.' He clicked his fingers at the wine waiter and pointed to their glasses. 'Now, shall we discuss *Peter Pan*? I have seen the show before, on Broadway, but I didn't enjoy it as much as I did this evening's performance and that has to be down to the actress who played Tiger Lily.'

During the meal Judy was aware of the large party from the theatre, principally because the producer, director and leading actors persisted in complaining long and loud about everything from their plates being cold to the slow response of the wine waiter when it came to refilling their glasses, to the salt cellars being damp. They had been seated at a long table at the end of the room. And although she was sitting with her back to them, Judy suspected that their complaints stemmed from the head waiter's delegation of the theatre's table to a subordinate's care, so he could bestow his full attention on Aled James and his table.

She didn't dare turn around to look at her fellow performers, but when Lennie went to the cloakroom he returned by a roundabout route, so he could give her a broad and sympathetic wink. She responded with a small smile that was noticed by Aled.

'You get on with Smee, Miss King?' he asked in amusement.

'Lennie – the actor who plays him – was very kind to me and all the other new girls during rehearsals. He knows all there is to know about stagecraft and he has a marvellous sense of humour,' she added, trying to forget the acidic comments Lennie had made to Jeremy.

'He was good,' Aled mused thoughtfully. 'Stan Peterson suggested that I employ a comic for the club as well as a singer. Perhaps I should talk to this Smee and see what he's like out of character.'

'He stole the show from Captain Hook,' Micah commented.

'He certainly got more laughs.' Moody would have never dared voice his opinion if he hadn't drunk two glasses of champagne which had gone straight to his head.

'That wasn't too difficult given the stilted performance of the actor playing the role,' Aled said loudly. He'd suspected from the way Jeremy Dupois was leaning towards their table that he was listening in on every word that he and the others were saying. He was sure of it when Jeremy turned purple. 'Max?' Aled hailed the head waiter who was hovering attentively at his elbow. 'I think we're ready for coffee and the dessert trolley now. And brandies?' He looked around at his guests.

'Not for me, thank you. I have to be up early in the morning,' Micah refused.

'And we'll be painting wonky lines on the wood and walls of your club if we have any,' Tony added.

Aled showed off the contents of the dessert trolley as if

he were personally responsible for the elegant confections, then waited until everyone had made their choice from the creams, mousses, soufflés and iced puddings before turning to Edyth and asking the question she sensed he had been waiting to broach all evening.

'Mrs Slater, I had the impression that you thought you knew me when you saw me at the theatre.'

'Did you?' she replied, aware that her answer would irritate him.

'I did. I also happened to see someone who looked just like me at the carnival. Is he a friend of yours?'

'No, Mr James.'

'Please, call me Aled.' He laid his hand over hers on the table. She pulled it away and looked to Micah for support. He was engrossed in conversation with Jed and Moody. But as though he sensed her appealing to him, he turned and slipped his arm around her shoulders. She had never felt closer to him and gave him a grateful smile.

'An acquaintance perhaps?' Aled pressed.

'My brother.' She dropped her spoon on her gooseberry fool and pushed the bowl away from her.

'You don't like it?' Aled noticed that she had scarcely touched her dessert.

'It's a little rich for me.'

'His name? Your brother's name,' he repeated when she didn't answer him.

She looked Aled directly in the eye. 'Harry Evans. Do you know him?'

'I believe I do. If he is the man I am thinking of, we were foster brothers when we were children, in the Rhondda Valley.'

'You are from the Rhondda?' Edyth had been born in Pontypridd but she knew her parents had moved there from the Rhondda Valley after her elder sister Bella's birth. She also knew that Harry's father had died before Harry was born and a few years before her parents had married. But it wasn't something that her parents – or

Harry – had discussed with her and her sisters, other than when they had told them that Harry's fortune came from his real father's family.

'Clydach Vale.' Aled watched her intently. 'My mother used to look after children whose parents could not care for them. That's how I met Harry. He was one of her foster children.'

'I think you must be mistaken. I can't imagine my mother handing over Harry, or any of us children, to someone else to bring up, not even for a short while,' Edyth said tartly.

'I believe your mother was in hospital at the time, but,' he gave her one of his cold smiles, 'I may be mistaken. I was only a child myself. Tell me, Mrs Slater, what does your brother do for a living?' After making extensive enquiries Aled knew as much about Harry's personal circumstances as any member of his family – and probably more about his business and financial affairs than anyone other than Harry and the trustees of his estate – but he continued to probe.

'My brother works in a family business.'

'And what would that be?' Aled persisted.

'Shops,' Edyth replied shortly.

'Big? Small?' He widened his frosty smile when Edyth gave him a hard look.

'It's no secret, Mr James, my brother owns Gwilym James.'

'The chain of department stores.' Aled nodded sagely. 'I can see now why you bought the bakery. You clearly come from a family of entrepreneurs.'

'My father brought all of us up to earn our own livings, Mr James.'

'Please, call me Aled.'

'Very well – Aled.'

'You are married, Mrs Slater?'

'My husband and I are separated.' Knowing from Micah's enquiries that Aled had been living in the

Windsor Hotel for a couple of weeks, Edyth didn't doubt that he'd picked up all the Bay gossip, including the full story of her failed marriage.

'You are very young. You couldn't have been married long.'

'A few months.' She looked to Micah again, but Jed had commandeered his attention.

'I'm sorry,' Aled commiserated.

'Marriage doesn't always work out.'

'Someone told me that you have applied to have your marriage annulled.' He spooned sugar into his coffee.

'You are well informed.'

'Perhaps we could have dinner one evening.'

'I don't think so, Mr James.' Edyth nudged Micah's ankle beneath the cover of the table. 'I keep very early hours as I have to be up every morning at four to open the bakery.'

'Surely not on Sundays, which leaves Saturday night?'

'On Sundays I am up even earlier to update my account books,' she lied.

Micah looked ostentatiously at his watch. 'I think it's time I walked you and Judy home, Edyth.'

Aled reached for his cigar case and offered it around the table. 'Allow me to send for taxis for all of you, Micah.'

'Please, don't disturb yourself, Aled.' Micah rose from his chair. 'It's only a ten-minute walk from here to Goldman's.'

'We must be off too, Mr James.' Judy's uncles and Moody pushed their chairs back and rose to their feet.

'We have to be up even earlier than Edyth,' Tony said. 'Mr Powell wants us to finish the conversion of the Sea Breeze in record time and what Mr Powell wants, Mr Powell gets.'

'For the sake of my club I'm glad to hear it.' Aled watched Micah crumple his napkin and drop it on his plate. 'I'll walk you to the door.'

Edyth allowed the attendant to drape her stole on her shoulders. She offered Aled her hand. He lifted it and kissed her knuckles.

'Thank you for a lovely dinner and a lovely evening, Mr James,' she said with more politeness than warmth.

'The first of many we'll enjoy together I hope, Mrs Slater. I trust that you,' he looked at the others, 'all of you, will come to the grand opening of the club and often afterwards to hear Miss King sing.'

'We certainly will,' Jed answered. 'Our niece is very precious to us. Thank you for the dinner, Mr James.'

Aled smiled graciously as the others gave him their thanks, then taking Judy's stole from the cloakroom attendant, he draped it around her shoulders. 'You'll let me know your answer when you've had time to consider my proposition?'

'I don't need time, Mr James; I would like to accept it.'

'Subject to contract,' Micah qualified cautiously.

'That goes without saying, Micah. I trust this is the beginning of a very profitable relationship for both of us, Miss King. We must do this again and very soon so we can toast our future – together.'

Edyth watched Aled lift Judy's hand to his lips and kiss it. Despite the warmth in the air, she shivered. Aled James had been kind and generous to all of them and exceptionally so to Judy. She was being ridiculous. After all, what did she have to base her dislike of him on, except a peculiar likeness to Harry – and a more abrupt and businesslike personality?

'Goodnight, Mrs Slater.'

'Goodnight, Mr James.' Edyth took Micah's arm and walked away.

# CHAPTER NINE

Aled returned to the dining room to tip and thank the head waiter. He was heading for his suite when Stan Peterson waylaid him.

'There's someone sitting at our table that you should meet.'

'It's a bit late in the day to do business, Stan,' Aled said.

Stan lowered his voice. 'He's a major wheeler-dealer on the Bay. His family own the largest shipping company. They're into all sorts, *and*,' Stan reduced his voice to a whisper, 'he's been asking questions about you, your employees and the old Sea Breeze.'

'His name?' Aled enquired shortly.

'Charlie Moore.'

'Of Moore's shipping agency.'

'You know him?'

'I've heard of the agency.' Aled recalled the long, cold hours he'd stood day after winter day on Penniless Point, along with all the other unemployed men and boys who were desperate for work, waiting for a Moore's representative to turn up.

'We're at the coffee and brandy stage. Would you like to join us? As our guest,' Stan added, hoping that Aled wouldn't discover that the 'our' was Charlie Moore. Charlie and his cronies frequently bankrolled Stan's first-night dinners for the cast, in return for theatre tickets, invitations to theatrical parties and introductions to the chorus girls.

Deciding he couldn't afford to ignore 'a major wheeler-dealer' on the Bay, Aled followed Stan back to his table. Stan relinquished his chair so Aled could sit next to Charlie.

'Mr Charles Moore, Mr Aled James.' Stan effected the introduction and its significance wasn't lost on Aled. He set no store by etiquette but he knew the likes of Charlie Moore did. The fact that Stan had said Charlie's name first put Charlie on a socially superior level. Stan went to the end of the table and sat next to Jeremy Dupois, whose mood hadn't improved with the advent of brandy and cigars.

'Mr James, or may I call you Aled? Everyone calls me Charlie.' Slightly the worse for drink, Charlie rose to his feet and offered Aled his hand.

'You may, Charlie.' Aled shook Charlie's hand and took Stan's chair.

'You're setting up business on the Bay?' Charlie spoke slowly and deliberately, in the manner of the habitual drunk.

'I am. But no doubt Stan Peterson has told you that.'

'Good man, Stan. Have a brandy.'

Aled watched the waiter fill Charlie's brandy balloon but he signalled the waiter to put no more than a splash into his. 'The shipping business is slow at the moment, or so they tell me. Has it affected Moore's?'

'I'd be lying if I said it hadn't.' Charlie laughed as one of the chorus girls leaned across the table to talk to Lennie. Her low-cut dress fell, exposing her nipples. 'What an eyeful, eh, Aled,' he chortled.

'You're not worried?' Aled asked.

'She's not mine so she can stand on the table, strip off and do the Hula Hula naked for all I care.'

'I was talking about your family's business.'

'Oh that,' Charlie said carelessly. 'I've diverted some of the family's funds into other things. Can't afford to lose income at a time like this, old boy. Need to keep up appearances and there's nothing like a good time – eh?' Charlie dug his elbow into Aled's ribs.

'There isn't.' Aled decided of all the 'crache' expressions, 'old boy' was the worst.

The chorus girl leaned back and adjusted her bodice. Disappointed, Charlie turned back to Aled. 'Stan says you're turning the Sea Breeze into a nightclub.'

'Given that Moore's offices are only up the road, you probably inspected the plans at the council offices.'

'I did.' Charlie narrowed his eyes and pursed his mouth. 'I also heard that you've bought gambling, drinks and entertainment licences by wining, dining and entertaining members of the various council committees – with Anna Hughes' assistance.'

'I have the licences but I resent your implication as to how I got them.'

'We're both men of the world. Let's not pretend that we don't know how it works. And just so we're not at cross purposes, I have a business proposition for you.'

'What kind?' Aled asked warily.

'You'll need insurance.'

'Against what?'

'The people of Tiger Bay. They're a rough lot, and they're not like us.'

'"Us" being?' Aled enquired.

'Hard-working businessmen. Everywhere you look on Tiger Bay you see Negroes, Lascars, Somalis, Chinese . . . not to mention all the half castes. They'll take one look at your club and want a piece of it for themselves.'

'I doubt it. I'm aiming more up market than the common seaman can afford.'

'All the more reason for them to be jealous. And they're capable of anything,' Charlie warned. 'Attacking your customers inside and outside the club, arson – even murder.'

'And I thought you were a businessman,' Aled mocked.

'No businessman worth his salt would sink so low as to use the old Mafia protection racket.'

'It's insurance . . .'

'What's the going rate for a thug on the Bay? Five pounds a week. Ten?'

Charlie flushed angrily. 'I'm offering you a good service.'

'I don't need it.' Aled looked pointedly at Aiden and Freddie. As usual, they weren't far away. They'd dined at an unobtrusive corner table close to the kitchen door. The moment they saw him looking at them, they dumped their napkins on their plates and left their seats. Aled shook his head and they sat back down again. 'Those two are all the insurance I need, Charlie.'

'They're not local. They don't know who's who around Tiger Bay.'

'They're quick learners. They proved that when they worked for me in New York. Where do you think I made the money to open my club?'

'You'll need operating capital. I can let you have preferential rates.'

'I'm sure you can, but I've all the money I need.'

'Only a fool sets up a high-risk business like a nightclub with his own money,' Charlie declared.

'Then I'm a fool,' Aled agreed evenly.

'You're running poker tables, roulette, blackjack – what happens if a gambler breaks the bank?'

'I pay him. Word soon gets out if a casino reneges on debts. On the other hand, if he's cheating, I'll call the police. Fraud is still a crime in this country, isn't it?' Aled enquired conversationally.

'How much money do you have?' Charlie demanded bluntly.

'Enough.'

'First friendly warning: steer clear of the turf if you value your health.'

'Thank you for the brandy, Charlie.' Aled opened his

cigar case, offered it around to the men and women at the table and Charlie last of all.

'I'm serious,' Charlie emphasised.

'I never doubted you were. Anything else I should steer clear of?' Aled struck his lighter and lit his own cigar.

'There's no reason why we shouldn't get along,' Charlie blustered in a friendlier tone. 'My family have had an office on the Bay since 1840.'

'Things have changed since then.'

'Not that much,' Charlie snarled, 'and we don't need Yanks coming in to change them.'

'That's where you've made your first mistake, Charlie. I'm not a Yank. I'm as Welsh as you are and I've lived on the Bay before.'

'When?'

'A few years ago.'

'It couldn't have been for long, or I'd remember you.'

'It was long enough for me to remember you, Charlie.' Aled left the table and beckoned to Freddie and Aiden. They crossed the dining room and joined him.

'I'll be seeing you, Aled.' Charlie looked Aled squarely in the eye.

'I don't doubt it, Charlie.' Aled took the hat Freddie handed him. 'You picked up the car earlier, Freddie?'

'Yes, boss.'

'Get it, we're going for a drive.'


'You don't want to tangle with Charlie Moore, Aled; he's a nasty piece of work.' Anna Hughes reached for the brandy and soda siphon at her elbow and topped up Aled's glass and her own. They were sitting companionably side by side on the large sofa that faced the cold hearth in the front parlour of her house.

'The man is thick as two short planks,' Aled said, reverting to one of his childhood expressions.

'Or, to be crude, thick as dog shit and twice as nasty, as the saying goes, but he has henchmen who are even thicker and they outdo one another to get a pat on the head from him.'

'How rich is he?'

'His family have enough money to pave their lavatories with gold, or so people say. But his grandfather died last month and from what I've heard, neither Charlie nor his father has the sense to hang on to what the old man made.'

'And the bottom is falling out of the shipping trade, so the Moores won't be making a new fortune.' Aled sipped his brandy thoughtfully.

'Charlie has extravagant tastes. A couple of months ago he started "insuring" local businesses.'

'Yours?' Aled asked astutely.

'He takes one of the girls whenever he wants to. He used to pay but,' she shrugged her shoulders, 'he hasn't for the last six months. I made it clear that the concession only applies to him, not his henchmen and I pay the girl – usually Gertie, as it happens – a couple of bob whenever he comes. It's only fair that the house bear the expense.'

'You're a fool, once that sort of thing starts—'

'A Tunisian who owned one of the cafés on Bute Street and the opium den above it refused to pay Charlie's insurance,' she interrupted. 'The next day the police raided it. There'd been a tip-off that he was serving meths in teacups. That resulted in an article in the *Western Mail*, along the usual lines of Tiger Bay – full of dens of iniquity, loose diseased women, drunks, thieves, robbers, drug addicts, criminal half-caste children.'

'I remember reading similar articles around chip wrappings fifteen years ago. The powers that be's attitude to Tiger Bay hasn't changed since I was a kid. But I gathered that much when I talked to the city councillors.'

'The reporter argued that a relaxation of the licensing laws in the regulated pubs was needed to combat the problem, although the police raid hadn't come up with a single scrap of evidence that the man was serving anything other than tea and coffee – in the café, that is. The following week the café was burgled. But not by thieves. Nothing was taken but all the furniture and fittings were smashed.'

'The café's out of business now?'

'Not as result of that night. The other traders in Bute Street knew what was going on so they rallied round and helped the owner replace everything. The night after it reopened it was broken into again and set on fire. The owner got the message. He shut up shop for good.'

'Do the other businesses on Bute Street pay Charlie's insurance?'

'Not all of them. Charlie may be thick, but he knows which way his bread is buttered and where to get the jam. He leaves the small-profit places alone. The grocers, greengrocers, bakers, butchers and ironmongers don't interest him. He targets the ones that flout the law: the pubs that stay open beyond licensing hours, the cafés that serve the illegal booze the sailors bring in, the opium dens and the knocking shops run by pimps. Rumour has it half the police force are in his pocket. It doesn't pay to cross him, Aled.'

'He warned me to stay away from his turf.'

'Every bookie's runner on the Bay works for Charlie.'

'I've met Charlies before. He may be the front man but he's not the brains. Is his father behind him?'

'I doubt it. He drinks, but not as much as Charlie and he's an outwardly respectable local politician. You won't catch him getting his hands dirty. But there are a couple of men who've worked for the Moore family for years. They're brothers – John and Tom Smith.'

'And what were they called when they were born?' Aled set his glass on the table next to him.

'No one knows. Rumour has it they suggest most of the enterprises to Charlie and hire the thugs they need to run them.'

'So, Charlie's just a front for the Smiths? The employer fronting the hired men doesn't sound right to me.'

'If there's anyone else behind Charlie Moore I don't know who it is. What I do know is that Charlie hasn't anything better to do than come down to Bute Street every day, pretend to work in his office, get drunk and pick up the money from his little enterprises.'

'As I said, I've met the sort before. There are hundreds of them in the slums of New York.' Aled finished his drink, rose to his feet and put his glass on the mantel-piece.

'Gertie might be free and if she isn't you could always see one of the other girls.'

'No thanks, Anna. I have plans to make.'

'Tiger Bay doesn't need a war,' she said seriously.

'I have no intention of starting one.'

'But you won't pay Charlie insurance for your club?'

'No, Anna, I won't.' He reached for his hat and angled it on his head. 'See you around.'

'The next time you want information?'

'If you're feeling neglected have dinner with me tomorrow evening in my suite?'

She smiled. 'I'd like that.'

'You're a good friend, Anna. Goodnight.'

Anna watched Aled leave the house. One of 'Aled's boys' had already opened the door of a new, leather-upholstered luxurious Bentley. Anna closed the curtains, switched out the light and went into the kitchen. As always a fresh pot of tea stood on the table. She poured herself a cup, lit a cigarette and reflected just how far she – and Aled Cooper – had come in the last fifteen years.

Two weeks after Judy's debut, Micah walked past the mid-morning queue that snaked out of Edyth's bakery and down the pavement of Bute Street. He tipped his hat to the waiting women.

'Good morning, ladies.'

'It was a lovely morning before you jumped the queue, Micah Holsten. That's not very Christian, and you a pastor,' Doris, who lived in the same street as Helga and the King brothers, shouted when he stepped inside the shop.

He leaned out of the door. 'I'm not here to buy anything, just deliver a message to Mrs Slater.'

'We'll search you when you come out, to make sure, Micah,' Doris threatened.

'And check inside your mouth for crumbs,' a wag added.

'You'll find nothing.'

'It'll be fun looking. It's been a long time since I laid hands on a strapping virile young man like you.' Doris puckered her lips and blew Micah a kiss.

'Keep it clean, Doris,' a woman with young children at the back of the queue admonished.

The shop was crowded and it was as much as Micah could do to squeeze through to the counter. Two of Judy's aunts were serving customers as quickly as they could while Judy's eldest cousin, Kristina, was busy arranging rows of bread rolls filled with ham and cheese on trays.

Edyth was packing cardboard boxes with sausage rolls, pies and pasties that she was lifting from the display plates with tongs. She saw Micah, nodded and carried on counting the pasties. 'Six . . . seven . . . eight . . . nine . . . ten—'

'He's back,' Micah interrupted, on the premise that ten was an easy number to remember.

'Who's back?' She dropped the tenth pastie into the box, closed it and made a note in a book next to the box.

'David.'

'Have you seen him?'

'Not yet, the captain sent a note to tell me the *Vidda* had berthed and David was sick.'

'Sick?' She looked up in concern.

'Seasick,' he explained. 'Apparently all the way to Norway and all the way back. Some people aren't cut out to be sailors.'

'Poor David,' Edyth murmured sympathetically. 'He was so set on seeing the world.'

'He was more set on something else,' Micah whispered before raising his voice. 'I thought I'd better check with Moody that it's still all right for David to move into his room in Helga's.'

'Moody's in the kitchen.' Edyth turned to the waiting women. 'I'll be with you as soon as I can,' she apologised before opening the flap in the counter for Micah. He followed her through to the back where Moody was brushing the crusts of a tray of unbaked meat pies with a mixture of milk and beaten egg.

'Is business this good, or are the boys just practising their baking?' Micah cast his eye over the vast amount of stock that was either on its way into the ovens or on its way out of them.

'It's boomed since George Powell's men moved into the Sea Breeze.' Edyth shifted a tray of Welsh cakes to the table nearest to the door. 'We're selling six times as much as we did before they started work on the place. And before you tell me, I know it can't last.'

'Are you running to the bank with the profits or distributing them among the poor?' Micah asked.

'Running to the bank. If I can pay off a chunk of my overdraft it will give me a buffer for when the nightclub opens and trade drops off.'

'You'll burn your mouth, Micah,' Moody warned when he filched a sausage roll from a tray that had just come out of the oven.

'David's back, is it all right if he moves into your room with you?' Micah blew on the roll to cool it.

'Only until he finds another berth. And you can tell him from me that he'd better start looking right away.' Moody turned to one of his apprentices who dropped an empty tray. 'They'll hear that in Cardiff Castle never mind out front. You trying to scare the customers away?'

'David won't be going back to sea, he was seasick on both voyages.' Micah gingerly nibbled at the edge of the roll.

Moody grinned. 'Some men just aren't cut out to be sailors.'

'That's exactly what I said to Edyth. See you later at the mission? We're short of a waffle cook tonight.'

'I'll be there.' Moody went to the small oven to check a batch of fruit cakes.

Micah pressed his hand on the door to prevent Edyth from opening it. 'I need to finish this roll before Doris sees me. I told her I was only delivering a message,' he explained.

'Isn't lying a mortal sin?'

'Possibly for Catholics. We Lutherans are allowed to tell as many white lies as we like.'

'And stealing sausage rolls comes under the category of "white lies"?'

'I'll pay for it later,' he winked at her, 'in kind.'

'I can't wait to see what that might be,' she said with a smile.

'Perhaps when David's had time to recuperate he'll go back to the farm.'

'I doubt it. Harry and Mary didn't want him to leave and after the trouble he had arguing with them to gain his independence I don't think his pride will allow him to admit defeat and go back.'

'Either way, I think you should talk to him, Edyth,' Micah said seriously. 'Unless, that is, you'd prefer me to talk to him for you.'

She shook head. 'No, David's part of my family. We won't be able to avoid seeing one another. The sooner this problem is sorted between us, the better it will be for everyone's sake.'

'Including mine. Are you going to visit him this evening after you've shut up shop?'

'Yes,' she said decisively.

'I'll meet you at Helga's and walk you back.'

'Thank you.' Apart from the opening night of *Peter Pan* when they had both been in the theatre, Micah had made the most of Judy's absence by spending every evening except Sundays with her in the rooms above her shop. But he was always careful to leave before Judy arrived, walked home by one of her uncles.

'Save me a pastie for supper?' Micah pushed the last chunk of sausage roll into his mouth.

'If you're good, two.'

'I'll be good, miss.' He looked up, saw Moody and the boys watching them and decided against kissing her. 'Time to fetch the wandering boy and take him to Helga's.'

'Be kind to him, Micah.'

'I can afford to be, I got the girl,' he whispered. He winked at her again and fought his way out of the shop.

'Micah, I warned you that I was going to search you.' Doris had worked her way up the queue to the doorway.

'Another time.'

'Promises, promises, that's all I ever get,' she complained to his retreating back.

'And service, Doris. It's your turn, when you've finished flirting with Micah. The usual? One Welsh bap and half a dozen Welsh cakes?' Edyth asked.

Micah strolled down Bute Street to where he'd parked the mission's van. The fine weather hadn't abated since the carnival and it was a beautiful warm summer's day. The sky was a pale washed blue, the sun was shining and he was tempted to forget the mission and all the errands he had to run on behalf of his parishioners, fetch his saxophone and take it down to his boat so he could play it on deck. He imagined sitting with his back to the cabin, the sea glinting with reflected sunlight all around him and the fishy smell of the salt-laden dock air. It would certainly be more peaceful than where he was.

Bute Street teemed with life. Sober-suited, bowler-hatted clerks and businessmen walked briskly and purposefully in and out of the imposing doorways of the Victorian-built banks and down towards the magnificent façade of the Exchange. A group of women stood gossiping on the corner of Custom House Street outside Thomas the tobacconist's. Delivery boys steered bicycles plastered with the logos of Patterson's the butcher's and Reese and Gwillim's the grocer, in between horse-drawn carts and the sleek black motor cars of the wealthy.

Half a dozen Chinese seamen were playing Sic Bo, the Chinese dice game the locals had adopted and rechristened Dice Bowl, on the doorstep of the Chinese Seamen's home. Somali seamen had spilled out of the cafés and were sitting on window sills, teacups in hand, taking the air. And everywhere, gangs of children roamed, making the most of the fine weather and the school holidays. Some were headed across the street in the direction of the canal, others towards the sea front, or the railway line behind him, but a fair number lingered outside the shops, looking to make a penny or two by carrying messages, or holding the horses of the delivery carts.

His spirits fell when he saw a crowd of elderly seamen outside the Corys Buildings at Penniless Point. There were fewer than usual because most of the younger, fitter men were working on the conversion of the Sea Breeze. There was little chance of any of them picking up work this late in the day because the shipping and docker agents and captains looked to take on crew before dawn. But having nowhere else to go and nothing better to do, they had obviously decided to wait simply because a slim hope was better than none.

Micah loved Tiger Bay, the diversity of the population,

the friendliness of the natives, their wit, intelligence and willingness to help their neighbours. After only six years of living on the dockside he couldn't imagine moving anywhere else. But he was also aware that although Edyth was happy in Bute Street for the moment, she might not always be. The question of their future – that's if they had one together – hung over their relationship, tainting every private moment they spent together.

If she should decide to sell the baker's and move away from the Bay he had no way of staying close to her unless she married him. And while she continued to refuse even to consider the idea, he was left in limbo, unable to make plans that included the both of them and unwilling to make any that excluded her.

Turning his back on the crowd of unemployed men, he climbed into his van, drove slowly down the street and turned at the dock, continuing along the quayside. He looked along the rows of berthed ships, finally spotting the *Vidda* in prime position close to the railway sidings. Dockers were hard at work, unloading the logs she'd brought in and piling them on to the empty wagons that waited to be pulled back up to the pitheads.

Lars Nordheim was on deck. When he saw Micah leaving his van he walked down the gangplank to meet him.

'Micah, old friend.' He lifted him off his feet in a bear hug. 'I hope that sister of yours has been baking for our return.'

'I don't doubt she's killed a few eels and a goose or two. How is David?' Micah asked.

The captain looked grim, held out his hand and waved it from side to side. 'I've seen some cases of seasickness in my time but he has to be the worst. He couldn't even keep water down. You gave me a healthy young man. I'm returning a skeleton.'

'Sorry, I didn't mean to offload deadweight cargo on to

you. He must have been worse than useless, because the crew had to look after him.'

The captain slapped his hand across Micah's shoulders. 'He didn't cost us any food. And one good thing has come out of it. Your young man has discovered that a sailor's life is not for him. He's vowed never to go to sea again.' He beckoned Micah forward. 'He's still below deck.'

David was lying white and still on the bunk that he hadn't left on the outward or return journey. His eyes were closed and the captain had to shake him twice before he opened them. He looked up, wide eyed and startled, at Micah.

'Micah's here to take you on to dry land,' the captain said heartily. 'A day or two to find your land legs and you'll be as right as rain.'

'Thank you,' David murmured; all trace of hostility and sarcasm gone.

'Can you walk?' Micah asked.

'I'll try.' David tried to move but from the way he swayed it was obvious he was suffering from vertigo.

'You take the right arm, I'll take the left, we'll prop him up on our shoulders,' the captain suggested. 'Terje, bring his kitbag.'

Micah noticed the seaman for the first time when he stepped forward from behind the bulkhead. 'Thank you.'

'Terje looked after David for most of the voyage.' The captain heaved David to his feet.

'Then double thank you.' Micah braced himself to take David's weight, but the captain was right, the boy had been reduced to skin and bones.

'David was no trouble. I've one his age at home,' Terje said gruffly, clearly unwilling to be thought of as kind.

Micah and the captain half dragged, half carried David on to the deck and down the gangplank. Even on dry land he swayed like a drunk. Micah opened the passenger door of the van with his free hand and he and Lars bundled David inside.

'Don't worry about your van if he starts retching, Micah, there's nothing in his stomach to bring up.' The captain stood back when Micah closed the door.

'Want a lift to Helga's?' Micah knew both seamen lodged there along with most of the *Vidda*'s crew whenever they berthed in Cardiff for longer than two days.

'No, thank you, we've still a few things to do here. But tell Helga we'll be up in time for one of her high teas.' Lars licked his lips in anticipation.

'Will do.' Micah climbed into the driver's seat, started the engine, drove away from the docks and into the network of back streets. He glanced at David. The boy looked so ill and wretched Micah searched his mind for something comforting to say to him.

'Captain Nordheim's right, you'll be fine once you get your land legs back.'

'So everyone keeps telling me,' David whispered hoarsely through cracked lips.

'I hear you've vowed never to go to sea again.'

'Not even on a rowing boat on Roath Park Lake,' David concurred.

'Sorry it didn't work out.'

'At least I tried.' David opened his eyes and looked at Micah. 'I've had time to do a lot of thinking. There isn't much else to do when you're being tossed and turned inside a ship that refuses to stay still, other than think and pray for death because you feel too ill to live.'

'I'm glad your prayers weren't answered,' Micah said dryly. 'You're too young to die.'

'That doesn't seem to stop me from trying. First in Pontypridd—' He looked keenly at Micah. 'Edyth told you about that?'

'Only after you ran out of the bakery yard, when you

saw me kissing her. She was desperately worried about you, and I couldn't understand why.'

'And now again on the boat, although that wasn't a conscious decision. But if I hadn't been too ill to crawl to the side and fling myself overboard I might have had another go.'

Micah decided to change the subject. 'You said you did some thinking. I hope they were good thoughts.'

'Not really. I've made a fool of myself over Edyth – twice.'

'I wouldn't say that. You simply fell in love with her, and I, of all people, find that perfectly understandable. But none of us has any control over who we fall in love with.' Micah found it difficult not to sound as if he were crowing.

'Edyth must think I'm a complete idiot,' David mumbled.

'She doesn't think anything of the kind,' Micah said seriously. 'In fact when I told her that you were back just now—'

'Why did you do that?' Anger flared in David's voice.

'I had to go to the bakery to see Moody. I wanted to check if it was still all right for you to share his room. With the *Vidda* in port I knew Helga's house would be full to bursting. The crew don't like staying anywhere else.'

'What did Moody say?'

'That you could share his room.' Micah decided it wasn't a good time to pass on Moody's message about finding another berth as soon as possible. 'Obviously Edyth was there. Did you expect me not to tell her that you were back?'

'I suppose not,' David muttered. 'Did she say anything?'

'That she wanted to talk to you and she'd come and see you this evening.'

'To tell me that I've behaved like a bloody fool.'

'To tell you that she loves you very much – like a brother. And, knowing Edyth, she'll want to help you. Now that you're not going to sea again, you have a few decisions to make about your future.'

'I'm not going back to the farm,' David stated firmly, confirming Edyth's suspicions.

'It's your choice, but you'll need a job and the only person who's hiring on the dock at the moment is the builder George Powell. He's converting a hotel on Bute Street into a nightclub. He's looking for craftsmen, but last I heard he was still taking on a few labourers. When you're feeling up to it you could go along and ask him if he has anything going. Judy's uncles are working for him; they might put in a good word for you.'

'I know a bit about carpentry.'

'You're experienced?' Micah said in surprise.

'Not time served or anything like that, but Harry's Uncle Victor is a fair carpenter – he taught Harry a bit, and Harry taught me.'

'Given the amount of work to be done on the hotel in the next few weeks, George will probably drag you in there as soon as you can stand.' Micah stopped the van outside Helga's house. 'But first we have to get you inside, and from the look of you into bed.'

'I won't argue with you.'

'I'll take your kitbag in and warn Helga you're here so she can make up your bed. Then I'll come back for you.'

'Micah?'

'Yes?'

David then said two words Micah had never expected to hear from him.

'Thank you.'

# CHAPTER TEN

'Thank you, Mr James. That was a lovely lunch.' Judy set her knife and fork on the plate and looked across the table at Aled. It was the sixth lunch he'd invited her to in the Windsor Hotel since she'd signed a contract with him. Micah and her uncles had checked it over before handing it to a solicitor who had assured them that it was the most generous theatrical contract he'd seen. But the solicitor's endorsement hadn't stopped her uncles from warning her to be sure to always remain in public with Aled James, and *never* visit him in his suite.

But whenever Aled James had invited her to lunch, it was always on the clear understanding that they would eat in the public dining room. She was aware of the two men who constantly shadowed him. It was difficult to ignore them when they were never more than a few paces from him at any one time, and always sat at the next table to them in the restaurant. On the rare occasions Aled referred to them, he called them his 'employees' although she knew people on the Bay had christened both men James's 'bruisers'.

As for Aled James's attitude towards her, it was generous, respectful – and formal. He never called her anything other than Miss King and she addressed him as Mr James. And the lunches he arranged weren't social. He had brought song sheets of the latest American music to all of them, so they could discuss her repertoire when the club opened and he left the sheets with her afterwards so she could practise the scores in what little free time she had in between performing in the theatre.

'It was a good lunch.' Aled forked the last piece of meat from his plate to his mouth. 'I must remember to order the pork and apple sauce again sometime.' He glanced at his watch. 'There's no matinée this afternoon so you have to be at the theatre at what? Six o'clock?'

'At the latest, management gets annoyed if we're late.'

'You haven't made any plans for this afternoon?' he checked.

'No.'

'In that case we'll go shopping.'

'Shopping for what?' she questioned.

'Stage wear, I'm contracted to pay for your costumes, remember. I did warn you I would be very particular about them.'

'I remember,' she said warily.

'Where do you usually buy your clothes? That gold dress, for instance. The one you wore at the carnival.'

'I borrowed it from one of Mrs Slater's sisters. That and the gown Edyth was wearing were bridesmaids' frocks.'

'Which is the best high-class ladies' outfitters in the city?'

'I don't know of any outside of the large department stores and most turn coloured people away.' It was the first time she had brought up the subject of her Negro blood. She felt unaccountably embarrassed for mentioning it, because unlike most white people who had lived outside of Tiger Bay, he had never drawn attention to it – or treated her or her family any differently because of it.

'Oh, they'll serve you,' he countered confidently. He looked around for a waiter. 'If you want a chaperone we could stop off and ask Mrs Slater to accompany us.'

'She'll be busy in her shop.'

'One of your aunts?'

Judy shook her head. It was broad daylight, they were going into the city and she couldn't think of anywhere more public.

'Max,' Aled greeted the head waiter when he glided over. 'Two French coffees and two champagne ices please.'

'An excellent choice, Mr James.' Max bowed and left.

'You spoil me, Mr James. I've never eaten so well or had so many ice creams.'

'A special lady deserves spoiling. Have you any colours in mind for your stage gowns or do you want to see what's on offer?'

'I'll wait and see what's on offer.'

'And you really don't have any particular shop or dress designer in mind?' he pressed. 'As you're going to be the showcase for my club, I assure you, the benefit will be all mine.'

'To be truthful, Mr James, I've never bought a new frock in my life, apart from my work overalls, and they all came from Bute Street. My grandmother and I used to make all our clothes.'

'Thank you, Max,' Aled said when the head waiter set the coffees and ices in front of them.

Judy sipped the coffee and realised there was an extremely generous measure of cognac in it. 'This will go straight to my head at this time of day.'

'That's why I ordered it. A young girl should be a little light headed when she goes shopping. It will make her bold and reckless. And bold and reckless makes the most head-turning choices, Miss King. That is exactly what I'm aiming for in the Tiger Ragtime. An impact that will turn heads, be talked about, and not easily forgotten. I want your gowns to upstage the costumes of the chorus girls. They'll provide the,' he raised his eyebrows, 'the "Ooh la la" factor, and you'll supply the class.'

'You have a lot of faith in me, Mr James,' Judy said nervously.

'I do,' he agreed. He covered her hand with his own and squeezed it lightly. 'And it's well placed.'

It was the first time he had touched her. Judy gazed

into his eyes. Edyth had said they were cold, but she could see warmth in their deep blue depths – warmth and something that made her spine tingle, her throat tighten and the blood rush to her cheeks.

'To use the Welsh expression, David looks like death warmed up.' Helga lifted two cups and saucers from her Welsh dresser and set them next to the teapot on the kitchen table.

'It's nothing a couple of days on land won't cure.' Micah looked at her critically. 'You're going to have a baby, aren't you?'

She whirled around. 'Edyth told you.'

'Edyth knows?' he asked in surprise.

'I told her and she promised not to tell you . . . '

'She didn't. I saw Ruth Jenkins leaving when I came in. She happened to mention that you're paying her to work here six mornings a week and I couldn't think of any other reason why you'd employ someone to help you in the house.'

'It could be because I'm doing so well. I have so many regulars unable to get berths out of Cardiff I'm considering renting the house next door.'

'What about the Morrises?' Micah was fond of the young couple who lived next door to his sister. They had helped Helga many times by accommodating the overflow from her lodging house.

'They're returning to Merthyr. His father has TB and he's taking over the family barge. Jobs are everything these days.'

'You can say that again. Even with George Powell hiring every spare man with any building experience, there was a crowd at Penniless Point this morning.'

'I saw the men there when I picked up my bread from Edyth's.'

'I thought Moody brought it home.'

172

'He does, but it's a fine day, I felt like a walk. Besides it's good exercise, for me and the little one.'

Micah smiled at the mention of the baby. 'So when is this niece or nephew of mine going to put in an appearance?'

'Not for months.'

'How many?'

'Five,' she revealed reluctantly. 'What about you and Edyth?'

'What about me and Edyth?'

'Any sign of the annulment of her marriage yet.'

'No,' he replied, 'and even when it comes I'm not sure Edyth will want to marry me. She keeps on saying she's happy with things the way they are between us.'

'Wise girl.'

'Don't tell me you're on her side,' he complained.

'What happens to her bakery if she marries you, Micah?'

'Have you been talking to her about me?'

'No.'

'The bakery is the excuse she gave me for not wanting to marry me. As if I'd interfere.'

'How could you not interfere?'

'What do you mean?' he demanded defensively.

'Being pastor of the Norwegian Church isn't a job, it's a vocation and a lifestyle rolled into one. How often do people around here say, "Get Micah, he'll know what to do"? Births, deaths, marriages, fights, arrests, arguments between the West Indians and the Scandinavians, the Arabs and the Italians, the gamblers and the sore losers, the poor, the destitute, the dead and dying sailors – you've made every problem on the Bay your problem. You have no time to spare for a wife or family, especially if they lived outside the mission.'

'Edyth would move in with me.'

'Into your tiny bedroom in the mission, when she has a

shop with several very comfortable rooms above it in Bute Street? The girl would be mad.'

'All right, living in the mission wouldn't be ideal,' he agreed, 'but I could rent somewhere closer than the bakery.'

'You'd expect Edyth to run a house, look after you and still get up at four in the morning and supervise the shop all day?'

'Put like that, I can see it would be difficult.'

'It simply wouldn't work, Micah. It would be, "Edyth, pop around to Mrs Jones's because she's just had a baby. She's feeling low and needs help with the housework." Or, "There's been a death in number twenty-six and the family's distraught. They can't cope with the undertaker and the funeral arrangements, go and sort it out for them, will you, while I go on board a ship and write a letter for a seaman who's dying and wants to say goodbye to his family." Or, "Could you do Mrs Williams' shopping for her. The doctor told me that her ulcerated leg is playing up and she can't move."'

Micah fell silent, every instance was something he had asked Helga to do in the last few days and he realised just how much he relied on her to take over for him when he had to deal with more urgent matters.

'I know why you took the post of pastor when it was offered to you, Micah.' She handed him a cup of tea.

'I took it because I thought I could make a difference to people's lives in the same way our father did in the Gdansk mission. A seaman's life is hard, not just for him but for his family. All those separations and the uncertainty of long silences without a letter or a word of communication. Never knowing whether a loved one is going to walk back through the door or not.'

'You took it because you wanted to do anything except what you should be doing.'

'Not that again, Helga, please.' He abandoned his tea on the table and walked to the window. Turning his back to her he stared out at the yard. A washing line full of bed linen hung drying in the hot, still air. He couldn't remember a time he'd visited Helga when her washing line hadn't been full except Sundays and he thought guiltily of the hours she'd spent helping him at the mission when she probably should have been doing her housework – or writing to her husband who rarely managed to spend more than one month in twelve at home.

'If you finished your training you could leave the mission and move in with Edyth. She has a more comfortable home than you could ever hope to provide, especially while you continue to live at the mission on the pittance the Lutheran Church pays you.'

'Enough, Helga.'

'You won't think about it?'

'I made my choice six years ago.'

'And you're not prepared to make another now?' When he didn't answer her, she shrugged her shoulders. 'I don't know why I waste my breath. If you're not prepared to change your ways for the woman you love, you're certainly not going to change them for me.'


'Please, Mr James, let's leave,' Judy begged. They had been sitting in the waiting area of one of the largest, plushest and most fashionable department stores in Cardiff for more than ten minutes, during which time half a dozen elegantly dressed women had walked in and been served by sales assistants.

'No, Miss King,' I will not leave.' Aled beckoned to Freddie. 'Freddie, come with me; Aiden, stay with Miss King.' Aled walked directly to the floor walker who was standing at the top of the stairs. 'You! Get the store manager for me. Now!'

'Sir.' The young man stared at Aled as though he'd taken leave of his senses.

'I'm sorry,' Aled apologised sarcastically, 'I was under

the impression that you would have had to speak and understand English to get a position at this store. I want to see the manager. Now!'

'Is there a problem, sir?' The sharp-featured, black-garbed female supervisor of the department glided towards them.

'We have been waiting ten minutes to be served. During which several people who arrived after us have been waited on.'

The supervisor looked from Aled to Judy and Aiden. When she spoke she lowered her voice. 'That girl and man are coloured, sir.'

'So am I,' Aled said. 'The last time I looked in the mirror I was a fetching shade of pale pink.'

'It's not me personally, or even management, sir,' she murmured, 'it's our customers. They wouldn't patronise us if they knew we allowed people like that to try on our stock.'

'People like what?' Aled said loudly for the benefit of everyone within earshot.

As they were attracting attention the supervisor tried and failed to draw Aled aside. 'You know what I mean, sir.'

'No I don't,' Aled bellowed.

'Sir . . . '

'Explain yourself, madam.' Aled stood, arms crossed and obdurate.

The supervisor coughed. 'They clearly have Negro blood, sir. As I said, it's not me . . . or even management . . . '

Aled turned to Aiden. 'I want the name of everyone in management in this store.'

'Sir . . . ' The woman touched his arm.

Aled shook off her hand. 'Everyone, Aiden.'

Aiden pulled a notebook from his pocket and went to the staff board at the top of the stairs. The supervisor tried to step in front of him. He simply picked her up, moved her aside and began writing.

Aled returned to Judy and offered her his arm. 'We have to go elsewhere, Miss King. On close inspection the gowns here are somewhat shoddy.' He swept Judy past the supervisor, down the stairs and out of the store so quickly she had to run to keep up with him. He didn't stop until they reached the pavement. He looked up St Mary Street past the grand Edwardian fronts of the rival department stores, towards the crenellated towers of Cardiff Castle and muttered, 'Bastards!'

Unsure she'd heard Aled correctly, Judy remained silent. He released her arm, and paced to the edge of the kerb. When he looked back at her he was calm.

'Is that the first time you have been refused service in a store, Miss King?'

'Yes.' A double-decker tram pulled up in front of them and she read the advertisements plastered on its sides. It was easier to consider the merits of a tea that promised to cure indigestion than think about the embarrassment she had just suffered.

'They will regret their attitude.' There was an undercurrent to Aled's harsh American vowels, and Judy realised that for all of Aled James's mannered politeness, he would make a formidable enemy.

'As I told you, Mr James, I've never shopped in Cardiff city centre before. Whenever I've needed to buy clothes I've always gone to the stores in Bute Street.'

'Well, we're not returning to Bute Street. Not yet.'

The tram moved on, two men on bicycles passed them and steered their machines towards the railway station. Aled resumed his study of the street. A large blue sign plastered on the side of the tallest, largest and most imposing building caught his eye. 'Gwilym James. Isn't that department store owned by Edyth Slater's brother, Harry?'

Judy was surprised that Aled James knew Edyth had a

brother. 'Mr Evans works there, as does Edyth's mother and uncle, but I don't think Mr Evans owns the store.' Judy had assumed from the way Edyth's brother and his family dressed, that he was reasonably well-to-do, but she couldn't imagine any person being wealthy enough to own a store the size of Gwilym James.

'I believe he not only owns this store, but several others. Shall we go inside and find out how he treats Gwilym James's coloured customers?' Aled asked.

She tried to summon up enough courage to ask if they could forget about buying evening gowns in the city centre, at least for that day. But before she did, Aiden was escorted out through the doors behind them by two men.

Aled smiled. Both men were slighter than Aiden and shorter by a full head than Freddie who had remained with him and Judy.

'These gentlemen,' Aiden indicated his escort, 'asked me to leave when they saw me writing down the names on the board, boss.'

'Before or after you finished making the list?' Aled questioned.

Aiden held out a sheet of paper, Aled took it from him and, without looking at it, folded it into his pocket.

Freddie stepped up alongside Aiden. The men looked warily from Freddie to Aiden and retreated.

'We're going to Gwilym James.' Aled held out his arm to Judy again. 'Miss King.'

Judy reluctantly complied and Aled whisked her purposefully towards the door of the department store. The uniformed doorman opened it for them, touched his cap, and said, 'Good morning, Mr Evans, sir, madam.'

Aled smiled. 'I am not Mr Evans.'

'I like the accent, sir, you sound just like they do in the films.' The doorman closed the door behind them.

'Could you point us towards ladies' evening gowns?' Aled asked.

'I see, sir, it's a test.' The man grinned. 'Third floor, sir, where they've always been. The lift is to the right of the store.' The doorman tipped his cap to a middle-aged woman who was leaving. 'Thank you for shopping with Gwilym James, madam.'

Aled headed across the ground floor to the lift. 'Third floor,' he ordered the young boy who opened the door.

'Yes, Mr Evans, sir.'

Aled allowed the boy's mistake to pass without comment.

The boy followed them into the lift and pressed the button. When they reached the third floor the doors opened, and the boy shouted, 'Ladies' fashions, evening and bridal wear, millinery, accessories and leather goods.'

Judy took a deep breath and steeled herself for further insult. She hadn't been aware of just how much her family, friends and neighbours in Tiger Bay had protected her from racism until she had been dismissed from her first job as 'daily' to an elderly widow. Increasing frail, her employer had decided to hire a live-in maid, and had offered the post to an Irish girl at a higher wage than she'd been paying Judy to live out. The widow couldn't have made it more obvious that although she was prepared to allow Judy to scrub her floors, she was not prepared to allow her to live in her home.

Desperate for work, before Edyth had employed her, Judy had taken every occasional cleaning and menial job she had been offered while auditioning for chorus work and minor roles in all the repertory and touring company in South Wales. The closest she had come to success was to be invited to a second call-back, only to be told, 'Thank you but no thank you.' The colour of her skin was never mentioned but from the whispers she had overheard she was aware that some of the auditions would have had different outcomes if she had been white.

She knew she was being cowardly but she was loath to

invite further embarrassment. Aled had insisted on making a point, and had made it, but if it had been down to her she would have preferred to have slunk out of the last department store unnoticed.

'Evening gowns?' Aled asked the floorwalker.

'Mr Evans, sir,' the boy smiled at what he assumed was a joke, 'you know it's the last department straight ahead of you.'

'Judy, how lovely to see you.' Harry and Edyth's mother, Sali Evans, walked towards her, a floor supervisor following at their heels. Both Sali and the supervisor were stylishly and elegantly dressed in the Gwilym James's female floor managers 'uniform' of black tailored costume and white blouse.

'How are you, Mrs Evans?' Judy asked eagerly, relieved to see a familiar and friendly face.

'I am fine, thank you for asking, Judy.' Sali kissed Judy's cheek. 'Edyth wrote and told me that you had a new job singing in a nightclub. I do hope you have come here to look for stage costumes. We took delivery of the new autumn evening gowns this morning and some of them would suit your slim figure perfectly. Wouldn't they, Miss Johns?'

'They would indeed,' the supervisor concurred.

'Miss Judy King, my daughter Edyth's close friend and right-hand lady in her bakery, Miss Alice Johns, who is in charge of the ladies' fashion department.'

'Pleased to meet you, Miss King.' The supervisor shook Judy's hand.

Aled, who had remained in the background while Judy had been talking to Sali, stepped forward and raised his hat. 'As we have come to purchase stage costumes for Miss King, Mrs Evans, I am glad to hear that you already have the new season's gowns in stock.'

Sali looked at him and the smile died on her lips.

'Mrs Evans, you do remember me?'

Sali continued to stare, mesmerised by Aled's resemblance to Harry.

'You look exactly like Mr Evans, Mr Harry Evans, that is, who owns the department store. Doesn't he, Mrs Evans?' Alice Johns asked excitedly. 'In fact, you could be his twin, sir.'

'So people used to say when we were boys,' Aled said. 'My mother looked after Harry for a few months when you were ill and unable to care for him yourself, Mrs Evans. It must be more than twenty years ago now.' Aled knew exactly to the day how long it had been, but he chose not to emphasise the fact. 'I remember you picking Harry up from Bush Houses in Clydach Vale, which is where we lived at the time. He held out his hand. 'Aled James. I changed my surname to my father's.'

'Mr James.' Sali shook Aled's hand but she couldn't bring herself to utter any platitudes such as, 'pleased to see you again'. She remembered Aled, but she also remembered his mother and that was a part of her and Harry's past that she would have preferred to have left buried and forgotten.

'You look like Mr Evans but you don't sound a bit like him,' Alice chattered. 'You talk like a film star.'

'So I've been told. I've spent the last few years in America.' Aled sensed Sali's discomfort and smiled. 'We're looking to buy at least a dozen evening gowns for Miss King, Mrs Evans, as well as day clothes, coats and accessories. In fact, we're here to purchase an entire new wardrobe for her.'

'I don't need day clothes, Mr James,' Judy demurred.

'Yes, you do.' Realising he'd spoken sharply and the inference that could be drawn from his insistence, he added, 'I own the nightclub Judy will be singing in and I'm contracted to buy her stage costumes.'

'Edyth wrote and told me that the club will be opening soon in Bute Street.' Sali leaned against a pillar for support. Aled's resemblance to Harry was so strong she found it unnerving, particularly as his eyes were hostile.

'I'm calling it the Tiger Ragtime. You and your husband must come to the opening as my guests so you can see Miss King's debut.'

'Thank you,' Sali murmured politely.

'As Miss King will be representing the Tiger Ragtime both on and off the stage she will have to look well turned out and fashionable at all times.'

'We'll do all we can to ensure she looks both.' Sali took Judy's arm. 'Let's go into one of the private rooms. I'll get the girls to model the gowns for you to narrow your choice so you won't have to try on too many.'

'I'll order coffee and biscuits, Mrs Evans.' Alice scanned Judy's figure. '34–22–34?' she asked.

'How did you know?' Judy blushed.

'It's my business, madam. I'll bring the evening gowns first. It won't be long before word gets out that they've come in. And once it does, our account customers will swarm in like ants on honey. Have you any particular designers in mind?'

'I don't know any designers,' Judy confessed.

'Dior, Chanel, de Regny,' Aled replied, surprising Alice with his knowledge of fashion.

'Colours?' Alice enquired briskly.

'White, cream, black, brown, gold, silver, green to match Miss King's eyes, and,' Aled studied a crimson silk strapless gown draped on a model in the centre of the room, 'scarlet, and that model. It is silk?'

'It is, sir,' Alice confirmed.

'Accessories, stoles, shoes, handbags, hats . . . '

'I get the picture, sir.' Alice scurried off. She had served many wealthy customers in her time, but she had never seen a man so certain of what he wanted. Not even the elderly baronet who set aside a day at the beginning of every new season to purchase his young mistress's lingerie.

Judy had expected the 'private room' to be an office. She was amazed when Sali showed them into a sizeable and comfortable sitting room that reminded her of the residents' lounge in the Windsor. It was decorated with green and cream striped wallpaper, oil paintings of city landmarks, and furnished with leather armchairs, mahogany side tables and, somewhat incongruously in a sitting room, a clothes rail.

A uniformed waitress brought in a tray of coffee and petits fours and Alice walked in ahead of two young assistants who were the same height and build as Judy. They wheeled in a second rail full of calico-draped gowns.

Sali sat alongside Aled and Judy as Alice donned white gloves and unbuttoned calico covers from gown after gown so the assistants could display them. After only ten minutes, Judy was bewildered by the array of velvet, silk, satin, organza and lace frocks, but Aled looked at each in turn and approved or dismissed them within a few seconds. The ones he approved of were modelled by the girls. He selected about three-quarters of them to be hung on the empty rail so he could check the quality of the fabric, the stitching, the seams and the cut.

To Judy's surprise her uncles would have approved of Aled James's choice, with the possible exception of the low-cut, strapless crimson silk. Most had sleeves, either long or short, and all were floor length. And to her astonishment he didn't ask the price of any of them.

The empty rack soon became full, as gown after gown was set aside for her to try on. A green satin with a flowing skirt, a classically draped Grecian white silk that Aled liked so much he asked to see it in every colour they had. A long black beaded shift with a matching beaded jacket, sequinned gold, silver lamé, deep burgundy velvet, cream lace, and Aled asked the assistants to drape matching silk and velvet stoles across every gown he chose.

Alice took Judy into an adjoining fitting room to try on the gowns Aled had picked out. She modelled twenty, and to her embarrassment he insisted they buy all of them and the matching stoles.

'Mr James, I couldn't possibly accept all these,' Judy protested after he asked Alice Johns to replace the covers on the ones he had chosen.

'You signed a two-year contract, Miss King. I intend to get my money's worth out of you.' He glanced at his watch. 'You'll need underwear, cosmetics, jewellery – and fur coats,' he added decisively. 'A long one for evening wear, an elbow-length evening cape for warmer weather and a short coat for day wear. But we shouldn't buy anything in a hurry. You have a matinée tomorrow?'

'I do,' Judy confirmed.

'Could we return the day after tomorrow at the same time, Mrs Evans, to look at day wear and furs?'

'Unfortunately I will be in our Pontypridd store that day,' Sali apologised.

'But I will be here and I'll have everything ready and waiting for you, sir. Will you be taking these gowns with you, Mr James?' Alice asked.

'No, I'll pay for them now, but I would like you to hold them and everything else we buy until the builders have finished decorating Miss King's dressing room in the club, then they can be sent on there. You shouldn't have to keep them for longer than two weeks. He removed a card case and his cheque-book from the pocket of his suit and handed her a card. 'The address of the club. I also want to set up an account for Miss King.'

'We'll hold these gowns until your account is set up, Mr James,' Sali offered. 'Miss Johns will see to it and have the necessary papers prepared for you to sign when you come in the day after tomorrow.'

'Thank you, Mrs Evans.' He gave Alice Johns an apologetic smile. 'I am afraid we are making a lot of work for you, Miss Johns.'

'Not at all, sir, it's always a pleasure to dress a beautiful lady.'

Aled glanced at his watch again. 'Time to get the beautiful lady to the theatre. I'm sorry, Miss King, we've no time for tea.'

'I don't think I could eat one after that lunch, Mr James.' Judy left her seat.

'Good day, ladies. Thank you for your help.' He tipped his hat to the assistants and Sali and Alice.

As Aled and Judy walked away he overheard Alice Johns say, 'He's a proper gentlemen just like Mr Evans, for all he talks like an American picture.'

His smile widened when he heard Sali's reply: 'He is, Miss Johns, but I have a feeling that Mr James is a very different kind of businessman to Harry.'

'Lunch again in the Windsor, the day after tomorrow?' Aled asked Judy when they were sitting in the back of the car and Freddie was chauffeuring them to the theatre.

'Please don't feel that you have to, Mr James.'

'I enjoy your company. Don't you enjoy mine?' he asked frankly.

'Of course I do, it's just that,' she found the courage to say what was on her mind, 'I feel dreadfully guilty for taking all those clothes from you.'

'They're not clothes, they're stage costumes,' he asserted.

'My grandmother used to say that the only person who should buy a woman's clothes, besides herself and her parents, is her husband.'

'I'm not offering to marry you, Miss King.'

Judy blushed crimson. 'I wasn't suggesting . . . '

'I know you weren't. I was making a joke – a bad one. And your uncles and Micah Holsten wouldn't have allowed me to write your stage costumes into your contract if they considered there was something wrong with the idea, now, would they?'

'No they wouldn't have,' she agreed, 'but there's nothing in the contract about fur coats and day clothes.'

'So, you're going to turn up at the stage door of my club wearing last year's mac over your stage costumes?'

'Who'll see me?' she challenged.

'The photographers from the local and national newspapers. This club is only the beginning for me, and you, Miss King. I intend to make you a star, and in the next couple of years open more clubs, in London and other places. And you'll be headlining in all of them.'

'London?' She looked at him in amazement. 'You never said anything to my uncles about London.'

'That's because at the moment my plans are just that – no more than ideas in my head. And, given the size of my investment, I have to get the Tiger Ragtime up and running and turning a profit before I start expanding.'

'Do you want me to park the car, boss?' Freddie slowed down as they turned the corner and approached the theatre.

Aled glanced out of the window. 'I'll tell you in a minute, Freddie. Are you still getting on with Lennie Lane?' he asked Judy.

'Yes,' Judy said in surprise. 'Why do you ask?'

'Because I think I'll go in and have a word with him. The club needs a comic; he has a history in show business and knows what it's about. And all the reviews I've read of *Peter Pan* have singled out his performance and complimented his comedy skills, timing and adlibbing.'

'He comes out with new gags and routines every night.'

'Really?'

'They're not always appreciated by the others on-stage with him.'

'He enjoys winding up Jeremy Dupois?' Aled guessed.

'Yes,' she conceded.

'As I haven't much time for the pompous either I will go in with you and have a word with him. Yes, Freddie, you can park the car.'

Freddie pulled in to the side of the road, switched off the engine and opened the back door.

Aled stepped out and offered Judy his hand. She took it. 'We'll have no more argument about day clothes and fur coats?' He handed her the gloves she'd left on the seat.

'Do you mind if I check with my uncles first?'

'Frankly, yes. It's my decision, and now you've signed the contract you're my property.'

'Your property, Mr James?' Her eyes blazed in indignation.

'Only professionally, Miss King, only professionally,' he reiterated, his smile taking the sting from his words.

# CHAPTER ELEVEN

Edyth carried a tray up the stairs of Helga's house, balanced it on her knee and knocked on Moody's bedroom door.

'Come in.' David's mumbled reply sounded weak, even through the door. She opened it and peered inside. He was lying in bed, his face as white as the pillowcase beneath his head. He looked at her. 'Micah said you'd call in to see me.'

'When he told me you'd been ill I had to see you and, as Helga's serving high tea, I volunteered to bring this up for you.' She lifted a cup and plate from the tray and set them on the bedside table next to him.

'I can't keep anything down.'

'Dry toast and Oxo, swallow both and you won't see them again.'

'Is that a promise?' he enquired sceptically.

'Having helped my mother nurse my four younger sisters and small brother through all their childhood ailments, I guarantee it.' She pulled a chair up to the bed and sat down. 'Bit of a let-down having to abandon your plans of a seafaring career because of sea-sickness.'

'It's put an end to any thoughts I had of following Francis Drake and Captain Cook's voyages around the world,' he agreed. 'You and Harry have every right to say, "We told you so, Davy, now get back to the farm where you belong."'

'I won't say it, and knowing Harry as I do, he won't either.'

'Why not? I've made a right piggy mess of everything.'

'No, you haven't,' she contradicted. 'You wanted to go to sea, you went and you found out that a sailor's life isn't for you. That sounds like progress to me. Now all you have to do is find out what you are good at.'

'It wasn't just the sea. I had hoped that with Peter gone we—'

'I didn't intend to fall in love with Micah, especially when I'm still legally married to Peter,' she interrupted, 'but I couldn't help myself any more than Micah could.'

'Or I could, the first time I looked at you,' he said sadly.

She wanted to tell him that what he felt for her wasn't love. She knew it wasn't because he didn't know her, any more than she had known Peter before she had married him. The day she realised she didn't love Peter was the day she'd understood the meaning of the phrase 'falling in love with love'. But at the time it had all seemed so perfect. She'd been eighteen, Peter had been handsome and she'd just been chief bridesmaid at her eldest sister Bella's wedding. And she'd so wanted a man to love and adore her, the way Toby loved Bella.

She suspected that when David had first met her, he was ready to fall in love just as she had been at Bella's wedding. And David had fitted her into his image of what an ideal wife should be just as she had fitted Peter into her image of ideal husband.

'When Peter left Cardiff I decided to concentrate on making a life for myself, which was why I bought the bakery. I certainly wasn't looking for another man. But then Micah and I met, and after we got to know one another—'

'He proposed and you accepted,' he interrupted.

'No, not yet and possibly not ever. As I have no idea how long I'll remain married to Peter, I'm in no position to make plans to marry again. I simply live each day as it comes.'

'With Micah?'

'We try to spend some of our free time together,' she replied, reining in her irritation with David for pursuing the argument. 'And I do love you, too, just not in the way you want me to.'

'Like a brother.'

'Like a brother,' she echoed, refusing to rise to his bait. 'And like a good sister, I'm on your side. I haven't spent more than a few days on your farm but when I did it struck me as a lonely place. Even more so, now I'm living on the Bay surrounded by people.'

'The farm's all right.' He felt he had to say something in defence of the place where he had spent the first twenty years of his life. 'Provided you prefer sheep, cows and chickens to people.'

'And you do?'

'I haven't had time to find out yet. Up until now I felt that I haven't had any choice about the way I've lived.'

'Born on a farm and into farming you haven't. But the world's changing, people are no longer bound by what their fathers and mothers did.'

This time, he was the one who changed the subject. 'That Oxo smells good.'

'If I plump up your pillows you can sit up and drink it.'

He leaned forward while she arranged the pillows behind his back. 'Micah told me there are building jobs going in Bute Street.'

'Did he?' She had taken such a dislike to Aled James she didn't want David going anywhere near the man. She didn't like the thought of Judy working for him either, although she had been forced to admit that it was a good entry into show business for her.

'I hope I get one of them.' He sat back and she handed him the cup.

'If you do, you won't be working there long. The conversion should be finished next month.'

'All the more reason for me to get on my feet tomorrow.' He sipped the Oxo.

'I suppose it will be a stop gap, that's if you do get a job there,' she qualified. 'Have you given any thought to what you want to do long term?'

'I thought about nothing else all the time I was on that damned ship . . . sorry,' he apologised. Harry had tried to curb his cursing, especially around women, but he hadn't managed to stop it completely.

'Living on Bute Street has taught me to put up with the odd "damn". Moody's training two of Judy's cousins as apprentices. I couldn't afford to employ you for more than a few weeks or pay you very much while you trained . . .'

'Come on, Edyth,' he stretched out his hands, roughened by years of farm work, 'can you honestly see me baking bread and making cakes?'

'No,' she replied truthfully, 'but there's delivery work.'

'You have a driver.'

'At present, but Jamie wants to go to sea eventually like his father.'

'By which time I hope to have long since found a job. No family handouts, Edyth,' he refused firmly. 'Not from Harry and certainly not from you.'

'Unlike Harry, I haven't much to hand out.' She gave him the plate of toast. 'Try a bite.'

He obediently nibbled the crust. 'It must be great to be rich and never have to worry about money.'

'If you're thinking about Harry, he might not have money worries but he has plenty of the other kind to occupy himself with. Like business and family. I remember what he was like before Will was born. He couldn't eat or sleep because he was convinced that either Mary or the baby was going to be taken ill during the birth.'

'I suppose you're right.' He took a larger bite of toast.

'I know you're happy living here with Helga but if ever you need somewhere to live I have four bedrooms and only two are being used at the moment.'

He eyed her over the edge of the toast. 'Can you see us living under the same roof?'

'If it's gossip you're worried about, Bute Street isn't like Pontypridd. In fact, it's not much like anywhere I've ever been to or heard of. The people who live here are broadminded. Given the number of nationalities and the differences in their customs they have to be. They think no more of an Imam calling the Muslims to prayer in the early hours than they do of the Catholic boys clattering round the street in their hobnail boots at six o'clock on a Sunday morning on their way to early mass.'

'And they wouldn't say a word about two young people who weren't married living together?'

'It wouldn't be two, it would be three. Judy might not be working for me any more, but she's still living with me. Besides, you're my brother's brother-in-law. We're practically related.'

'I have enough money to last me for a while and I want to do things on my own terms, and that includes living here.'

'I understand.' What Edyth understood was that David wanted to be independent and, after all the arguments she'd had with her parents in order to gain her own freedom, she sympathised with him.

They were both relieved when there was a knock at the door and Micah walked in. 'I heard you two talking, I hoped it would be a good sign but you really do look better than you did this morning, David.'

'I feel better.' David waved the toast in the air. 'Eating and drinking.'

'I have some good news for you. I spoke to George Powell and told him about you.'

'Who's George Powell?' David asked.

'The builder I mentioned who's converting the Sea Breeze Hotel into a club. He's desperate for carpenters and he said he'll start you as soon as you can drag

yourself over to Bute Street. If you're reasonably profi-
cient he'll pay you five shillings for a twelve-hour shift, if
you're only fit for labouring he'll drop it to three.'

'Bute Street – I could walk there in the morning.'

'Give yourself a day or two to get your strength back.'
Edyth left the chair and returned it to the corner of the
room.

'And if you feel strong enough at the end of the week
you could come with us to see Judy in *Peter Pan* on
Saturday,' Micah suggested. 'Helga was so taken with the
play the first time she saw it, she wants to see it again.
She's booked a box and we're going with her and Moody
but we could easily squeeze in an extra chair.'

'Please don't feel that you have to mollycoddle or
entertain me,' David said guiltily, realising just how
much trouble he'd caused Edyth and her friends.

'We're not. We want to see Judy perform again and
there aren't that many tickets left. Judy said the last two
weeks of the run are fully booked.'

'It wouldn't hurt you to say, "Thank you, Micah, I'd
love to come and see *Peter Pan* with you,"' Edyth teased
gently.

David looked up at Edyth and she braced herself for
one of his caustic retorts. Instead he smiled, and said,
'Thank you, Micah, I'd love to come and see *Peter Pan*
with you.'


'I don't like the idea of David working for Aled James,'
Edyth said when Micah walked her home from Helga's.
They passed the old Sea Breeze, and although it was after
ten o'clock, the sound of hammering and sawing echoed
from inside the building.

'If he gets a job – and that's a big *if*, David wouldn't be
working for Aled James, he'd be working for George
Powell,' Micah pointed out. 'And it's a big *if* because
much as George is under pressure from Aled James to
finish the conversion, there's only so many semi-skilled

labourers he can take on. Word's got around. While I was talking to George this afternoon, half a dozen unemployed miners turned up. They'd walked down from Maerdy and Tonypandy and were prepared to take a shilling a day. They thought they'd landed in heaven when George said he'd pay them three. George warned them he wouldn't be able to keep them on after the conversion is finished but that didn't stop them from signing up. He told me that other than the Sea Breeze he has nothing lined up except his annual painting and maintenance contracts with the banks. And that will mean going back to his usual half a dozen tradesmen. It will be a big drop from the two hundred who are working for him now. That's bad news for the docks.'

'And the bakery. It's not just the loss of the workmen's trade from the Sea Breeze I'm worried about, but the cutbacks families will make when the men are thrown out of work.'

'We'll survive. Not just us – everyone,' Micah said optimistically. 'It's what people do in hard times.'

'You sound like a Dickens happy ending. I thought Scandinavians were supposed to be miserable.'

'Not this Scandinavian. Although, as I can't even remember Norway I'm not sure I qualify as one.'

'I'm not only worried about David,' Edyth blurted uneasily. 'He may be working for George Powell, but Judy will be working directly for Aled James and—'

'You can't stand the man.'

'How do you know?' She stopped walking.

'Because it's written all over your face every time you look at him.'

'It's really that obvious?'

'Perhaps not to someone who doesn't know you,' Micah said. 'But it is to me.'

She shivered. 'I know I'm probably being ridiculous, but I think he's evil.'

Micah took her arm, tucked it into his elbow and they

carried on walking. 'That's a bit strong. I know Aled looks like Harry and acts as though he owns the world, but he's never been anything other than polite to Judy, or, come to that, you, me and the Kings.' A sudden thought occurred to him. 'Judy hasn't complained to you about him, has she?'

'No. He's taken her to the Windsor for lunch a few times, and sorted out some song scores for her, but that's all. When I asked, she said that he's always behaved like a perfect gentleman towards her.'

'But you had to ask?'

'Yes, because I have a funny feeling about him.'

'I'm not saying you should ignore your funny feelings. If you did, I'd suffer, because one of your funniest feelings is towards me.'

'I love you . . . ' she began absently, still thinking about Aled James.

'And you love Aled James?' he broke in.

'Don't joke, Micah, he really frightens me.'

'He's just a poor boy made good who likes to throw his money around and exercise the power it's given him,' he dismissed. 'As for you loving me, I sometimes have difficulty believing it, especially when you tell me that you won't marry me.' He walked her down the side of the shop and through the yard to the back door.

'Not that again, Micah,' she pleaded.

'Absolutely not – until the day Peter sends those papers and then I'll nag you until you capitulate.'

'Are you coming in?' she asked.

He shook his head. 'I have to get back to the mission. The crew of the *Vidda* were there when I left, opening bottles of aquavit, ordering waffles and settling in for the night. I can't expect Moody to stay up until the early hours cooking for them.' He slipped his fingers beneath her chin and lifted her face to his. 'Sleep tight, my love, see you tomorrow.'

She stood on tiptoe and kissed him. He wrapped his

arms around her and she rested her head against his chest.

'I hate saying goodnight to you, Edyth,' he murmured, reluctant to tear himself away.

'I don't like it any more than you do.'

'Then . . . '

She summoned all her will power. 'I won't move into the mission, Micah, and that's my final word on the subject.'

'Goodnight, my love.' He dropped a kiss on top of her head. 'And sweet dreams.'

'The same to you, and I hope yours are all about me.' She watched him walk away, opened the door and stepped into her kitchen. She had her hard-won independence, but sometimes – and always late in the evening since Judy had started working in the New Theatre – she found it very lonely.

Two days later, David stood back and watched George Powell inspect the skirting board he had fixed to the newly plastered wall on the ground floor of the old Sea Breeze.

'You haven't done a bad job of these joints.' George ran his fingers over the corners. 'Not bad at all.'

David frowned, despite Jed King's encouraging smile, he took George's 'haven't done a bad job' as an insult.

'You can start first thing tomorrow morning.' George Powell rose stiffly to his feet and straightened his back.

'I could start right away,' David offered eagerly, angry with himself for sleeping away most of the first full day he'd spent ashore.

'All the jobs have been allocated for the day. Tomorrow you can begin work on the skirting boards on the second floor, cutting and fixing. If you do a good job on those, I'll move you on to the banisters. There are enough of those to keep you and every other carpenter here busy until the day we complete.' George looked up at the ceiling. The centre had been torn out of the building to the roof and all the rooms on the ground floor, except the lavatories and offices, had been knocked into one large space. The three floors on all four sides rose in tiers around the perimeter, supported by scaffolding. To their right, the scaffolding had been replaced by columns, and workmen were tearing down the supporting walls that were no longer needed.

'Fifty per cent of the floor area on the first, second and third floors has gone to create that high ceiling. Mr James has ordered four electric chandeliers from Waterford. They'll be the largest I've ever seen and bright enough to illuminate the ground floor and the mezzanine areas on the floors above. They're coming in next week from Ireland. This is going to be some building when it's finished,' George said proudly.

'It looks like a big chapel to me,' David commented with more honesty than tact.

George laughed. 'I'll have to tell Mr James that one. If it's a chapel he's creating, it'll be a temple to gambling and drinking.'

'What time do you want me here in the morning?' David asked.

'Six o'clock, Micah did say you weren't a time-served apprentice.'

'I'm experienced but I haven't completed an apprenticeship.' David would have liked to have given him a different answer but he knew his age was against him.

'I pay my carpenters five shillings a day, my labourers three. I'll pay you whatever I think you're worth – somewhere between the two – after you've put in a full day's work, all right?'

Needing the job, David nodded agreement. 'Yes.'

'Twelve-hour shift, six in the morning until six at night, half an hour for dinner at twelve and two ten-minute tea breaks at ten and three. If you don't bring your own food, we can put in an order with Goldman's the baker's for you and dock it from your wages at the end of the week. Pay day is Friday. You'll get whatever you're owed then. If you haven't any tools, book them in and out with your foreman, any losses have to be paid for and I'll take those out of your wages too.'

'Thank you, Mr Powell.' David shook hands with the man.

A shout of 'Watch out!' preceded a wall crashing down from the first floor.

David ducked out through the door and walked past the scaffolding and tarpaulins that shrouded the front of the building. He looked at the watch that Mary and Harry had given him, thought of home, then remembered it was no longer 'home'. He had walked away from the farm. And the last thing he could do was return there and admit to Mary and Harry that he was a failure who was a useless sailor.

Feeling very alone, he debated what to do. He could go and see Edyth but judging by the length of the queue outside her baker's shop she was busy. He could return to Helga Brown's house, but when he had left, she and Ruth had been cleaning the house from top to bottom and he'd have nowhere to sit. Judy wouldn't be working in the bakery, but he suspected that she'd probably be sleeping after performing in the theatre. That left Gertie.

He smiled, it wasn't Monday morning, but it was early on a Thursday. She shouldn't have that many other callers at this time of day. He felt in his inside pocket for his wallet. He'd taken one of the pound notes from his locked suitcase. He hoped it would buy him all the time he wanted for the week. But much as he liked Gertie and wanted to see her again, he sensed it would be prudent to change the note into silver before he went looking for her.

'The young man who thought I was Harry Evans, I believe.' David looked up to see Aled James. Dressed in a starched white shirt and collar, beige tie, cream linen suit and panama hat, he was better turned out than the bankers heading down into Mount Stuart Square. 'Do you remember talking to me on the day of the carnival?' he asked when David didn't answer.

David was intimidated by Aled's air of authority but he would never have admitted it to Aled – or anyone else. 'Yes, I do and in those clothes you look even more like Harry Evans.'

'And how do you know Harry Evans?'

'Why do you want to know?' David asked warily with a countryman's innate distrust of strangers.

'Because I know him too. We used to be friends when we were boys,' Aled said, straying into the realms of fantasy.

'Harry is married to my sister.'

Aled looked at the tarpaulin-shrouded doorway behind David. 'You've been in the old Sea Breeze?'

'How do you know?'

'I'm no Sherlock Holmes, but you have dust on the shoulders of your suit.'

David glanced at his jacket and tried to brush it off with the flat of his hand but it clung stubbornly to the cloth and all he succeeded in doing was smudging it. 'I was looking for a job.'

'Did you find one?'

'I start work tomorrow.'

'I'm surprised that you don't work for Harry in one of his shops.'

'I don't want to work for Harry,' David answered quickly, too quickly he realised when he saw the expression on Aled's face.

'So, you want to be independent, Mr Harry Evans's brother-in-law.' Aled offered David his hand. 'I'm Aled James. George Powell is converting the Sea Breeze for me.'

'I didn't know.' Impressed, David shook Aled's hand.

'What do you intend to do once the conversion is finished.'

'I'll find something.' David hoped he sounded more confident than he felt.

'I'm looking for likely young men to work in the Ragtime.'

'What's a ragtime?'

'It's what I'm calling this club when it's finished, the Tiger Ragtime.'

'Doing what?' David asked.

'I have a few different jobs going.' Aled glanced at his watch. 'I've an appointment shortly, but if you're interested I can spare half an hour now. We could have a drink in the Packet and talk about it.'

Trying to look as though it wasn't the first time he'd been asked to have a drink in the middle of the day, David said, 'I don't mind if I do.'

'Judy, this is a surprise, and a timely one. I've been wrestling with the mission's accounts and they don't look good. Too many waffles being eaten and not enough contributions coming in to pay for the eggs and flour.' Micah left his desk and walked out in the hallway of the mission to meet her. 'But I don't doubt there's enough eggs and flour here now for me to offer you a waffle lunch.'

'No thank you, Pastor Holsten, I'm having lunch with Mr James in the Windsor at one.'

'Coffee, then?'

'That would be nice.' A burst of laughter echoed down the stairs and she said, 'Could we drink it in your office?'

'Of course, I'll bring it down, make yourself at home.'

When Micah returned a few minutes later Judy had hung the jacket of her beige linen suit on the back of the visitor's chair and was sitting, beating time with her finger as she read a song score.

'Do you ever stop working?' He set the tray on the desk.

'Mr James and I have been planning out my act for when the club opens. This is "Just a Crazy Song". It's brand new, I think he must have either brought the score over with him from America or bought it from one of the seamen here.'

'Did he tell you that he's invited me, along with your uncles, aunts and Edyth to the opening night of the Tiger Ragtime?'

'Yes, you will come?'

'Unless I'm shanghaied.' He poured two cups of coffee and handed her one before returning to his chair behind his desk. 'Help yourself to milk and sugar.'

'Thank you.'

She took her time, sugaring her coffee, pouring milk into it and stirring it but he didn't try to hurry her. It was obvious something was bothering her and after what Edyth had said about the way Aled James made her feel, he wondered if Judy was also afraid of the man.

'It's about the contract I signed with Mr James,' she said finally.

'You're sorry you signed it?' Micah asked in concern. He recalled the solicitor warning him that although the contract was a good one it was watertight. If Judy didn't perform for any reason other than illness Aled could sue her for every penny she had. Tony had raised a laugh by pointing out that the only pennies Judy was likely to have when *Peter Pan* finished in the New Theatre, were the ones Aled James paid her.

'No, of course not,' Judy said quickly. 'It's about the clothes.'

'Clothes?' Micah looked at her blankly.

'The stage costumes.'

'Oh yes, I remember, Aled James has to pay for them. And that's a problem?'

'We went to Gwilym James the day before yesterday

and he bought me twenty evening gowns. They were so expensive they didn't even have price tags.'

'It's his club, Judy. He wants his singer to look her best. Did he choose them?'

'With Edyth's mother and the supervisor's help.'

'You don't like them?'

'Any girl in her right mind would like them.'

'They're too revealing?' he asked, remembering Jed King's reservations.

'Not at all, although one is fairly low cut.'

Micah waited, there was obviously more, but he was a patient man, and he wanted Judy to tell him in her own words without prompting. After he'd watched two minutes tick by on his wristwatch, he ventured, 'You don't want the clothes?'

'I don't mind the evening gowns. Mr James explained that I have to look well groomed because I'll be representing his club.'

'A glamorous club does need a glamorous star. But if it's not the frocks, Judy, what is it?'

'He wants to buy me a whole new wardrobe, not just evening gowns, but day frocks, suits, accessories – and fur coats. I'm meeting him for lunch now because he's arranged for us to go back to Gwilym James. He even told the supervisor to select some fur coats for me to choose from. He insists I need three—'

'Three!' Micah interrupted her mid-flow.

'A short one for day wear, a long one for evening wear and an elbow-length cape for summer.' She picked up her coffee cup and saucer. Micah could see she was nervous from the way her hand shook.

'Most girls would jump through hoops for three fur coats?'

'I don't want Mr James buying me one, let alone three. Evening gowns I can understand, but not day clothes. He even asked the supervisor to open an account for me so I can go in and chose new underwear.'

'Have you talked to Edyth about this?'

'No, she's been so busy in the bakery since the workmen started converting the club that she has hardly any free time. Besides, nine times out of ten when I come home from the theatre, she's in bed and she gets up hours before me.'

'What about your uncles?'

'They're working such long hours in the Sea Breeze I don't like bothering them.'

'As I said, most girls would love the idea of having a whole new wardrobe bought for them,' he pointed out mildly.

'Girls like Anna Hughes, you mean.'

'So, that's it. You feel like a kept woman.'

Her green eyes flashed angrily. 'Yes, I do.'

'Judy, no one who knows you would ever mention you and Anna Hughes in the same breath,' he said swiftly.

'What's the difference? Aled James is spending a fortune on me and showering me with expensive things that I could never afford to buy in exactly the same way that Anna Hughes's customers pay her and buy her things to . . .'

'Has Aled James ever tried to kiss you?'

'No?'

'Has he ever suggested anything inappropriate?'

'No.'

'So all he's done so far is give you twenty evening gowns and the promise of a new wardrobe.'

'He hasn't given me anything yet. He asked the supervisor to hold on to everything until my dressing room in the club is finished. Then he wants everything sent there.'

'And there you have your answer,' he said in relief. 'He's not giving you anything that you won't wear either in the club or outside when you're travelling to and from the club or out on club business. All you have to do is keep everything he gives you in your dressing room, except for the outfit you wear back and forth to work. That way, all the clothes remain his property. When you're not working you can wear your own clothes. Just regard this wardrobe he's buying you as your uniform.'

'A uniform is what I'd be wearing if I was a waitress or a chambermaid.'

'There's no difference, Judy. You're working for the man and he's telling you what you can and can't wear. That's a uniform. And if, at end of the contract, you want to walk away from him and the club, leave all the clothes there and no one can possibly think of you as a kept woman.'

She thought about what he'd said for a moment. 'That sounds like common sense, Pastor Holsten.'

'That's because it is, and don't you think it's time you started calling me Micah? You're not thirteen any more.'

'All right, Micah, it sounds like common sense apart from the expense. Fur coats and evening gowns cost a fortune.'

'Which Aled James is spending for the benefit of his club.'

'That's what he said when I told him that I didn't want fur coats.'

'Then he and I are in agreement. Think about it, Judy, if you don't get to keep the clothes in your home then you can hardly count them as yours.'

'And you really believe that everyone will see it that way.'

'What other way can they possibly see it?' He looked out of the window. 'It's a fine day; I'll walk you to Stuart Street and the Windsor for your lunch date.'

'You don't have to.'

He reached for his hat. 'I was thinking of calling in on my sister anyway.'

'She's been complaining that you visit her far more often than you used to.'

'If she expects me to ignore the fact that I'm about to become an uncle she can forget it.' He offered her his arm. 'Let's go, you don't want to be late.'

'No, I don't.'

'Are you sure that you're happy with the idea of working in Mr James's club?' He wasn't sure why he'd asked the question and he had absolutely no idea what he'd do if she said she wasn't.

'It's a great opportunity.'

'Yes it is, but it'll be hard work and long hours.'

'And more money than I've ever made before ... Micah. Money my family can use.'

'One thing I've discovered since I've been in the Bay is that one member of a family can't keep a whole tribe and the Kings are a tribe. Besides, your uncles wouldn't be very pleased if they knew that they and their children were one of the reasons you took the job in the club.'

'I'm far more selfish than that. I took it for me.'

'You always were more ambitious than the rest of us in the band put together.'

'And you think that is wrong?'

'Absolutely not. Especially in someone with your talent,' he said quickly.

'Did you know that Mr James has plans to open clubs in London?' Now that Micah had set her mind at rest about the wardrobe Aled James was buying her, she couldn't wait to tell him about the future Aled was planning for his club – and for her.

'No, I didn't.'

'He said he'd want to me to headline in all of them, eventually.'

'And incidentally make him a lot of money. I always knew you were destined for great things, Judy.' He waved to a group of seamen across the road. 'Just don't forget where you came from.'

'As if I could.' She looked at half a dozen small girls

who were playing hopscotch on the pavement. 'It only seems like the other day I was doing that.'

'It only seems like the other day I was watching you,' he said wryly.

# CHAPTER TWELVE

'I could really earn as much as a pound a day?' David sat with both hands clamped around the pint of beer Aled had bought him, but he made no effort to lift it. He was too amazed by what Aled was telling him.

'You could, and in time I have no doubt that you will, but it might take a while. And to start with, it's a job you can do while working on the building site. All you have to do is refer to a list of races, the horses that are running in each race and the odds against them winning. Plus, of course, you'll have to keep a book of copies of all the betting slips you've issued and a note of the amount you've collected, and the winnings you've paid out.'

'But betting and gambling are illegal.'

'There's a handsome profit to be made and no bookie's runner who's ever worked for Aiden has gone to gaol, or will. Why don't you try running a book for us for a couple of weeks? If you prove you can handle it, there may be a permanent job at the end of it for you in my club.'

'As a bookie's runner?' David asked.

'No.' Aled finished his brandy. 'Inside my club everything will be legal and above board. I'll need croupiers, card dealers, crap game organisers and a whole lot more – a bookie's runner is a good way in to any one of those jobs. Are you doing anything this afternoon?'

Deciding Gertie could wait, David answered, 'No.'

Aled opened his card case. 'Go to the White Hart in James Street. Aiden Collins is running a training school for people who want to become bookie's runners. Give him this card, and tell him that I think you have the makings of a runner. He'll soon work out if I'm right or not. How is your basic arithmetic?'

'I've never had trouble adding up money.' David wasn't boasting. He hadn't learned to read and write until Mary had met Harry and Harry had taught him alongside the rest of the family. But he'd always been able to work out what the farm was owed at the livestock sales.

'Aiden will check how good your calculations are. We won't let you loose with the books until we're sure you're up to it. Now, I'm meeting a lady and I can't keep her waiting. Don't forget: the White Hart, James Street. Ask for Aiden Collins and they'll show you to the room he's booked.'

'Just one thing, Mr James.'

Aled jammed his panama on his head and turned around. 'Yes.'

'You said I'd have to keep a note of the winnings I pay out. What happens if there's more money to pay out than I've taken in bets?'

Aled laughed. 'There never is, boy. And that's your first lesson as a bookie's runner. The punters sometimes win, the bookie always does.' Still laughing, Aled left the pub and headed down to Stuart Street and the Windsor.

As David was the only inexperienced would-be runner who turned up for Aiden Collins's 'school' in an upstairs room of the White Hart, Aiden kept him behind after he had run through what he expected of his bookie's runners. He saw the other three men out, closed the door behind them, motioned David back to his chair and sat opposite him.

'Let's go over it one last time. But before we do, you understand that we only take bets to win. No place and it doesn't matter who is asking.'

It wasn't the first time Aiden had mentioned the word

'place' but, too embarrassed to ask, David hadn't a clue what it meant. He nodded agreement and repeated the basics Aiden had drummed into him, in the hope of at least sounding intelligent. 'I only take bets to win.'

'I want to bet on Flash Lightning in the three o'clock at Aintree tomorrow afternoon. The odds are?' He handed David a cheap child's exercise book and looked expectantly at him.

David flicked through the handwritten book, found the race and the list of horses he wanted. 'Flash Lightning is 3 to 1.'

'I bet a shilling, Flash Lightning wins. I get?'

'Four shillings.'

'Which is?'

'Your original shilling plus three,' David suggested tentatively, his head swimming with the facts and figures Aiden had thrown at him.

'I want to place a bet on Green Bay in the three thirty. The odds are?'

'Even.'

'I've put on half a crown. Green Bay wins.'

'You get your half a crown back plus half a crown, which makes five bob.'

'You catch on quick, kid,' Aiden muttered. 'Lemon Top in the four o'clock.'

David checked, 'it's the 1 to 3 favourite.'

'I bet three shillings. I get?'

'Your three shillings back, plus a shilling.'

'Never forget the second number is the bet, the first the winnings – but only if the horse wins the race outright. Wins, not placed second or third.'

'So that's what "place" means,' David blurted thoughtlessly.

'That's what it means.' Aiden didn't smile. He gave David a second book with a blue cover. A sheet of carbon paper separated the first two pages. 'The pages are double numbered. Place the carbon between them. Make sure you have the same number on the top and bottom copy. You don't want to go issuing slips out of sequence. You write down the punter's name – preferably a nickname, they're more difficult to trace should the book ever fall into the wrong hands – the time of the race, the horse, the odds and the amount you've taken. You give the top copy to the punter. The bottom stays in the book. You NEVER take it out. It's our only proof the bet was placed. And if the punter doesn't have his copy of the slip, there is no pay-out. Not even if the punter is your brother and you remember him placing the bet, otherwise he could present the ticket at a later date and claim twice. You're a bookie's runner not a charity. I'll be here at seven o'clock tomorrow evening to help you check your books and the slips you've issued. Tell your punters: pay out starts at seven thirty. Not one minute before. You'll need this.' Aiden handed him a grey canvas bag.

'What's this for?' David looked inside the bag. It was empty.

'The money you take. Keep it safe. Inside your shirt would be a good place while you're working. If it's hot enough to take your shirt off, make sure the top of the bag is tied tightly then slip it inside, not outside your trousers. The boss gets cross when money goes missing, and,' he eyed David coldly, 'the one thing you don't want to do is make the boss cross. Especially on your first day.'

David took the empty bag, folded it and pushed it into his suit jacket.

'When you start work tomorrow morning, let one or two people know – but casually – that you're prepared to place bets. Word will get out without you advertising. You take the money, you issue the slips. No credit. If you haven't any change to give the punter after he's placed his bet, you make a note of what he's owed at the top of his slip and tell him to collect his change later whether or not his horse has won. You walk away from anyone who offers to pay you at the end of the week when he gets his wages. You ALWAYS take the money upfront. Get it?'

'Yes.'

'You finish your shift on the building at six?' Aiden questioned.

'Yes.'

'The boss is particular about how his people look, so wash and change into your suit before you come here to pay out the winners. And this is the only place you pay out. No matter how hard the punters press you or how pathetic their hard-luck story, you only pay out at the end of the day and you only pay out behind closed doors with either me or Freddie standing behind you. There are two reasons for that. One, if there's a challenge to a race result it will be made in the first half hour. Either Freddie or me will have heard it on the wireless and we will have made a note of it. We'll have a full list of the final results when you turn up to pay out and we'll check your pay-outs against them before you hand over any cash. Two, if the coppers catch you paying out in the street, or on the building site, they'll nab you as soon as look at you and then you'll end up in the cage. So where do you pay out?'

'This room and nowhere else.'

'This room is rented until Friday. After that we'll move on to a different pub. And we'll continue to move on to a new place every week. That way we stay one step ahead of the law.'

Despite Aled James's assertion that none of his runners had ever gone to gaol, David had to ask the question. 'What happens if the police stop me and find the money and the books?'

'They won't.'

'But if they do,' David persisted.

'You open your mouth to ask for your lawyer and then keep it firmly shut until he arrives.'

'I don't have a lawyer,' David was unfamiliar with the American term.

Aiden handed him a card. On it was printed AIDEN COLLINS – ATTORNEY AT LAW. 'You tell them I can be reached at the Windsor Hotel.'

'You're a lawyer?'

'All the one you're ever likely to need, boy.' Aiden picked up his hat from the stand. 'You know what to do?'

'I think so.'

'You'd better know so, boy. The boss doesn't like sloppy work or people who make mistakes.'

'I'll try not to make any.'

Aiden lifted his finger to his hat. 'Try hard. See you tomorrow. Seven, sharp.'

'I'll be here.'

David watched Aiden leave, then walked to the window. Aled James had promised he'd make real money when he had recruited him, but after meeting Aiden Collins he wasn't at all sure that he was doing the right thing in becoming a bookie's runner. Like Harry, Aled had an air of what his sister Mary called 'class'. Aiden looked like a roughneck who wouldn't hesitate to beat a man to a pulp – or worse – if it suited him.

Driving all thoughts other than the money Aled had promised he'd make from his mind, David flipped his cap on to his head, picked up his jacket, stuffed both books into the pocket and left the room.

Harry Evans was discussing the recent stock take with his Uncle Joey, who had been appointed to the post of managing director of the chain of Gwilym James's department stores and Timothy Grove, the manager of the Cardiff store, when there was a knock at the door. Timothy shouted, 'Come,' and the assistant manager looked around the door.

'Mr Harry Evans wanted to know when Mr James arrived, sir,' he said diffidently.

'I did.' Harry left his chair.

'Miss John has shown Mr James and Miss King into private room two, on the third floor, sir. The girls were wheeling in the garments that Miss John had set aside for them when I left. Shall I bring Mr James up here, sir?' the assistant manager asked.

'No, thank you. I'll go down and meet him.' Harry glanced at Timothy. 'You did say the conference room was free all day?'

'It is, sir, but if you'd prefer to use my office—'

'The conference room will be fine. Thank you. I'm not sure how long this will take.'

Harry hadn't taken Joey into his confidence, but the fact that Harry hadn't talked about the mysterious 'Mr James' had led Joey to suppose that whatever his nephew wanted to discuss with the man was important – and probably personal.

'I can take over here, Harry,' Joey offered.

'Thank you.' Harry reached for his jacket and hat.

'We'll be having tea in the restaurant if you're free to join us, Harry.' Joey winked at the manager. 'I enjoy shaking up your staff.'

The manager, who knew Joey well, said, 'I've noticed. Every time you eat a meal with us, waitress breakages go up twenty per cent.'

'See you later.' Harry left the office. He automatically checked the carpets for dirt and the walls and mirrors for smudges. Joey might be his uncle, but he had worked his way up to his present position from that of trainee assistant manager in the Pontypridd store. And Joey had taken care to pass on all the knowledge he had gleaned along the way to Harry.

Harry took the lift down to the third floor, chatted to the lift boy and discovered that, like all lift boys who'd been in the job for more than six months, the lad hoped for promotion to the sales floor. He left the lift, walked down the corridor and knocked on the door of the second private room he came to. Miss Johns opened it.

'Mr Evans, sir.' She looked from Harry to Aled James. The similarities between them were less marked when they were standing side by side. Their height and colouring were the same, but Aled's face, creased by lines of experience, appeared harder, and the chill in his eyes was more pronounced when it was set against the warmth in Harry's.

'Mr Evans, it is nice to see you.' Judy left her chair and offered Harry her hand. He took it, squeezed it, leaned towards her and kissed her cheek.

'How are you?'

'Fine, thank you, Mr Evans.'

'I have tickets for *Peter Pan*. I'm bringing Mary and the children down to see it the weekend after next.'

'I hope you enjoy it, Mr Evans.'

'If it's half as good as my sister said it was the last time I telephoned her, we'll do just that. And speaking of Edyth, how is she?'

'Busy in the shop when I left this morning.'

'I intend to go down there and see her after I've left here this afternoon.' Harry turned to Aled, who was lolling back in his chair smoking a cigar.

'It's been a long time, Harry.'

'It has,' Harry agreed. 'Can you spare me a few minutes when you've finished here?'

'Possibly, if Miss King requires fittings for alterations once she's chosen her day wardrobe.'

'Some of the evening gowns might fit better if they were taken in at the waist, Mr James,' Alice Johns suggested.

'They might.' Aled flicked ash into the tray Alice had placed at his elbow.

Harry spoke to the supervisor. 'I'll be in the conference room, Miss Johns; perhaps you could ask one of the assistants to show Mr James upstairs when you've finished here.'

'Yes, Mr Evans.'

Harry closed the door and walked away. Memories that had lain dormant for over twenty years rose, unbidden and unwanted, into his mind. Just as David had said on the day of the carnival, he and Aled could be twins. But when he had last seen Aled his surname had been Cooper and, he had been five inches taller and several pounds heavier than him. An advantage Aled had used to punch and beat him every chance he could get. And for years he had relived that pain and humiliation in his nightmares.

David stopped at Edyth's bakery after he left the White Hart but any hopes he'd had that he'd be able to buy her tea and cakes in one of the cafés in Bute Street were dashed when he looked through the window and saw her packing enormous cardboard boxes with rolls, sandwiches and baked goods. Moving on swiftly, lest Jamie or one of Judy's aunts recognise him and force him to make small talk, he went into the first café he came to and sat at a table out of sight of the window. His appetite had returned with a vengeance, so he ordered pie, chips, bread, butter and coffee. And while he waited for his food, he thought about Gertie.

He closed his hand over the pound note he'd tucked into his shirt pocket. His meal would come to sixpence and although he had plenty of change he resolved to pay the cashier with the note, so he'd have silver on hand to give her. Harry had warned him about women like Gertie, but he thought that what she had given him had been worth every penny of the two shillings he had paid her last time. Would she charge him the same again? Would she allow him to stay longer if he paid her more money? Would she be free to see him? What would he do if she wasn't?

His meal came and, still thinking about Gertie, he ate quickly, paid his bill, stepped outside, and suddenly realised that he had no idea where she lived. He could find his way around the wilderness of the Brecon Beacons, no problem at all, but the built-up dockland was a different kind of wilderness, one where he hadn't yet learned to recognise any landmark except the Pembroke Castle pub a few doors along from Helga's house.

He walked up and down Bute Street for ten minutes, looked round every corner and down every side street but failed to distinguish one row of terraced houses from another, or indeed one house from another. They all had front doors that opened directly from the pavement, a sash window alongside it and two sash windows on the first floor.

He turned back and walked further down Bute Street towards the docks. Try as he may, he couldn't recall if there had been anything different about the street or the house Gertie had taken him to. All he could remember was Gertie herself. He could conjure every detail of the green, white and pink pattern on her thin cotton dress. The way the flimsy fabric had clung to her breasts and legs, outlining them clearly while she'd strolled on ahead of him, her feet thrust into white, peep-toe sandals. The nails on her fingers and toes were painted a crimson that shone even through her white stockings.

Blood pounded around his veins at the memory. He had to find her. He simply had to! He stood still, looked around again and saw ABDUL'S written above a corner shop. He was sure Gertie had been standing outside it when she'd called to him – he'd turned back and seen her – they had talked for a few minutes, he had agreed to follow her and they had walked on for five or ten minutes. He turned full circle . . . the only question was in which direction . . .

'You look lost, boy.' A burly uniformed police officer loomed over him.

Intimidated, David muttered, 'I'm looking for a friend.'

'Male or female?' the officer enquired.

'A girl . . . ' David fell silent when he realised Gertie

wouldn't thank him for bringing her to the attention of the police.

The policeman grinned. 'One of Anna Hughes's tartlets?'

'I don't know Anna Hughes,' David bit back defensively.

'This girl – did she offer you a nibble of nectar, a dip of delight, a portion of paradise?' The officer taunted. David squirmed in embarrassment and the constable relented. 'Turn left back on to Bute Street, boy, take the next left, first right and it's the house with birds woven into the net curtains.'

David practically ran from the officer. He followed his directions and found himself in a street that looked no more familiar than any of the others he'd been in for the last half an hour. As he couldn't remember what side of the road Gertie's house was, he walked up and down both sides of the terrace before spotting a front window covered by nets with peacocks woven into the design.

He walked up to the front door, touched the door knocker and the door swung inward. He leaned self-consciously inside the porch and knocked. The quarry-tiled floor was wet and, judging by the smell of soda, newly scrubbed. A narrow table holding a saucer full of coins stood below a row of hooks that held an assortment of ladies' summer straw hats and flimsy, lightweight scarves.

A well-dressed man didn't so much as brush past him, as push him aside. The man walked down the passage without turning around, or acknowledging his presence and disappeared through a door at the far end. David waited a few minutes before leaning forward and knocking a second time. That time he elicited a reply.

'If you're the milk man or the bread man, take your money from the table and go. If you're looking for company then you can bloody well come in. If you're not, you can stand out there all day for all we care. Just stop your bloody banging,' a woman's voice shouted.

He stepped forward as a middle-aged red-headed woman left the room at the end of the passage with the man he'd seen enter a few minutes before.

'You looking for someone?'

'Gertie,' David answered timorously. When she continued to look at him he felt he had to add something so he said, 'I'm a friend of hers.'

'What kind of friend?'

Without giving David time to answer, the woman opened the door behind her and yelled, 'Gertie, customer,' before taking the man's arm and leading him up the stairs.

Gertie wandered out into the passage. She was wearing a thigh-length dark blue rayon robe and navy blue slippers with white pom poms and was holding a cup of tea in one hand and a cigarette in the other.

'David, I wondered where you'd got to.' She opened her arms wide, balancing the tea in one hand and the cigarette in the other, and leaned forward, inviting a kiss.

'I went to sea.' Feeling self-conscious he kissed her cheek, and breathed in a peculiar mix of strong tea, rose petal scent and nicotine.

'And how was the sea?'

'It didn't suit me.'

'I'm glad. I get to see more of my regulars if they're ashore.' She frowned. 'You do have a job?'

'Starting tomorrow, working on the old Sea Breeze,' he said proudly.

'You and three-quarters of the men on the Bay,' she dismissed carelessly. 'But you have your pay from the ship, right?'

'They didn't pay me.'

'They bilked you?'

'I don't understand.'

She moved back towards the door. 'They did you out of your wages.'

'No, I knew before I went that I wasn't going to get any.'

'Then why did you go?'

'To get experience,' he explained.

She rammed the door with her hip, and opened it. 'I don't give out free samples.'

'I have savings.'

She brightened. 'Five bob?'

'It was two last time,' he reminded her.

'For five bob you can have me all afternoon. Until seven o'clock,' she added cautiously.

'I have to be back at my lodgings for supper at half past six.'

She checked her watch. 'Four bob until six?'

'Two shillings and six pence until five,' he offered.

'You drive a hard bargain, David . . . '

'Ellis,' he finished for her. 'What's your second name?'

'What do you want to know for?' she demanded suspiciously.

'Just wondering.'

A man walked through the front door and stood behind David.

'You're holding up the traffic, David. You know your way up.' She held up her cup. 'I'll dump this in the kitchen and I'll be with you.'

David nodded to the man who looked right through him as if he wasn't there. It was then David realised that they were in the house for the same purpose, something most men, especially if they were married, wouldn't be eager to advertise. He walked up the stairs and looked at the doors at the top. Although there had been only two windows at the front of the house there were four doors.

'Why are you waiting?' Gertie was beside him.

'I wasn't sure which was your room.'

'That's not very flattering. How many girls have you visited since you were last here?'

'None,' he protested.

Gertie opened a door to her left and walked inside. 'Close the door behind you,' she ordered when he didn't make a move. 'I don't want to give the other girls' clients a free eyeful.' She stood at the side of the bed, kicked off her slippers and held out her hand. 'Half a crown.'

He took two shillings and a sixpence from his pocket and handed them over. She untied the belt on her robe and dropped it at her feet. He barely had time to register that she was naked beneath it before she pulled him down on to the bed.

'Gertie ... I can undress myself,' he remonstrated when she started unbuttoning his flies.

'All part of the service, lover boy.' She licked her lips, moistening them. 'Two of my regulars have left the area, and I'm out to replace them. For six bob a week you can have both their slots.'

'That's the one,' Aled said decisively as Judy stood before him in a floor-length sable coat. 'We'll take it and the mink cape and the fox fur for day wear.'

'You know quality when you see it, Mr James.' Alice Johns transferred the three furs to the rack that held the day wear Judy had chosen – or rather Aled had chosen for her.

'How long will the fittings take, Miss Johns?' Aled rose to his feet.

'At least an hour, Mr James. Miss King has a very slim waist and most of the gowns will need to be taken in. Would you like me to send word to you in the conference room when we have finished?' She picked up a box of pins.

'I should be back before then, Miss Johns, but if I'm not, I'd appreciate it.'

'Show Mr James to the conference room,' Alice ordered one of the assistants.

Aled picked up his hat and followed the girl into the corridor and through a door marked STAFF ONLY. She led him to the conference door, knocked and announced him before leaving.

Harry had deliberately sat at the side of the long table because he hadn't wanted to put Aled at a disadvantage. But Aled had no compunction in taking the chair at the head of the table. He sat and looked at Harry sitting four chairs below him.

Harry rose to his feet. 'Would you like some coffee?' He lifted the pot from the tray. 'It's fresh. One of the waitresses brought it up a few minutes ago.'

'I'll just have an ashtray.' Aled reached out and dragged one of the large onyx ashtrays towards him. He looked around. The floor was wood block, the walls papered in a pale green and cream abstract pattern. A map of Cardiff dated 1854 hung on the wall. Next to it was an old print of the Castle, but in pride of place facing the head of the table was an oil portrait of the man who had founded the company, Gwilym James. It had been painted half a century before when he had been middle aged. He looked Victorian, benign, and comfortable with his advancing years. Next to it was a photograph, a black-and-white studio portrait that could have been taken of either one of them. A young, fair-haired man sat behind a desk, pen in hand, inkpot and papers in front of him.

Aled raised his eyebrows. 'That, I take it, is Daddy?'

'You only have to look at the photograph to realise he fathered both of us,' Harry agreed.

'I wonder what he'd make of us sitting here together looking at his picture.'

'I have no idea. I didn't know him any more than you did.'

'Of course, he died before you were born.'

'Did you ever see him?' Harry asked curiously.

'No. And I wish my mother had never set eyes on him. She was stupid enough to work in Gwilym James in Pontypridd. She even thought she was lucky to get the job.' Aled looked coolly into Harry's eyes. 'He seduced her, along with God only knows how many other women.'

'My solicitor told me when I started working for the company that after Mansel James's death, fourteen women claimed he had fathered their children. Annuities of a hundred and four pounds a year were paid out to all of them until their children reached the age of sixteen.'

'And that makes it right?' Aled questioned angrily.

'No, it doesn't and I didn't say that it did.'

'You were the only one of Mansel James's children to inherit any of his wealth.'

'All I inherited from my father was his personal possessions. His watch, cuff links and tiepins.'

'His fortune, the companies—'

'Mansel James had no fortune. If he'd lived, his aunt, Gwilym James's wife, would have left him hers, but he was murdered before she died. His personal fortune was small and left to her. She passed his jewellery on to me.'

'Very convenient,' Aled sneered.

'After Mansel James's death, Mrs James left the companies and her money to me in trust. She was our father's aunt by marriage and my mother's great aunt. Having no children of her own she loved my mother like a daughter. She wanted to provide for her and she thought the best way of doing that was to set up the trust in my name. And that is exactly what she did.'

'And you think that because you were related to this aunt twice over you had the better claim?'

'I claimed nothing. She simply set up the trust in my name. I won't inherit a thing until I'm thirty.'

'Then you've a few more years to go.'

'And in the meantime, I'll work for the company.'

'But hardly on the same terms as every other employee. I dare say you can cajole the trustees into paying you as much money as you want.'

'There's only so much money a man can spend on living, Aled.'

'Very true.' Aled set his lighter down next to the ashtray. 'And I'm Mr James not Aled. I changed my name to our father's.'

'So my mother told me.'

Aled flicked open his cigar case and removed one without offering it to Harry. 'I decided that I couldn't possibly bring any more shame to it than our father already had.'

'If you feel that way about him, why use his name?'

'Because I needed to change it from Cooper. It became too well known in the wrong circles in America.'

'Judging by your accent you've obviously spent a lot of time there.'

'Enough to make a great deal of money.'

'Miss Johns mentioned that you're building a club in Bute Street and Judy King is going to be the resident singer.'

'That's right.'

'She's very talented.'

'So we do agree about something.' Aled exhaled twin rows of smoke. 'Miss King also lives with your sister, Edyth Slater. She's pretty, your sister, not conventionally so, but I find her attractive. Pity about her broken marriage.'

'You've met my sister?' Harry pulled out the chair to Aled's right and sat down.

'I took her out to dinner. Didn't she tell you?'

'Edyth and I have both been busy lately.' Harry resolved that no matter what happened in the store that afternoon he would make time to see Edyth.

'I've also met your brother-in law, David. In fact, he's working for me – indirectly.'

'David doesn't know the first thing about running a nightclub,' Harry said quickly.

'No, he doesn't – yet. But he knew enough about carpentry to impress my builder who hired him. As for running a nightclub, I didn't know anything about running one when I started.'

'Have you been deliberately seeking out my family?' Harry asked bluntly.

'What if I say yes?' Aled rejoined coolly.

'Why did you come back here?'

'To Britain or Wales?'

'Cardiff.'

'I didn't know that you would be here, but given that I knew you'd inherited the family fortune I guessed you wouldn't be too far away. And, as I said, things were getting too hot for me in America.' He looked back at Mansel's photograph. 'My roots are here. Did you know that Americans set great store by their roots? Some are so busy looking back at the "old country", wherever it might be, they haven't the time to make a new life for themselves. That didn't apply to me. But I admit, it's good to be living in a country where I feel completely at home.'

'Given the life we led in Bush Houses, I didn't think you'd be the nostalgic type.'

'I'm not, but I capitalised on other people's homesickness. I made it my business to find out what they missed from their old lives, got hold of it and made a fortune selling it.'

'Like what?'

'You don't expect me to give away my trade secrets, do you?' Aled said smoothly.

'Did your mother go to America with you?'

'She died years ago.'

'I'm sorry.'

'Where were you, when you were twelve years old?' Aled enquired conversationally.

'At school.'

'Lucky you. Sitting in a nice cosy classroom all day, going home every night to Mam in the mansion our father grew up in.'

'I was in boarding school,' Harry said flatly.

Aled laughed mirthlessly. 'Of course, you would have been put into a posh kids' school. Don't try telling me that it was tough on you.'

'No more for me than any other boy.' Harry was determined to remain calm in the face of Aled's taunting.

'When I was twelve, I was unloading potato barges on the docks for pennies. And when I wasn't doing that, I was watching my mother die slowly in a stinking room at the back of a whorehouse. She was too weak from disease and starvation to turn over on the mattress I scavenged from a tip for her, let alone stand on her own two feet.'

'I'm sorry.'

'Are you?'

'Yes.' Harry met Aled's steely gaze.

'So, if you had been in a position to help us, you would have?'

'If you'd allowed me to.'

'Oh, I would have allowed you to all right, for my mother's sake. I don't have to tell you what she was, but a dog wouldn't have been allowed to die the way she did.' Aled flicked the ash from his cigar into the ashtray. 'But the manager of Gwilym James in Pontypridd wouldn't lift a finger to help her. One of my mother's friends wrote to him. She told him that my mother was destitute and dying but he wouldn't give her a single penny.'

'If your mother made a claim she would have received an annuity—'

'My mother never received a brass farthing from Mansel James or anyone connected to him,' Aled said frostily. 'The only money we ever had was what she earned looking after other people's brats – like you. But when the miners came out on strike in the Rhondda, no one could afford to pay her to look after their kids. It was then she found herself with a choice: starve or sell herself to put food on the table. Have you any idea how that made her feel? Or me?'

'I've already said I would have done something if I could have. But I wasn't in a position to then.'

'But your mother was. Your mother didn't have to get dolled up every night to trawl the pubs to pick up men and do whatever they wanted of her just to keep out of the workhouse. Your mother was already working for Gwilym James when my mother was dying, living in the mansion in Pontypridd that had been our father's with your stepfather and sisters—'

'You know a lot about my family,' Harry broke in suspiciously.

'I made it my business to find out.'

'Before or after you went to America?'

'I left Cardiff for America the day I buried my mother,' Aled continued without answering Harry's question. 'It seemed a good idea at the time to get out of this place. It didn't seem so good when I was horsewhipped by the drunken second mate before we were even out of the Bay.'

'If it's money you want—'

'That's all you can think about, isn't it? Our father's money.' Aled squashed his cigar in the ashtray. 'I don't want a penny of it.'

Uncertain how to respond to Aled's bitterness, Harry remained silent.

'I've learned two lessons in life. The first is money is only important when you haven't any. And, as you said earlier, there's only so much a man can spend in one lifetime. The second is that once you have more money than you need you can use the surplus to buy anything or anyone you want. And I intend to use my wealth to do just that.'

'To buy people?'

'Influential people, who can give me what I want,' he reiterated.

'Like your club?'

'I have my gambling, alcohol and live entertainment licences, so there's no point in you trying to pull any political strings to stop me.'

'I didn't intend to.'

'No?' Aled asked sceptically.

'No,' Harry replied firmly.

'I've also bought your brother-in-law. I think David Ellis might prove to be quite an asset.'

Harry broke into a cold sweat. 'You hurt David or any member of my family—'

'Did I say I was going to hurt him – or Edyth Slater?' Aled pushed his chair back from the table and rose slowly to his feet. 'She's your sister, Harry, not mine. And, with her husband gone, "footloose and fancy free" as the saying goes.'

'Aled, please—'

'Watch your back, Harry Evans,' Aled cut in ruthlessly. 'Watch it everywhere you go, David Ellis and Edyth Slater are just the beginning.'

'We're brothers . . . '

'That, Harry Evans, is something I will never forget.' Aled returned his gold cigar case and lighter to his pocket and left the room.

# CHAPTER THIRTEEN

Gertie opened her eyes to see David watching her in the gloom of the curtained bedroom.

'Enjoy that?' she smiled lazily.

'What do you think?' He wrapped his arm around her naked body and cupped her breast.

'I like to leave a man satisfied.'

David deliberately pushed all thoughts of Edyth from his mind. He loved her – had loved her before he had seen her kissing Micah – but the last person he wanted to talk about Edyth to was Gertie. His feelings for Edyth had been and still were sacred to him. The way he felt about Gertie was anything but. And now he knew how it felt to make love to a woman, he didn't want to think about Edyth making love to Micah or Peter – that's if she ever had.

He'd overheard Harry explaining to Mary why Edyth had applied to have her marriage annulled instead of simply divorcing Peter. Harry had said that Peter had never wanted to sleep with Edyth, something he found unbelievable after making love with Gertie.

'What you thinking about?'

Sensing that Gertie was waiting for a compliment he said, 'I never in a million years thought that it could be this good between a man and a woman.'

'That's because you probably never saw any women besides your sisters on your farm,' she teased.

'I saw plenty on Sundays when we went down the valley to chapel.'

'Sour old matrons in black that smelled of mothballs

and lavender water, wearing their Sunday, pickle-onion-sucking, disapproving face.'

He laughed. 'You have a funny way of putting things.'

'It's true though, isn't it?' she challenged.

'Some of the older women were like that,' he conceded.

'And the younger ones?'

'There was never much time to talk to them after chapel, although there was a little cracker working in the grocer's shop in Pontardawe, with come-to-bed eyes. I used to look forward to delivering eggs and butter there every Wednesday.' He lay back on the pillows, smiling at the memory.

'And?' She dug him in the ribs.

'And nothing. I just used to look at her.'

'Her come-to-bed eyes, you mean.'

'One of the delivery boys christened them that. I never had the courage to find out if his description was accurate.'

'So, all you did was worship her from a distance,' she snorted in amusement.

'There wasn't much else I could do given that the farm was miles from the village. It used to take me an hour and a half to drive down there in the horse and cart in daylight to make the deliveries. It would have been an all-night effort if I'd invited her out for the evening. Not that there was anywhere I could have taken her other than the chapel social.'

'We lived in the Rhondda and there were lots of places to go, besides the chapel socials: picture palaces, dance halls, roller-skating rinks, concert halls, Italian cafés, and walking on the mountains, which we did more often than anything else because it didn't cost anything.'

'Did you go out with a lot of boys in the Rhondda before you came here?' he asked curiously.

'One or two.' She took a pack of cigarettes from her bedside table, opened it and pushed one between her lips.

She picked up a box of matches and glanced at David. 'Sorry, I should have offered. Do you want a ciggie?'

'That depends on what you're going to charge me for it.'

'You – you – monster!' Her anger turned to laughter when he made a face at her. 'I suppose I do go on a bit about money. But I have to pay Anna three quid a week to live here, and I send a pound a week home to my mother.'

'Three pounds!' he exclaimed. 'I pay Mrs Brown seventeen shillings and sixpence. And that includes my washing, a cooked breakfast and a cooked high tea every day.'

'Mrs Brown doesn't have to pay the coppers to look the other way when you walk down the street. And it's all found here. All meals, washing, coals, gas.' She pointed to the fireplace that had been boarded up to house a small gas fire. 'Anna even pays our doctor's bills. She takes care of us. It can be tough down here, making a living the way we do, when you're on your own.' She slipped another cigarette into her mouth, struck a match on the side of the cabinet, lit both and passed one to David.

'Thanks.' David took it and inhaled. He had smoked the cigarettes and cigars Harry had offered him enough times to know that he didn't like the taste of tobacco but he didn't want to risk hurting Gertie's feelings.

'You got any brothers as well as sisters?' Gertie asked.

'Two brothers, why?'

'Just wondering.' She plumped up the pillow behind her and sat up, deliberately allowing the sheet to fall to her waist. She was proud of her breasts and enjoyed David's blatant admiration. 'I'm the eldest of ten but two died when they were nippers. One of TB, one of typhoid.'

'That must have been tough.'

'Not as tough as when my dad got killed in the pit just before our youngest was born. He fell in front of a tram.

Didn't stand a chance – or so his buttie told my mam. One minute they were standing together talking, the next a runaway tram came crashing towards them and knocked him flying. Mam was determined not to go into the workhouse or put us in there, so we had to survive on ten bob parish relief, which covered the rent, and what she could make scrubbing out the local pub and taking in washing, which meant I had to leave school to look after the little ones.'

'How old were you?'

'Ten.'

'You're lucky you went for that long. I didn't go to school at all.'

'You never learned to read and write?'

'My brother-in-law taught me a couple of years ago.'

'I was a good scholar,' she said earnestly and David sensed that she wasn't boasting. 'The headmaster told my dad I was clever enough to win a scholarship to go to college. He said I could become a teacher. But,' she picked up an ashtray from the cabinet, flicked her ash into it and handed it to David, 'I had to give up on that idea when Dad was killed.'

'Are you sorry?'

'No,' she giggled. 'Women teachers are supposed to live the life of dried-up spinsters. They're not allowed to marry, and I like what we've just done too much to give it up. As for doing anything else, this is a damned sight easier and better than skivvying for my keep plus a couple of quid a year below stairs in some posh London house. Or scrubbing out filthy pubs and taking in washing like my mam has had to do for years and still does.'

'What about your brothers and sisters. Now you've left home who is looking after them?'

'Molly, she's the next one down from me. When she got to be as good as me in taking care of them and helping Mam with the washing and housework, Mam said I had to go out and earn my keep. Mind you, she didn't mean here. Just after I registered with a domestic agency one of the girls in our village came home to visit her mam and dad. She was living with Anna at the time, although she's moved on to London since. She had lovely clothes. Silk frocks, new shoes – not boots – and a fur coat – real fur and she had a matching fur hat, gloves and scarf. She told me that I could earn a lot more here than I could in service. Mam was furious when she found out I'd talked to the girl. She told me that if I went with her she'd never allow me over her doorstep again. But I came down here anyway, and ever since I've sent Mam a pound a week. She wrote to tell me that she doesn't like where it comes from but she's never sent it back.'

David squashed his half-smoked cigarette into the ashtray. 'When I came down here Harry warned me about places like this and girls like you. He'd laugh if he could see us now.'

'Why?' she demanded, instantly on the defensive.

'Because this room and this house, or what I've seen of it, is so ordinary.'

'What did you expect?'

'I don't know.'

'Yes, you do.' She laughed again, an infectious chuckle that made him laugh as well. 'You expected roomfuls of naked girls that you could take your pick from, exotic dancing and snakes.'

'I definitely didn't expect snakes. But you can't blame me for imagining all sorts. There was nothing like this—'

'On the farm?' she finished for him.

'Or in Pontardawe or Brecon.'

'You can take it from me that if there are men around there'll be a "house." And Brecon has soldiers stationed there, doesn't it?'

'Close by.'

'Then I take that back. There won't be one house there'll be dozens.' She crushed the remains of her cigarette on top of his, removed the ashtray and slid back down in the bed. 'I like you, David. You're easy to talk to. Can I call you Dai?'

'If you want to.' He moved restlessly away from her when she slid her hand between his thighs.

'I haven't had a Dai before.' She propped herself up on her elbow and looked down at him. 'You going to become one of my regulars?'

'What would that mean?' he asked warily.

'Coming to see me a couple of times a week. Not going off with one of the other girls if I'm busy, and waiting for me downstairs until I'm free. It's cosy in our kitchen and there's always a fresh pot of tea on the table.' She kissed the base of his neck.

'That doesn't sound too bad.' He played with her nipples.

'And in return, I'll be good to you. Awful good,' she murmured, moving her body slowly and languorously over his until she drew him inside her.


'That was a good afternoon's shopping.' Aled offered Judy his arm after they left Gwilym James.

'I dread to think how expensive an afternoon's shopping,' Judy qualified.

'That's for me, not you, to worry about. And we have time for tea in the Park Hotel.' Aled turned to Freddie, who looked hot and ill at ease in his woollen chauffeur's jacket and cap. 'We'll walk to the Park and, as it's only a few minutes from there to the theatre, you can go back to the Windsor. I'll telephone you there if I need you again today.'

Freddie tipped his cap and returned to the car.

Aled waited for a motorcycle and side car to pass before crossing the road. 'I spoke to George Powell this morning. Your dressing room will be finished by the middle of next week. I'll give it a day or two to make sure the paint is dry before asking Gwilym James to send the clothes there. And you'll need a dresser – someone who knows how to apply theatrical make-up, and cut and style hair, as well as care for quality clothes. Do you have anyone in mind?'

'One of my aunts?' Judy asked hopefully. 'I could teach them about stage make-up.'

Aled shook his head. 'I want someone who knows every trick in the theatrical trade, not an amateur. What about the wardrobe mistress in the theatre?'

'She's been in the New Theatre for ever and although she knows clothes she knows nothing about make-up.'

'The make-up artist?'

'There isn't one. We apply our own, even Peter Pan and Captain Hook. But there is Mandy. She's the head chorus girl, and she knows everything there is to know about make-up and clothes.'

'But she's a dancer.'

'She told me that she's thinking of hanging up her dancing shoes after this run.'

'Mandy's the tall blonde who always takes centre stage in the dance numbers?'

'Yes,' Judy confirmed.

'She is getting on a bit for the chorus,' he said callously. 'Does she live on the Bay?'

'No, she's from West Wales but she's played all over the country. England as well as Wales.'

'A well-travelled lady indeed,' Aled commented with a smile. 'I'll have a word with her after I've spoken to Lennie.'

'You offered him the job of comic?'

'Yes, and he's taken it on principle but we still have a few details like salary to thrash out.'

The doorman bowed to Aled before opening the door of the Park Hotel. Aled acknowledged the man and strode into the foyer as if he owned the place. Half a dozen people were waiting to be attended to at the desk. A bell boy was loading luggage on to a trolley next to the lift. Two old ladies were sitting side by side on a sofa, gossiping. The receptionist glanced up, saw Judy and froze.

Judy's grip tightened on Aled's arm when every head in the room turned in their direction. All conversation ceased. She met the receptionist's look and steeled herself for another scene. But Aled walked her straight to the lift. The bell boy moved the trolley away from the door; the lift boy stepped out and lifted his hand to his pork pie hat.

'Good afternoon, Mr James.'

'And good afternoon to you, Tommy.'

Judy saw Aled slip something into the boy's hand. She'd noticed that Aled tipped wherever he went but always surreptitiously and, from the service he received whenever she was with him, she suspected, generously.

They left the lift on the second floor. Aled walked down the corridor, took a key from his pocket and opened a door.

'You have a room here?' Mindful of her uncles' directive never to be alone with Aled James, especially in a hotel room, Judy hung back.

'A suite I use as an office,' he explained. 'The Windsor is too far from the centre of the city for some people's convenience.' He picked up a telephone from a desk set in front of the window and dialled a single number. 'Room service? Tea for two, but bring a pot of coffee instead of tea ... That's right, sandwiches, scones and cakes. You recognise my voice? Then you'll know to bring it to Room 22.' He replaced the receiver and held out his hand. 'Give me your jacket. I'll hang it in the wardrobe.' He opened a door and walked into an adjoining bed-room.

'There is a bedroom here?'

'And a bathroom. The restaurant is crowded with gossiping middle-aged, middle-class civil service wives and widows at this time of day. I thought we'd be more comfortable here.' He opened the window. She joined him and looked down on the street below. A boy was standing on the corner, holding an armful of newspapers and shouting '*Echo*'. Well-dressed men and women strolled arm in arm, enjoying the warm summer sunshine. A street cleaner pushed a brush along the gutter, his stained and ragged blue canvas overalls shabby against the summer cream, white and pastel finery of the shoppers.

'This suite and the one in the Windsor must be costing you a fortune,' she said, awed by the elegance of the furniture and decor.

'A small one, but together they're cheaper than buying a property, and they'll do until the club opens. Once that is underway I'll have time to look around and organise a more permanent office.'

'In the city or Tiger Bay?'

'Both. There'll be an office suite in the club next to your dressing room.' He sat in one of the brown leather armchairs and opened his cigar case. 'You're happy with your repertoire?'

'I'll be happier still after I'd had a chance to practise it.'

'I've hired an orchestra leader. Stan Peterson recommended him, so he should know how to handle musicians. He's arriving next Monday and he'll be holding auditions in an upstairs room in the White Hart next week. Aiden's sorting it, so tell your uncles to have a word with him if they if they want to apply.'

'I'll pass on the message.'

'You don't think they'll be interested?' He reached for his lighter.

'It's a regular job and everyone on the Bay is looking for one of those. But an Argentinian ship is leaving the docks at the end of the month. My Uncle Tony has been taken on as ship's carpenter and he's recommended Uncle Jed and Uncle Ron to the skipper, although it's not certain they'll get berths.'

'Your uncles would prefer to go to sea than stay at home and play in a band?'

'The sea's their profession, the band's a hobby. Just as Pastor Holsten – Micah – said: the Bute Street Blues are amateurs.'

'Except for you.'

'Sometimes when I wake in the night I have to pinch my arm to convince myself that I am performing on a professional stage.'

'The only wonder is that you weren't picked up by an impresario sooner. I'm glad I came along when I did. When I spoke to Stan Peterson on opening night he was talking about offering you work in London.'

'He did,' she said briefly.

'The bastard – pardon my French – the swine,' he amended in response to the startled look in her eyes. 'Did he offer you more money?'

'Not until after he asked what you were paying me.'

'You told him?'

'Shouldn't I have?' She turned the question back on him.

'I suppose there was no reason not to. Did he offer you more?'

'He offered me the same plus three pounds a week lodging allowance.'

'And you turned him down?'

'Obviously,' she smiled, 'as I signed a contract with you.'

'Why?'

'Because I love Cardiff Bay. It's my home, I know practically everyone there. And I like living with Edyth above her baker's shop. It's close to my family and,' she smiled grimly, 'I might need their kindness if I fall flat on my face on opening night in the club.'

'You won't,' he said confidently.

'But if I do, I can always go back to working with Edyth in her shop.'

'That's the last thing you'll be doing. Good, our tea – or rather coffee.' He opened the door and a waitress wheeled in a trolley.

'Shall I pour for you, sir?'

'No, Miss King will. Thank you.' Aled signed the chit the girl handed him and slipped her a coin before closing the door behind her. 'Mine's milk and two sugars.'

'I remember from the lunches.' She picked up the coffee pot. 'It seems odd to drink coffee at this time of day.'

'I lost the habit of drinking tea in America. They drink coffee at all times of the day – and night.' He took the cup she handed him and watched her set a plate and knife on the table beside him. 'You look quite at home.'

'Serving tea? I should do. I was a maid for long enough after I left school.' She took her coffee and a cucumber sandwich and sat in a chair opposite his. 'Thank you,' she said simply.

'What for?'

'Not trying to get served in the restaurant downstairs. They wouldn't have waited on me.'

'Like the Windsor, they wouldn't have dared not to, the amount I pay them for the use of this room.'

'If they had, it would have been unwillingly and only after an unpleasant scene.'

'At the risk of sounding tactless, it's time you developed a thicker skin.' He lifted two ham sandwiches on to his plate.

'I'll try.'

'You haven't come across prejudice before?'

'Never in Butetown.'

'And outside it?'

'The only times I ever left it, apart from auditions, was on outings with my grandmother or uncles and aunts when I was small. Looking back, I realise how much they must have shielded us children from unpleasantness.'

'I knew you hated me making a scene in that first

department store we went to, but life won't get better for Negroes, or any coloured people, unless you yourselves make a stand. There's a society in America called the Society for Advancement of Coloured People.'

'I've heard of it. Uncle Jed reads a lot of political papers.'

'Then you must know that people and their attitudes won't change unless you force them to sit up and take notice of the injustice that's being meted out in your direction.'

'If you're trying to tell me that I am a coward, I know I am.'

'Not always, Stan told me that you had a go at the theatre manager over the way he treated your family and friends on opening night.'

'I snapped at him, that was all.'

'And there's been no problem with your friends and family from the Bay coming into the New Theatre since?'

'No, but that's mostly down to Micah Holsten and Mr Peterson – and you. Uncle Jed told me that you were the one who suggested that Mr Peterson deal with the situation.'

'Bigots despise the poor every bit as much as they despise coloured people and I was poor for long enough to develop a dislike of prejudice. Don't let the cakes go to waste.' He lifted a chocolate éclair on to his plate.

She took another bite of her cucumber sandwich. 'What's America like?'

'That's like asking, what's Europe like. It's a big country and some parts of it are as different as Russia is from Scotland. I spent most of my time in New York but I visited New Orleans a couple of times. That's where I learned to appreciate jazz and good blues singers like you.'

'I love listening to the records the sailors bring in. If they have something new they take it to the Norwegian

Church Mission, so Micah can play it on the gramophone. That's where the band practises and if Micah likes a piece we try to put it into our act.'

'Talking about practising and rehearsing, I've decided to open the club on a Saturday night. A week to the day after *Peter Pan* closes. That will give you six days to rehearse with the orchestra and get used to them, provided the conductor can get one together next week.'

'It will be good to have some practice time, although it will also give me more time to get nervous.'

'After seeing you on-stage I don't believe you have a nerve in your body.'

'You haven't seen me in the dressing room before I go on. I'm a quivering jelly,' she confessed.

'Which solidifies once you hear your cue?' he guessed.

'How do you know?'

'Because I've seen you perform six times.'

'Six?' she questioned in surprise.

'It pays to do business with Stan – free seats in the boxes are just one perk.' He glanced at his watch. 'It's time to get you to the theatre, and have a word with Lennie Lane and this Mandy of yours.' He went into the bedroom, retrieved her jacket and held it out.

She slipped her arms into the sleeves. 'Thank you, Mr James.'

'Don't you think it's time we dropped "Mr James" and "Miss King" and called one another by our Christian names?'

'You're my boss,' she reminded him.

He smiled. 'Do you want to call me "boss" like Freddie and Aiden?'

'If that's what you want me to call you?'

He bent his head and kissed her chastely on the cheek. 'Aled will be fine. Let's go.'

She stood and fingered the spot he'd brushed with his lips while he wheeled the tea trolley outside the door.

Had she imagined the kiss? Or was she reading far more into it than he'd intended?

'Aled James is your brother?' Edyth fell back into her chair and stared at Harry in amazement.

'My half-brother.' Harry left his easy chair and paced to the window of Edyth's upstairs sitting room. He thought for a moment, debating how much to tell Edyth about the conversation he'd had with Aled. All he could do was repeat Aled's veiled threat 'watch your back, Harry Evans. Watch it everywhere you go', which when repeated in broad daylight sounded ridiculous. Especially in the calm comfort of Edyth's sitting room, which was furnished in old-fashioned, good quality furniture, which the Goldmans had left.

'Why didn't you tell me about him before now? Do Mam and Dad know he's your brother?'

'I'm not sure about Dad, but Mam knew about Aled, because I lived with him and his mother for a short while when Mam was in hospital. But it was a long time ago, before she married Dad.'

'Aled James said that his mother had looked after you when you were little but I didn't believe him.'

'You know that my father was murdered before he could marry Mam?'

'Mam told all of us that when she explained about your inheritance.'

'And you've seen the photographs I have of him, so you know I look just like him. What you don't know is that one of the first things the family solicitor told me when I started working for the company was that my father was a philanderer who'd fathered several children and the company had paid annuities to all the women who'd made claims. He tried to be kind, and suggested that not all the women were telling the truth, but it was impossible to prove either way after my father had been killed. And the firm paid out rather than have my father's name and reputation dragged through the courts. Aled was just one of many. It's an odd feeling to know that I have brothers and sisters out there I've never met and may never meet, particularly when I think how close we all are.'

'I'm sorry, Harry,' Edyth sympathised.

'But to get back to Aled, although he's done well for himself, he is very bitter. From what he told me, he and his mother lived in extreme poverty and she died young. He also insists that his mother never received a penny from Gwilym James.'

'But he can't hold that against you,' she cried.

'Not logically,' he agreed. 'But people who hold a grudge are never logical. Aled knows that David is my brother-in-law and he told me that he's employing him. I tried to see David before I came here but he wasn't at Helga's and Helga said she hadn't seen him since early this morning. Aled also knows that you're my sister—'

'I told him,' she interrupted.

'I'm afraid that he might try and hurt one of you.'

'How can he, Harry? He certainly can't touch me and he'd hardly be hurting David by employing him.'

'That depends on what Aled is employing David to do.'

'I know David is hot headed but I can't see him doing anything illegal.'

'Have you seen him today?'

'No, but I do know that he was going to try to get a job with George Powell who's converting the nightclub. Micah asked George to take David on. Perhaps that's what Aled James was talking about. In which case, as Micah said, David will be working for George Powell and only indirectly for Aled James.'

'You've talked to Micah Holsten about Aled James?'

'Yes, Aled took Micah as well as me and Judy's family to dinner in the Windsor on Judy's opening night.'

'So that's what Aled mean when he said he'd taken you to dinner.'

'I certainly wasn't alone with the man.'

'You don't like him?'

'He makes me uneasy, Harry. I don't have a reason for feeling the way I do about him. It's just . . . '

'What?'

'Promise you won't laugh.'

After his meeting with Aled James, the last thing Harry felt like doing was laughing. 'I promise, Edie.'

'He looks so much like you but he's not you. It's almost like he's a mirror image in every sense. You're good and he's evil.'

'You think Aled James is evil?'

'I said my feelings about him weren't based on reason.'

'I know Judy is working for the man, but please, promise me that you won't see more of him than you absolutely have to.'

'I assure you, I don't and I won't. Would you like tea?' she asked when he left the window.

He shook his head. 'No, I want to get home tonight. Mary's happy at the farm but I'm never happy about staying away from her for too long.'

'You two are lucky to have found one another.'

'We are. I'm sorry things didn't work out between you and Peter,' he added sincerely.

'Some things aren't meant to work out.'

'You seem friendly with Micah Holsten.'

'Very.' She smiled broadly. 'Which is why you don't have to worry about me seeing too much of Aled James.'

'You're . . . '

'I love Micah and he loves me.'

'And?' he pressed.

'Micah wants to marry me when my marriage to Peter is annulled. But I'm talking it one step at a time. Annulment first.'

'Have you told Mam and Dad about this?'

'How can I, when I'm still legally married to Peter?'

'They wouldn't mind, Edie. In fact they'd be delighted.

243

The whole family have been worried about you living down here alone. But then there's David and he's—'

'David saw me kissing Micah so he knows that Micah and I are in love. He was angry at the time but we've talked since.'

'And he's all right with it?'

She shook her head. 'You know David, he's angry with both Micah and me, but Micah is convinced he'll get used to the idea.'

'I'm pleased for you, sis. I really am. I liked Micah Holsten the first time I met him. You must bring him to the farm for a holiday so we can get to know him better.'

'And leave the baker's shop and the mission to run themselves?' she asked. 'It will be easer if you bring Mary and the children down here.'

'I'll put it to her but I'm not promising anything. It's time I was on my way – I told Helga I was going to call in again on her in the hope of seeing David. Look after yourself, sis.' He hugged her. 'You've come a long way from the clumsy girl who was forever falling over and breaking her bones.'

'I'm still clumsy.'

'Maybe, but you've proved that you have what it takes to run a business.'

'I'll see you out.' She picked up her cardigan from the back of a chair.

'You don't have to.' He fetched his hat from the hall rack.

'I usually go for a walk about this time in the evening.'

'In the direction of the Norwegian mission?' he guessed.

'No. In the direction of a boat Micah has berthed on the docks. He practises his saxophone there most nights.'

'The bakery is doing all right, isn't it, Edie?' Harry asked seriously as they walked down the stairs.

'Business is booming. I've even managed to pay a chunk off my overdraft, but I know it can't last. The men converting the Sea Breeze eat as much as we can produce these days, but trade will fall off as soon as the work's finished.'

'And then?'

'Like everyone else on the Bay, I'll have to tighten my belt.'

'Sis . . . '

'Offer me money, Harry, and I'll never talk to you again.'

'Stubborn little thing, aren't you?'

'Just like the rest of my family.' She closed the door behind her and followed him through the yard.

# Chapter Fourteen

Aled left the theatre feeling pleased with the world in general and himself in particular for the deals he had struck with Mandy and Lennie. The sun was a deep orange ball in a cloudless blue sky that promised a fine dawn in the morning. And, if the dry weather continued for just one more week, George Powell had told him that all the supports and alterations to the roof of the new club would be finished.

A few more days to put the interior finishing touches and the Tiger Ragtime would be ready for the first customers to walk through the doors, provided Aiden had enough trained croupiers ready to run the tables. Hopefully the orchestra leader would be up to scratch and would take on a sufficient number of competent musicians – he thought of the chorus girls and Judy. They at least were ready to perform.

Deciding to walk back to the Windsor Hotel he continued down Bute Street, tipping his hat and exchanging pleasantries with acquaintances. He couldn't help but contrast his present with his past. People will look with unseeing eyes when a ragged, barefoot boy crosses their path, but waiters, barmen, unemployed men and women hoping to find work will always be respectful to a man who might be in a position to offer them a job.

Halfway down Bute Street he saw Edyth walking towards the docks and quickened his pace to catch up with her. As he had told Harry, she was a good-looking woman, but certainly not in the conventional sense. Her mouth was too wide and her features too strong to be thought of as pretty. But he was attracted to her – and she was separated from her husband.

In his considerable experience separated, widowed and divorced women were ridiculously easy to seduce. They missed the intimacy of sex. A few compliments and small presents were usually enough to gain admittance to their beds. And his seduction of Edyth Slater would serve another purpose: it would infuriate Harry Evans.

'Mrs Slater.' He lifted his panama from his head when he caught up with her.

'Mr James.'

'It's a lovely evening.'

'It is,' she answered shortly.

'Are you going for a walk?'

'Just down to the sea.'

'May I escort you?'

'I'd hate to take you out of your way.'

It was obvious from the look she gave him that she didn't want him to accompany her but they were in the middle of a street crowded with early-evening idlers and he knew that like most well-brought-up middle-class girls, she'd be loath to make a scene. 'You wouldn't be. I'm going to the Windsor.' He offered her his arm. 'I took Judy shopping this afternoon.'

'She told me that you wanted to buy her fur coats and day clothes.' She capitulated and took the arm he offered her.

'As I told Judy, I will get more use out of them than her. Everywhere she goes she will be representing my club. And I intend to use her as a hostess at the formal and informal lunches I am planning for various organisations and charities as well as the council. I don't just intend to open a nightclub here in Cardiff, I intend to become a part of the community.'

'And do good works?' Aled James's use of 'Judy' as opposed to 'Miss King' wasn't lost on Edyth.

'Isn't that what all businessmen – good businessmen – do? Take your brother, for instance.'

'He called on me today. He mentioned that you two had met.'

'Did he?'

She looked him coolly in the eye as they passed the Exchange and drew alongside the turn to Stuart Street. 'You go that way, I believe, *Mr* James.' She pointed in the direction of the Windsor.

'I'll walk you to the sea.'

'There is no need, but thank you for the offer,' she refused firmly.

'Would you take pity on a lonely bachelor and have dinner with me one evening?'

'No, Mr James, but thank you for asking.' She broke into a broad smile and he smiled back, unaware that Micah Holsten was standing behind him.

'I hope I haven't kept you waiting, Micah.' Edyth relinquished Aled's arm and took Micah's.

'Not at all, Edyth, I was just chatting to Old Bill. His charabanc business is thriving.' Micah raised his hat. 'Mr James, if you'll excuse us.'

Micah and Edyth walked away, leaving Aled standing on the pavement looking after them. It was then Aled realised that he'd never stood a chance with Edyth Slater, for the simple reason that she was already spoken for.

David's back and thigh muscles were aching from crouching low over the floor of the Sea Breeze for most of his twelve-hour shift in the old hotel. And his hands were raw and bleeding from the skinning he had inadvertently given them while sawing and sanding lengths of skirting boards, in between taking more bets than he had anticipated from his fellow workers. He wondered if Aiden Collins would be pleased with the money he had bagged. It seemed a vast amount to him but he had no idea what a bookie's runner was expected to take in a day.

He had done exactly as Aiden had asked him to. Left the site at the end of the day and returned to Helga's to wash and change into his suit. After barely eating half a dozen mouthfuls of the sausage and mash Helga had prepared for her lodgers' tea, he had headed for James Street and the upstairs room of the White Hart.

He found Aiden sitting with his feet propped on a corner of a desk reading the evening edition of the *South Wales Echo*.

'It's just as you said, Mr Collins.' David pulled the canvas cash bag from inside one of his best linen shirts. 'I only had to tell one person I was taking bets and the men flocked round me like chickens at feeding time. Especially at break.' He set the bag on the table in front of Aiden.

'The books?' Aiden held out his hand, David took them from his pocket and placed them on the desk. Aiden flicked through them before taking a small notebook from his own pocket. 'Have you checked the cash against the entries you made?'

'I didn't have time in work. And I was in my lodgings only as long as it took me to eat and change.'

'Pull up a chair. Count the money. I'll tally the books.' Aiden took a pencil from his pocket and began to add up the columns of figures David had entered.

David tipped the bag out on the opposite side of the table to the one Aiden was working on. He started piling pennies, halfpennies, threepences and sixpences into shillings, and the shillings, half a crowns and florins into neat stacks of pounds. For ten minutes the only sounds that could be heard in the room were the clink of coins, the scratching of Aiden's pencil and their breathing.

'How much was in the bag?' Aiden laid down his pencil and looked expectantly at David.

'Seven pounds, thirteen shillings and sixpence.' David looked at Aiden in concern, worried that he had somehow lost money despite the care he had taken to look after it.

'Which is exactly what I make it.'

David weakened in relief. 'That's good to hear.'

'You're not used to handling money?' Aiden asked.

'Only what we get when we sell the farm produce to the local shops in the Swansea Valley and then it was always simple and straightforward. More or less the same amount every week.'

'Have you tallied the winnings?'

'No.' David shook his head.

'I have. We'll be paying out two pounds nine shillings, which leaves a clear profit of five pounds, four shillings and sixpence, of which,' he pushed a stack of shillings in David's direction, 'one pound, one shilling is your share, which is slightly more than the percentage due to the runner, but the boss believes in rounding up not down.'

'This is mine?' David stared at Aiden in astonishment.

'Didn't the boss tell you that the runner takes twenty per cent of the profit?'

'He said I'd be well paid.'

'I'd say that isn't bad for a day's work.'

'No – no, isn't, in fact it's bloody great,' David concurred.

'So you're pleased with how your first day went?'

'Yes, but what happens if everyone backs a winner and I make a loss not a profit?'

Aiden gave him the same pitying look Aled James had when he'd asked the selfsame question. 'Take it from me. Unless the runner is on the take, there is always a profit.' He nodded to David's cut. 'Put it away before the punters come in to pick up their winnings. Do you owe anyone change?'

'No. There was plenty around the site today.'

'That will alter when the work dries up.' He handed David a book. 'The odds for tomorrow's races.'

David pocketed it along with his winnings.

'The boss will be pleased with this. He'll probably want to see you about a regular job when the work on the club is finished. In the meantime, it might be as well if you concentrate on the book instead of the building.' Aiden lifted a briefcase from the floor and, after separating the 'winnings' that had to be paid out, scooped the rest of the money into it. He closed the case, returned it to the floor and handed the empty canvas bag to David.

'You think the boss will give me regular work, running a racing book?' David asked.

'The boss may have something else in mind for you, but you'll have to talk to him.'

David's hand closed over the guinea in his pocket. He had earned almost as much in a day as he had expected to earn on the site in a week.

Aiden heard the clink of coins in David's pocket. 'If you want to earn more you could go round the pubs in the evenings, and spread the word. Just as you did on the building site. But be careful. Not all the law wear uniforms and those that don't hang round pubs to see what they can pick up. Don't approach any strangers, especially those who are well built and over six feet tall.' He looked up as Tony King walked in. 'Is this our first customer?' he asked David.

'Green spirit. Five to two in the second race today at Aintree.' Tony laid down his ticket.

'Pay the man, David.'

David counted out seven shillings and handed them to Tony.

'Pleasure doing business with you, David.' Tony grinned.

'It's a pleasure to do business with you, Mr King. If you're looking to put some of that on a dead cert tomorrow, rumour has it Dark Oak running in the two thirty is a good bet,' Aiden said.

'I'll bear that in mind, Mr Collins. Bye, David.' Tony left.

David picked up the next betting slip. 'I didn't know that you knew the Kings, Mr Collins.'

'I made it my business to get acquainted with most of the people on the Bay.' Aiden looked up as two more men came up the stairs. 'Let's see you do another pay-out, boy. The sooner I get you working on your own, the more time I'll have to concentrate on gearing the casino up for business.'

Edyth was leaving her shop by the back door when Micah walked into the yard.

'Am I that late?' she adjusted the silk scarf she'd draped round her neck and fastened it with a pin.

'No.' He frowned absently. 'I'm looking for David. Is he here?'

'I haven't seen him since I visited him in Helga's the night he came back from Norway.' Micah's sombre expression concerned her. 'Is he in trouble?'

'Not yet, but the fool soon will be. Tony King called into the mission as pleased as punch because he won five bob on the horses.'

'That's nice for Tony.' Tony was the wildest of Judy's three uncles and Edyth knew that his wife, May, would be furious if she suspected that her husband had risked his wages gambling after being unemployed for months.

'And guess what? The bookie's runner who took his bet was David. He's working for Aiden Collins, one of Aled James's henchmen.'

'Oh Vladivostok!' Edyth's blood ran cold when she recalled the conversation she'd had with Harry the day before.

'You knew about this?'

'Not about David being a bookie's runner. But Harry came to see me yesterday. Aled James is his half-brother.'

'His half-brother . . . ?'

'Not my father's son.' Edyth had denied the obvious and now that she'd said that much, she felt she had to explain further. 'Harry's father was murdered before he could marry my mother.'

'So he's illegitimate?'

Recalling what Micah had said about wanting his children to bear his name, she snapped, 'You have a problem with that?'

'I thought you knew me better, Edyth. It's what people are, not how they're born, that's important.'

Mollified, she continued. 'When my father married my mother he adopted Harry and when my sisters and I, and my younger brother came along he treated all of us the same. We really are one family. No one ever considered Harry to be any different from the rest of us. My parents told us about Harry's real father when we were old enough to understand, because they didn't want any secrets in the family. And also because they wanted us to know why Harry was going to inherit a fortune and we weren't. Harry doesn't just work for Gwilym James. When he reaches thirty in four years' time his trust will be dissolved and he'll inherit the company along with some property and other businesses.'

Micah whistled. 'A wealthy man indeed.'

'You want to know the worst thing about having a wealthy brother?' she asked seriously.

'Tell me?'

'He tries to help everyone. Me – David – he won't let any of us stand on our own two feet.'

'Isn't that only natural? He obviously cares for all of you and doesn't want to see you struggle. What's so awful about that?'

'A lot, when you want to make your own way in life,' she said in exasperation. 'Anyway, to get back to the point, from what Harry told me yesterday, his real father was something of a ladies' man. Harry has quite a few half-brothers and probably sisters. Aled James is one of them and he blames Harry and our family for his mother's early death. Apparently he and his mother didn't get any of his father's money. Harry said that Aled is bitter and he threatened to hurt Harry by getting at me and David. Employing David as a bookie's runner would be one way to do it. If David gets caught taking bets by the police he could go to gaol, couldn't he?' she asked.

'He could,' Micah concurred.

'The stupid fool!' she exclaimed angrily. 'Mary told me that David's always been headstrong. But something like this could destroy him – he's used to wide open spaces not prison cells, and the shame would devastate Mary.'

'Someone needs to talk sense into David before word gets out that he's a runner, because once it does, the police will mark him for arrest. Have you any idea where he could be?' Micah asked Edyth urgently.

She shook her head. 'The only place I can think of is Helga's.'

'He wasn't there a few minutes ago. Helga said he came in from work, washed and changed into his best suit, barely touched his tea and ran back out again. Tony said that David had paid him his winnings in the White Hart. I called in there on my way to Helga's but David and Aiden Collins had already left.'

'Then we'll just have to wait for David in Helga's,' Edyth said determinedly. 'As he's lodging there, he's bound to return there sooner or later.'

'Do you think he'll listen to us?'

'No, but that's not going to stop me from trying to talk sense into him,' Edyth said forcefully.

'Close-knit clan you Evanses, aren't you?' Micah smiled.

'Absolutely,' she agreed firmly, 'and whether David likes it or not, as Harry's brother-in-law he's a full family member, even if his surname is Ellis.'

'Have you got to go – right this minute?' Gertie complained when David left her bed.

He sat up and rummaged on the floor for his clothes.

They were tangled up with Gertie's but he managed to free his vest, underpants and shirt. 'It's after nine o'clock and I have to be up early in the morning to go to work.' What he didn't tell her was the reek of her scent on top of the fish and chip supper and beer he'd bought them was making him nauseous. He was also intent on taking Aiden Collins's advice and calling in on one or two pubs on the way back to Helga's to spread the news that he was available to take bets.

'Come and see me tomorrow.' She sat up, linked her arms around his waist and pressed her cheek against his bare back.

'If I have time.' He was suddenly and, in view of the way he had felt about Gertie an hour ago, inexplicably irritated with her. He felt that she wasn't in the least bit interested in him, only in the contents of his wallet.

'What do you mean?' she cried indignantly. '"If I have time." What kind of an answer is that for a regular to give a girl?'

'Just what it says. I'm holding down two jobs—'

'Goody.' She locked her arms even tighter around his waist. 'All the more money for me.'

She couldn't have said anything worse in his present mood. 'I have to keep myself too, you know.'

'Why so cross, Dai?' She watched him pick up his suit trousers from the floor and step into them.

'Because all you ever talk about and all you ever ask for is money. And there's pink face powder all over my jacket and my trousers.' He tried to brush it off but it became ingrained in the suiting. He looked down at the floor. 'Don't you ever clean this place?'

'I work all the hours God sends—'

'I wouldn't call what you do work,' he said acidly.

'Then what would you call it?' When he didn't answer her, she said, 'I provide a service the same as the doctor and the dentist.'

'They have set fees that don't go up every five minutes.'

'First rule of Anna's house: every girl has to look to her own future.'

'By fleecing her customers.'

'That's a vile thing to say.' Her bottom lip trembled. 'I gave you your money's worth, didn't I?'

'You did when you charged me two bob. Tonight it was half a crown for the same, and supper and drinks. What will it be tomorrow?'

'You're in a bad mood. I'm not talking to you.' She flounced back on to the bed and pulled the bedclothes over her head.

David found his shoes beneath Gertie's frock and laced them on. He checked his pockets – and his wallet to make sure that no more of his money than he had intended had 'accidentally' fallen in the direction of Gertie and her piggy bank. When he was sure it was all there he opened the door. As he did so, Gertie pulled the sheet down, uncovering her face.

'See you tomorrow?' she pleaded.

He remembered how he had felt when he had walked into the room and softened a little. 'Perhaps, I've told you I have two jobs.'

'And they keep you so busy, you can't make time for little me?' she whined.

'I can't make firm plans.'

'But if you come here and I'm busy – you'll wait?'

Her begging made him wonder if Anna's other girls were charging less for the same service Gertie was providing. 'I'll see how it goes.'

'Please . . . '

'Night, Gertie.' He closed the door behind him and ran down the stairs. The red-haired woman he'd seen earlier, and, from her age, had presumed was Gertie's 'Anna', opened the kitchen door and looked out into the passageway.

'You just left Gertie?'

'Yes,' he confirmed.

'I've seen you before, haven't I? Are you one of her regulars?'

'I don't know,' David answered uneasily, anxious to leave the house.

'If you've visited her more than once, you must be.'

'I have to go.' David went to open the door but she joined him and leaned against it, preventing him.

'What's your name?'

David wasn't sure why she was asking, so he used the nickname Gertie had bestowed on him. 'Dai.'

'You can't be a sailor in that suit.'

'I'm not. I'm working on the old Sea Breeze.'

Anna then repeated what Gertie had said when he'd told her the same thing. 'You and every other man on the Bay. God help the lot of us when it's built.'

'Goodnight, Miss ... Mrs ... ' David faltered, it seemed disrespectful to call a women so much older than himself by her Christian name.

'It's all right; you can call me Anna without any other handle. Everyone else does on the Bay.'

'Good night, Anna.'

'I heard you and Gertie having words. She's not trying to bilk you, is she?'

That word again – bilk. 'I'm not sure what you mean, Anna.'

'Charge you too much?'

'I gave her half crown.'

'That's top whack, Dai; I hope she gave good service.'

'She did.'

He must have sounded grudging because she said, 'Any problems, come to me. The last thing I want is for this house to get a bad name. And you don't have to tell me. I know Gertie can be greedy.'

David stepped outside, breathed in several lungfuls of warm, sea-scented air and headed purposefully for the lights of Bute Street. One of the open-air 'casinos' was operating in full swing beneath a street lamp and a circle of twenty or more onlookers were watching half a dozen men crouched at the foot of the lamp playing poker. When David drew closer, he saw that one of the players was Tony King.

'David, my lucky mascot. Thanks to you I'm in the game.'

'You winning?' David asked, interested.

Tony pointed to the small heap of coins on the pavement in front of him. 'See for yourself.'

'Carry on at the rate you have done today, Tony, and it'll be Rockefeller move over,' Abdul, who was playing next to Tony, joked.

'It might be by midnight.' Tony fished a watch from the top of his neighbour's pile of winnings and checked the time. 'Do me a favour, Davy boy.'

'That depends what it is,' David replied warily, expecting Tony to ask him for a loan.

'Pick up Judy for me. It's my turn to walk her home from the theatre and I don't want to interrupt the game. These beggars will only mess with my cards if I do.'

'As if we would,' Abdul protested indignantly.

'You would,' Tony said calmly.

Steve Chan shrugged his shoulders. 'We would.'

The others nodded good-natured agreement.

'I was going to call in a few pubs on my way back to Mrs Brown's.' The last thing David felt like doing was arguing with Judy after quarrelling with Gertie. And if past experience was anything to go by, argue was all he and Judy ever did.

'To do some advertising for your new venture?' Tony guessed.

'How did you know?'

'I could see that you'd had a successful day when I picked up my winnings. Being a bookie's runner can make you a lot of dough, as long as you remember to wear running shoes at all times.' He glanced at a boy standing on the corner. 'No sign of any men in blue?'

'No, Tony,' the boy yelled back.

'Good lad. Tell you what, Davy boy: me and the boys will do your advertising for you, if you go to the New Theatre and meet Judy. A walk on dry land will do you good if half of what I heard about your voyage to the North is right.'

David made a face. 'All right, but you won't forget about the advertising?'

'We won't.' Abdul threw down one card and drew another.

'Do you have a problem?' Mandy asked when she walked to the stage door and found Judy, who'd left the dressing room ten minutes before her, standing in the entrance looking up and down the road.

'It's my Uncle Tony's turn to walk me home and he hasn't turned up.'

'Want me and the girls to go with you?'

'You're all going the other way,' Judy reminded her.

'I owe you a favour for getting me that job in the Tiger Ragtime. Besides, we don't mind, do we, girls?' She turned to the rest of the chorus behind her. 'A breath of fresh sea air will do us all good after that stuffy theatre,' she coaxed.

The silence said more about the girls' lack of enthusiasm than a list of excuses would have.

'It's all right,' Judy insisted. 'I'm perfectly happy to walk home by myself. It's just that my uncles insist on meeting me. In fact, it would be nice to break the pattern. Once I do it by myself, they may allow me to walk home alone every night. It's barely half an hour to my lodgings.'

'If you're sure that you're happy about it. I've heard stories about Tiger Bay,' Mandy said doubtfully.

'So have I,' Judy smiled confidently, 'I was born there

and I've lived there all my life. It's nowhere near as bad as people try to paint it.' Not wanting to delay any longer, or make Mandy feel any guiltier than she already did, Judy walked past the front entrance of the theatre towards Queen Street.

'Judy?'

She turned and saw David standing outside the main entrance of the theatre. 'What are you doing here?'

'Waiting for you. Your uncle was busy so he asked me to pick you up.'

'Busy?' Judy reiterated. 'You mean he was playing cards in one of the open-air casinos.'

'That's right.'

'Auntie May will go wild if she finds out he's been gambling. She'll throw him out and then he'll have to sleep in either Uncle Jed's or Uncle Ron's shed because their wives won't have him in their houses when he's quarrelled with May.'

'Why not? He didn't look drunk when I saw him.' David caught up with her.

'Uncle Tony drinks, but he hardly ever gets drunk. Gambling is his problem. A couple of years ago, Uncle Jed allowed Uncle Tony to sleep in his kitchen after he lost his entire week's wages on a horse. Auntie May heard about it from the neighbours and came looking for Uncle Tony the next morning. When she found him snoring in Uncle Jed's easy chairs in his kitchen, she lost her temper and threw all of Uncle Jed's and Auntie Bessie's china at Uncle Tony's head. It took Uncle Jed two voyages to the Caribbean to earn enough to replace everything and two weeks for Uncle Tony's cuts to heal.'

'Vicious lot, your family.' David had difficulty imagining someone breaking the entire china of a house over another person's head.

'Only to one another and they love each other underneath it all.' She caught hold of his arm, although he hadn't offered it to her. 'I can't believe Uncle Tony sent you to walk me home. I wish my uncles realised I've grown up. If I can hold down a job in the theatre, I'm perfectly capable of walking myself home.'

'Tiger Bay's a dangerous place.'

'To outsiders maybe. Not to people who grew up there. I'd only have to cry out for half the residents to come and see what was the matter.'

'Look,' he said in exasperation, 'I didn't have to come to get you.'

'I know.'

'So, are you going to complain about your uncles all the way back to Edyth's?'

'I'm sorry, that was unfair of me.' She had given him an apology but she couldn't resist adding a gibe. 'Almost as unfair as you were to me when I met you at the station and I told you that I had found you lodgings. But if it's any consolation, I'm cross with my uncle not you.'

'I did rather bite your head off when you met me at the station,' he said grudgingly.

'Is that a "sorry" for the way you behaved?'

'Yes.'

'Are you getting paid daily on the site? Because if you're not, I can't see how my uncle can afford to play poker. Since the last incident, Auntie May makes a point of taking everything except sandwich money off him when he works.'

'Any food we order is taken out of our pay at the end of the week before we get it.'

'So that's how he got his stake. The crafty devil.'

'He also bet a couple of shillings on the horses today and won.'

'He told you?'

'I took his bet,' David said, proud of his new job.

She stopped dead in her tracks. 'You're not working as bookie's runner for Charlie Moore?'

'No.'

'Thank goodness.' She breathed a sigh of relief for

Edyth's sake. 'That's a mug's game if ever there was one. Uncle Tony worked for him for a couple of weeks and ended up in court. He was fined twice as much as he'd earned.'

'He didn't go to gaol?' David asked.

'No, it was his first offence.' She looked up at him sideways. 'What do you want to know for?'

'Because I'm working as a runner for Aiden Collins.'

'The Aiden Collins who works for Aled James?'

'The Mr James who's building the nightclub, I don't know of another one, do you?' He led her across the road and down into Bute Street.

'Don't you know it's illegal to take bets, you stupid boy?'

'I am not stupid,' he said fiercely.

She lowered her voice as they passed a crowd leaving the Salvation Army Citadel. 'If the police catch you they'll throw the book at you, lock you up and toss the key in the dock.'

'They won't catch me,' he said confidently. 'And even if they do,' he added somewhat illogically given his assertion, 'Mr James promised me that no runner of his has ever gone to gaol.'

Judy was torn between loyalty to Aled James for giving her a job and loyalty to Edyth without whose help, friendship and love she wouldn't have been able to stay in Tiger Bay. And naïve, irritating and maddening as David was, he was still a member of Edyth's family. 'That's easy for Mr James to promise. He's just come from America and hasn't had any runners working on Tiger Bay before now that I know about.'

Sensing the logic in what Judy said, David fell silent.

'You are an idiot,' Judy continued to scold him. 'Edyth said you had a job on the building site. Why didn't you stick to that?'

'I'm doing the two at the moment. Mr James said I could earn extra running a book for Mr Collins and if I did well, there might be a permanent job at the end of it working for him in his nightclub. Everyone knows that the building work will be finished in a couple of weeks, and then Mr James will need people to run the gaming tables. I can do it if I'm shown how, Judy, I know I can. I made a guinea out of the money I took in bets today and that's without the money I made working on the site—'

'Keep your voice down,' Judy hissed when she saw heads turn in their direction. 'Don't you know that there are people down here desperate enough to beat a man up for the price of a cup of tea and a bun? Honestly, David, you're a real baby,' she lectured as if she was middle-aged and he was a wayward child.

'I am not, I . . . I . . . ' He almost boasted about his exploits with Gertie before realising that it wasn't something he could tell a girl. Or Harry or Micah or Judy's uncles. He had a feeling that even Tony would repeat Harry's warnings about loose women if he tried.

'I suppose I should make allowances for you. Edyth told me that you grew up on an isolated farm.'

'There's no need for you to feel sorry for me just because I grew up on a farm,' he snapped testily.

'I don't. The truth is, I'm envious. I've never stayed in the country but I've been on day trips to Leckwith fields and Creigau. They seemed so green, peaceful and beautiful after the docks. The only flowers you see down here are in people's back yards – and between the coal sheds, dog kennels and the Ty Bachs there's not much room left. The last time I went to Creigau, I was twelve. I picked masses of primroses. I even dug up a few roots, although I knew I shouldn't have,' she confessed. 'My grandmother planted them in her garden and every spring after that they reminded me of the trip.'

'The country might be nice for a townie to visit but it's a lot different when you're born on a farm. From the day I could walk I was expected to work and work bloody hard,' he swore. He saw her shocked expression and said,

'Sorry, bad habit. Harry has tried to stop me swearing but all I've heard on site today is cursing and I've started doing it again without thinking.'

'It's hard not to swear when that's all you hear around you,' she conceded. 'I never used to swear when I lived with my grandmother but everyone swears all the time in the theatre. The actors, the director, the producer, the musicians, even the chorus girls. They don't bat an eyelid. Show-business people seem to think no more of swearing than they do of breathing. They do it more than anyone else I've ever met, even seamen. But my uncles always watched their language around my grandmother. Towards the end of her life she was very frail but they were still terrified of her.'

'How come you were brought up by your grandmother?' he asked.

'My mother died when I was a baby and my father was at sea.'

'Is he still at sea?'

'I don't know and I don't care.'

David knew from the tone of her voice not to trespass further. 'My mother and father died young.'

'Who brought you up?'

'My sister as much as anyone, although, looking back, I suppose we brought one another up although she's older than me by four years. My mother died less than a year after my father, and she made Mary promise to do everything she could to keep the farm going and the family together. As we have two younger brothers and a sister it was tough going until Mary married Harry.'

'He's nice, but then Edyth and all her family are.' She blushed when she thought of Edyth's confession to Micah that David had fallen in love with her and hoped that David didn't think she meant anything by the throwaway remark.

'Yes, they are,' he agreed.

'So, are you coming to see me in *Peter Pan* now you

are back from your adventures on the high seas?' she asked.

'Some adventures,' he sneered. 'And I'm coming next Saturday. Mrs Brown has booked a box and she's invited me, Moody, Micah and Edyth to join her, although they've all seen you before. What's it like to be on-stage?' he asked curiously.

'Everything and more that I ever dreamed, when the audience are applauding, and cheering me at the end of my big number. And the clothes and the make-up are as glamorous as I thought they would be. But the fighting, backbiting and bitching between the cast backstage has to be heard and seen to be believed. So it's not all glitz and glitter. And some of the people are so nasty they make you look like a soft pussycat.'

'What do you mean?' he said angrily.

'You've just proved my point. Look at you now, spitting and hissing like a cornered tomcat.'

'I am not,' he said indignantly.

'I'm sorry; I didn't realise that this is how you normally behave.' She looked at him and a shaft of light fell on his face from a street lamp. He glared at her for a moment. She smiled and slowly he smiled back.

'My mother always used to say that I was too hot-tempered for my own good. And I know I became even worse after she died. We didn't have it easy. Just because Mary and I were young, people – cattle dealers and people like that,' he explained not wanting to go into details, 'thought they could cheat us.'

Judy knew that was the closest she would get to an apology from him for his bad temper. 'So you played,' she deepened her voice, mimicking Jeremy's Mr Darling, 'the angry hard man.'

'Sort of.' He looked down the wide street of two-, three- and four-storey buildings. 'And I'm not used to living among all these people. But that's not to say I won't get used to it.'

'Snarling at people because you're not sure of yourself isn't going to make you any friends. And before you jump down my throat again, I know exactly how you feel.'

'No, you don't,' he contradicted.

'At the risk of sounding like a pantomime chorus, oh yes I do. You're in a strange place, surrounded by people you don't understand because you're not used to their ways and you're not at all sure what you should do next.'

'Clever, aren't you?'

'I know because it's exactly how I feel in the theatre. I'm not used to actors and their ways. And now that I'm one of them . . . '

'You're not sure you want to be?' he guessed.

'Oh no. After fighting so hard to get a part on-stage, I want to be one of them all right. It's just that sometimes – it feels so strange.'

'Like me being here in Bute Street instead of the farm or on the Brecon Beacons.'

'Home sweet home.' Judy stopped outside the bakery yard and looked up at the windows. 'The lights are out. That means Edyth's in bed.'

'Where I should be, if I'm going to get up early tomorrow to work on the site.'

'I don't have to be up until midday,' Judy said.

'Lucky you.'

'I wasn't boasting. But I can never go to sleep straight after coming back from the theatre. Too wound up by all the applause and excitement of knowing we've pulled off another successful performance against all the odds. You don't fancy a cup of tea, do you? I'll make it in the bakery kitchen so we don't disturb Edyth.'

David hesitated for a split second. 'That would be nice, thank you.'

'If we're lucky there may even be a doughnut left,' she whispered as she opened the door, stole inside and switched on the light.

# CHAPTER FIFTEEN

'This sitting up waiting for David is getting to be a habit.' Micah left his chair when the hands on Helga's clock pointed to ten o'clock. 'Another few hours and you'll have to be up and working, Edyth.'

'I can't go home without seeing David.'

'He's been a stupid silly boy today. He'll still be a stupid silly boy tomorrow,' Helga said philosophically. 'I don't know why you two insisted on waiting for him. Surely you don't think for one minute that he's going to listen to either of you.' She removed her needle from the patch she'd been stitching and jabbed it into her needle book.

'As usual, you're probably right, Helga.' Micah stretched his arms above his head.

Helga folded her quilt and held out her hand to take Edyth's needle. 'Of course I'm right. Edyth, it's time you were home and in bed. And don't bother to come back here, Micah. The boy's telling-off can wait until tomorrow.'

'You always were a bossy boots, Helga.' Micah picked up Edyth's cardigan and held it out to her.

'One more thing, if you're going to tell the boy off, I'd rather not be around while you do it.' Helga finished folding the quilt and pushed it into the cupboard. 'I have to carry on living in the same house as him and it might be as well if I don't hear what you have to say. That way he can think I'm still on his side. Or at least neutral.'

'I just hope he's all right.' Edyth took the cardigan Micah handed her and slipped it over her frock.

'That boy seems to have nine lives and as far as I know he's only used two of them,' Micah observed.

'Four,' Edyth corrected. 'There are a few accidents you don't know about.'

'I'll take your word for it.'

Helga straightened and rubbed her aching back. 'You two look good together,' she said, smiling when Micah wrapped his arm around Edyth's waist.

'We know we do.' Micah winked at Edyth. 'Ready?'

'I suppose so. But I really would rather wait until David gets back.'

'If he's in one of the pubs having a good time buying rounds with whatever he was paid to run the betting book—'

'I know, he could be gone for hours,' Edyth interrupted.

'So let's go, you need your beauty sleep.'

'And you don't, Micah?' Helga asked.

'Pastors can lie in bed all day if they choose to, because they won't be missed.'

Helga kissed Edyth then Micah. 'See you both tomorrow, but remember what I said about not dragging me into your argument with David.'

'I will,' her brother replied.

Micah and Edyth left Helga's and walked out on to the pavement. Like most warm summer evenings in the Bay the street was almost as busy as it was in the day. Children were playing, neighbours were sitting on window sills gossiping, a group of youngsters were standing in the middle of the road practising a jazz piece on an assortment of home-made instruments, including paper-covered combs, spoons and saucepan drums.

Micah looked up at the sky. 'Make the most of this weather – it can't last. The rains will start at the end of August.'

'Now you can predict the weather?'

'I come from a long line of seamen who lived their entire lives by the weather.'

'I didn't know.'

'I told you my grandfather was a fisherman.'

'So you did, but I didn't realise he was one of a line.'

'Have you ever thought that our generation and perhaps the ones before us are the lucky ones?' he said thoughtfully. 'Not all of us are bound by what our fathers did. Take David, he's left his family farm. As the eldest son that would have been unheard of in Wales a hundred or even twenty years ago. My father set tongues wagging in our home village when he became a pastor instead of going into the family fishing and farming business.'

'The Great War changed things for so many women. My mother has friends who worked in the munitions factories and they carried on working in shops and offices when the factories closed simply because there was no one left for them to marry.'

'Your mother is exceptional; she is married, has a family and works in a full-time job.'

'In a family business,' Edyth reminded him. 'And she always put us children first.'

'I wasn't criticising, Edyth,' he said. 'I just wondered if that was why you bought the bakery. To be like your mother.'

'I bought the bakery because I wanted to do something besides live off my parents, as so many girls do until a man knocks on the door and asks them to become a wife. But then,' she smiled wryly, 'I rather messed up any ambition I had to be a good wife when I married Peter.'

'You've achieved what you wanted to now: your independence. And you had a choice as to whether or not you bought the bakery. It wasn't a business you inherited. But perhaps I'm not entirely right,' he said thoughtfully. 'You, David and I had a choice, but for most of the girls on the Bay there are generally only two options, service or helping their mother run the house, and then only if their mothers can afford to keep them.'

'Or a third,' Edyth said, looking at a girl wearing thick make-up who was leaning against the wall of a house smoking a cigarette. The girl saw Micah and lifted the hem of her skirt to her thighs.

'That option is not open to decent women.'

'Anna Hughes and her girls told me the only option they had was to sell themselves, or starve. In my opinion that's not a choice.'

'Don't tell me you still have tea there?'

'Not since Peter left the Bay and I stopped being a vicar's wife, but only because I haven't had time for afternoon tea parties with anyone.' She led the way through the yard to the back door. 'Are you coming in? I'll make coffee in the kitchen so as not to disturb Judy.'

'That sounds tempting.'

'When I last looked there were a couple of pasties left.'

'You've sold me on the idea.'

Edyth opened the door and they saw Judy and David sitting at the large scrub-down table, a teapot, cups and a plate of pasties set between them.

'We've been looking everywhere for you, young man,' Micah said sternly.

'If you're going to give him a lecture on his new career as a bookie's runner, Micah, I've already done it.' Judy went to the cupboard and fetched two more cups and saucers for Micah and Edyth.

'Did you take any notice?' Edyth asked David.

Judy answered for him. 'None whatsoever.'

Twenty minutes later, Micah and David left the bakery. And, as Edyth had prophesied, none of them had succeeded in persuading David to give up working as a bookie's runner – not even Edyth's threat of writing to Harry, although she had made it clear she would do just that before going to bed that night. The only concession, if it could be called a concession, that David had given them, was he'd look around for a legal job – while he continued to work as a runner.

Micah and David were walking back towards Helga's house when Micah said, 'You have to be more careful, David.'

'No more lectures,' David pleaded. 'I've told you, I've made too much money on my first day as a bookie's runner to drop the job. And it's work that might lead to a full time position. I don't need anyone to tell me that jobs are going to be scarcer around the Bay than flying pigs when the work's finished on the Sea Breeze. You're also forgetting that Aled James said he'd look after me.'

'Even though Aled James has no experience of the way things are done on the Bay?'

'He bought his nightclub, didn't he? He knew how to get the licences he needed. From what the men on the site told me today, that couldn't have been easy.'

'David. I'm not going to go through all that with you again,' Micah said wearily. 'Edyth, Judy and I have all warned you. You won't listen to us, so be it on your own head.'

'Then why should I be more careful?' David asked.

'That scent I can smell on you. It's the one Anna Hughes and her girls use. It's sweet, it's sickly and everyone on the Bay can recognise it half a mile off. You're risking more than your wallet in that house. You're risking your health and that is far more serious. Once you lose that, it may take a long time to recover it, that's if you ever do.'

'The girl I see is young . . . '

'Youth is no guarantee of good health in that profession.'

'She's—'

'Likely to give you any and every disease her last customer was suffering from. Just give it some thought before you see her again, there's a good lad.'

*

'I suppose this is the last order we will be packing for the old Sea Breeze.' Judy's aunt, May, dropped a box of pasties into the cardboard crate Edyth was filling with rolls and baked goods.

'The last for the old hotel,' Edyth concurred, 'and unfortunately for business, I can't see us making up many for the new Tiger Ragtime.' Edyth tried to be philosophical. Her profits had soared courtesy of the workmen who had effected the transformation of the old hotel into the new club, but although she was optimistic by nature, she couldn't see the nightclub staff buying a fraction of the goods that the men on the building site had done.

May checked the contents of the box against the scribbled order. 'It's a small box compared to the one we made up yesterday.'

'Tony told me the workmen finished everything that needed to be done late last night. The only people going in this morning are the cleaners Aled James hired to put the finishing touches to the place ready for the grand opening tonight. This buffet is his thank-you to them for coming in early this morning.'

'You looking forward to going to the opening?' May asked.

'I'm looking forward to hearing Judy sing, and spending some time with your family, but since I started running the bakery I've lost my enthusiasm for late nights. This candle's getting too old to burn at both ends.'

May laughed. 'You're only nineteen.'

'Some days, like today, I feel ninety.' Edyth glanced at the clock. It was only half past six but she felt as though she had already done a full day's work. 'As it's quiet, I'll take my breakfast break. But if it gets busy, give me a shout.'

'I will.' May lifted the box they'd packed on to the back counter next to the till to await collection.

Edyth pushed open the door to the kitchen and found

Moody sitting with the postman, Bobby Harding. They were eating jam doughnuts and drinking tea. Bobby had been accustomed to taking his 'second breakfast' with Mordecai Goldman before Mordecai had sold the shop to Edyth and he had seen no reason to alter his routine simply because the business had changed hands.

'Tea's fresh.' Moody fetched another cup for Edyth. 'Would you like a doughnut or a French breakfast roll?'

'Both, thank you, Moody. Eating might keep me awake.' Edyth sank down on a chair opposite Bobby. 'This morning seems to be lasting for ever and I've only been working for an hour and a half.'

'Time passes more slowly when you're not busy.' Moody poured Edyth's tea. Knowing she didn't take sugar, he pushed the milk jug towards her.

'And we won't be for a while, unless someone decides to convert another building nearby.' Edyth took a doughnut from the plate on the table.

'I can't see that happening.' Bobby opened his mailbag and flicked through the mail.

'There might be another Mr James landing in the dock this minute.' Moody wiped a dab of jam from his chin with his finger.

'I don't think so. Aled James is one of a kind,' Edyth declared.

'Post to cheer you up, and judging by the number of letters, somebody loves you.' Bobby dropped a bundle of mail on the table in front of Edyth.

'Thank you, Bobby.' Edyth looked at it. There was one from Mary and she knew before she opened it that her sister-in-law would have filled nine-tenths of the pages with enquiries about David. What he was doing? Was he eating enough and properly? Was he making friends? Harry had made her promise not to write any news that might worry Mary about David. As a result Edyth had come to dread every letter she received from her sister-in-law because she felt as though she was lying when she answered it – and that had been before David had taken a job as a bookie's runner.

There was a letter from her estranged husband's aunt, Alice Beynon. Edyth smiled and set the letter aside as a treat to be read over lunch. She and Aunt Alice had become good friends and, as Alice was an amusing and witty correspondent, she looked forward to Alice's weekly epistles, which were full of wickedly accurate and caustic comments about Peter's sanctimonious and hypochondriac mother.

There was a bill from the coalman and another from the wholesaler, which she knew would be for last month's flour. It would be enormous but she took comfort in the thought that it would be covered by the increase in last month's sales.

There was also a large fat brown envelope, postmarked Buenos Aires, addressed in a hand she recognised only too well.

She murmured, 'Thank you,' to Moody when he set a French roll in front her, took a knife from the drawer in the table and slit the packet open before dropping the knife into the bowl of utensils waiting to be washed. She removed the bundle of papers it contained and glanced at them.

'Bad news, Mrs Slater?' Moody asked when she remained silent.

'No, Moody, just business.' She bundled the papers together with her other letters. 'Bills for the coal and flour and the like.'

'I wouldn't like to pay our flour bill for the last few weeks,' Moody said feelingly.

'It's large,' she agreed, 'but as there was very little wastage, we sold enough goods to meet it.' She left her chair and held up the bundle of papers. 'I'll put these in the office before I lose them.'

Moody nodded and topped up his own and Bobby's cup, emptying the teapot. Edyth went into the small ante room off the kitchen and deliberately allowed the door to swing shut behind her. She dropped her personal letters and the bills on top of her in-tray. Then she looked at the contents of the large envelope again. On the top sheet in large bold print was, **ANNULMENT OF MARRIAGE OF PETER GEORGE SLATER AND EDYTH RHIAN SLATER NEE EVANS.**

A note fell from inside the typewritten pages.

*Dear Edyth,*

*This is your copy. I have sent the originals to my solicitor and asked him to file them. By the time you read this we will no longer be married.*

*I am sorry for all the pain and trouble I have caused you. Please don't spare me another thought. I am well and as happy as I can be in this life. I will be sailing out of Argentina for a new country very soon, and although I now no longer use the name, I will send you what love I can and all sincere good wishes for your future, this last time as Peter Slater.*

'Sincere good wishes for your future' – the future – her future as a single woman. She opened the bottom drawer in her desk where she kept the old bills that she had paid. She lifted them out, set them aside and dumped the papers and the envelope into the bottom before replacing the bills on top.

She was free. The moment she and Micah had been waiting for had actually happened. There was nothing to prevent them from marrying – nothing at all except her own reluctance to move into the mission and take second place to his life and profession.

She closed the drawer, turned and looked in the mirror she had hung on the back of the door. She patted her hair into place, forced a smile and went out to finish her breakfast with Moody and Bobby.

Edyth was just putting a final dab of powder on her nose when she heard a knock on the door that led directly from the street to her rooms above the shop. As everyone on the Bay used the back door of her baker's shop as an entrance, even to her private rooms, she went into her living room, opened the window and looked down. Harry was standing on the pavement beneath her in his evening suit.

'Harry, what on earth are you doing here?' she called down.

'I thought I'd attend the grand opening of the Tiger Ragtime. It is tonight, isn't it?' he checked.

'Yes,' she confirmed.

'I saw it advertised last week in the *South Wales Echo* but I didn't make a note of the date. Do you know if it's invitation only?'

'I'm not sure, but my invitation said "and guest" so you can come with me if you haven't your own. Hang on a minute and I'll come down. Or better still, why don't you walk around to the yard and come in through the shop's kitchen?'

'Will do.'

Edyth returned to her bedroom, sprayed herself with lily of the valley scent, and picked up her stole. She walked into her small upstairs hall just as Harry was climbing the stairs.

'Where are Mary and the children?' she asked.

'Safe and sound at the farm, or at least they were when I telephoned there from Gwilym James this afternoon.'

Edyth opened the door to her sitting room. Harry walked in, stripped off his jacket, unbuttoned his waist-coat, loosened his bow tie and sank down on the sofa. 'It's hot out there. Talk about Indian summers and heat-waves. I've never known anything like it so late in the day or the year. It's September next week and there's no sign of the weather breaking.'

'So it would appear, for all of Micah's predictions of rain. I've never known summers like this one and last.'

'Next year it will probably tip down with rain all through June, July and August to make up for it.'

'Can I get you something?' Edyth asked. 'I only have beer, sherry and brandy, but I could make you a meal or a sandwich . . .'

'I've only just eaten, but a glass of water would be good. I don't want to start drinking alcohol this early. If I do, I'll fall asleep before we even get to the club.'

Edyth went into her small upstairs kitchen and poured Harry a glass of water from the pitcher Judy filled every morning. She carried it into the sitting room and gave it to him.

'Thank you. I'm parched. I thought a stroll down Bute Street would be pleasant after working in the office all day, but the street has doubled in length since the last time I walked it.'

'It seems to grow when you're tired.' Edyth arranged the skirt of her long black silk frock so it wouldn't crease and sat opposite her brother. 'I thought you knew that I always left the back door of the shop open.'

'I assumed that with the club opening and half of the people of Cardiff heading into Tiger Bay tonight, you'd have the sense to lock it.'

'I probably should have.' Edyth remembered Micah saying the same thing to her on the day of the carnival.

Harry finished his water, set his glass down and smiled at her. 'You look very glamorous, sis.' He sniffed. 'You smell nice too.'

'You say anything about it not being my usual eau de tennis and I'll clock you.'

'Ever wondered what "clock you" means?'

'No.'

'Neither have I until now. And that joke wore thin a long time ago.'

'What possessed you to come to the opening of the

Tiger Ragtime? I thought after the conversation you had with Aled James you wouldn't want to go near him or his club.'

'I was working in the Cardiff store. The meeting I had with the manager overran and I thought, why not stay overnight with my loving sister in Tiger Bay, who keeps reminding me that she has two spare bedrooms that I can use anytime? And incidentally see Judy's debut.'

'And talk to David,' Edyth added quietly. She had sent the letter telling Harry of his brother-in-law's exploits in a plain brown business envelope that she had asked Judy to address, lest Mary get suspicious.

'If I can find him.'

'That shouldn't be difficult. David went to Aiden Collins's "gambling school" every day last week. After training bookie's runners Aiden moved on to instructing the unemployed in the finer points of card dealing, roulette and rolling dice.'

'So Micah told me.'

'You've spoken to Micah about David?' she asked in surprise.

'Yes.'

'When?' she asked.

'On the telephone every day this week,' he confessed.

'And he told you that we couldn't do anything to dissuade David from working for Aled James.'

'Yes.'

'We have tried, Harry,' she said apologetically, 'but you know how stubborn David can be.'

'I do,' he said in a resigned voice.

'Yet, you had to come because you thought you'd have more success than us?'

'I know I won't.' Harry ran his fingers through his thick blond hair. 'But I have to try, although I know it's useless. I also happen to know that you've been writing to Mary, and thank you for not telling her exactly what her beloved brother's been up to.'

'Does David write to Mary?'

'A once-a-week duty letter to her and the others, which is full of stories about the Bay, the people he's met and the variety of shops and ships and anything and everything that isn't personal. I wish he wouldn't. He's got Matthew and Luke so excited about the glamorous life they think he's leading that they're both talking about leaving the farm and coming down here to join him as soon as they're old enough.'

'Matthew's – what? – eleven and Luke is only six,' Edyth said. 'It will be a while yet before they'll be able to leave the farm.'

'That doesn't stop them talking about it, and it upsets Mary. David mentioned in his letter that he has a job in the nightclub but he said he's working as a barman. Micah told me that he's working on the roulette wheel.'

'As Micah seems to know everything that's going on around here, I'd be more inclined to believe him than David. You do know that even if you see David in the club tonight, he may not want to talk to you.'

'Yes, but as I said I have to try. I owe it to Mary – and David, in the absence of any closer family – to try to steer him into a legal occupation.'

'Given the shortage of jobs there's nothing wrong with working in a nightclub that's licensed for gambling,' Edyth said in David's defence.

'There's a lot wrong with being a bookie's runner. All Mary can talk about is what they'll do when David returns to the farm.'

'I hate to dash your and Mary's hopes, Harry, but I've talked to David a few times since he's come down here and the one thing he is adamant about is that he won't return to the farm.'

'I know.'

'And that's all Mary writes about in her letters.'

'I know that too.' Harry picked up his empty glass and

looked at it. Edyth took it from him, went into the kitchen and refilled it with water.

'You sure I can't get you anything to eat?' she asked.

'I'm sure, thank you.' He took the glass from her. 'I knew that David was intent on leaving the farm for some time before he finally went. And before you say anything, it wasn't just that he thought he was in love with you, Edyth. He was restless. Every glimpse I gave him of the world – the pictures in Pontardawe, the beaches on the Gower, shopping trips to Swansea, the visits to Pontypridd – made him hungrier for even more new experiences.'

'So what happens when Mary realises that he isn't coming back?'

'I don't know.' Harry cradled his glass of water. 'When I married Mary I thought we would live on her family farm for a few years, six or seven at most, until David was old enough to take over the running of the Ellis Estate. Then Mary and I and our children and her younger brothers and sister would move to the house the trustees built for me in Pontypridd. But I've had to face facts.' He took a deep breath. 'Mary would wither away if she left that farm. She belongs there – she's rooted there,' he added slowly. 'She fought and struggled to keep it in the family for so long when she should have allowed the bailiffs to take it, she's unable to let it go. She insists she only did it to keep the farm in the family, and it was all for David and her brothers and sister, but it wasn't. She did it for herself and I love her too much to take her away from there now.'

'But where does that leave you, Harry?' Edyth asked in concern.

'Where I am now. I'll continue to run my businesses from the farm as much as I can so I can spend every spare moment with Mary and the children. And it's not as if Mary isn't prepared to travel. She's happy enough to spend a few days in Pontypridd from time to time.' He smiled deprecatingly. 'I even managed to get her there for a whole week last month when I had urgent business with the board and my solicitor, but by the end of it she was pining for the Beacons.'

'You're sacrificing a great deal to keep your wife and children happy.' She had a sudden stab of guilt. If she loved Micah so much, how could she allow him to carry on thinking that she wasn't free to marry him? Wasn't that tantamount to lying? And wasn't a lie doubly bad when it was told to the one person you loved above all others?

Harry smiled. 'No, I'm not. I've got what I wanted most out of life: the person I love, and the bonus of two adorable babies. I really am blissfully happy.'

'Doing all that travelling?'

'I get to see the country and when I get fed up of my car breaking down on country roads I can always take the train. I've no idea if it's true that the railway line was put into Craig y Nos for Madam Patti on the express order of the late king, but if so, I take my hat off to him. It's certainly made my life a lot easier.'

Edyth jumped up as a door closed downstairs. 'That will be Micah.'

'Does he have his own invitation to the opening?'

'Yes, so you could be his guest or mine,' she reassured him. 'We arranged to meet Judy's family and Micah's sister and Moody at the club.' She glanced at her watch. 'It's only a ten-minute walk down the road, and we're not due to meet them for another hour. Are you sure you don't want a sandwich before we go?'

'I had a huge tea in the store, but thank you for asking. I'm not cramping you and Micah's style by coming here, am I?' he asked when he heard Micah's step on the stairs.

'Far from it. And I'd like you two to get to know one another better.'

'He's a good bloke.'

'You never said that about Peter.'

'I never thought Peter was a good bloke.'

'He wasn't a bad one, either,' she said seriously.

'But he was no good for you, sis.'

'I hope that's not me you're talking about,' Micah said as he walked in.

'Who was it that said, "Eavesdroppers never hear any good about themselves"?' Edyth left her chair and kissed Micah lightly on the lips. 'Hungry, thirsty?'

'I could murder a glass of beer and a smoked pork sausage.'

'The beer I can manage, the sausage I can't.'

'But I can.' Micah pulled a packet from the pocket of his evening jacket. 'One of the sailors brought it in this afternoon. His mother made it and it tastes like heaven. Hello, Harry, good to see you.' Micah shook Harry's hand.

'It's good to see you too. I take it this sausage is already cooked.'

'No, we Norwegians like our food raw and bloody, didn't Edyth tell you?'

'Enough teasing. Beer and sausage, Harry?' Edyth asked.

'It will make an honorary Norwegian of you, and give you special Scandinavian powers,' Micah joked.

'If it will help me to persuade David to be sensible give me the smallest of small portions please, Edyth,' Harry answered.


'This dressing room is fabulous, the best I've ever seen.' Mandy laid out sticks of greasepaint on a marble slab. 'And I've played the London theatres. Not that I ever had a dressing room of my own, ever, and none of the shared ones were a patch on this. But I visited the star quarters for cast parties. And no matter how big the name they were never given a sitting room, a walk-in wardrobe for their costumes or a bedroom – and as for a bathroom with plumbed-in hot and cold water – that is real luxury.'

'This suite is identical to Mr James's office suite next door. Perhaps it was just as cheap to put in two as one.'

'I can't see that. The bath, toilet and washbasin alone must have cost a pretty penny without all those fancy tiles.' Mandy tied a silk kimono over Judy's dress to protect it. 'Sit down and I'll start on your make-up.'

Mandy picked up a stick of base foundation just as there was a knock on the door.

'You girls decent?' Aled called.

'I can't imagine what you think we're doing, Mr James,' Mandy answered.

Aled opened the door. He looked at the few inches of white silk showing beneath the black kimono. 'You decided on the white Grecian classical dress, Judy?'

'It was the one you suggested I wear on opening night,' Judy reminded.

'You don't have to do everything I say. Keep your robe on over your dress, there's something I'd like you to see in my office. Mandy, fetch some more vases from the storeroom, will you? I've a feeling the ones here aren't going to be enough to take all of Judy's bouquets.'

'Certainly, Mr James.' Mandy disappeared down the corridor.

Mystified, Judy followed Aled into his office. There was a window behind his desk and he had angled the Venetian blinds in front of it so he could look outside without being seen. He beckoned Judy forward.

'You see those people trying to get in to the club.'

Judy was already nervous and she began to shake when she saw the size of the crowd queuing to get in.

'There's hundreds.'

'I didn't bring you here to see the size of the crowd. But those people, there, on the right, with Aiden and Freddie. Recognise them?'

Judy saw half a dozen men and four women who appeared to be arguing with Freddie and Aiden.

'That woman seems familiar,' Judy murmured.

'She should do. She refused to serve us in the first department store we went in when we were buying your stage costumes. She and her colleagues are now getting a taste of what it feels like to be on the receiving end of discrimination.'

'You saw them trying to get in and sent Aiden and Freddie out to stop them?'

'No. I asked Aiden to make a note of the names of everyone in senior management in the store.'

'I remember.' She looked at him.

'I sent them complimentary tickets to the opening, to make sure they'd come.'

'You invited them just so you could turn them away?'

'Yes.' He saw the troubled expression on her face. 'You don't approve?'

'No, I know just how humiliated they feel. And they won't know why they are being turned away.'

'Yes they will.' He closed the blinds. 'I told Aiden and Freddie to tell them exactly why they are being turned away. I also told them to tell them that their complimentary tickets will be honoured on the day they start serving coloured people in their store and not before.'

'And you think that will make them change the store's policy?' Judy smarted at the memory of the supervisor referring to her and Aiden as 'people like that', but it still didn't make what Aled had done right in her eyes.

'I thought it was worth a try. You're obviously not so sure.'

She bit her lip. 'No, I'm not.'

'It was probably childish of me to want revenge, but from where I'm standing,' he flicked the blinds again so he could see out, 'it not only feels good, it feels right.'

'My grandmother used to say two wrongs don't make a right.'

'She was undoubtedly a wise woman and more generous and forgiving than me.' He looked at her. 'I'm sorry. I should have known you'd disapprove.'

'You're my employer. It's not for me to approve or disapprove of anything you do, Aled.'

'I wish you'd stop thinking of me as your employer,' he said seriously.

'That's difficult when you pay my wages.'

'You're going to open with "You're Driving Me Crazy".'

'I am.' She smiled, happy that he'd changed the subject.

He kissed her forehead. 'Go out there and kill them.'

'Break a leg, you mean,' Lennie shouted through the open door.

'Come in, Lennie,' Aled invited. 'I was just about to open a bottle of champagne.'

'I drink after a show, not before, thank you, boss.' Lennie came in and gave Judy an enormous hug. 'Not nervous, are you, darling?'

'A condemned man waiting for the hangman couldn't feel any worse,' Judy admitted.

'After all the rehearsing you've done, you could do your act in your sleep,' Lennie encouraged.

'Then why have I forgotten all the words to my songs?' Judy asked, suddenly panic-stricken.

'We'll go through them while I finish your hair and make-up,' Mandy said, coming into the room with a bouquet of two dozen roses. 'And while you recite them you can smell these. They've just arrived.'

'You've already filled the dressing room with white lilies and roses,' Judy reproached Aled.

'These are nothing to do with me,' Aled said. 'And my congratulatory bouquet won't be delivered to you until after the performance – and on-stage.'

'He's hedging his bets in case you corpse on-stage. If you do he'll save the florist's bill,' Lennie quipped. He saw Judy's stricken face. 'Sorry, bad joke. You're going to be fantastic.'

'Here's the card.' Mandy handed it to her. Judy opened

the envelope and read the message as she followed Mandy back to her dressing room.

*Sorry for all the arguing. If you sing like you did at the carnival, everyone in the audience will love you, including me, David Ellis.*

'Two dozen red rosebuds. Best quality.' Mandy smelled them before handing the bouquet to Judy after she'd sat down. 'Someone knows the way to a girl's heart.'

'Not really, they're from a friend.' Judy returned the card to the envelope.

'I've never had a friend send me two dozen red roses. Not a disinterested one, that is,' Mandy warned. 'Now, do we use the gold stick on your eyelids or the rich cream?'

# CHAPTER SIXTEEN

Harry waylaid a waiter, ordered a round of drinks for the table he, Micah and Edyth were sharing with the King family, Helga and Moody, then looked around for David. Edyth saw him turn his head.

'David's upstairs.' She glanced up at the mezzanine that ran around all four sides of the room.

'What's he doing up there?'

'The gaming machines and tables are there. David's been telling people that he's working the roulette table, but he's a kind of apprentice. Watching and learning.' Micah slipped his hand inside his collar and adjusted it.

Edyth saw the gesture and smiled. Despite the electric ceiling fans attached to the chandeliers it was even warmer inside the club than outside and all the men looked distinctly uncomfortable in their starched collars.

Harry rose to his feet. 'I think I'll have a quick walk round before the show starts.'

Micah rose alongside him. 'I'll come with you.'

'I'm happy on my own,' Harry said.

'I don't doubt you are, but I'm a pastor. It's my duty to see if any of my flock are here.'

'So you can hold an impromptu service?' Harry derided.

'I have my prayer book in my pocket.' Micah patted his dinner jacket.

'I take it Edyth told you about the threat Aled made,' Harry said as they walked up one of the staircases to the second floor.

'Yes,' Micah replied shortly.

'And that's why you're playing bodyguard?' Harry challenged.

'Hardly. Aled wouldn't dare try to hurt you or David in here. It's his home territory and far too public. The man's arrogant, knows who to bribe and operates on both sides of the law, but one thing he isn't is stupid.'

'As he's my half-brother, I don't know whether to take that as a compliment or not,' Harry said doubtfully.

'Good heavens above.' Micah stopped at the head of the stairs and stared at the array of mechanical and electric gaming machines Aled had installed on the second floor. 'I heard Aled had imported machines from America. I had no idea he'd brought in this many or that they'd be so . . . ' He blinked at the flickering coloured electric lights.

'Pretty?' Harry suggested.

'I suppose some people will think they are.'

'People who can afford to lose money, maybe,' Harry said doubtfully. 'But I can't imagine who they might be in this day and age.'

'People gamble, whether they can afford to or not,' Micah said flatly. 'Some idiot or other proves that adage every day on the Bay. There's David, over by the roulette table in the far corner. See him?'

'Yes.'

'And the Catholic priest is playing at the blackjack table. I'll remind him that he'll have to add gambling to his list of sins at his next confession.'

'See you downstairs.' Harry apologised to a group crowding around one of the electric machines, pushed his way past them and made a beeline for David.

David saw Harry coming. As soon as his brother-in-law drew close enough for conversation, he snapped, 'I'm working, Harry.'

'So I see,' Harry said. 'I wish I could get a job where I could stand and watch people.'

'I could be operating this table next Tuesday.'

Not wanting to antagonise David, Harry said, 'You must get a break some time. Can we talk then?'

'I'm on duty all evening.'

'Afterwards?'

'The club doesn't close until two o'clock, and then there's a staff party. I probably won't get away until three or four in the morning.'

'I'm staying the night with Edyth. Perhaps we could have breakfast together tomorrow in her rooms?' Harry persisted.

'I'll want a lie-in.'

'I'm not in a hurry to leave. The trains will be on Sunday service and won't start running regularly until the afternoon. You have to eat, so why don't you come to Edyth's for a late breakfast and lunch combined?'

'I may be busy.' David moved closer to the table and away from Harry but Harry refused to be deterred.

'If you won't meet me in Edyth's I'll get up early and camp outside your bedroom door. I'm sure Mrs Brown will let me into her house if I ask her. And I'll stay there for days if I have to.'

'You only want to lecture me.'

'I want to talk to you, not lecture you,' Harry countered. 'And you can't avoid me for ever. The more you try the more determined I'll become.'

'All right,' David conceded sullenly. 'I'll be at Edyth's tomorrow.'

'What time?'

'Around midday.'

'I'll be waiting. And I warn you now, if you're not there by one o'clock I'll come and find you.'

'Success?' Micah asked when Harry rejoined the others downstairs.

'David's agreed to talk to me tomorrow.'

'I wish you better luck than Edyth and I had.'

'I remember what it felt like to be David's age.' Harry sat at the table.

Micah laughed. 'You sound a hundred years old. Yet Edyth told me you're only twenty-five.'

'Twenty-six, but being married and having two children ages a man. There's nothing like responsibility to make you take life more seriously.'

'I can't wait to find out.' Micah saw Edyth's hand resting on the table and laid his over it. She saw him looking at her and turned away.

The curtain on the small stage rose. Lennie Lane walked on to an orchestral fanfare. Micah wondered if it was his imagination or if Edyth really was avoiding meeting his steady gaze.

While Judy was singing 'What is this Thing Called Love', Edyth looked around the nightclub. People who had been in the old Sea Breeze before and after the conversion had told her that the place was unrecognisable in its present guise. Given the Victorian layout of the other buildings she had visited in Bute Street, she could believe it. Aled James had ordered George Powell to rip out the centre of the building to create a ceiling that soared four storeys to a new glass done that had been placed over the centre of the roof. Four enormous glittering electric chandeliers hung from the perimeter, shedding diamonds of light that illuminated the furthest corners of every floor.

Judy's voice soared upwards, past the gamblers on the first- and second-floor mezzanines, who were leaning, games and gaming machines abandoned behind them, as they listened, rapt, to her singing, to the revellers who had walked to the topmost floor to view the interior of the club from the highest vantage point. If Aled was concerned that Judy's performance was affecting business, he gave no indication of it. He was standing on the ground floor close to the stage, his back to the bar, facing

Judy and the orchestra behind her, as absorbed as everyone else in the club.

Every one of the tables was full of meticulously groomed and expensively dressed revellers. And, although Edyth didn't know many people outside of Tiger Bay, she believed Harry's assurance that Aled James had attracted the cream of Cardiff Society and those who lived in the suburbs beyond.

Judy sang the last note. The orchestra died into the silence that occasionally follows an exceptional perform-ance, then Micah and Jed rose simultaneously to their feet and began applauding. Within seconds every person in the club was doing the same.

Lennie Lane walked on-stage, short, rotund and comic in contrast to Judy's slender, elegant classical figure.

'The Tiger Ragtime's headliner, ladies and gentlemen, Miss Judy King.' He held out his arm. The applause escalated to deafening proportions when some of the younger men began stamping their feet and whistling.

Judy took another bow and one of the chorus girls came on-stage with a massive bouquet of white roses. Judy took them and, overcome with emotion, fled from the stage.

'I apologise in advance on behalf of the management, ladies, gentlemen and gamblers,' Lennie pursed his tiny button mouth, which was almost lost between his chipmunk cheeks, 'but you will have to make do with me for the next ten minutes.' He cracked a dozen or so jokes before ending with a rousing rendition of 'Tiger Ragtime'; the audience joining in with his, 'Where's that Tiger . . . '

'Who's that Tiger . . . ?'

'Judy was a success.' Tony tried to refill everyone's glass from the bottle of champagne Aled James had sent to their table, but Harry and Edyth clamped their hands over the tops of theirs to prevent him.

'Did you doubt she would be?' Micah asked. 'She always was too good for the Bute Street Blues.'

'Speak for yourself,' Tony reprimanded with mock seriousness. 'I'm a consummate musician. It's not been easy all these years making allowances for you lot.'

'You wouldn't have had to make allowances if you'd been playing the same tunes as the rest of us,' Jed bit back.

Lennie finished his song. 'Our headliner, Miss Judy King,' he waited for the applause to die down, 'will return in one hour. Until then, please go upstairs and take a look at the machines and gaming tables – but I warn you, anything more than a look will cost you. For some lucky people that money will be repaid hundreds of times over and when it is, a crate of champagne to be marked "for the attention of mine host Lennie" and sent backstage will be very welcome. If you want a drink, please alert our waiting staff and they will be with you. If you want to dance, grab the prettiest lady next to you because if you don't,' he waggled his eyebrows suggestively, 'I will.'

Tony left his chair. 'Which of you gentlemen would like to take a tour of the upstairs with me to admire my carpentry?'

'None of them,' Tony's wife May answered for all the men at the table. 'Because they all know it's not your carpentry you want to admire, it's the gaming machines Mr James has had installed.'

'Are you accusing me of lying?' Tony asked blandly.

'Yes,' May replied bluntly.

'And you call yourself a Christian woman, May.'

'What has that got to do with anything?' May asked.

'Suspicion, suspicion,' he repeated, 'and me an honest man.'

'This is you, Tony King, we're talking about?'

'I've given you a month's wages. I'm heading out to

Argentina in two days. A man's entitled to a little relaxation.'

'Relaxation, yes. Gambling no.' May looked at the stage. The orchestra had struck up 'Putting on the Ritz' in foxtrot time. 'I can't think of a better way to relax than by dancing. Husband,' she extended her arm, 'the floor, please.'

'Good job I'm not a boxer or that request would have a different meaning.' Tony grimaced but followed her to the polished wooden floor in front of the stage where a few couples were already dancing.

'The star of the evening.' Jed rose to his feet as Judy approached and kissed her cheek. She had covered her dress with a white silk shawl. Her eyes were sparkling, but her hand shook when she took the glass of champagne Jed handed her.

'You were a triumph,' Edyth complimented sincerely. 'In a few years, people will be wanting to know us because we know you.'

'That will be the day,' Judy answered. 'I still can't believe we pulled it off. You should have heard the mistakes the orchestra and I made this afternoon. I don't know who hit the most wrong notes.' She sipped her champagne. 'I'm on again twice more this evening, but I only have two songs to sing after twelve o'clock and as they're the last of the evening and won't start until twenty minutes to two, I don't expect you to stay.'

'We wouldn't miss it for the world,' Edyth assured her.

'I won't be home much before dawn. Aled's organised a staff party, but he's such a perfectionist I've a feeling it won't be all congratulations. The last time I saw him he was talking to Aiden Collins about taking the rough edges off the table service and the entertainment.'

'I haven't noticed any rough edges on either!' Jed protested.

'That's because you don't own the club,' Judy replied. 'Lennie told me backstage that Aled's written a list of complaints three pages long to the orchestra leader. But as it's the first time they've performed together they're bound to get better.'

'It must be wonderful to only see the good side of everything,' Micah commented. 'I swear if the undertaker buried someone alive you'd say he was only practising and he'd get it right next time.'

'I would not,' Judy said indignantly.

'You were magnificent tonight; a credit to the Kings. Pearl King would have burst with pride if she had been here.' Jed slipped his arm around Judy's shoulders.

'Thank you, Uncle Jed.' Tears started into Judy's eyes at the mention of her late grandmother.

'And absolutely no sign of nerves,' Edyth added, knowing just how jittery Judy had been before she had left the house.

'It feels as though my whole life has been building up to this moment.' Judy's eyes shone, suspiciously damp. 'I still can't quite believe that it's actually happened.'

'Judy?' Aled walked up to their table. 'I'm sorry to break in on you when you're with your family and friends but a reporter from the *Western Mail* would like to a word with you.' He turned to the table, and managed to speak to Judy's uncles and aunts without apparently noticing Harry. 'I do apologise for taking her away.'

'We understand,' Jed said. 'Show business first.'

'Second and third,' Aled added. He signalled to a waiter. 'A round of drinks for this table.'

'You don't have to do that,' Harry and Micah objected at the same time.

'My pleasure and penance for monopolising the star. And don't worry about Judy getting home, Jed. Aiden and Freddie will take her and Mandy in the car.'

'Some mothers would worry about those two bruisers taking young girls home,' Jed's wife Bessie commented after Aled had whisked Judy away.

'Not with Aled James breathing down their necks and watching every move they make, they wouldn't.' Jed finished the champagne in his glass. 'Anyone else want a beer?' He looked around for a waiter.

'Two here, please, and I'm paying, seeing as how you got me in here for free.' Harry held his hand up and a waiter came running, Harry gave him an order and the man disappeared. The band finished the foxtrot and paused for a few seconds before sailing into the Charleston, which brought a crush of people on to the dance floor. 'If Aled James keeps people coming in at this rate, he's going to make a fortune,' Harry observed.

'He's certainly spent one to bring them in.' Micah glanced up at the glass dome and chandeliers. 'As for Judy, she's going places after tonight. No more Bute Street Blues Band for her, Jed, or probably us.'

'It couldn't have lasted, Micah. Tony and Ron are off to Argentina the day after tomorrow.'

'Not you?'

'No.' Jed looked at his wife. 'The captain didn't want any crew over forty on his boat.'

'That's tough,' Micah sympathised.

'Vic the beer, who runs the pub in our street, hasn't been too well lately and I do the odd shift to cover for him.'

'Not that the odd shift pays the rent but a little is better than nothing,' Bessie broke in. 'And word's got out that Jed is a passable barman. Once trade picks up in the dockside pubs more landlords might send work Jed's way.'

'It could be a while before the pub trade gets back to what it was a couple of years ago,' Micah said cautiously.

'We'll just have to tighten our belts a bit more. It's been easier since our Kristina has started working for you full time along with our Jamie, Edyth. And it's not all bad news. The boys are growing up into quite a handful. They're steady enough compared to some but they're at an age where it helps to have their father around to keep an eye on them. And that goes double for our Jamie,' Bessie said emphatically.

'He's a good delivery boy.' Edyth felt duty bound to come to Jamie's defence.

'And an argumentative son,' Bessie added.

'When push comes to shove, family is everything, even when everyone's quarrelling.' Jed cleared some of the champagne glasses so the waiter could set the beer on the table.

'It certainly is,' Harry agreed.

'And if you don't go to sea with Tony and Ron you'll be on hand to keep an eye on Judy as well as your own children,' Micah reminded.

'She's nineteen. I had been married three years and had three children when I was her age,' Bessie said tartly.

'I was married at eighteen,' Edyth said. 'And after the disaster that was my marriage, perhaps it's just as well that Judy's uncle is staying around to keep an eye on her.'

When Freddie hauled the third crate of champagne on to the table in the staff rest room, Judy and Mandy slipped away.

'I must be getting old,' Mandy yawned when she followed Judy into her dressing room. 'Only four in the morning and I'm ready to leave a party.'

'You and me both.' Judy closed the door.

'You have an excuse for being tired; you've been rehearsing all hours this week.'

'And you've been arranging my clothes.'

'As they were delivered in pristine condition and covered with calico, all I had to do was make a note of which was which on the covers, hang them on rails and set out your make-up.' Mandy opened a drawer in the dressing table, removed a sheet and shook it out on the floor. 'In the middle, please.'

Judy obediently kicked off her heeled shoes and stood

in the centre. Mandy took a large paper bag from the dressing-table drawer. 'This is just in case. We don't want to get greasepaint on the frock.' She slid the bag over Judy's head, unbuttoned the back of the frock and slipped the sleeves from Judy's arms. Judy wriggled out of the gown and stepped clear of it. While Mandy checked the frock for perfume and make-up stains Judy reached for her plain black cotton button-through dress.

'All this gown needs is an airing and a pressing before it's hung away. I'll do both on Tuesday.' Mandy hung the dress on a rail inside the door of the walk-in wardrobe. 'You should take some of these flowers home. The club won't be open again for two days and they'll soon die in this heat.'

Judy looked around the room. 'I'll take the red roses, the violets and the white roses. You take the mixed roses and lilies.'

'I didn't earn them.'

'Edyth's living room is very small. As it is I'll have to break up the roses and divide them between my aunts.'

'If you're sure.' Mandy buried her head in a bouquet and inhaled the scent.

'Miss King.'

'Come in, Freddie.' Judy had made friends with Freddie during the last week when she had spent every day rehearsing with the orchestra. She had discovered that beneath his rough exterior he could be a kind and gentle man.

'Boss sent me to drive Miss Mandy home to Grange-town.'

'Thank you, Freddie,' Mandy said gratefully. 'I couldn't walk a step.'

'You could drop me off on the way, Freddie,' Judy suggested.

'The boss is coming to see you, Miss Judy. He's talking to a man who has a radio show. They want you to go on it.'

'What did I tell you?' Mandy picked up her handbag. 'You're on your way to the top, kiddo.'

'Thanks, Mandy, and not just for saying that.' Judy gave her a hug.

'Then for what?'

'Calming me down and getting me on-stage in one piece.' Judy pushed the largest bouquet into her arms.

Mandy winked at her. 'Be nice to the radio producer. See you on Tuesday.'

Hoping Aled wouldn't be long, Judy looked at her flowers again and re-read David's card. Replacing it in the envelope she pushed it into her handbag and opened the door of her walk-in wardrobe. The rows of evening gowns, day frocks and fur coats hung shrouded like ghosts on the rail. On a shelf was the jewellery box that Aled had packed with expensive, well-designed pieces of glittering paste.

She had everything a rising singer could want and more. But she felt most peculiar. Flat – and somehow empty.

'Freddie and Mandy left the door open so I guessed you'd already changed.'

She turned. Aled was standing in the doorway behind her. 'Freddie said you were with someone from radio.'

'He's gone off with one of the chorus girls. I've arranged for us to have lunch with him on Monday – tomorrow.'

'I suppose it is, although Sunday hasn't dawned yet.'

'There was another reason I wanted to keep you here.' Aled removed a small box from his pocket and handed it her. 'Go on, open it.'

She lifted the lid on an exquisite pair of glittering gold and diamond drop earrings.

'They're not paste. That's real gold and real diamonds. I thought you'd like to have something more permanent than flowers to remind you of tonight.'

'Thank you seems inadequate. I was just looking at all

the clothes and—' She stopped mid-sentence and brushed her cheek. She couldn't believe it when she lifted her hand away. It was wet. 'I have nothing to cry about.'

'Except sheer bloody weariness,' he said. 'Sorry, that just slipped out. I've spent too much time around builders lately.'

'It did go all right tonight, didn't it?'

'You're asking me, after three standing ovations, each of which lasted a full five minutes.'

'We're in Tiger Bay. My home territory. That's just my neighbours being kind.'

'Not many of your neighbours could afford the few tickets that were sold after the invitations went out. The standing ovations came from the crache not the natives.'

'What if I never give another performance like that again? What if my voice goes and I . . . ?'

'What if you turn into a frog overnight? What if the sea rises and drowns Butetown? What if the world ends?' He laughed. 'Want a final glass of champagne? It might help you sleep.'

'No, thank you, I've had enough champagne. I'm too tired to think, yet I know that once I lie down I won't be able to sleep. I feel . . . restless . . . edgy . . . '

'You don't have to wait for Freddie to drive you home. I could walk you.'

'I'd like that,' she said gratefully. 'Just what I need. Fresh air and the smell of the sea.'

'It's the wrong way, but I could walk you down to the docks before you go back to the baker's.'

'Please.' She looked again at the earrings nestling on their bed of dark blue velvet. 'They're too grand for this frock.'

'They are,' he agreed. 'Put them in your handbag and wear them to lunch on Monday. You've put the key I gave you to the club safe?'

'Yes.'

'Wear one of the smart day frocks – the black one

299

might be best and the fur cape. You don't want the radio producer to think you don't know how to dress.'

'In case he thinks he can get me cheap. One of Mandy's maxims,' she explained when he looked puzzled.

'Mandy's right.'

'She knows everything there is to know about show business.' She lifted her old mac from the back of the door.

'If you took the fur cape you wouldn't have to come back for it.'

'I'd still have to come back for the frock. And it's a warm night. Too warm for furs. Besides, the cape is worth more than a year's wages to most people down here. I wouldn't blame someone for hitting us over the head to steal it. The pawn money would keep a family of twelve for six months.'

'So you're not going to enjoy wearing the furs?'

'To the right place perhaps, like the Windsor on Monday.'

'If you're that concerned about wearing them around the Bay I'd better send Freddie to pick you up.'

'If you do, people will think I'm flaunting your car as well as the cape.'

'So, you can't win with your neighbours. Is that what you're saying?'

'I doubt many of the women will consider the clothes you've bought for me as being of more benefit to the club than me.'

'But you'll wear them?'

'When it's appropriate and I'm on club business,' she said, remembering her conversation with Micah.

'Some women would enjoy showing off fine clothes and fur coats in front of their friends and neighbours.'

'I'm not "some women".'

'So I've discovered.' He took his cigar case from his pocket and lit one as they left the club. 'Last chance, home or to the sea?' he checked.

'The sea.' She looked up at the sky, the soft grey light of dawn heralded a new day, but the ghost of the full moon still hung low overhead, silvery pale and misty although the stars had faded.

They walked on down Bute Street in silence, passing sailors, Chinese gamblers and tarts clinging to the arms of the last customers of their night as they steered them back to their rooms. When they reached the end of the street they turned left towards the Pier Head and West Dock.

Judy folded up the collar of her coat against the breeze blowing in from the sea.

'I sense the first chill of autumn.' Aled drew on his cigar for the last time and tossed it into the water.

'The cold will be welcome after the heat of this summer.'

'I'll remind you that you said that next January. And I guarantee you'll have no qualms about wearing your fur coat then, if we decide to take an early-morning walk to the sea.'

She stood and stared at the giant hulls of the ships berthed in the Bay. 'When I was small I used to spend hours down here, wondering where the ships had been, where they were going, and trying to imagine all the things they had seen.'

'After spending time in various ports of the world, I think perhaps it's just as well that you couldn't imagine half of the things they'd seen,' he said dryly.

'Like that.' She indicated a group of sailors lying slumped on the pavement with their backs to the wall of the building behind them, empty bottles strewn round their feet.

'There are drunks and poverty in every port in the world; they attract the dross from miles around. Anyone capable of walking to one will, in the hope of making money, either working on board a ship or,' he glanced at an underdressed, over-painted woman who would never see middle age again, 'out of the sailors.'

'My grandmother tried to teach me to ignore the seedy side.' Judy looked towards the West Dock and the Norwegian Church. Even at that hour, the sound of singing emanated from the building.

'Micah Holsten must be holding a service.'

'That's an alcohol-fuelled sea shanty, not a hymn.' she smiled. 'Micah never refuses admittance to anyone, especially not to those who haven't the price of a bed in a doss house. His chairs aren't that comfortable, but they're under a roof and cleaner than the pavement.'

'Ready for bed now?'

She took one last look at the ships and realised that she was suddenly and desperately tired. 'No matter what problems I had when I was growing up, I believed that if I could get on one of those and sail away, I would leave all my worries behind. I remember telling Uncle Jed how I felt and he said that no matter how far someone sails, they take their troubles with them.'

'He was right,' Aled agreed.

'Did you take your troubles with you when you left here?'

'Who told you that I used to live on the Bay?'

'Everyone knows. I didn't realise it was a secret.'

'It's not. I left when I was a boy because my mother died. As I didn't have any other relatives my only problem was poverty. I thought the cure for that lay in the colonies, or so I must have been told on one of the rare days I attended school.'

'You made a fortune.'

'Not in the colonies.' He looked back up Bute Street. 'I never thought when I left that I'd be able to come back and book a suite in the Windsor.'

'You never went into the hotel when you lived here?'

'Did you before I took you?' he asked.

She laughed. 'I couldn't have afforded a cup of coffee

in there. And that's supposing they would have served me.'

'The closest I got to the Windsor when I was a boy was to stand outside and offer to shine the porter's shoes. Nine times out of ten he chased me off.'

'Is the same man on the door now?' she asked curiously.

'He's old enough, but if he is, he doesn't remember me and I certainly don't recall him.' He offered her his arm and they began to walk back up Bute Street. 'It's odd coming back here after so many years.' He looked around. 'Large and imposing as the buildings are, they look smaller than when I left. Perhaps I should have just taken a look at the place and moved on.'

'Do you regret investing all your money in the club?'

'No, and I didn't invest it all,' he corrected her. 'Walking down here at this time of day reminds me of the times I used to crawl out of bed and go to Penniless Point to look for work in the hope of earning enough money to buy breakfast. It makes me feel twelve years old again.'

'You can't mean that after tonight.'

'Yes, I can.'

'After the club opening and everything else?'

'How grown up do you feel?' he asked her.

'Not very,' she admitted. 'After Mandy helped me dress, did my hair and make-up, I looked in the mirror and felt as though I was playing dressing up.'

'And how old were you when you last played that game?'

'About twelve,' she said with a smile.

'So we're not that different after all.' They drew near Edyth's baker's shop and he followed her through the yard to the back door. 'You have two days off. What are you going to do until Monday lunchtime. Sleep?'

'Probably.'

'I'll send Freddie with the car at eleven o'clock on Monday morning. He'll take you to the club, wait while you change and bring you on to the Windsor. Lunch will be in my suite, but Lennie Lane and a few other people will be there. I take it that will be all right.'

'Yes.' She cringed. It was as though he had known about the warning her uncles had given her, never to go alone to his suite.

'Goodnight, my lucky star.' He wrapped his arms around her and kissed her. And that time she was left in no doubt as to its intensity – or his passion.

# CHAPTER SEVENTEEN

David sat in Edyth's sitting room and picked at the bacon, eggs, mushrooms and sausages she had put in front of him. Harry sat across the table, watching him eat while the food grew cold on his own plate.

'So, no matter what anyone says you intend to carry on working for Aled James as a bookie's runner?' Harry challenged, braving the silence that had fallen after he had brought up the subject.

'It's good money and a lot more than I ever earned working on the farm.'

'The farm is yours—'

'Was mine, Harry,' David corrected strongly. 'Now I've left, I want no part of it.'

'You do realise that you could end up in gaol?'

'Aiden Collins told me that he and Mr James will look after me. Aiden even gave me his card. He's an attorney, look.' David handed Harry the card.

Harry read it, then tossed it down on the tablecloth in disgust. 'I doubt very much if Mr Aiden Collins is an attorney at law, but even if he is, his qualifications wouldn't be recognised in this country. We have solicitors and barristers in Britain, not attorneys. And if you do get picked up by the police for running a book, I rather suspect Mr Aiden Collins and Mr Aled James will be nowhere to be seen.'

'You don't know them like I do, Harry.' Ignoring the tight knot that had formed in his stomach, David forked two mushrooms and half a sausage into his mouth.

Harry dropped his napkin beside his plate, rose from

the table and went to the window. He looked back at David. 'You really think Aled James will look after you?'

'Yes, I do,' David asserted.

'I assure you, the only person Aled James will look after is himself. And that's coming from his half-brother.'

Edyth glanced from Harry to David. She left her chair and picked up the teapot. 'This is cold, I'll make fresh.'

'You don't have to leave,' Harry said.

Edyth recalled what Helga had said about having to live with David after Micah had lectured him. 'This is between you two, not me.' She turned and looked back at David. 'No matter what happens, you are always most welcome here, David, you know that.'

David dropped his knife and fork on to his plate. 'Thank you.'

She left and closed the door behind her.

'You and Aled James are half-brothers? I know you look alike . . . '

'My real father, as opposed to my stepfather, wasn't averse to fathering bastards. And he didn't care what happened to them,' Harry said crudely, tired of making excuses for a father he had never known.

David turned bright red, not at the thought of Harry's father fathering bastards but at what he had been doing with Gertie. Now he had got to know her better, he didn't even like her. And the idea of her having his child, and bringing it up in Anna's house, horrified him.

'I'm sorry if I embarrassed you.' Harry returned to his chair and sat down.

'You didn't. It's just that . . . ' David had always found it easy to talk to Harry, even about personal matters, when they had both been living on the farm. But much as he wanted to discuss his mixed feelings about Gertie with someone, he felt that Harry wouldn't understand, not after all the warnings he had given him about loose women. And a confession about Gertie would only give Harry one more reason to be angry with him.

'What?' Harry asked eagerly.

'Nothing,' David mumbled, shame-faced.

'There's absolutely no point in my trying to talk to you, is there?' Harry asked irritably. 'You're not going to change your mind about working for Aled James.'

'Not until I find another job,' David agreed.

'And you won't be coming back to the farm.' It was a statement not a question.

'No, I won't.' David was surprised that Harry knew and accepted the fact. 'Does Mary know?' David picked up a piece of bread so he didn't have to look Harry in the eye.

'No.'

'She'll accept it, given time.'

'All of us can get used to almost anything given time,' Harry said finally. 'I did what I set out to do. I came down here and tried to talk sense to you. If you refuse to listen to me I can't make you.'

'I'm old enough—'

'To go to the devil in your own way, David. Yes, you are.'

'You've been talking to Micah Holsten, haven't you?'

'You saw us together last night, so of course we've been talking to one another,' Harry replied caustically.

'About me?'

Harry sighed. 'He told me that he'd had no luck in persuading you to stop working as a bookie's runner either.'

'And that's all he said?'

'You want more?' Harry's temper rose at David's selfish attitude and his lack of consideration for the feelings of his brothers and sisters. 'No matter what you think, the entire population of the world doesn't spend all its time talking about David Ellis.'

'I never thought it did.' David carried on buttering a piece of bread.

'And that's all you can say?'

David looked up and finally met Harry's steely gaze. 'What else do you want me to say, Harry?'

'Nothing.' Harry left his chair. 'I'm going to see if Edyth's made that tea.'

'Harry, if I could find another job that paid decent wages, I would take it,' David conceded.

'You could work in Gwilym James, here in Cardiff—'

'No family handouts,' David cut in, repeating what he'd said to Edyth. 'Besides, can you see me bowing and scraping and sirring and madaming customers?'

'No. But I can imagine you unloading stock.'

'You've given me and my family enough. I want to make my own way, Harry.'

'If one more person says that to me, I'll scream.' Harry opened the door.

David lifted the empty sugar bowl and waved it at Harry. 'Tell Edyth we need more sugar, will you please, Harry?'

Harry hesitated for a fraction of a second and David wondered if he'd pushed his brother-in-law too far. But Harry returned and snatched the sugar bowl.

'If you hadn't said please I would have smashed this over your head. You do know that?'

'I do now,' David said quietly.

'Oh, David, I want that blue dog. Please, it's absolutely darling . . . '

'It's also half a crown and it's not worth tuppence,' David said crossly. Bored and restless after leaving Edyth's, he had returned to Helga's to find everyone out. There was a note on the table asking him to join Helga and his fellow lodgers at the mission. Instead he had locked all his money except for a pound in silver in his suitcase and visited Gertie. After half an hour in her bed, she had persuaded him to take her on the short train journey to Barry Island so they could walk along the beach and visit the funfair.

'But it's adorable and it would look so-o-o good with all my other little kitties and doggies . . . '

'I'm not buying it for you, Gertie, so you can shut up about it.' Angry with himself for not parting on better terms with Harry; furious with Gertie for coming out with him dressed in the hallmark clothes and make-up of her profession; and irritated by her pleading to buy her every worthless knick-knack in sight, he was very close to losing his temper.

'This has been a horrible trip,' she snapped. 'The tide's in so there's no sand to sit on. The fairground is packed. There are queues at every ride worth going on and the fish and chips you bought me were cold.'

'They were hot when I gave them to you.'

'Then you put too much vinegar on them and that cooled them down.' She beamed at a couple of soldiers in uniform who were eyeing her. 'Hello, Tommies.'

'And hello to you, little lady,' one of them answered.

'If you want to go to work, go to work,' David snarled. 'You don't need me along.'

'A girl has to make a living.'

'I'm not stopping you from making it.'

'There are times when I think you don't care this much,' she clicked her fingers in the air, 'for me.'

'How can I care for someone who sees me as a money machine? Every time you take me up to your room you hold out your hand for half a crown.'

'Why, you . . . ' She slapped David soundly across the face.

'Trouble, little lady?' One of the soldiers wrapped his arm around Gertie's waist.

'How can it be trouble for her when she hit me?' David demanded rationally.

'Seems to me that a lady wouldn't hit a gentleman for no reason.' The soldier smiled at Gertie.

'Take the lady with my compliments, but I hope for

your sake that you have deep and well-filled pockets,' David said.

'I'll get you for that, damn you, David Ellis,' Gertie yelled at him as he walked away. 'You wait and see. I'll get you for that . . .'

With Gertie's threats ringing in his ears, David walked straight to the railway station. When he reached the ticket office, he reached for his wallet in his inside pocket. It wasn't there. He felt every pocket in his suit to no avail.

Cursing, because the wallet had been a present from Harry's parents, he searched his shirt pocket. He found sixpence. He looked up and down the road. There was nothing for it except to start walking.

'I've been conducting guests up to Mr James's suite all morning.' The porter straightened his sleeves when the lift reached the third floor of the Windsor Hotel and stepped back to allow Judy to precede him. Once they were out of earshot of the lift boy he started talking non-stop. 'You're the fifth person I've taken up in the last hour, madam. Mr Lennie Lane was the first to arrive. I saw him – and you, madam – in *Peter Pan*. You were both really good and it was a marvellous show. My little sisters couldn't stop clapping their hands to make fairies come alive for days. Mr Lane's a real card. He had the lift boy in stitches on the way up with his impressions of an angry train.'

'An angry train?' Judy repeated. Lennie had told her many jokes, but she had no recollection of an angry train.

The porter made a series of hooting noises. Judy listened politely although she didn't find them remotely amusing.

'Of course, it goes without saying that I'm not as good as Mr Lane.' He paused obviously expecting a reply.

'Few people could be.'

'Everyone on the Bay is talking about your performance in the Tiger Ragtime on Saturday night. I heard that you're better than Bessie Smith—'

'I don't think so,' Judy interrupted, blushing at the comparison to the famous American Blues singer.

'That's what my brother said. And he should know. He's working in the Ragtime as a barman. He said the place is bigger than most palaces and you could have heard a pin drop there when you were singing. And once the applause started there was no stopping it. He said that he and the other workers expected the roof to blow off.'

'Your brother works in the Tiger Ragtime?' After only a month 'on-stage' Judy was finding it easier to deal with criticism than praise and she was anxious to change the subject.

'Thanks to Mr James. He's made a real difference to me and my family – and not only in the tips he gives me here for the errands I run for him. We got to talking a couple of weeks back. I told him that my father had died at sea two years ago and my mother was finding it hard to make ends meet with seven of us at home and only me in work, so he told me to send my eldest brother Neil, to see Mr Aiden Collins. I did, and that's how our Neil got to be working in the Tiger Ragtime. Now there are two of us bringing home wages, the family's not doing too badly. My mother's even scraped together enough to get my eldest sister apprenticed to a tailor.'

'Who else have you taken up to Mr James's suite this morning?' Judy asked, curious as to the identity of Aled's other lunch guests.

'As I said, Mr Lane, and there was the estate agent, Mr Arnold, the builder, Mr Powell, Mr Peterson, the theatrical impresario – but as he stays here so often he's practically one of us – I mean the regular guests, not the staff. And,' he lowered his voice, 'a man from the BBC. The receptionist told me who he was. She said he compères the Monday-night music show on the wireless. And now you, madam. You're the last one I was asked to look out for. But you've spent so much time here with Mr James, the staff regard you as a regular as well.'

As Judy continued to follow the porter down the corridor to Aled's suite she wondered how she could have allowed herself to feel intimidated by the staff in the Windsor the night Aled had invited her and her family to dinner. The porter was so eager to please, that apart from the occasional 'madam', he reminded her of her young cousins when they were trying to coax pennies out of her to buy sweets. Recalling his mention of the tips Aled had given him, she debated whether or not to give him sixpence.

It hadn't occurred to her to give any of the staff money before. Whenever she had gone anywhere it would have been appropriate to tip, she'd been with Aled, and he had put his hand in his pocket. Then she remembered her uncles and their families, and decided that if she had any pennies to spare, they should go in their direction.

The porter knocked on the door of Aled's suite and showed her in. A waiter was serving drinks, but Aled rose to his feet as soon as she entered.

'Judy, looking lovely as always.' Aled took the fur cape he had insisted she wear and handed it to the waiter who carried it into the bedroom. 'Gentlemen, I think after Saturday night you all remember Miss Judy King.'

Stan Peterson was the first to grab her hand. Instead of shaking it, he kissed it. 'I hear you were a great success on Saturday. I'm only sorry I wasn't able to see your debut, but it was the opening night of *The Student Prince* in the New Theatre and as the producer I had to be there.'

'Was the show a success?' Judy asked.

'Not as much of one as *Peter Pan*,' Stan admitted ruefully, 'and we've nowhere near the same number of advance bookings. We'll be lucky if it runs two weeks and covers the cost of the scenery. Old Heidelberg doesn't come cheap.'

Aled moved Judy on. 'Mr Raymond Smith, the radio producer.'

'Everyone calls me Ray, Judy, and I was at the club on Saturday night. That's quite a talent you have there. I'm sure our listeners will go for it. I was just telling Aled that you must come down to our London studio. If you travel on Sunday, we can rehearse on Monday, transmit Monday night and you can travel back on Tuesday in time to play the Ragtime on Tuesday night.'

'I didn't know it was settled,' Judy said to Aled.

'It isn't – yet.' Aled signalled to the waiter to refill everyone's glasses. 'The final decision rests with you.'

'But before you make it, please consider, no matter how large an audience you have in the club, if you broadcast you will be reaching at least a thousand times that number and probably more, Miss King,' Ray said earnestly.

'I don't need any persuading on that score. Radio is every performer's dream booking,' Judy smiled.

'It is,' Lennie agreed, 'which is why I need you to persuade Ray that we come as a package, Judy. Beauty and the Beast.'

'More like Snow White and the smallest dwarf,' Stan broke in.

Judy thought the reference to Lennie's height cruel, but Lennie was the first one in the room to laugh.

'Miss King,' George Powell shook her hand, 'it's a pleasure to meet you after seeing you on stage on Saturday. I thought Mr James too exacting over the specifications of the club until I saw you perform. Then I realised he wanted everything to be perfect to do justice to you.'

'If the club is perfect, Mr Powell, that has to be down to your efforts.'

'And the men who work for me,' he said, knowing that three of Judy's uncles had been part of the building team.

Aled moved her on. 'You must know Mr Arnold?'

Judy knew of Geoff Arnold, as did everyone on Tiger Bay, but the estate agent hardly moved in the same circles she did. She shook his hand.

'And me, darling, we may have already spoken but I insist on being in the receiving line.' Lennie held out his arms and tried to sweep Judy off her feet as much as anyone six inches shorter than she was could have. When he failed, he stood on tiptoe and kissed her cheek instead. 'Now, come and sit next to me.' He dropped on to the sofa and patted the cushion beside him. 'We'll both have a nice *large*,' he eyed the waiter, 'glass of the Windsor's excellent sherry as an aperitif and I'll try out all the new jokes I've written on you.'

'Knowing you, Lennie, on all of us.' Aled watched the waiter serve Judy a sherry and the rest of the guests another round of drinks.

There was a knock at the door and two waiters entered to put the finishing touches to a circular table that had been set up in front of the window.

'So what does it feel like to be an overnight success, Judy?' Ray asked.

'Like most overnight successes, Judy has been working very hard to achieve that end for some time.' Aled looked at her. 'Am I right?'

'I've been singing with my uncles' band, the Bute Street Blues for the last four years.' She sat next to Lennie to stop him patting the cushion and looking at her with imploring eyes.

'How old were you when you started?' Ray took the chair opposite them.

'Fifteen, but I was singing before then, in school and church concerts.'

'And how old were you when you cracked your first joke, Lennie?' Stan asked.

'The minute I was born. My mother took one look at me and didn't stop laughing for a week. Apparently I looked exactly like my father. For years afterwards she said her only consolation was that I'd been born a boy.' Lennie pulled down a lock of his bright red hair and squinted up at it. 'She said she had nightmares for years at the thought of a fat round female dwarf with carrot-coloured plaits.'

One of the waiters coughed discreetly. 'Lunch is served, Mr James.'

Aled took charge. 'Judy, you sit next to Ray. Lennie, you'll never allow anyone to talk serious business anywhere near you, so you may as well sit on Judy's left. Gentlemen, shall we start?'

The men waited for Judy to sit before taking their seats.

'Knights of the round table, I give you Guinevere.' Lennie raised his glass to Judy and all the men toasted with him.

'I suppose that makes Aled King Arthur,' Stan leered suggestively, to Aled and Judy's annoyance.

'Hardly, they're not married so he can't be Arthur.' Lennie looked at the first course the waiter was serving. 'Salmon mayonnaise, how yummy. I l-o-v-e pink food. Of choice that's all I would eat.'

'You'd starve,' Judy said, grateful to Lennie for switching the conversation from her and Aled.

Lennie considered for a moment. 'As well as salmon, prawns and shrimps, I could eat blancmange, rare beef and lamb and raspberries.'

'All together in the same sandwich no doubt,' Aled chipped in facetiously.

'No – well, not unless it was sandwiched together with the pink bits of a Battenberg cake and raspberry jam. Want me to make one for you?' Lennie pursed his mouth and rolled his eyes upwards.

'No thank you. And unless you want someone to be ill,

I suggest you drop this conversation.' Aled passed the salt down the tables.

'To go back to the Round Table theme, Lennie, who do you see yourself as?' Ray asked.

'That's easy.' Lennie reached for Judy's hand and kissed the back of it. 'Lancelot, I couldn't possibly be anyone else. My great good looks wouldn't allow it. Besides, he's by far and away the one with the happiest ending. He outlived Arthur and got the love of Guinevere—' The end of his sentence was drowned by laughter.

'Lancelot could have been small,' Lennie said with mock seriousness.

'Did you take lessons from Little Tich?' Ray asked. 'He's the only other comedian I've heard of who made capital from his lack of height.'

'I saw him on stage once when I was even shorter than I am now. Knee high to a footlight as it were,' Lennie answered. 'But to go back to serious matters. You need me on your wireless show, Ray?'

'Why?'

'As a foil to Judy's glorious voice. First rule of show business: the crass always alternates with the divine. You can't give an audience too much of a good thing. They'll go on expecting it, and then where will you be? Set an impossibly high standard and you'll soon be stuck for acts. You'll be spending the next ten years scouring the countryside for more Judys, and take my word for it,' he added conspiratorially, 'without success. Our Judy is one of a kind.'

'That I believe.' Ray looked at Judy.

She shivered at the thought of the power Ray wielded. He seemed a nice, ordinary man. She found it most peculiar to think that her voice could be beamed into every home in the country that possessed a wireless, on his say-so.

Lennie's non-stop banter continued throughout the second course of roast chicken, bread sauce, asparagus in cream sauce and potato chips. Aled sent frequent signals to the wine waiter who had remained to replenish their glasses with iced champagne, hock and, when they insisted on it, water. And by the time they began eating the final course of cherry flan and cream, Lennie wasn't the only animated person at the table.

'All right, Mr Lane, I admit defeat, you're a natural and I'm impressed.' Ray pushed his empty dessert plate aside. 'You're welcome to accompany Miss King to London.'

'As her squire, boot boy, footman or bodyguard?' Lennie demanded.

'All four if it makes you happy,' Ray answered.

'And when we get to the studio?'

'I'll give you two two-minute compère slots.'

'How much air time is Judy getting?' Lennie looked enquiringly at Ray.

'Four four-minute song slots.'

'I know my place.' Lennie rubbed his hands together in a Uriah Heep impression. 'She's the star and I'm the lowly link. But I know how to be grateful for small mercies – and cheques.'

'I'll make it my business to see that you get exactly one quarter of what we pay Miss King,' Ray assured him.

'And all expenses paid to London? That includes a first-class ticket on the train and a room in the same hotel as Judy. Make it a good one. I want to be on the same floor as her, not packed off into the attic or the cellar just because I'm small.' He shed a few of the crocodile tears that he had honed during the *Peter Pan* run when Jeremy's Captain Hook had bullied Smee.

'I'll tell the hotel: no cellars or attics,' Ray said seriously.

Judy found Ray and Lennie's banter amusing, but she couldn't help noticing that Aled, Geoff Arnold and George Powell had been engrossed in a private conversation throughout most of the lunch and she wondered what they had found to talk about now that the club was built.

The waiters cleared and removed the table after dessert and coffee. The wine waiter offered petits fours, more coffee and brandy in the sitting area, but Ray was already looking for his hat. He retrieved it from Aled's bedroom, glanced at his watch and made his apologies.

'I'm sorry, Aled, but I have to get back to London. I've fixed a tentative date with Judy and Lennie for the middle of next month. I'll get my secretary to confirm it in writing when I return to the office. You'll be travelling up with Miss King and Mr Lane?'

'That depends on pressure of business.' Aled opened the door for the waiters who were carrying out the last of the glasses, plates and empty bottles.

'I hope you can come, but I'll understand if you can't. Dinner in Claridge's, on me, if you can make it?'

'That bribe is enough to make me try very hard to clear my diary.' Aled shook hands with him.

'Goodbye, everyone,' Ray called out and left.

Geoff Arnold, George Powell and Stan Peterson took the producer's departure as their cue to leave and, as Lennie had already wangled an invitation from Stan to go backstage to the New Theatre to see an old friend who was playing Kathie in *The Student Prince*, the four men left together. Aled shut the door on them and looked at Judy.

'And then there were two,' he said lightly.

'There'll soon be one, because it's time I was going too.' She looked around for her handbag.

'Because you have something to do this afternoon or because your uncles warned you never to be alone with me in my suite.'

'How did you know . . . ?' Her voice trailed in embarrassment.

'Because it's what I'd say to my daughter if I had one. I would never allow a girl of mine to remain alone in a hotel room with an unscrupulous scoundrel – or, in Tiger Bay terms, a wide boy like me. Do you have something arranged for this afternoon?' he reiterated.

'No, but I've a rehearsal booked with the orchestra for tomorrow morning to see if we can iron out some of the problems you listed on Saturday, so thought I'd go through my song scores this afternoon.'

'The problems aren't with you, they're with the orchestra. It was the musicians who were hitting the wrong notes.' He poured himself another brandy and held the bottle up to her.

'No, thank you.'

'Sherry?'

'I'm not used to drinking alcohol, especially in the middle of the day.'

'I'm glad to hear it. Stan Peterson told me that there's nothing like drink to ruin a singer's voice, and given the number of people he's worked with, he should know.' He sat next to her on the sofa. 'I think that lunch went well. Ray was keen on getting you on to his variety show. I'm not sure he was as keen on hiring Lennie but I knew that once Lennie met him, Ray wouldn't stand a chance. Lennie's an expert at wangling himself jobs.'

'It was good of you to introduce us to Ray, Aled. After all, there's nothing in it for you.'

'That's where you're wrong. When you get to know me better you'll realise that I never do something for nothing. It's not in my mercenary nature. You will be introduced on air as the headliner from the Tiger Ragtime in Butetown and Lennie as the compère. That should boost attendance at the club.'

'How much do you want to boost it?' she asked. 'The place was bursting at the seams on Saturday.'

'Only because I gave out two hundred free invitations to the crache. The Ragtime needs more publicity if it is to become the "must be seen at" place in south-east Wales. And if you'd read your contract properly you'd know that I get ten per cent of any fees you're paid for outside performances – and that includes wireless.'

'I know, but I doubt ten per cent of my fee would pay for one of the evening gowns you bought for me.'

'It would pay for two actually, but who's counting.' Aled propped his legs on the coffee table in front of him.

She looked at him, sensed what was about to happen between them but felt powerless to prevent it. He leaned towards her and kissed her. She was aware of the sensation of his lips, warm and tender on hers, his hands cupping her face, his thumbs caressing the soft sensitive skin beneath her ears.

Thoughts whirled around her head without coherency, pattern or reason. Aled was everything she had ever dreamed of in a man: handsome, wealthy, not that she had ever thought that much about riches until she had seen firsthand the lifestyle it could buy. Rooms in the best hotels, fine clothes, service and deference, which after her experience in the first store she and Aled had tried to shop in she had learned to value.

Aled was well travelled, commanded respect from everyone he came into contact with – she tried to forget the existence of Aiden and Freddie. He was worldly, sophisticated, knew how to get the best from people, and yet had none of the airs and graces she associated with the Welsh crache. And because he, too, had grown up in Tiger Bay he understood her and seemed to know instinctively how she felt and what she was thinking.

'That was you kissing me back?' he checked when he finally released her.

'Yes,' she whispered.

He looked into her eyes. 'I don't want you to climb into my bed out of a misplaced sense of gratitude. I meant every word I've ever said to you. What I've done for you I've done for myself and my club, not you. But,' he touched her lips with his fingertips, 'you're very beautiful and beautiful young girls always have had an overwhelming effect on me.'

She continued to look into his eyes. The moment was so unlike any she had imagined, she didn't know what to say. Whenever she had thought about making love for the first time, she had imagined being swept up in a moment of wild unrestrained passion, not sitting calmly discussing the situation with the object of her desire in a suite in the Windsor Hotel.

His eyes, deep blue and teasing, gazed relentlessly into hers. Before she had time to think of a reply, he kissed her again, and that time his hands roamed over her body, evoking strange new sensations that sent the blood coursing headily around her veins.

The palms of his hands burned her skin through the thin silk of her dress. He caressed her back, her breasts, and she wasn't even aware that he had unbuttoned her bodice until her dress fell open to her waist. Her cheeks burned when he slipped down the sleeves and the thin straps of her petticoat exposing her breasts.

'Perfect.' He thumbed her nipples and kissed each in turn. 'Shall we continue this in the bedroom?' he whispered huskily. Without waiting for her to reply he lifted her in his arms, carried her through to the bedroom and dropped her on to the bed. He locked the door behind them.

He undressed her slowly, sensuously, his hands lingering over her naked thighs and breasts. And when he had finished he turned back the bedclothes and laid her in the centre of the bed, watching her, while he stripped off his own clothes. He continued to look into her eyes, when he lay beside her.

He caressed her again, slowly, tenderly until the moment her passion rose to meet his. Then he lifted her on top of him. She cried out.

'I'm sorry . . . I should have been gentler . . . you're a virgin . . . '

Tears lay wet on her cheeks. His face was blurred but she could see that his eyes were still focused on her. 'It's all right, Aled. It really is. I love you.'

'Darling little Judy.'

It wasn't until afterwards, when they were lying, spent, side by side in the bed, that she realised that he hadn't spoken one single word of love to her. Or if he had, he had whispered it too softly for her to hear.

# CHAPTER EIGHTEEN

David was enjoying a late lunch of pie and beer at a secluded corner table in the Gentlemen Only bar of the Mount Stuart pub, the nearest public house to the dock gates in Bute Crescent. He had gone there at Freddie's suggestion after helping Aiden supervise the morning bar stocktake at the club. Someone had told Freddie that the Mount Stuart was the first stop sailors made after leaving their ships and that there might be a few punters among the newly arrived crews.

David was filling out his second betting slip of the day when Gertie burst into the bar, flanked by a 'rookie' constable.

'That's him,' she screamed, pointing her finger at David. 'That's the bookie's runner. Look, he's filling out a betting slip right now.'

'Gertie, out!' the barman shouted. 'No ladies or,' he gazed frostily at her, 'any of your sort allowed in here.'

'What do you mean, my "sort"?' Hands on hips, she rounded on him.

'Let's see that book, boy.' The constable, who looked no older than David, walked up to the table and snatched the book from David's hands.

'You can't do that,' David blustered. 'That's my property—'

'Is it now?' The constable removed a notebook and pencil from his top pocket and repeated as he wrote. *'When I removed said book from the table, suspect said, That's my property . . . '*

The man who had been placing the bet slunk away

323

under cover of the altercation and David wished that he could have done the same.

'Tut tut tut.' Keeping a firm grip on the book, the police officer walked to the door, opened it and blew his whistle. 'I'm surprised at you,' he said in a disappointed tone to the barman. 'Allowing a bookie's runner to do business in the Mount Stuart. The sergeant won't be pleased. He told all of us newcomers that this was a well-run house.'

'It is, when you coppers don't come in here looking for trouble. And that's a dark corner he's sitting in. I couldn't see what he was doing.'

'Or the men walking up to him, I suppose?' the officer demanded in a sceptical tone.

'People come into pubs to have a friendly chat. Fine barman I'd be if I asked them what they were talking about.'

Two more officers rushed through the door. They stopped and looked round. 'Where's the fire?' one of them asked the rookie.

'Here.' The officer grabbed David's arm. 'On your feet.' He hauled David upright and handed the betting book over to the oldest constable. The constable flicked through it.

'My, my, my, it's amazing the things people do in pubs in broad daylight. And right under our noses.' He looked at David. 'We're going to take a little stroll to the Maria Street police station, boy. You too, Gertie.' He nodded to his colleague who grabbed Gertie just as she was about to sidle out of the door.

'Let me go!' Gertie shouted ineffectually at the constable who clamped his hand on her arm. 'I told you what you need to know. You caught him red-handed. You don't need me.'

'We always need people who give us tip-offs, Gertie,' the senior officer said. 'And I'll tell you something else.' He placed his head very close to hers. 'Anna Hughes isn't going to like this. She'd rather die than grass on anyone in the Bay, even a customer who bilked her. As for you, boy,' he turned to David, 'you should have paid the lady what she wanted.'

'I did, and she stole the rest.' David gave Gertie a contemptuous look. 'Bloody tart wanted every penny I had and she got it. Cleaned me out last night. Took my wallet, my train tickets and almost a quid—'

'No swearing now, boy,' the constable admonished, 'or we'll have to charge you with using indecent language as well as running a book. As for your wallet, you got any proof the lady took it?'

'She was with me in Barry Island. We quarrelled, I left her and when I got to the station it was gone.'

'You walked through the fairground? Pushed your way through the crowds?'

'It was crowded there,' David admitted.

'Then any one of a hundred people could have taken your wallet. Did you report it stolen to the police in Barry?'

'What was the point?' David asked.

'The point is we often get the wallets back. Not the contents, just the wallets. They can incriminate a thief. Give me a description?'

'Black, calfskin. Two pockets at the back for notes, there was ten bob in it and about another eight or nine shillings in a button down pocket for change.'

'Any distinguishing marks?'

'My initials, DE, in gold in the bottom left-hand corner. It was a present,' David said defensively.

'We'll send the description to Barry the next time we contact them. You never know, something might turn up. You got anything else you want to say in your defence?' the middle-aged officer asked.

'Just one thing.' David handed him Aiden's card, which he always kept in the top pocket of his shirt. 'I want my attorney.'

'We don't have those, but one of us will go down and get Mr Aiden Collins, if that's who you want to see, boy. But now it's time to introduce you to the delights of our Maria Street station and the cells.'

'You're not putting me in no cell,' Gertie screamed.

'We don't put witnesses in the cells, Gertie,' the officer said cheerfully. 'They get nice comfortable interview rooms, with tea and ciggies on tap so they can tell us everything they know. Like who exactly put you up to shopping this boy.'

Judy woke to see Aled standing next to the bed in a white bathrobe. His hair and face were wet and he was holding out the largest and thickest white towel she had ever seen.

'I thought you might like a bath so I ran you one.'

'Thank you,' Judy folded back the bedclothes and blanched. 'I'm sorry, there's blood on the sheets.'

'Don't concern yourself. I'll telephone housekeeping, they'll come up and change the bed.'

'Then they'll know—'

'One of the reasons I live in an expensive hotel is to buy discretion. Here.' He wrapped the towel around her and held her close. 'Thank you, that was a very nice after-lunch interlude.' He kissed her and pushed her gently towards the bathroom door. 'Bath salts are in a blue and gold jar on the windows sill. I'll be in to wash your back . . . '

'Don't you dare. What if someone comes and sees you?'

'One, no one can get into the suite unless I allow them to. And two, after what we've just done there can't be any modesty between us, can there?'

'No,' she said cautiously, 'I suppose there can't.'

'There's tooth powder and new toothbrushes in the cabinet.' He picked up her handbag and handed it to her. 'Presumably you'll need your hairbrush, cosmetics and perfume.'

'Thank you.'

'I'll leave your clothes on the chair.' He slicked back his wet hair with a comb.

She started, dropping her handbag. 'Was that a knock at the door?'

'It was, but the outside door.'

'The hotel staff know I'm still here . . . '

'I told you I pay for their discretion. Go into the bathroom. Lock the door. I'll deal with this.'

'Please don't.'

'Why ever not?'

Whoever was at the door knocked a second time.

'You're in a dressing gown in the middle of the day, Aled.'

'I have been known to take a bath in the afternoon and even sleep when I'm tired. But I have never been known to explain myself to anyone.' He left the bedroom and closed the door behind him.

Judy listened at the door for a moment, heard Aiden's distinctive voice and did as Aled had suggested.

The first indoor bathroom Judy had ever used was the small downstairs one in Edyth's house and it was positively utilitarian compared to the luxurious brass fittings, mahogany dados, and thick white-tiled splendour of Aled's. She found the jar of salts he had mentioned and added a handful of the turquoise crystals to the water. The room was immediately filled with the scent of violets. She dropped the towel, stepped into the warm water and slid down, luxuriating as the warmth stole through her body.

She lay back and closed her eyes. Aled had been so gentle – so practised – she realised. But she could hardly expect a man like him to be as naïve and innocent as her. And it was only now, when she relived every kiss, every caress and every tender touch, that she was acutely conscious that he hadn't uttered one word of love. Not even a murmur that could be mistaken for one. But then she couldn't imagine any of her uncles saying anything that they would have regarded as 'soppy' to her aunts, not even in their most private and passionate moments.

Love wasn't a word men used easily. But no man could make love to a woman the way Aled had to her and not feel something for her. Could he?

'You're sure about this?' Aled asked Aiden.

'I asked the constable who came to find me. He said that a rookie had been given information by one of Anna's tarts, a young girl called Gertie. She'd even taken the rookie to the Mount Stuart to point out the bookie's runner, so he wouldn't arrest the wrong man.'

'And the runner was David?'

'Yes, and he was there at Freddie's suggestion.' Aiden looked at Freddie who was standing uneasily in front of the door, shifting his considerable weight from one leg to the other.

'You told David to go to the Mount Stuart?' Aled asked sternly.

'Yes, boss.'

'Why?'

'Because this young girl came up to me and said she knew sailors who'd just come in and wanted to place some bets but couldn't find any runners to place them with.'

'Gertie?' Aled asked.

'Don't know her name, boss. She was really young. Looked about fifteen. I thought she was straight . . . '

'It's not your fault, Freddie, but for future reference, don't assume that anyone, man or woman or child, in the Bay is straight.' Aled went to the telephone. 'Aiden, you go down to Maria Street, see if you can find any of the coppers we know, and organise bail for David and any other of our boys they've picked up. I'll call my solicitor and get him to meet you down there. Freddie, get the car.'

'We going somewhere, boss.'

'Yes,' Aled said shortly. 'To Anna Hughes's house to ask Gertie exactly who put her up to wrecking our turf.'

David stood back as the officer unlocked one of the reinforced metal doors in the stone wall of a corridor that was studded with a dozen or more just like it. Humiliated and battered by a rough strip and body cavity search, and the confiscation of all his personal belongings, including his watch, cuff links, belt, shoelaces and money, he felt totally demoralised. The constable yanked out the enormous bunch of keys and heaved the door open. He took a small key from a chain on his belt, unlocked the handcuffs from David's wrists and pushed him into the cell.

David shivered from more than the chill in the air when the door slammed shut behind him and the ratchets turned home. He blinked to adjust to the gloom. A narrow steel bench, six feet long, was secured by chains and bolts to the stone wall on his left. Ahead of him a set of metal bars fronted a strip of window that bordered the ceiling, but the glass beyond it was so thick with grime it was impossible to see anything except the dirt. He took a step forward. Behind the steel bunk stood a metal bucket with a lid. Then, he sensed he wasn't alone.

He turned to his right. A second steel bench, identical to the first, was fastened to the wall opposite him. Two young men were sitting silently on it, two feet apart, their backs against the wall, their faces dull and expressionless. David recognised them: they had both been fellow students at Aiden's 'turf school' in the White Hart.

David had never spoken to either of them but he found their presence reassuring after the casual, jocular brutality of the police officers.

He ventured, 'Hello.' When that drew no response he added, 'How long have you been here?'

One man made a razor movement across his throat

with his finger. His companion covered his mouth with his hand and pointed to the door. David nodded that he'd understood and sat on the empty bunk. He propped his back against the wall and the cold from the stone seeped through his suit jacket into his bones. Emotionally drained by the shock of his arrest, mortified by the process that had taken away every shred of his dignity and terrified by what the immediate future might bring, it required more strength than he could muster to sit upright.

Somewhere, outside the door, he could hear a woman screaming and a man shouting. A drunk was singing 'Land of Hope and Glory', his voice wavering from an overdose of alcohol and emotion.

David had been locked up a dozen or so times in his life. Once in a workhouse ward when he'd had his younger brother, Matthew and twenty other boys for company; and afterwards, when the workhouse had hired him out to a farmer who had imprisoned him in a cellar every night. Accustomed to the wide-open spaces and fresh air of the Breconshire hills, he had hated the loss of freedom and ever since, any kind of confinement made him feel physically ill. The cell wavered about him and his chest grew tight as he struggled to draw breath into his lungs.

Despite the cold, his skin burned and his mouth was dry. He unbuttoned his collar, breaking a stud in the process. It dropped to the flagstone floor with a rattle he was certain could be heard outside the cell but neither of his companions moved a muscle.

He stared up at the strip of light that was their only link to the outside world. While he was debating whether or not to walk over to it in the hope of seeing into the street, one of the men left the bench and walked to the bucket in the corner. He lifted the lid and a foul stench permeated the still, damp air.

Used to mucking out the cow sheds and pig sties on the

farm, David still gagged. He tried to hold his breath. But the smell seeped into his nostrils, nauseating, polluting his lungs and mouth. He retched and turned his head sideways, spewing the beer and pie he had eaten in the pub on to the steel bunk.

The man sitting opposite him rose and hammered his fist on the door. A barred grill opened at eye level.

'What's the noise about?' a gruff voice demanded.

'Sick man in here.'

A few minutes later the door opened and a constable handed David a bucket and mop. 'You made the mess, son, you clean it up.'

Trembling, weak and shaky, David staggered to his feet. He wiped the back of his mouth with his hand. 'How long am I going to be kept here?'

'As long as it takes, boy.'

'Have you sent for ... ?' David couldn't remember what Aiden had called himself but he did recall that the police hadn't been impressed by the American word. 'Mr Aiden Collins?'

'We've sent for him.' The constable pointed to the mess David had made. 'When you've finished, knock on the door. I'll bring you a bowl of water so you can wash your face,' he added, not unkindly.

David set about mopping the bench, which wasn't easy. The mop had a long handle and it proved difficult to wield without hitting the walls. And the whole time he mopped, he felt faint and was forced to lean against the wall simply to remain upright.

His fellow cell mate finished using the bucket and replaced the lid. David wasn't sure whether it was his imagination or the stench really lingered in the air. His second companion had returned to his seat on the bunk and retreated back into his self-contained, uncommunicative state. The constable returned with a bowl of water. He dumped it on the bench David had finished cleaning.

'No soap and towels, but the water's cold.'

David plunged his head into it and ran his fingers through his dark curls, pushing them away from his face.

Another officer loomed in the doorway. He pointed to the man sitting on the bunk. 'You, follow me.'

David went to the door.

'Not you, boy.' The constable who had given him the water pushed him back. 'Your turn will come.'

'Can I stand out here, just for a minute?' David begged as he gulped in mouthfuls of air. The corridor stank of institution disinfectant but compared to the cell it was a rose garden.

'Not even for a minute, boy.' The officer placed the palm of his hand on David's chest and pushed him back into the cell. David winced when he heard the key turn and the ratchet drop home again.

'The worst sound in the world.'

David looked to his remaining companion.

'The last time they caught me running a book I got six months' hard labour.'

'Six months!' David didn't even want to try to imagine being locked up for that long. 'Mr James told me no runner of his had ever gone to gaol.'

'Very probably that's true.' The man then made the same observation Judy had. 'But then Aled James has never run a book in the jurisdiction of the Maria Street police station in Tiger Bay before.'

Swathed in the massive towel, Judy left the bathroom to find Aled still in his bathrobe, talking on the telephone. He saw her standing in the bedroom and closed the living-room door. Ten minutes later he walked into the bedroom and, oblivious to her embarrassment, stripped off his robe, and opened the wardrobe door.

'I have to go out and I need the car. I'll ask the desk clerk to order a taxi to take you back to Edyth Slater's.'

'I can walk,' Judy protested.

'You'll take the taxi.' He climbed into a clean set of

underclothes and lifted out a linen shirt and her fur cape. 'You'll be wearing this.' He tossed the cape on top of her clothes on the chair. 'And it was you who told me that a pawnbroker would advance enough money on it to keep a family for six months. The last thing I need is for you to get attacked on your way home.'

'People know me in the Bay. It's the middle of the afternoon. My uncles—'

'Taxi, or I'll lock you in here,' he threatened.

'I'll take the taxi.'

He sat on the bed and slipped his sock suspenders over his feet. 'I like a woman who takes orders.'

'That isn't me,' she began irritably, then she saw him frown. 'Has something happened?'

He buttoned his shirt. 'David Ellis has been arrested.'

'David—' Judy's eyes rounded in horror. 'For running a book?'

'Yes.'

'I begged him not to take the job.'

'And you blame me for offering it to him?' He flicked through his suits and chose a sober, dark grey pinstripe.

Judy wanted to say no, but in all conscience couldn't. 'He's only a boy . . . '

'He's the same age as you. When I was nineteen I was doing a lot worse than running a book. He wanted to make real money. I gave him the chance to earn it.'

'Outside of the law,' she reminded him bitterly.

'The law's an ass. No one can make the kind of money I've earned legally. And that goes for all our so-called "betters" from the local Welsh crache, to the kings, queens, lords and ladies who put on airs and graces courtesy of their bulging bank accounts, wallets, castles and great houses. All their wealth proves is that their ancestors were bigger and more successful thieves than our great grandfathers.'

She knew it might make Aled angry but she still had to

ask the question uppermost in her mind. 'Have you ever gone to gaol?'

'No, but I would have if I'd stayed in America.'

'What did you do?'

'Stop short of murder. If I hadn't, I wouldn't have had to leave.' He flicked through his ties and pulled down a plain grey silk from the rack.

She summoned the courage to ask one more question. 'Will David go to gaol?'

'Not if I can help it.' He sat on the bed, pulled up his socks, clipped them on to his sock suspenders and began lacing his shoes. 'Aiden said the police picked up David and two other runners who were working for him.'

'Don't you mean for you?'

'The turf's Aiden's sideline. I bankroll it and take a cut, but he runs it.' He stepped into his trousers and buttoned his braces on to the waistband.

'If you put up the money, the business is yours.'

'I have no intention of arguing the point with you. But I will say this much: David and the others should never have been arrested. I paid the man at the top a great deal of money to make sure the local bobbies turned a blind eye to their activities.' He looked at her keenly. 'Who ran the book before I arrived?'

When she didn't answer him, he said, 'You must know. Your Uncle Tony likes a gamble even if your other two uncles don't. There must have been times when he asked you kids to put money on a horse for him.'

'He always used to send us to John or Tom Smith. They're both Charlie Moore's men.'

'You really think Charlie was behind the runners?' He shrugged on his waistcoat and buttoned it.

'That's what everyone on the Bay says.'

'I'm not so sure, I've met the man and he's an idiot.' He picked up his wallet, lighter and cigar case from the dresser.

'He's hateful.' Judy shuddered.

'You've met him?' he asked in surprise.

'He attacked me once, in a cloakroom when the band was playing at a private party. If Edyth hadn't come along when she had, he would have raped me.'

He reached out and stroked the side of her face. 'I'm glad he didn't because violence would have changed you. And we might never have been able to enjoy this afternoon.'

She laid her hand on top of his. 'Aled . . . '

He shattered the moment of intimacy by pulling his hand out from under hers. He moved in front of the mirror and busied himself, pushing collar studs into his shirt and cuff links into his sleeves. 'You've just given me one more reason to teach Charlie Moore a lesson.'

'Don't, he's influential . . . '

'So am I,' he said flatly.

'Did he have David arrested?'

'Not so anyone can accuse him outright. One of Anna Hughes's girls pointed David out to a rookie cop. David's been messing around with her ever since he came down to the Bay. She's young and pretty, if you like the painted floozy look.'

'Gertie?'

He looked back at her from the mirror. 'I didn't think respectable young ladies had anything to do with the Anna Hugheses of this world.'

'I only know Gertie by sight, but I know Anna well. Everyone on the Bay does.'

Aled recalled Anna saying that Judy had bought dresses from her. 'Don't worry about David; I'll get him out of gaol.'

'Are you sure?' Judy asked in concern.

'I'm sure,' Aled reiterated forcefully. 'Even if the police insist on taking him and the others to trial they can't refuse to set bail. Do you fancy dinner here tonight? And I mean in this suite,' he added so there would be no mistake.

'What would I tell my family – and Edyth?'

'That you're dining with me in the Windsor Hotel. Eating isn't a crime – everyone has to do it.'

'But they'd know that we didn't eat in the dining room.'

'How?'

'Waiters talk.'

'I'll have their jobs.'

'Please don't make trouble for anyone.'

'Then tell your family and Edyth the truth,' he said irritably.

'That we're carrying on?'

He smiled at the old-fashioned expression. 'Is that what we're doing?'

'It sounds better than you've taken me to be your mistress.'

He fell serious. 'I didn't think that I'd "taken" you anywhere you didn't want to go, Judy.'

'You didn't,' she admitted.

'Tell them whatever you want,' he said carelessly, 'that's if you want to have dinner with me here. But I wouldn't be too worried about Edyth Slater, if I were you. As she's "carrying on", as you so quaintly put it, with Micah Holsten she can hardly say anything about us.'

'You know everything there is to know about everyone on the Bay, don't you?'

'I make it my business to find out.' He put the finishing touches to the knot on his tie, picked up his jacket, looked at his panama and settled on a more serviceable trilby. 'I'll send Freddie to pick you up at the baker's around seven. If you feel the need to use an excuse, say we're working on the repertoire for your broadcast.' He kissed her lips. Pulling down her towel, he stroked her breasts and murmured, 'That's to keep me going until dinner.' Then he left.

Judy sank on the bed and looked at the door. The

unthinkable had happened. She had promised her grandmother that she would never make love to a man until she was married and now – now – she was living in sin.

No, she wasn't. Living in sin implied that two people were living under the same roof, which she and Aled certainly weren't. She had become Aled James's mistress and if Pearl King were still alive she knew that her grandmother would regard her as a fallen woman.

She had allowed – no, not allowed, that suggested some kind of pressure – she had willingly made love to a man who hadn't as much as hinted that he loved her or might at some time in the future consider marrying her.

Ignoring the lift, Aled ran down the stairs into the foyer. Freddie was waiting for him in the car outside the entrance.

'I've sent a solicitor to the Maria Street police station to meet Aiden and told him to post whatever bail the police set.' Aled climbed into the back seat.

'They won't bail until the morning, boss.'

Unused to having his plans thwarted, Aled's face darkened. 'How do you know?'

'A copper was waiting for us in the foyer when we left your suite. He was looking for Aiden. He said that David will have to go to the magistrates' court and they won't be meeting until tomorrow morning. They'll set his bail, and until then he'll have to stay in the cells.'

'There has to be some way to get him out.'

'Not before morning, boss. A rookie constable arrested David in the Mount Stuart in front of everyone in the Gentleman Only. There's no way it can be kept quiet. And the copper hadn't just been sent there to look for Aiden. He'd been told to warn you to stay away from Maria Street for your own sake as well as David's and the other two boys.'

'After you've dropped me off, go to the station and see Aiden. Talk to him yourself and don't take no for an answer, whatever excuse the police try to give you, understand?'

'Yes, boss.'

'Tell Aiden to get anything David wants and make sure he has a cell to himself and a decent meal tonight. After you've done all you can for David, drive Aiden to Anna Hughes's. Tell him to walk straight in and meet me in her kitchen.'

'I will, boss.' Freddie pressed the ignition. The engine roared into life. He leaned back in his seat. 'I take it you still want to go to Anna Hughes's place?'

'As quick as you can make it, Freddie.'

'Micah, I wondered when you were going to turn up.' Inspector Cummings wandered out of his office, a cup of tea in one hand and a Chelsea bun in the other. 'Want one? Constable Murphy's wife just sent down a batch from upstairs.'

'No thanks. I've heard that you're holding David Ellis.'

'Popular young lad that one. His solicitor and Aiden Collins are with him and the arresting officer and the sergeant in the interview room now.'

'You got him for running a book?'

'You a betting man?'

'You know I haven't two halfpennies to rub together,' Micah answered.

'That's never stopped a man from gambling. If he hasn't the money he gambles with thin air. The trouble starts when the bookie won't take thin air as payment.'

'Are you or are you not holding David Ellis?' Micah questioned impatiently.

'He's being charged now and he'll be held overnight for the magistrates in the morning.'

'Release him into my custody.'

'Give me one good reason why I should do that, Micah?' the inspector asked.

'As a personal favour to me. I've done enough for you

over the years – patching up the drunks in the cells and coming out at all hours to act as an interpreter whenever you've needed one.'

'It's been useful having a pastor who speaks ten languages on the Bay; the only thing is, I'm not too sure you've always translated what I've said correctly or, come to that, whatever the people we were questioning said to you.'

'Have you ever been left with a mess to clear up as a result of my translations?'

'No, but there is such a thing as the letter of the law. And we have just told the fancy solicitor Aled James hired to represent David Ellis that we're keeping Mr Ellis in the cells overnight.'

'Since when has anyone in this station liked fancy solicitors, or listened to what they have to say?' Micah asked. 'Please . . . '

'Tell you what I'll do,' Inspector Cummings beckoned Micah forward and lowered his voice to a whisper, 'if you disappear for a couple of hours and come back at eight o'clock after the senior officers go off duty I'll release him into your custody on two conditions.'

'What are they?' Micah asked suspiciously.

'That you keep him in the mission overnight.'

'Done.'

'And get him to the court by eight thirty tomorrow morning.'

'Agreed.'

'And don't tell anyone about it or crow that you can wrap me round your little finger.'

'Would I do that?'

'No, Micah, you wouldn't, which is why I'll grant you the first favour you've ever asked of me. Just make sure that you don't ask me for another in a hurry,' the inspector said seriously.

# CHAPTER NINETEEN

As Anna was lolling on the sofa, Aled sat on one of the stiff, Rexine-covered chairs in her front parlour. The absence of dust on the mantelpiece and the Victorian walnut table and chairs in front of the window suggested that the room was cleaned on a regular basis. The musty smell, however, indicated that it was rarely, if ever, used.

'If what everyone on the Bay is saying is right and David was caught red-handed with his book and betting slips in the pub, there's no way that the police will be able to ignore it, Aled, no matter who you have bought,' Anna warned.

'Someone put your Gertie up to this.'

'Possibly,' she conceded cautiously.

'Definitely, Anna. She must have a regular—'

'More than a dozen at the last count,' Anna interrupted.

'You're not going to help me, are you?' Aled said testily.

'I look after my girls, I give them sound advice. If they choose to ignore it, that's their affair.'

'Gertie's ignored it?'

'She was brought back here by the police this afternoon. They searched her room and found David's wallet. Gertie insisted he left it there when he visited her yesterday before they went to Barry. Apparently David insisted he had it in Barry and used the money in it to buy their train tickets. As it's her word against his they've let her off with a caution. But I warned her if she brings the police to my door on official business again, she's out.'

'Never mind that she's committed the worst crime someone on the Bay can. Especially a girl in her profession. She's grassed to the police, Anna.'

'You don't know that.'

'How much more proof do you need?' Aled hadn't raised his voice but there was an undercurrent of steel in his quiet tone.

'Talk to Gertie about it, not me. I've said all that I'm going to say to her today. She's upstairs. You know her price; two bob will buy you an hour.'

'Is anyone with her now?'

'Her number-one regular. He calls to see her most days, not that he pays.'

Aled remembered what Anna had told him the last time he'd spoken to her. 'She's with Charlie Moore?' he guessed.

'If you want to talk to Gertie when they've finished, be my guest. You want to talk to Charlie Moore, do so outside my house. I don't want any more trouble here. Not today – or ever.'

Edyth grasped the telephone in her hand and shouted down the line. 'No, Harry, please don't leave the farm and travel down here, not tonight . . . There's nothing you can do that Micah hasn't already done for David . . . Micah has been to the police station . . . He's arranged with the inspector for David to be released into his custody at eight o'clock tonight and Micah and I will go to the magistrates' court with David tomorrow morning . . . The bakery is the least of my worries, trade has slackened off and Kristina and the boys can manage without me for a couple of hours . . . Harry . . . please.' She turned around and looked imploringly at Micah, who was leaning in the doorway of her office, listening. 'Micah is with me now . . . talk to him . . . it would be better, Harry, as he is the one who has made all the arrangements . . . Remember, David is going to be feeling

341

very ashamed of himself and embarrassed after all the warnings we gave him not to work as a bookie's runner . . . Yes, here's Micah.' She handed the telephone receiver to Micah. 'The line is terrible. You'll have to shout.'

To give Micah privacy, Edyth went upstairs. Judy was kneeling on the window seat in the bay that overhung the street in the sitting room. She had changed out of the expensive black day dress she had worn to lunch in the Windsor Hotel and was wearing one of her own dresses. A simple floor-length cream shift belted low at the hip with a wide cream and brown belt. The style had been fashionable two or three years before, but it suited her slim figure.

'Are you going out again?' Exhausted more by the news of David than her long day in the shop, Edyth sat in one of the easy chairs that flanked the fireplace.

'To a business dinner at the Windsor Hotel. I didn't tell you earlier because it seemed wrong after hearing the news about David. Aled has arranged for me to sing on the wireless.'

'That's marvellous, Judy,' Edyth said enthusiastically. 'It's just the kind of good news I need after what's happened to David.'

'We'll be going through the repertoire I'll be singing in the studio. I have four four-minute spots, which means four songs. And the producer is anxious that they should show off the range of my voice. Lennie has been given two two-minute compère spots in the same show.'

'I am so pleased for both of you. I wish you had told me earlier.'

'It was awful to see you and Micah looking so upset.'

'I'm beginning to think that's the normal effect David has on people.'

'I could ask Aled to arrange this dinner for another evening and stay here,' Judy offered.

'Absolutely not.' Edyth shook her head. 'There's nothing you could you do if you stayed. Micah has done everything that can be done now the worst has finally happened. David chose to ignore the advice we gave him. He's been arrested and he's going to have to suffer the consequences.'

'I feel sorry for him. I'm fond of David,' she said absently, suddenly realising that she meant what she'd said, for all of David's irritating ways.

'We all are. Is Aled James going to be hosting this dinner?'

'Yes. As he pointed out to Lennie and me, he gets ten per cent of any fee we earn working outside of the Tiger Ragtime, and that includes wireless performances.' Judy crossed her fingers behind her back and hoped that Edyth wouldn't ask for a list of the other guests.

'David worked for Aled and look where he is now,' Edyth warned.

'David said that Aiden runs the bookie side of the business.'

'Aiden Collins might be concerned with the day-to-day running of the bookie's business but I bet he was running it with Aled's money.'

Judy couldn't contradict Edyth or say anything in Aled's defence, when on Aled's own admittance he had bankrolled Aiden. 'You're probably right.'

Edyth went to the window seat, sat beside Judy and caught hold of her hand. 'I know that Aled James has given you the break into show business you were looking for and that working in the club is the culmination of all your dreams. I couldn't be more pleased for you that you're going on the wireless. You've worked hard for your success, Judy, you deserve it. Just one thing, please, don't get any more involved with Aled James than you have to.'

'How can I not, Edyth? He's my boss.' Judy felt the blood rushing into her cheeks. She turned aside, but not quickly enough.

'My God!' Edyth clamped her hand over her mouth.

'I'm stupid as well as blind. You're already involved with Aled, aren't you?'

Judy met Edyth's steady gaze but she couldn't lie to her friend. She said nothing.

'Judy, darling, I love you as much as I love my sisters. Truth be known, a lot more than my younger sister, Maggie. But then she always was the most difficult one of the five of us. I'd hate to see you make the same mistake as David, and trust the wrong man, only to get hurt.'

'I won't be going to gaol.'

'No, you won't,' Edyth agreed, 'but look at what's happened to David and learn from it. Men like Aled James use women and discard them with no more thought than they'd give to a worn-out suit. You only have to look at the way Aled behaves, the way he throws money around. The men around him – Freddie Leary, Aiden Collins – everyone knows they're hired thugs. That night in the hotel, the way the head waiter and everyone else fawned over Aled. They only do that because he has bought them with his tips and tickets to his nightclub. Judy, darling, now that David's been arrested you don't need me to tell you what the man is capable of. Please, I'm begging you, don't see any more of him than you have to.'

'I work for him. I see him in the club five nights a week.'

'But you don't have to have lunch and dinner with the man.' Edyth lifted her legs on to the seat and wrapped her arms around her knees.

'I do when he arranges meetings and lunches with BBC producers and impresarios like Stan Peterson. It's business, Edyth.'

'I can see that I've spoken too late. I should have said something sooner.'

Judy felt remorseful enough without having to cope with Edyth's guilt. 'You couldn't have stopped it from happening.'

Edyth left the window seat and returned to the chair. 'You saw what my marriage to Peter was like. If you get involved with the wrong man as I did, you could be letting yourself in for a lot of heartache.'

'I'm old enough to know my own mind, Edyth.'

'I thought I was when I married, Peter,' Edyth said with a touch of bitterness. 'I just don't want you to end up unhappy and full of regrets.'

'I doubt I'll end up regretful,' Judy said wryly. 'I've gone into this with my eyes wide open. I know that men like Aled James use women; I also know that they're not the marrying kind.'

'You know that,' Edyth said wonderingly. 'And yet—'

'And yet I made love to him,' Judy said defiantly. 'It wasn't one-sided, Edyth.'

'You love him?' Edyth asked wonderingly.

'I suppose I must do.' Judy was as amazed by the idea as Edyth.

'How could you? You've just said he's not the marrying kind and that means you'll never be anything more to him than a mistress.'

'Like you with Micah?' Bitterly ashamed of the silence that followed her outburst, Judy said, 'I'm sorry. I had no business to say that. But a person would have to be blind and deaf to live in this house and not know what was going on between you and Micah Holsten, Edyth.'

'I know I'm not treating Micah fairly.' Edyth suppressed a pang of guilt at the thought of the letter that lay hidden in her desk. 'But that doesn't excuse what Aled is doing to you. I've told you that he's Harry's half-brother. He threatened to hurt Harry. And he's doing just that. He can't get at Harry directly so he's getting at him through the people Harry loves. David, me, you . . . the man is evil and vicious.'

'He's also capable of kindness. He knows Bay people. He tries to help them by giving them jobs—'

'Like David,' Edyth couldn't contain her anger at the

thought of Harry's brother-in-law sitting in a prison cell because Aled James had persuaded him to break the law.

'Edyth, the last thing I want to do is quarrel with you,' Judy pleaded. 'You gave me a home and a job when I needed them most. But I'll understand if you want me to move out after what I've told you about Aled and me.'

'If I asked you to move out, would you move in with Aled?' Edyth asked.

'No.'

'Because he wouldn't have you?'

'Because I wouldn't live with him even if he wanted me to. A man like Aled needs his freedom. I'd cramp his style.'

'He probably has other women.' Edyth knew the suggestion would hurt Judy but that didn't stop her from making it.

'I know.'

'And you don't care. My God, have you no pride?'

'While I don't know about them, I can't care,' Judy said practically. 'Do you want me to move out?'

'No. I want you to stay. You looked after me when Peter left. The least I can do is be there for you . . . ' Edyth couldn't finish the sentence.

'When Aled flaunts a new mistress in front of me?' Judy suggested.

'I don't understand you,' Edyth said sadly.

'I don't understand myself. I only know that I couldn't stop myself from falling in love with Aled and now that we've made love I want to wring the last drop of happiness from the relationship while it exists.'

'Does he love you at all?' Edyth asked.

'I don't know. I suspect not, but I like to think he cares for me a little, although I know I'm probably deluding myself.'

'I hope I'm wrong but I suspect that Aled James is incapable of loving anyone except himself.' Edyth heard Micah's step on the stairs and went to open the door.

'Edyth?'

'Don't worry, I won't tell Micah or your uncles about you and Aled. But given the way things are in the Bay, I suspect that they'll find out sooner than you'd like them to.' Edyth opened the door. 'Did you persuade Harry not to come down here tonight?'

'I did.' Micah walked in and sat on the sofa. 'But he's meeting me and David in a café early tomorrow morning before we have to go to the magistrates' court. And he asked me to tell you that he doesn't want you there. If all goes well, we'll bring David straight back here.'

'And if it doesn't?' Edyth had to ask.

Micah looked from Edyth to Judy. 'There's no need for you both to look so tragic. It will go well. It has to.' He glanced at his watch. 'Another hour and I can go down to the station and pick David up. My bed in the mission might be hard and David may be used to a better supper than waffles, butter and preserves in Helga's, but mission hospitality isn't quite as bad as that of the Maria Street police station.'

Edyth left her chair and went to the door. 'What are David's chances in court – the truth, Micah?'

'That depends entirely on the magistrates. It's out of our hands.'

Edyth forced herself to concentrate on practical problems as they were the only ones she could do anything about. 'As you're going to the station in an hour, can I get you something to eat?'

'A sandwich and a cup of tea would be nice.'

'I'll lay the table for you.' Judy left the window seat.

'Please don't bother; I'll make up a tray. Besides, the car will be here for you soon.'

'You're going out?' Micah asked Judy.

'To the Windsor, for dinner,' Edyth answered for her. 'Judy is going to be singing on the wireless and she needs to sort out her repertoire.'

'Congratulations, I always knew you'd get there,' Micah said sincerely.

'Thank you.' A car horn sounded outside. Judy looked out of the window, saw Freddie and waved. 'That's my ride. I won't be late, Edyth.'

Edyth grasped Judy's hand as she passed her on her way to the door. 'Good luck with choosing your songs.' She kissed her cheek. 'And look after yourself,' she whispered in her ear.

Judy choked. 'Give my love to David,' she said to Micah before running down the stairs.

'I will.' Micah looked at Edyth. 'For all her good news, Judy seems a bit tearful.'

'She's upset about David and it's a lot to take in. A few short weeks ago she was working dawn till dusk in the bakery and playing in the pubs for shillings.'

'And now she's heading for the high life.'

'I only hope she's happy there and can live it as long as she wants.' Edyth went into the kitchen.

Micah followed her. 'That's an odd thing to say, Edyth.'

'I'm worried about her.'

'Don't be. After her success in the club last Saturday Aled James needs her more than she needs him. He'll look after her better than he did David.'

'I hope you're right, Micah,' she said fervently. 'Sandwiches.' She lifted the loaf from the bread bin and set it on the chopping board. 'Cheese or ham?'

Tired of talking about Gertie and upset by Aled's allegations, Anna made tea for both of them and took hers upstairs to her room, leaving Aled to wait for Gertie in the kitchen. For once it was deserted. Aled sat in one of the easy chairs next to the range, picked up a copy of the *South Wales Echo*, flicked through it and waited for the sound of footsteps on the stairs. He left his chair and went into the passage that led into the hall three times only to see other men leave before Charlie Moore walked straight down the stairs and out through the front door. Charlie didn't look back. Aled was glad, he wanted to be certain of his facts before he confronted the man.

Deciding to give Gertie a few minutes to dress before going upstairs to see her, Aled returned to his chair. No sooner had he sat down, than Gertie wandered into the kitchen in a thigh-length see-through green negligée, green French knickers, and a pair of white stockings held up by sequin-encrusted garters.

She took a cigarette from an open packet on the kitchen table, filched a spill from the wooden holder on the mantelpiece, and bent over the fire to light it. She didn't see Aled sitting still and quiet with the newspaper folded on his lap until after she'd lit her cigarette. She shook out the spill, threw it on the fire and gave him her wide professional smile. 'Have you come to see me?'

'Who else?' he asked softly.

She flicked up the corner of her negligée and lifted the leg of her knickers. 'You know the way to my room.'

'For what I want to do to you, down here is fine, Gertie.'

'This is the public room, anyone can walk in. I wouldn't want the other girls to see us at it. Not in here. But if you're into people watching—'

'As far as I'm concerned the whole world is welcome to watch what's about to happen here. Sit down, Gertie.'

'If you want me to strip . . . '

'You couldn't be wearing much less than you are now.'

'Want to make a bet on it?' she whispered provocatively.

'Sit down,' he repeated. He hadn't raised his voice but when Gertie looked into his eyes, the blue had turned to unflinching steel. She sat.

Aled reached into the inside pocket of his suit, removed his wallet, opened it and peeled off a large white five-pound note from a roll tucked into the back. He held it up in front of her.

'Five pounds . . . ' Her eyed rounded.

'Which could be yours.'

Gertie ran her tongue over her lips to moisten them. 'What would I have to do to earn it?'

'Give me information.' He watched beads of sweat form on her forehead.

'What kind of information?' She lifted her chin, putting on a show of bravado.

'You can tell me exactly who ordered you to go to the coppers, and finger David Ellis as a bookie's runner.'

'I have absolutely no idea what you are talking about.'

'Yes, you do,' he contradicted calmly. 'You went into the Mount Stuart pub around two o'clock this afternoon with a rookie constable straight out of training school. You pointed out David Ellis to him and told him that David was taking bets.'

'It's no secret that David is a bookie's runner. He told me so himself.'

Aled sat back in his chair, took his cigar case from his pocket, removed a slim black cigar and tapped the cut end on the closed case. 'How long have you lived on the Bay?' he asked, conversationally.

'About a year. Why do you want to know?' she demanded.

'I'm surprised a year hasn't been long enough for you to learn the first unwritten law of Tiger Bay. You never grass on your neighbours, not even if they murder your father and rape your mother.' He took his lighter from his pocket, lit his cigar and drew on it. 'I'm asking you for the second time, Gertie. Who put you up to grassing on David Ellis?'

'No one,' she answered defiantly. But she saw him watching her rip at the bitten edges of her nails. She pushed her hands beneath her thighs and sat on them.

'I don't believe you.' He returned his lighter, cigar case and wallet to his pockets.

'It's true. David and I went to Barry Island yesterday and we quarrelled there.'

'I know. I also know that the police found his wallet in your room.'

'It was empty when David left it there,' she snapped pre-emptively.

'Really?'

'Yes, it was.'

'You said you quarrelled with David.'

'I did.'

'About what?'

'Nothing.' She squirmed uneasily on her chair.

'In my experience people rarely quarrel about nothing.' He flicked his ash into the grate.

'We were at the funfair. I talked to a couple of soldiers, that was all. David got jealous.'

'Because you were touting for trade.'

'I wasn't.' Her voice rose precariously. 'I was just being friendly, that's all. David took it the wrong way. He said some horrible things about me. And I wanted to get my own back on him,' she blurted furiously. 'That's why I went to the police this afternoon.'

'You wanted to get your own back on David enough to put him in gaol.'

'Yes.'

'Wasn't that a little extreme? Even for a tart.'

'I was angry.'

'You're sorry now?'

'No.' She tossed her head in the air and flicked her hair back from her forehead. 'David had it coming to him.'

He looked her in the eye. 'I am now asking for the third and last time: who put you up to fingering David and the others?'

'What others?'

'Don't play games with me, Gertie,' he threatened coldly.

'No one put me up to anything—'

'Come in, Aiden.'

Gertie turned her head and saw Aiden Collins standing in the doorway.

'Boss,' Aiden acknowledged.

'You heard me ask the lady a question.'

'I did, boss,' Aiden replied softly.

'Find out the answer. I'll be waiting with Freddie in the car.' He handed Aiden the five-pound note and his cigar.

Gertie shrank back even further into her chair and watched Aled leave. He closed the door behind him.

Aiden moved swiftly. Catching Gertie unawares he grabbed her by the shoulders and lifted her off the chair. Closing his right hand around both her wrists he yanked her arms high behind her back. She screamed.

'Talk; or we'll carry on this conversation upstairs in your room. People expect to hear screams coming from a whore's bedroom.' He drew on the cigar until the end glowed, crimson. Then he held it, poised above her face.

'It was Charlie Moore,' she gabbled hastily. 'He was running the book down here before you lot moved in . . . he wanted all your boys picked up . . . it was Charlie . . .'

Aiden inhaled on his cigar again; the tobacco crackled with the heat. He heaved her arms higher and she screamed again.

'Who is behind Charlie Moore?'

'No one is behind Charlie Moore. He has all the money he can spend. His family are rich. He was the most powerful man on the Bay before you and Mr James came here. Please,' she begged when he drew on his cigar again. 'That's the truth, I swear it.'

Aiden dropped her arms and released her. She fell back into the chair.

Anna walked in. She saw Gertie trembling and looked at Aiden.

'You should be more careful who you give house room to, Mrs Hughes.' Aiden flung the five-pound note on to Gertie's lap. 'Buy yourself a one-way ticket out of here. I hear they quite like Welsh girls in Cork.' He tossed the remains of the cigar on to the fire and left the house.

From the moment Micah picked him up at the police station, David kept expecting a lecture but Micah made a couple of innocuous remarks about the weather, drove him to the mission and left him with Moody, who made him and a crowd of seamen a waffle supper. The sailors produced a couple of bottle of aquavit to wash down the waffles and shortly afterwards they started singing. The party spirit was at its height when Micah reappeared to remind David that he had to be up early in the morning. He showed him to his own bedroom and left.

David tossed and turned on the thin mattress for most of the night, listening to the singing and raucous laughter of the Scandinavians. He felt he had only just closed his eyes when Micah came in and shook him awake. To David's surprise, Micah was already washed, shaved and dressed in a dark three-piece suit, sober tie and white shirt and collar.

'Here's a cup of coffee. I hope you take milk and sugar. There's a razor, shaving soap and ordinary soap on the washstand. I've brought warm water for you to wash. Don't be long. I want to get away by a quarter to seven. We'll breakfast on the way.'

'But I don't have to be at the magistrates' court until half past eight . . . ' David found himself talking to the door. He rose, washed, dressed and shaved in record time and left the bedroom. There was no sign of Micah in the public room that adjoined the bedroom. He went downstairs to Micah's office, which was also empty, saw that the front door of the mission was open and found Micah outside, warming up the engine of his van.

He climbed into the front passenger seat and stared sleepily out of the window as Micah drove up Bute Street. Halfway along, Micah pulled up in front of a café and killed the engine.

'Why have you stopped?' David asked, lack of sleep making him irritable.

'Breakfast.'

'I'm not hungry.'

'We're meeting someone.'

David looked in through the café window. He saw Harry sitting at a table. 'So this is where you two give me the "we told you so lecture".'

'This is where we have breakfast.' Micah opened the van door.

'Now I know why you didn't say anything to me when you picked me up at the police station last night. You talked to Harry on the telephone and the two of you decided—'

'We decided nothing, David,' Micah broke in. 'You made all the decisions that had to be made when you broke the law and got yourself arrested.'

'You may as well get it off your chest now.' David folded his arms.

'I've nothing to get off my chest,' Micah said. 'I said my piece when I discovered that you'd taken the job of bookie's runner. Harry, Edyth, Judy, me – we all tried to persuade you to change your mind, and stop working for Aled James, but you wouldn't listen to any of us. It's too late for recriminations now. All that's left for you, Harry and me to talk about is how best to deal with this bloody awful mess you've got yourself into.'

David was shocked. It was the first time he'd heard Micah swear. 'Neither you nor Harry have to do anything,' he said. 'Aiden Collins came to see me in the police station last night. He has got me a first-class attorney—'

'Solicitor,' Micah corrected. 'You're in Britain, not America.' He stepped out of the van on to the pavement. 'I'm hungry. Do you want me to order breakfast for you? They do a good full English breakfast here: bacon, eggs, sausages, tomatoes, mushrooms, fried bread and laver bread.'

'I'm not hungry,' David said sourly.

'It might be your last chance to eat for a while.'

'All right, I'll have the breakfast,' David agreed, embarrassed and angry at having put himself into a position where he was beholden to both Harry and Micah.

'How do you like your eggs?'

'Fried.'

'Tea or coffee?'

'Tea.' David added 'please' but by then Micah had entered the café and joined Harry.

David left the van, closed the passenger door and stood, shivering, on Bute Street. The chill in the air and the mufflers tied around the necks of the workmen painting the windows of a bank lower down the street announced the arrival of autumn. Even at this early hour the street teemed with traffic, and David wondered if the people on the Bay ever slept.

A milk cart had stopped at the side of the road opposite. Its khaki-coated driver was busy ladling milk from a churn into the jugs of a queue of housewives who were gossiping whilst they waited their turn to be served. A road sweeper was piling rubbish on to a giant dustpan. Half a dozen shabbily dressed men were walking, heads down, caps pulled low over their faces, towards Penniless Point.

David looked at the watch Micah had retrieved from the police along with the rest of his personal possessions. It was almost seven o'clock. Another hour and a half and he would have to be in court. And he didn't even know where it was.

Despite Micah's assurance, he braced himself for a dressing-down, pushed open the door of the café and went inside.

'David, sit down. Your breakfast is on its way.' Harry pulled out the chair next to him. An elderly waitress appeared with a pot of tea and one of coffee. She put them on the table.

'I'll bring your hot water now, gentlemen.'

'Thank you, Mavis. How's your husband?' Micah asked.

'Crippled with rheumatism, but thank you for asking, Micah. How's your sister?'

'Burgeoning.'

'You'll make a daft, soft touch of an uncle.' She bustled off.

'And how are you?' Harry asked David after she'd left.

'Fine.'

'Really?' Harry pressed.

'If you're going to have a go at me . . . '

Harry poured himself a cup of coffee. 'You've enough problems on your plate, David, without me adding to them.'

'So why am here?' David demanded.

Micah poured him a cup of tea and pushed it across the table towards him. 'To have breakfast.'

'I could have eaten that at the mission or Helga's.'

'Not Helga's.' Micah sugared his tea and passed David the bowl. 'The police insisted that you could only leave the station on condition you stayed at the mission.'

'We're here to show solidarity.' Harry buttered a piece of bread. 'No one should have to go into court alone. No matter what they have done. Pass the salt and pepper, David.'

Micah parked his van behind Harry's open-topped Crossley tourer outside the court at a few minutes before eight. David opened the passenger door and climbed out. The first people he saw were Aiden Collins and Freddie Leary who were waiting in front of the building with the solicitor he had seen at the Maria Street police station the night before.

Another man was standing a short distance away from the group. Dressed like a tailor's mannequin in a fine woollen three-piece suit, cashmere overcoat and trilby, he walked over and greeted Harry as he left his car.

'Mr Evans, sir, I'm Alfred Lewis, from Mr Richards's office.'

'Pleased to meet you.' Harry shook his hand.

'I am going to need some details from you regarding your brother-in-law's case, sir.'

'We'll talk inside and, please, call me Harry. Did you leave Mr Richards well?'

'As well as can be expected. He doesn't complain, but he hasn't been the same since his recent stroke.'

'I must call in and see him soon. David.' Harry took David by the elbow and drew him aside. 'This is the solicitor I have engaged to represent you, Mr Alfred Lewis. Alfred, this is my brother-in-law, David Ellis.'

'I told you, Harry, Aiden has already got me a solicitor. I'm sorry you had to come down here on a wild goose chase, Mr Lewis. If you'll excuse me, I must join Aiden and the others.' David practically ran over to Aiden.

'I'm sorry, Alfred,' Harry apologised. 'My brother-in-law is young, impetuous and, on occasions like now, downright ill-mannered.'

'He must be under considerable strain,' Alfred suggested tactfully.

'Nevertheless, he could have been more polite. It was good of you to come down here at such short notice, and obviously I'll pay your fee.'

'It was the least the firm could do, Mr Evans,

considering the amount of work your company puts our way.'

'Would you mind coming into court with us and sitting in the public gallery?' Harry asked. 'There are bound to be things that we, that is Pastor Holsten and I, won't understand.'

'Not at all.' Alfred shook Micah's hand. 'Pleased to meet you, Pastor.'

'Micah. Shall we go in? Between the press, interested parties, families of the accused and nosy parkers, the seats go early, and they won't allow anyone to stand in the magistrates' court.' Micah led the way inside the building, and Harry stopped and read the details of the cases pinned on board.

'Are these all due to be heard today?' Harry was daunted by the prospect.

Alfred Lewis studied the list. 'If the timetable goes to plan, your brother-in-law's case should be the last to be heard before lunch. If a prior case overruns we could be here until the end of the day. Or, if we are extremely unlucky, and more than one case drags on, David Ellis's case could be postponed until tomorrow, or even the day after.'

'Perhaps we should have brought a flask, sandwiches and camp beds, Harry,' Micah suggested, not entirely humorously.

# CHAPTER TWENTY

David stood in the dock and tried not to look as frightened as he felt. Three middle-aged magistrates, who wore whiskers that might have been fashionable in the Victorian era, were ranged on the bench above him. All appeared formidable. Only the man sitting in the centre had spoken during the proceedings, although he occasionally held whispered conversations with his two companions, which only served to heighten David's anxiety.

David had never felt as alone as he did in that dock. Not even when he'd been tending his sheep on the Beacons, miles from the nearest road, let alone farmhouse. But the solicitor Aiden had engaged for him and the other runners had insisted all three defendants be tried separately.

The magistrate spoke, and everyone in the courtroom fell silent.

'David Mark Ellis,' he began formally, 'we have considered all the evidence in this case. If you have anything further to say in your defence this is the time in which to say it.'

David recalled the advice the solicitor had given him and leaned on the rail in front of him for support. The magistrate pulled his glasses down to the end of his nose and looked over them. 'You wish to speak?'

'Yes, sir,' David whispered tremulously.

'What is it you wish to say?'

'I am very sorry I broke the law. I promise I will never take illegal bets from anyone ever again.' The solicitor had asked David to say more, but his mind had gone blank and he couldn't remember another word.

The spokesman conferred with his colleagues again. After a few moments he looked directly at David.

'David Mark Ellis, by entering a guilty plea to all the charges proffered against you, you have, on your own admission, broken the law. The only mitigating factor in your favour is that you have seen fit to make a full confession of your crimes. As this is your first offence, I have no doubt that you have been led astray by older men who have in all probability profited more than you from your wrongdoing. However, even taking all these things into consideration we cannot condone what you have done, nor can we be seen to be so doing. Therefore we will hand down a custodial sentence of six months' hard labour.'

David gripped the railing in front of him even more tightly. His head swam as he fumbled to find another interpretation of 'custodial sentence'. But whichever way he considered it, 'custodial' meant prison. He was going to prison! Where were Aled's promises now?

'The said custodial sentence to be suspended for one year. However, should you transgress and break the law during the year, in any way whatsoever, you will be taken into immediate custody and transferred to the nearest penal institution. In addition, we fine you the sum of one hundred and fifty pounds.'

The magistrate turned to the officers behind him. 'We will now break for one hour.'

David was acutely aware of Harry and Micah sitting on the public benches to his right. But he couldn't bring himself to look at either of them. Instead, he sought for and saw Aiden Collins moving to the back of the court. Aiden nodded and smiled at him. David only wished he could smile back.

One hundred and fifty pounds was a colossal amount of money. If he added his savings to the contents of his suitcase, he doubted he could have scraped together thirty pounds in total. And the last thing he wanted to do was ask Harry to loan him the money. But he decided that he could, and would, ask Aled James.

'David.'

He looked down. Micah was standing next to him. 'Come on, either Harry or I will drive you back to Edyth's.'

'You, please, Micah.' David was too ashamed to face Harry.

'As you wish. Edyth said she'd make a cold lunch for us that wouldn't spoil if we were late.'

David stood transfixed, staring at the empty bench where the magistrates had sat.

'David,' Micah touched his arm, 'it's time to go.' Micah looked round as they left the court. There was no sign of Harry or Alfred Lewis and he guessed that they were paying David's fine.

Harry said goodbye to Alfred outside the court and joined Micah who was waiting by his van.

'You didn't see David inside?' Micah asked.

Harry shook his head.

'He went back in. He said he wanted to thank his solicitor and say goodbye to Aiden. He's worried about his fine. I think he wanted to ask Aiden to lend him the money to pay it.'

'It's already paid.'

'You?'

'Someone had to.' Harry fished his keys from his jacket pocket. 'David hasn't that kind of money.'

'If you go to Edyth's, I'll drive David there.'

'He doesn't want to drive with me?' Harry guessed.

'He's feeling so guilty. I think he'd be happier if we chained him to a post and whipped him, or at the very least put him in the stocks and threw rotten vegetables at him.' Micah joked.

Harry saw David emerging from the court with Aiden and the solicitor who had represented him. 'At least the man Aled James hired had the sense to advise David to plead guilty.'

'Given the evidence, what else could he tell David to do other than go on the run?' Micah slapped Harry across the shoulders. 'Go on, I'll catch you up shortly.'

'You won't—'

'Have a go at him? Give him a row? Wipe the floor with him? Do any of the other quaint things you people say when you're angry with someone? No, Harry, I won't because the last thing I want to do is make David feel any more wretched than he already does.'

Harry went to his car and drove off. Micah sat in his van and waited for David, he didn't have to wait long.

'I'm sorry,' David apologised when he joined him. 'The clerk made me wait. He wanted to give me a receipt for my fine.'

'You paid it?' Micah said innocently.

'It's paid, so Mr James must have given Aiden or the solicitor the money to settle it.'

Micah didn't enlighten him. He started the engine and drove out into the road. 'Have you thought what you are going to do now, David?'

'Have lunch in Edyth's.'

'I meant for a job.'

'That's all settled. Aiden said they took delivery of a second roulette wheel this morning. It came in last night on a ship from America. It's mine.'

'Literally?' Micah asked dryly.

'To operate in the club.'

'You still intend to work for Aled James.'

'What happened wasn't his fault, or Aiden's. It was Gertie. I should never have got involved with her.'

'I'll second that.'

'Anyway, after yesterday, I'm through with her, for good.'

'I'm glad to hear it.'

'I wish Harry hadn't come to court,' David said.

'He came to support you, David.'

'I looked a right fool in there.'

'Possibly, because you behaved like one.' Micah slowed behind a horse and coal cart. 'You could at least have thanked him for being there for you and hiring a solicitor even if you didn't use him.'

'He only came to crow.'

'Did he?'

'Ever since he married my sister he's been trying to tell me what to do and how to do it. Where I should live, what I should do with my life. Just like Mary has ever since I was little. Well I'm grown up now; I can run my own life.'

'It seems to me that you're not doing a very good job of it at the moment,' Micah said evenly. 'But that doesn't matter, because there are a lot of people on your side. Just don't be too anxious to insult them. You never know when you might need them again.'

Edyth had set ham, salad, cheese and Moody's 'special' white milk rolls on the table. For dessert, Moody had baked a chocolate cream cake. But although the food was good, the atmosphere was strained and Edyth, Micah and Harry were relieved when David finished eating and insisted he wanted to go back to Helga's to change. None of them tried to stop him.

'It might have been easier if Judy had been here, but she had a rehearsal arranged with the orchestra.' Edyth ignored the peculiar look Micah gave her as she piled their dirty dishes on to a tray ready to carry out into the kitchen. 'She and David get on reasonably well. Or at least as well as anyone can with David.'

'He barges around like a ram in rutting season most of the time.'

'Harry!' Edyth looked at him, then laughed.

'Sorry, I've lived too long on the farm. I think like Mary, and it would appear I'm beginning to talk like her.'

'Why didn't you tell David that you paid his fine?' Micah asked.

'Because there's no point. If he can't see what's under his nose, I'm not going to tell him to look.'

Edyth was tired of talking about David. 'More coffee?' she asked as Micah took the tray from her and carried it into her upstairs kitchen.

'Please.' Harry left the table. 'But before you make it, can I borrow your telephone?'

'You know where it is.'

'In your office downstairs.'

'That's a big name for a little cupboard off the kitchen.'

'I need to telephone Aled James. Do either of you know where he is likely to be?'

'I'd say the Windsor hotel or the Tiger Ragtime,' Micah answered.

'Judy said that Aled has a suite in the Park Hotel in town that he uses as an office as well, but your best bet is the Windsor. If either of his hired thugs are there they will know where he is, and if they aren't there and Aled wants to be found he will have left a telephone number where he can be contacted. But,' Edyth set the sugar bowl in the centre of the table, 'if you are going to ask Aled to leave David alone I don't think you're going to have much success. Not the way David was talking over lunch about running the roulette wheel in the club.'

'I need to discuss a few things with Aled,' Harry said evasively. 'I won't be long.'

'I'll put the kettle on.' Micah parried Harry's smile. 'I'm trying to prove to your sister that I am domesticated and will make a good husband.'

'Don't go overdoing it or all the wives in the family

364

'will start expecting the same service.' Harry ran down the stairs.

'Is Judy really in a rehearsal in the club?' Micah asked Edyth when he returned from the kitchen.

'I believe so.'

'Because that's what she told you?'

'And because I saw some of the musicians walking past when I was serving in the shop. They were carrying their instruments.'

'Jed has heard rumours about Aled and Judy. Not all the staff in the Windsor are as discreet as they should be.'

'What kind of rumours?' Edyth's heart started thundering against her ribcage. She'd never been very good at lying.

'You don't know?'

'I know that some people on the Bay should mind their own business not other people's.' She sank down on one of her easy chairs.

'Has Judy told you that she's having an affair with Aled James?'

'She told me that she thinks she's in love with him.'

'Dear Lord.' Micah buried his face in his hands. 'I love that girl like a daughter and she deserves a lot better than Aled James.'

'Judy's nineteen, Micah, that's a bit old to be your daughter.'

'Like a younger sister then. She's a child . . . '

'She's the same age as David. They both think they know what's best for them. And they both want to run their own lives. As I did, not so long ago. We can't stop them from making mistakes.'

'I suppose we can't.' He sat opposite her on the sofa, reached out and took her hand into his, stroking the ring finger on her left hand. It was bare because she had stopped wearing the wedding and engagement rings Peter had given her when he had left her. 'It makes you wonder what our children will be like, doesn't it? What will we do if they mess up, Edyth? Will we be able to stand back and allow the Aled Jameses of this world to lead them astray?'

'We may have no choice. Because if they are anything like David and Judy they won't take any notice of what we say.' Edyth turned aside, hoping he wouldn't see the guilt in her eyes. When she was busy in the shop she managed to forget the letter hidden at the bottom of her desk drawer. But the moment she was with Micah its presence surfaced, throwing a dark shadow between them and poisoning every private moment they spent together.

'You do want children, don't you?' he asked, misunderstanding her silence. 'We have talked about it . . . '

'Yes, I want children,' she said quickly.

'Just as soon as those annulment papers come through. And they can't take very much longer. A ship came in from South America this morning. The captain had a good voyage. Even with the stops he had to make along the way, he did it in less than a month.'

'How do you know?'

'Because I walk down to the docks most mornings to see if any of the Argentinian ships have brought a letter for you. I love you, Edyth,' he said simply. 'I can't wait to make you my wife. You do feel the same way?'

She squeezed his hand. 'That's Harry coming up the stairs. I'd better go and make that coffee.'

Harry looked around the door. 'You two look comfortable. Don't disturb yourselves on my account. Aled can see me right away so I'm going to drive down to the Windsor now.'

Edyth rose from her chair. 'I've left the shop for longer than I should have already. Will you be back for tea?'

'No.' Harry shook his head. 'I'll see Aled then drive to Pontypridd. I have a couple of meetings arranged with the board. I'll spend the night with Mam and Dad and go back to the farm tomorrow.'

'Give everyone my love, and kiss the children for me?' Edyth hugged him.

'I will, sis.' He looked at her and Micah again. 'I can't wait for the next family wedding; it's going to be such a happy one.'

'That it is.' Micah laid his hand around Edyth's waist.

'I'll see you out, Harry. Unlike pastors, I have to work in the afternoon.' Driven by guilt, Edyth couldn't wait to get away from Micah and immerse herself in work.

'What about the coffee?' Micah called after Edyth as she ran down the stairs after Harry.

'Bring it down into the kitchen. We'll drink it there if I have time.'

Harry parked his car outside the Windsor Hotel and took his briefcase from the boot. He glanced around Stuart Street, saw the groups of idle men lounging on the corners of Louisa Street and George Street and did something he had never done on the farm or in Pontypridd. He locked his car.

He walked into the hotel foyer. The receptionist dropped his pen and closed the ledger he had been working in. 'Mr Evans?'

'Yes,' Harry answered, surprised at being recognised.

'Mr James is expecting you, sir.' The receptionist signalled to the bellboy. 'Take Mr Evans up to Mr James's suite.'

Given Aled's varied business interests, Harry expected him to be entertaining visitors, but he opened the door himself. And when Harry entered the sitting room he saw that it was empty. Aled tipped the bellboy sixpence before Harry had a chance to put his hand in his pocket, closed the door on the boy and motioned Harry to the sofa. A catalogue of gaming machines and a tray of coffee were set on the table in front of it.

'I have no idea why you wanted to see me, but never let it be said I'm a poor host. Coffee?' He indicated the tray.

'No thank you, I have just had lunch with my sister, Micah Holsten and David.' Harry offered Aled his hand but Aled chose to ignore it.

'Aiden came here straight from the court. He said he'd seen you and the pastor there. You paid David's fine.'

'I did.'

'Aiden would have paid it.'

'I'm not here to look for reimbursement,' Harry said quietly.

'I'm not offering.' Aled sat on the sofa and pointed to an easy chair. 'Sit down.'

'Thank you.' Harry set his briefcase next to the tray of coffee. He unlocked it and removed a file.

'If you've come to ask me to fire David, I won't.'

'I know.'

'Then you approve of him working for me?'

'No, I don't,' Harry said flatly. 'But there's no point in discussing it. David's too stubborn to listen to anything I have to say and while you believe that you're annoying me by employing him you won't let him go.' Harry pushed the file across the table towards Aled. 'That is a copy of the original paperwork in a Gwilym James file on our father. I had it made up for you.'

Aled opened the file. It contained a sheaf of papers. He picked up the letter that lay on top. 'This is dated over twenty-three years ago.'

'It's a copy of a letter from my mother to yours suggesting that she contact Mr Richards. He was our father's solicitor.'

Aled read the letter once, then more slowly a second time. 'As this is a copy how do I know that your mother ever sent such a letter to mine?'

'It's in the files, so your mother must have taken it to a meeting she had with Mr Richards. Look at the copy of the note beneath it and the bank statements in your mother's name.'

Aled went through the rest of the papers in the file. He

moved the catalogue and tray of coffee aside so he could spread them out on the table.'

'After my mother removed me from your mother's house, she wrote to your mother and told her to contact Mr Richards and ask him for an annuity, so you could both live, if not in comfort, at least not in want. There is no record of your mother writing back.'

'My mother couldn't read or write.'

'Then someone must have read my mother's letter to her. As well as my mother's original letter there is a note from Mr Richards detailing a visit your mother made to him shortly after she received it. He made arrangements for your mother to be paid an annuity of £104 a year. It wasn't a fortune but it would have been enough for her to rent a better house away from the colliery wasteland that surrounded Bush Houses.'

'But it couldn't have been paid—'

'As you see from the copies of Gwilym James's bank statements of their "special fund", which was set up before either of us were born to pay compensation to the victims of our father's indiscretions, the annuity was paid in full into a Capital and Counties bank account that bore your mother's name until your sixteenth birthday.'

Aled looked at the papers. 'I am certain that my mother never received a penny of this. If she had, we would never have lived the way we did. She wouldn't have died in squalor and I would certainly never have had to go to sea when I was twelve years old.'

'I spoke to Mr Richards on the telephone after I went through this account. He remembered your mother. He also said he took great pains to explain everything to her. He told her that she could go to the bank in Tonypandy every week and withdraw the two pounds, which she did for about three months. Then she went into the bank and told them she was moving from Clydach Vale to Cardiff. The bank arranged for the payments to be made from their Butetown branch. They were collected every week for almost ten years, Mr Richards assumed by your mother. He was very concerned when I told him that she had died when you were twelve. It is typical of the man's honesty and integrity that he blamed himself for not visiting your mother after she moved here from Clydach Vale to ensure that she was still receiving the money.'

'She never mentioned an annuity to me.' Aled frowned with the effort of remembering childhood events and conversations that he had tried so hard to forget. 'She said the only things my father ever gave her were some clothes and a few pounds, which didn't even keep her until I was born. She said he never even tried to see me.'

'Do you remember the time just before you moved from Clydach Vale to the Bay?'

'I remember her buying me cakes and new boots and clothes and I recall her telling me that we'd be all right when we moved to Cardiff. But after we'd been living in Tiger Bay for a few weeks, she was working the streets.' Aled left the sofa and walked to the window.

Harry looked past Aled to the view of the docks and the hulls of ocean-going steamers that could be seen between the buildings. He had a few painful memories of his own childhood, all stemming from the time before his mother had married his stepfather but he doubted that any were as traumatic as the ones Aled was carrying. However he remained silent, wary of showing any sympathy lest Aled take it as patronising.

'Not being able to read or write is a handicap,' Aled said quietly. 'It's a wonder I learned because I only went to school for a few months in Clydach Vale before we came down here and then I only went to the church school for six months. It was more important that I earn money than get an education. But I managed to get one anyway, in the best possible college: the slums of New York.' He turned and smiled grimly at Harry.

'I don't know what happened to the annuity.' Harry closed his briefcase and lifted it to the floor. 'I believe you when you say that your mother didn't receive it, but as you can see from the statements it was paid into a bank account bearing her name. Not that I can take any credit for it because all the arrangements were made by Mr Richards. He is a fair man who did all he could to ensure that no woman or child suffered as a result of being abandoned by our father. Either the money is still in the bank account or someone took it from there. You have the number and the name of the bank. As your mother's son and heir you can make enquiries. They wouldn't discuss the account with me or Mr Richards when we telephoned.'

'Can I keep the papers?'

'I made the copies for you.' Harry opened his wallet and extracted a business card. 'This is the address of the solicitor's firm that made the arrangements. Mr Richards, the man who saw your mother, is semi-retired but the other people in the firm should be able to help you if you have any queries.' Harry rose to his feet and picked up his briefcase.

'If the money was in the account and my mother knew about it, she would have used it. If it was taken out, it wasn't taken out by her and that means that someone stole it.'

'It looks that way. I'm sorry. It would have made a difference to your life, and your mother's.'

'And maybe even the way I feel about you,' Aled said thoughtfully. 'But if this solicitor opened the bank account in my mother's name, how could someone have taken it?'

'Your mother might have signed over the account to a third party.'

'Not knowingly. She wasn't very bright but she wasn't stupid.'

'I've told you all I can. You're welcome to study the originals of those documents. They're in Pontypridd but I can have them sent to the Cardiff store if it's more convenient for you. And you can call and see me any time. My door will be always open to you.'

'Even after what I did to David?'

'If it hadn't been you, it would have been someone else, given the way he's behaving. And it must have cost you a bit to keep him out of gaol.'

'You knew I paid a bribe?'

'I don't like the way the world works, but I am a businessman. I try to live in it honestly and fairly but I don't always succeed.'

'If attitude and integrity are anything to go by you have succeeded more than I have. I only wish I'd had your start in life so I could have done the same.'

'So do I, Aled.' Harry held out his hand and this time Aled shook it.


'What the hell are you doing here?' Charlie Moore demanded of Gertie when she burst into his office.

'I'm sorry, Mr Moore.' The clerk who dealt with Charlie's personal correspondence raced in after Gertie. 'I tried to stop her but she hit me.'

'I have to see you, it's urgent.' Gertie faced Charlie. Panting and dishevelled, she glared at the clerk. 'It's personal.'

'You can go, I'll deal with this,' Charlie snapped at the clerk. 'Close the door behind you.'

'Aled James came to see me last night, and he set one of his bruisers on me,' Gertie blurted as soon as they were alone. 'They know I put the finger on David Ellis and the others.'

'What's that got to do with me?'

'You put me up to it, and I told Aiden Collins just that.'

'You what!' Charlie's face darkened in anger.

'I said you made me do it. I wasn't telling him anything he didn't know,' she added defiantly. 'Everyone on the

Bay knows that you were running the turf before Aled James showed up and Aiden Collins took over.'

'I might have been running the turf, but no one could prove that it was me who suggested you shop David Ellis and the others. And, you didn't need much persuading,' he said acidly. 'You wanted to kill him two days ago.'

She shrugged her shoulders. 'I've calmed down since then. And I have to leave Tiger Bay. Aiden Collins told me to move on and I intend to do just that. But I need money to set myself up somewhere else.'

'You've made a bloody fortune from me over the last year,' Charlie said curtly. 'And you told Anna that I stopped paying you, so she'd give you extra.'

'How do you know?' she challenged.

'Because Anna told me the free service only applied to me, not to the Smith brothers.'

'You treated me worse than any of my other customers and I have the bruises to prove it.' She pulled up the sleeve of her dress to show him the blackened finger marks on her upper arms. 'Those are the reasons I charged you top whack.'

'I won't give you another penny, Gertie.'

'If you don't, I'll go to the coppers again and tell them that you put me up to shopping David because you run your own books. And I'll give them a list of your operators just as I gave them a list of Aled's. John and Tom Smith's names will be right at the top.'

'As if the police don't know who they are,' he sneered. 'I've paid them well to look the other way when John and Tom work the pubs.'

'Aled James paid the police well too, but the officers can't ignore people who go into the station and volunteer statements. If they could, they would have ignored me. But once it's down in black and white it's a different story.'

'Cunning little bitch, aren't you?'

'Just looking after number one,' she countered, 'because if I don't, no one else will.'

'And if I give you money you'll go and never bother me again.'

'That depends on how much you give me,' she said archly.

'How much do you want?' He opened a drawer in his desk.

'Fifty quid.'

'Not a hope in hell.' He slammed the drawer shut.

'Come on, Charlie,' she coaxed. 'If I don't get out of here I'm going to be found floating face down in the dock. You don't want my murder on your conscience.'

'The way you're behaving, I'm tempted to kill you myself. Fifty quid!' he sneered. 'No girl is worth that kind of money, Gertie.'

'I am, because if I don't get it I'll not only go to the police I'll go to your father. And I know you don't just run the bookies. You've all sorts of scams going. The brandy you smuggle in through customs for the pubs and clubs on the docks, the goods that fall out of ships' containers and find their way into your warehouses, the ten per cent of seamen's wages you demand every time you give a man a berth on a ship—'

'You can't prove any of that,' he broke in.

'But I can create a stink by talking about it. Especially to your father – upright councillor and citizen like him. He likes people to think he's honest. His career as a city father wouldn't last long once people found out otherwise.'

'Here.' He opened his drawer again. 'There's a tenner.' He handed her two five-pound notes. 'That's all I've got. Get out of here.'

'Drop the other forty into Anna's tonight or I'll—'

'You'll what?'

'Waylay your father when he comes to see Colleen. I wouldn't dream of taking him from her. But I'm sure he'd be interested in having a chat with me once he hears how much I know about his darling blue-eyed son.'

'You say one word to my father—'

'Oh, I'll say a lot more than one word, Charlie,' she warned. 'Forty pounds delivered to my room in Anna's this evening or I'll talk to your father. By the way, you don't have to bring it personally.'

Aled spent a long time looking through the papers after Harry left his room. He returned all of them to the file except a couple of Gwilym James's 'special funds' bank statements, locked them into the desk in his sitting room, walked up Bute Street to the club and sat in on the orchestra's rehearsal with Judy. The moment the orchestra leader saw him he started perspiring and several musicians hit wrong notes out of sheer nervousness. Aled left after ten minutes without making a comment. He walked back down Bute Street to his bank and asked to see the manager on an urgent matter.

'He'll see you right away, Mr James,' the clerk bowed and scraped as he showed Aled into the manager's office. 'But he asked me to tell you that he can only spare you twenty minutes as he has another appointment.'

Aled went in. The manager had already taken a decanter of malt whisky out of his cabinet and cut two plump Havana cigars.

Aled took the whisky and the cigar, produced the records Harry had given him and explained in as few words as possible what he wanted.

The manager topped up their glasses. 'I'd help you if I could, Aled, you know that. You're a damned good customer. Accounts the size of yours don't walk through the doors that often these days. Butetown might be the first place in the world that a million-pound cheque was written but it's been a long time since we've seen any transactions that size on the Bay. But, to get back to this old account of your mother's, we only keep records of transactions that go back five years. Everything older is sent to Head Office. You could try writing to them to see if they can help you. But the boys in Head Office are sticklers for doing everything by the book. They'll want to see a statement of your mother's old account.'

'If she ever received any, they've long since disappeared. I told you she died when I was twelve and we were living in rented rooms. Everything she owned, which wasn't much, was either thrown out or sold.'

'Perhaps you have her birth certificate?' When Aled shook his head, he said, 'Marriage certificate?'

'She wasn't ever married to my knowledge,' Aled divulged curtly.

'Death certificate?'

'I don't even have that. Have you always worked in this bank?'

'The Capital and Counties Bank, yes. My grandfather was and my father is a director. When my father was younger he managed the main Cardiff branch. I followed him into the business straight from public school.'

'Were you working in this bank sixteen years ago?'

'The bank yes, this branch no.'

'Could you give me the name of someone who was?'

The manager put his fingertips together and stared thoughtfully into space for a few seconds. 'The name that springs to mind is Geoff Arnold, the estate agent. He's rumoured to be worth hundreds of thousands. His father was an ordinary seaman; his mother took casual work unloading ships when the family hit hard times. But to look at him now, you'd never think that he started off as a humble clerk behind the counter here, would you?'

# CHAPTER TWENTY-ONE

'Do you have any messages for Mary or Martha or the boys?' Harry stood in Helga Brown's backyard watching David brush his shoes.

'Tell them that I'm thinking of them and that I'm fine—'

'Are you?' Harry interrupted.

'How many times do I have to tell you and everyone else that I won't work as a bookie's runner ever again?' David questioned testily.

'You want to make a career out of running a roulette wheel in a gambling club instead?' Harry couldn't resist the gibe.

'Not a career but it will do for the time being.' David straightened up and returned the shoe brushes and polish to the old biscuit tin Helga kept them in. He walked over to the cold tap set in the outside wall, turned it on, took a sliver of green household soap from a dish on the window sill and washed his hands.

'What happens after "the time being"?' Harry expected David to snarl 'I don't know', as he had done so many times before, but he surprised him.

'Eventually, when I've earned and saved enough money, I'd like to buy a business down here like Edyth – and not because she lives on the Bay. I know she's in love with Micah Holsten.'

'You don't mind?' Harry asked cautiously.

David shrugged his shoulders. 'I did when I first found out about them. But Micah's a good man and I'm used to the idea of them being together now. I'm lucky to have both of them for friends,' he added.

'You are.' Relieved, Harry felt that David had taken the first step towards maturity.

'I like the Bay. I like the people here. I like the fact that everyone is judged by what they do, not who their family are or the amount of money they have in their pocket.'

'At the risk of making you angry again, you took a big risk to make above average wages when you started working for Aiden Collins,' Harry ventured.

'I was stupid to do it. I know that now. I also know that it will take years to save enough money to buy a decent business, but it will give me something to work towards. In the meantime, I can earn a lot more working for Aled James than I can by joining the queue at Penniless Point.'

'What kind of business are you thinking of?' Harry enquired.

'A shop perhaps. Or a pub.' David smiled. 'A pub would be great – there'd always be people calling in and talking and games—'

'Like roulette so you could fleece your customers. You've learned the lessons Aled James has taught you well.'

'Not roulette,' David said impatiently, 'cards—'

'Which are illegal,' Harry reminded him.

'Only if there's money on the table.'

'Which there would be on the Bay.'

'Not in my pub,' David countered. 'And there'd be darts and dominoes for the old men.'

'You've really been thinking about this, haven't you?' Harry was amazed.

'The pubs here are fantastic, Harry. Not a bit like the ones in the Swansea Valley,' he insisted enthusiastically. 'There are people in them from all over the world. You should hear some of the stories the sailors tell. And the singing – everyone on the Bay seems to be musical.'

'And you think you'd be happy running a pub like that?'

David saw that Harry was serious. 'I don't know,' he answered cautiously. 'But what I do know is that I'm happier here, surrounded by people, than I was at the farm with only you, Mary and the family for company. I'm sorry, Harry, but I'm not coming back.'

'You've nothing to be sorry for. You're a young man, it's only natural you want to see something of life. And the farm is isolated and quiet.'

David had a rare flash of insight. 'You're not that happy living there either.'

'I don't live there all the time. I travel around a lot and occasionally manage to get Mary away. But there's one big difference between you and me. The woman I love is on the farm and I would do anything to stay close to her and make her happy.'

David went into the washhouse and lifted down his suit jacket from the peg on the back of the door. 'If I don't leave for the club now, I'll be late.'

'I'll give you a lift to Bute Street.' Harry followed him into the house.

'You calling in on Edyth again?'

'No, I'm on my way to Pontypridd to spend the night with my parents. I'll go back to the farm tomorrow.'

'You won't tell Mary about my being in court, will you, Harry?'

David looked so apologetic and frightened, Harry almost hugged him, but he knew that his brother-in-law would balk at any display of emotion. 'I won't tell her and I'll be careful not to take any newspapers home that carry the story. But my parents will probably find out what you've done. Ellis isn't a very common name in this part of Wales.'

'If they do, tell them I'm sorry and I won't ever do anything to bring disgrace on the family again.'

'I will.'

'I'm sorry for messing up, Harry.'

'We're all entitled to make a few mistakes.'

'I think I've made enough to last me the rest of my life. And, I promise you, Harry, I may still be working for Aled James, but no amount of money will ever tempt me to break the law again.'

'That's good to hear.' Harry knew that David meant every word he'd said, but the assertion wouldn't stop him from telephoning Micah Holsten and Edyth every few days, just to make sure that David was keeping out of trouble.


'If you've called in to set your guard dog on Gertie again, you'll have to wait, she's with a client,' Anna snapped when Aled walked into her kitchen, where she was sitting talking to her other girls.

'It's you I've come to see. Can we go into your parlour?'

Just when Aled expected Anna to refuse, she left her chair. She ushered him into her cheerless front parlour and looked around before sitting on the sofa. 'I don't know why I keep this room as a parlour. The only times it's been used in the past few years is when we've talked and we could go upstairs to my room. I should turn it into another bedroom and give it to one of the young girls working the streets. Do her and myself a bit of good.'

'You'd need thicker curtains,' Aled observed.

'I think I could run to those. But you haven't come here to talk about curtains. What do you want, Aled?' she asked bluntly.

'I found out something today about my mother.'

'If it's bad, I don't want to hear it,' she retorted loyally. 'Like me and every girl on the game, your mother did what she had to in order to survive – and to bring you up as best she could,' she reminded him acidly.

'It's nothing she did, but it might be something that was done to her. Apparently my father paid her—'

'Two pounds a week,' Anna broke in.

'You knew about that?' he said in amazement.

'She moved down here on the strength of it. One of her old friends from Tonypandy lived in rooms in Loudon Square. The woman – she's long moved on – told your mother all sorts of stories about life on the Bay. Your mother heard about the park in the middle of the square and Butetown being close to the sea and thought it would be an ideal place to find a bit of life for herself and bring you up. So she came down here and rented rooms in the same house as her friend.'

'In Loudon Square.' Aled had a sudden image of his mother, taking him to a window. *There's a bloody nice little park there, Aled, for you to play in. If the other kids push you around, you push them right back and clock them one, just like you did the kids in Bush Houses . . .*

'Two rooms, big ones with high ceilings.'

'You remember? You were only a nipper and you weren't there long.'

'No, we weren't.'

'Then the bastard – your father, that is – stopped paying the money. Your mother went to the bank one Friday and the clerk said it hadn't been paid into her account so she couldn't take it out. He knew she couldn't read or write so he said he'd try and find out what was wrong for her. Shortly after that she fell ill. I went to the bank a couple of times for her but there never was any more money. That's when I told her to move in here with me. Course, I was renting a room here at the time. I didn't own it.'

'This clerk, do you remember his name?'

'The one who offered to look into it for her was Geoff Arnold. He's done all right for himself, made a bloody fortune . . . ' She whirled around. 'He didn't?'

'I found out today that two pounds a week was paid

into my mother's bank account every week until my sixteenth birthday.'

'One thing's for certain: she didn't see much of it after the first few weeks she lived here.'

'Have you got her bankbook?'

'Don't you remember? After she died we went through her things. We burned most of the papers. You thought you'd never need them again.'

'Geoff Arnold? How wealthy is he?'

'He and his wife live in a big house out Rhiwbina way. They moved from Butetown ten years ago or more. Said the Bay wasn't fashionable enough for them any more. He has an office in Bute Street, but you'd know that. And he owns at least half a dozen of the big houses in Loudon Square, all split into rooms. The rents on those alone must come to a pretty penny. Do you really think he took your mother's money?'

'If Arnold told her that her money hadn't arrived she wouldn't have thought to go to anyone else in the bank and question what he'd said.'

'Neither did I and I wasn't ill like your mother. I could kick myself. I should have demanded to see your mother's bank statement.'

'You didn't have any reason to be suspicious,' he consoled. 'And if it wasn't for you taking us in, Mam and I would have ended up on the street.'

Anna took a packet of cigarettes from her pocket and lit one. It said something for the state of her mind that she didn't offer one to Aled. 'The bastard!'

'You talking about Geoff Arnold or someone else?'

'Geoff Arnold. He was one of your mother's regulars. He used to pay her five bob a week every Friday. Not that she didn't earn it ten times over the things he made her do. But she was grateful because it covered half the cost of her room here.'

'I wish I had proof that he pocketed our money.'

'Do you want me to ask around the Bay?'

'No.' Aled left his chair. 'I need to find out more before I challenge Geoff Arnold. And don't tell me to be careful . . .'

'You've fallen foul of Charlie Moore and it has cost you and your boys more than money. Rumour has it the two that were picked up the same time as David Ellis are going down.'

'The solicitor warned me that they'll probably get six months apiece as well as the fine,' he admitted.

'You're making powerful enemies, Aled. Watch your back.'

'I've a few well-paid boys to do that for me. And you. You're a good friend, Anna.'

'I could have been a better one to your mother. Two quid a week would have made a lot of difference to her back then.'

'If we'd had it I would never have gone to America, and if I hadn't, I would never have come back here with my pockets well lined. I probably would have stayed here and found work as a docker or a bartender—'

'You? Never.' She shook her head. 'You only have to look at you to see that you're destined for great things, Aled James.'

The door banged and Anna went into the hall. Gertie was tucking her hair under a beret.

'I'm going out. I won't be long, just reminding a man about a debt I'm owed.' She looked at Aled. 'Before you say another word, it's money I need to move on.'

'I thought Aiden gave you enough to do that.'

'He gave me enough to move, not to set myself up when I get there. See you, Anna. Any regulars of mine come in, keep them until I get back and don't let Colleen grab them, not until I'm packed and out of here. Don't worry, *Mr* James, I'll be out of Butetown by this time tomorrow.'

Aled tipped his hat to her and left the house. He followed Gertie to Bute Street. He'd been a pickpocket and a good one in his time. It was easy to slip a couple of fivers into Gertie's pocket before turning into his club.

'You shut down your roulette wheel for the night?' Aled asked David when he walked into his office at midnight.

'Ten minutes ago, Mr James.'

Aled looked to Aiden who was sitting next to Freddie. 'You and David go round the card tables, Aiden, take everything except the floats, put it together with the money already in the safe, take it down to the bank and lock it in the night safe.'

'Isn't it too early, boss?' Aiden asked. 'We usually go after the club is closed.'

'I've been looking at the tables. We've had a good night. I'd be happier if some of the money was off the premises now. Freddie, you drive them.'

'Boss, it's only a couple of hundred yards—' Aiden began.

'And I'd be happier if you had Freddie with you,' Aled interrupted sharply. 'Now start collecting that money.'

'Yes, boss. David.' Aidan led the way out of the door. They passed Judy, who was wearing the crimson silk dress Aled had insisted on buying.

'Only a couple more songs to go.' Aled smiled as he saw her. 'Do you fancy supper in my suite in the Windsor after the club closes?'

'Not tonight, Aled.'

'Anything the matter?'

'I'm tired, and I have to face Edyth when I go home.'

'She waits up for you?'

'No she doesn't, but she's a light sleeper and she knows about us.'

'How?' he questioned warily.

'Because I told her. I'm not very good at keeping secrets,' she explained.

'And what exactly did you tell her?'

'That we're carrying on.'

'And what did she say?'

'What I expected her to say.' Judy sat on the edge of his desk. 'She wasn't very happy.'

'Judy, please don't spoil what we have by starting a fight.'

'I'm not, I'm just telling you that Edyth knows.'

'If you can't make supper tonight, how about lunch tomorrow, in my suite?'

'I'll be more alive then. Shall I come round about twelve o'clock?'

'Make it one; I have a few things to do in the morning.' He opened his desk drawer.

'Even better, I can have a longer lie-in.' She jumped down off his desk. 'I'd better go and ask Mandy to check my make-up before I go on.'

Judy left the room and Aled lifted an envelope from his drawer. He opened it and read the 'letter' it contained for the tenth time since it had been handed to him as he had left the Windsor. The receptionist had told him that it had been hand delivered by one of the unemployed seamen who hung around the streets, but the man had only been able to give him a vague description that could have fitted any one of a hundred men. And given the message, there was little point in trying to track down the seaman. He knew who had sent it, although there was no handwriting, just letters cut from newspaper headlines and pasted on to a sheet of plain paper.

## AVOID TROUBLE – PAY YOUR INSURANCE

'Boss.' Aiden walked in and Aled returned the sheet and envelope to his drawer. 'We've counted and bagged the money. We're taking ninety pounds to the night safe.'

'You've made the entry in the ledgers?'

'Yes.'

'You're prepared for trouble if it comes?'

Aiden palmed a knife. 'Always, boss.'

'When you're done, you and David can come back here and help close up for the night. Freddie can drive Miss King home. While he's gone you can count and bag whatever's left above the float. When Freddie comes back, and not before, the three of you can make another trip to the night safe.'

'Yes, boss.'

'Aiden.' Aled waited until Aiden turned around. 'I didn't pay Charlie Moore's insurance.'

'I didn't expect you to, boss.'

David watched Aiden stash the cash bags they had filled with the night's takings into a briefcase and lock it. Aiden then wound a chain around both his wrist and the handle of the case and secured it with a padlock and steel chain. He handed the keys to the padlock and the briefcase to Freddie, who slipped them into the top pocket of his evening suit.

'The boss is panicking over nothing,' Freddie said in his Irish lilt. 'Tiger Bay is a kiddie's playground compared to New York.'

'I've never known the boss to get worried over nothing.' Aiden picked up the case and handed the key to the night safe to David. 'Let's go.'

Freddie went ahead of them and opened the car. David and Aiden climbed into the back. As they drove the short distance to the bank, David looked out of the window. Bute Street was quieter than the side streets. As usual, the open-air casinos on the street corners were crowded with both players and onlookers but the cool autumn weather had kept the women and children indoors and there were no musicians in sight. Winter was coming to the Bay and he suspected that it was going to be quieter than the summer had been.

Freddie stopped the car outside the bank. He felt in his pocket for the keys Aiden had given him.

'I'll open the night safe.' David left the car and looked

up and down the street. A street lamp burned brightly directly in front of the bank, but the corner that marked the junction with West Bute Street was shrouded in shadow. The only sounds he could hear were the ships' hooters and the cries of excitement from the gamblers some distance away.

He bent over the night safe, which was set low in the wall of the bank. A shadow moved. He turned. A skinny middle-aged woman was standing in front of him, dressed like most of the street walkers in too few clothes and too much make-up. She held out a cigarette.

'Got a light, lover boy?'

'Don't smoke,' David answered.

'Want something else?' She pulled down the neck of her low-cut dress and pushed out her flat chest.

'Clear off.'

'No need to be rude.'

Aiden climbed out of the back of the car. 'You're not wanted, miss. Buzz off.'

David turned back to the night safe but a heavy blow between his shoulderblades felled him to his knees. It was followed by a second blow to the back of his head. The world blurred into grey and black swirls. He was vaguely aware of someone screaming as he collapsed headlong on to the filthy pavement. It was only when he closed his mouth he realised the screams had been his own.

He lay in excruciating pain, unable to move a muscle. Shapes and shadows moved above and around him. He heard the dull thuds of fists hammering into flesh, interspersed with sharp gasps of breath. He tried to cry out again but failed to make a sound.

Something heavy fell on top of him. He struggled to move it aside and Aiden's face loomed barely an inch away from his. Aiden's eyes were open, staring, and something dark and sticky was oozing from his mouth. It took David a few minutes to realise it was blood.

*

'Turn him on to his back – I need pressure. Here!'

David lay curled in anguish on the pavement as Aiden was hauled off and laid alongside him. He watched Micah work frantically. He wanted to help, tried to help, but it was torture simply to draw breath.

Micah took off his jacket and crumpled it into a ball. He grabbed a constable's hand and pushed the jacket into it before pressing it down hard on to Aiden's chest. 'Come on,' he urged the rookie constable, setting his own hands over the officer's. 'A strong boy like you can press harder than that.'

Aiden turned his head and looked directly at David.

'Aiden?' David whispered.

Aiden's eyes glistened darkly like wet coal pebbles into his.

'Aiden?'

Aiden blinked.

'Keep talking to him, David,' Micah shouted. 'Keep talking. Aiden, look at David, Aiden, fight the pain . . . '

David kept whispering Aiden's name, although even as he watched, a cloud filmed Aiden's eyes. Aiden could still see him, David was certain of it, but it was as though someone was drawing a veil between them.

'Press harder,' Micah urged the officer as he continued to try to stem the flow of blood from Aiden's chest. 'Where the hell is that ambulance?'

'They'll be here as soon as they can, Micah.'

David looked up and saw that they were surrounded by a sea of uniformed police officers.

'Carry on pressing,' Micah urged, but even through his pain David sensed that Micah was speaking automatically, without thought as to what he was saying.

David heard Freddie's distinctive Irish drawl. 'One of you go to the Tiger Ragtime, get the boss down here. They cut the chain on Aiden's wrist and got our money. Over ninety quid . . . '

'Freddie, are you all right?' Micah asked.

'Flesh wound on my arm. Bastard shredded my new suit jacket,' he cursed.

'Trust a bloody Irishman,' one of the coppers said. 'His arm's been carved into dog meat and all he can think about is his suit.'

'Keep pressing down on that jacket.' Micah turned from Aiden to Freddie. He pulled the tie from around his neck and tied it tightly on the Irishman's upper arm before looking at David. 'Where does it hurt?'

'My back, my head . . . ' When Micah tried to move him, black shadows crawled upwards from the ground, smothering him, making it impossible for him to breathe.

'Don't you faint on me, David! David!' Micah's voice, high pitched, urgent, penetrated the fog that had closed in on David.

'The ambulances are coming.' One of the rookies blew his whistle as hard as he could and waved his arms in the air.

'There are enough of us standing around here, boy. I don't think you need to do that,' Constable Murphy, one of the older, more experienced officers said calmly.

An ambulance parked alongside them and a man climbed out.

'This one goes first. Knife wound to the chest has punctured the heart.' Micah pointed to Aiden. 'You,' he looked at the young officer who was still holding the blood-soaked jacket over Aiden's chest, 'get in the ambulance with him, and don't let that pressure up for an instant.'

'Me . . . ?'

'You, son.' Constable Murphy helped the ambulanceman get a stretcher out of the back of the van.

'Another ambulance is behind us, doctor,' the ambulanceman said, as he and his colleague prepared to move Aiden on to the stretcher.

'I'm not a doctor,' Micah said.

'You behave like one.'

Bells ringing, a second ambulance pulled up behind the first.

'We need a firm board on the stretcher here,' Micah called out as soon as the driver and his mate emerged. 'Spinal injuries and concussion. Freddie,' Micah finally looked at the Irishman, 'keep that tourniquet I've tied on your arm and get in with David, will you? I'm going with Aiden.'

Judy and Edyth jumped out of the Black Maria and ran headlong into the Royal Infirmary. It was only when they reached the deserted foyer and saw the empty corridors stretching around them that they realised they didn't have a clue which direction to go in.

A porter rounded a corner. He took one look at Judy in her crimson silk evening gown and Edyth in the work overall and coat she had thrown over her nightdress and stopped dead in his tracks.

'A relative was brought in tonight . . . '

'A knifing victim. Fight in Bute Street? Three men were injured.' Constable Murphy walked in behind them.

'Two are in theatre, one's in the treatment room. There are people in the waiting room.' The porter pointed down a corridor directly ahead of them. 'Want me to go with you?'

'No, we'll find them.' Murphy took hold of Edyth's arm and led the way.

Micah was standing in his blood-soaked shirt-sleeves outside a door at the end of the corridor, talking to a doctor wearing a surgeon's apron and hat. A mask was pulled down around the doctor's neck and there were blood splashes on his sleeves and the front of his apron.

'He didn't stand a chance,' the surgeon declared. 'The knife penetrated upwards from below the ribcage, straight into the heart, damaging the main artery. It's a wonder he lived until he reached here. You did all that could be done, but he was a dead man the moment that knife hit the blood vessel.'

Edyth caught the tail end of their conversation and ran towards them. 'Micah . . . David . . . ?'

Micah slipped his arm around Edyth's shoulders. 'I'm fine and David is being operated on now.'

Edyth turned deathly pale. 'The blood on your shirt . . . '

'Most of it is Aiden Collins's.'

'Who's dead?'

'Aiden,' Micah answered. 'David Ellis is the boy who was brought in with spinal injuries and concussion,' he explained to the doctor.

'I'm sorry, Miss . . . ?'

'Mrs Slater, I'm a relative.' Edyth clung to Micah.

'As Micah said, one of my colleagues is operating on him now. It may be some time before he finishes.'

'Can we see David,' Edyth begged.

'Not while he's in theatre.' The doctor indicated the waiting room. 'You'll be more comfortable in there.'

Judy was already in the waiting room. She'd taken the chair next to Aled James, who was sitting, slumped forward, on a hard upright chair. He glanced up as they walked in.

'You got here quickly, Aled,' Micah commented suspiciously.

'The police came to the club. They took me to the bank, you'd just left in the ambulances but my car was parked outside so I drove it up here.' He rose to his feet and offered Micah his hand. 'Thank you. Freddie and the doctors told me that you did everything you could to save Aiden's life.'

Micah shook his hand before helping Edyth on to a chair. 'Whatever I did, it wasn't enough. How is Freddie?'

'Preparing to have his arm stitched and be questioned by the police when I saw him a few minutes ago. They took him into a treatment room but they told me I could see him again later.'

'Did he see who killed Aiden?'

'Do you need to ask?' Aled answered.

'Charlie Moore's thugs?' Micah guessed.

'They made a mistake leaving Freddie alive. After seeing the way Aiden died he won't be afraid to testify in court.'

'Freddie – and you, Mr James – will need police protection,' Constable Murphy said from the doorway.

'I'll buy Freddie all the protection he needs.' Aled lifted his head and looked at Murphy. 'That's the only sure way that Freddie Leary will live to see the inside of a courtroom.' He turned and stared at Judy as if he were seeing her for the first time. 'When the police told me what had happened I ordered the boys who man the doors to walk you home.'

'When I came off stage and heard that David, Aiden and Freddie had been hurt, I had to come here with Edyth. I didn't know Aiden was dead. I'm so sorry.' Judy was sincere. She had been terrified of Aiden the first time she had met him but she had known him long enough to discover that he was blindly loyal to Aled. And because she also worked for Aled, he had regarded her as one of the people he should protect.

'I have to tell Harry about David . . . he'll never forgive me if I don't.' Edyth felt frantically in her coat pocket for pennies for a public telephone. 'Has anyone any change?'

'There's an office down the corridor that has a telephone they allow relatives to make calls from. I'll take you there, Mrs Slater,' Constable Murphy offered.

A nurse brought in a tray holding a teapot, sugar bowl, milk jug and half a dozen thick white institution mugs. 'The doctor ordered it,' she explained. 'If you are all waiting for David Ellis to come out of surgery, you'll probably be here until morning.'

*

At five o'clock, Judy felt that she had been condemned to sit in the waiting room for eternity. Every bit of her ached, especially the sides of her breasts confined by the boned strapless bodice of her gown. She felt ridiculously over-dressed for a hospital as well as freezing cold and over-exposed, given the Spartan surroundings of the icy waiting room. She had also left the club in such a hurry she had forgotten her stole.

When Aled saw her shivering, he emptied his evening jacket of his wallet, cigar case and lighter and draped it over her shoulders. She continued to sit next to him, her fingers locked in his, occasionally stealing sideway glances up at his face, stern and intractable. She sensed that he held himself responsible for Aiden's death and wished she could take some of the pain he was obviously feeling.

As dawn paled the light in the window from dark to pale grey, a porter wheeled Freddie past the open door of the waiting room. His round face was white beneath his shock of red hair. His arm was swathed in bandages and supported by a sling. A red flannel hospital dressing gown hung loosely over his shoulders. The police sergeant who was walking behind Freddie's chair signalled to Murphy and Aled. They rose and followed him. The wheels on the chair squeaked, growing fainter with distance until they ceased altogether. After ten minutes of silence Harry rushed in.

Micah took him outside. They held an urgent whispered conversation before rejoining Edyth and Judy. The surgeon didn't appear until half past six. He walked into the waiting room and removed his mask. To Micah's relief he was smiling.

'We've set David Ellis's collar bone, and wired two broken vertebrae. His spinal column appears to be unaffected. He has a hairline fracture of the skull—'

'What does that mean?' Edyth asked, too upset to interpret the technical language.

The surgeon looked kindly at her. 'It means that given

time, good medical care and nursing, David Ellis should make a full recovery without suffering any long-term ill effects.'

'All his medical bills will be covered.' Harry didn't like the fact that the degree of care given to a patient depended on the ability to pay hospital bills, but he was realistic enough to know it was the case.

'The office will be open at nine,' the surgeon informed him briefly.

'Thank you.'

'We've strapped Mr Ellis into a spinal corset, and put him on bed rest. A couple of weeks and he should be well enough to leave here, provided he has someone to look after him.'

'There'll be a queue of people willing and able to do that,' Micah volunteered.

'Can we see him?' Harry asked.

'He's in the recovery room. He'll be taken up to the ward shortly. I'd rather you waited until visiting—'

'Please,' Edyth begged. 'Just for one minute.'

'As there's no one else in the recovery room, you may look in through the window. But only for a few seconds,' the doctor warned. 'The anaesthetic hasn't worn off, so he's unconscious, but any disturbance could have a detrimental effect.'

'We won't make a sound,' Edyth promised.

Judy hung back. 'I'll wait here for Aled.'

'I'll stay with Judy.' Micah attempted to give Edyth an encouraging smile but she was too upset to return it.

Harry held out his hand, Edyth took it and they followed the doctor.

Judy huddled beneath Aled's jacket. 'I can't believe the change a day has made. Yesterday all I had to think about was what gown to wear for my act in the club . . . and now . . . Aled will have Aiden's funeral to organise. Freddie and David will have to be looked after . . . '

'By the hospital, not by you.' Micah went to her and opened his arms. She almost fell into them.

'I'm sorry,' she faltered as the first tears fell from her eyes. 'I'm not helping.'

'None of us are, because there's nothing that we can do.' Micah stroked her hair back from her face and held her the way he would have a child.

Constable Murphy returned and knocked on the open door. 'Micah, as you were the first person on the scene with any medical knowledge we'll need a statement from you. The hospital has given us the use of an office. Can you come with me now so we can take it down?'

Judy released him and stepped back. 'Go; I can see Harry and Edyth coming back.'

Micah waited until they entered the waiting room. 'How's David?' he asked.

'He looks like you'd expect someone to look who's just had an operation,' Edyth said. 'But you heard the doctor. He's going to be fine, which is more than can be said for Judy if she doesn't get some rest.'

'You do look exhausted, Judy,' Harry concurred. 'I'm taking Edyth back to the bakery. I think you should come with us and go to bed.'

'I'll wait for Aled . . . ' Judy began.

'He'll be a while yet, Miss King,' Murphy warned. 'They were only halfway through the statements when I left the office just now. And Mr James still had to complete all the formalities relating to Mr Aiden Collins.'

'I'd still rather wait.'

'Judy, formally identifying Aiden Collins's body and completing the forms could take all morning.' Harry took a pencil and notebook from his pocket. 'Write Aled a note. Constable Murphy will see that he gets it.'

'I will, Miss King,' the officer assured her.

'You'll be no use to Aled or anyone else if you don't get some sleep,' Harry warned.

Judy took the notebook and pencil and scribbled,

*Gone home, telephone me as soon as you can.* She thought for a moment and added *Love Judy,* not caring who saw it, but she gave the note and Aled's jacket to Micah, not Constable Murphy.

Harry took his keys from his overcoat pocket, and slipped off the coat. He folded it around Judy's shoulders. 'It's cold out there.'

'Thank you.'

'I gave the ward sister all the information I could about David while you were talking to the surgeon, Harry, but I didn't know the name of his doctor. I told her that you and Mary were next of kin, but I gave her my address and telephone number because I live closer to the hospital.'

'I'll fill in any gaps when I come back to open an account in the office. Let's go. Both of you are sleeping on your feet.'

'Not really,' Edyth yawned.

'Yes, really. Come on, my car is parked close to the front door.'

'I feel as though I'm abandoning David,' Edyth murmured.

'We both are, but in the best place.' Harry led Judy and Edyth down the corridor and out through the front door of the infirmary.

He had parked his open-topped Crossley tourer next to Aled's Bentley. He left the girls and stepped between the cars, intending to open the back and front passenger doors of the tourer, when someone ran full tilt through the gates and lunged at him.

Caught unawares, Harry staggered back and stared at the man who was waving something in front of his eyes. Something, long and thin and as crimson as Judy's dress. It took a few seconds for his numbed brain to recognise it as a knife.

He glanced down and saw blood seeping through his jacket and waistcoat. Edyth screamed and he saw a second man dragging her back away from him. The man wielding a knife was now bearing down on Judy. Harry threw himself between them.

The man tried to push him aside. Hampered by her long skirts and torn between a desire to help Edyth and Harry, Judy hesitated.

'The other boys didn't finish the job but we will. Say goodbye to your songbird, Aled James,' the man holding the knife hissed.

Harry summoned the last vestiges of his strength, and pushed Judy back towards the door of the infirmary. 'Run!' He blocked the man, preventing him from reaching Judy, and watched him sink the knife to the hilt in his stomach.

# CHAPTER TWENTY-TWO

Micah was walking out of the hospital when he heard Edyth scream and someone call Harry 'Aled'. He turned in time to see the man knife Harry. Micah shouted back into the foyer for help and ran to Harry.

Both assailants saw Micah charging towards them, the one holding Edyth threw her to the ground. She shouted, 'I'm all right,' and climbed to her feet.

Judy was pulling a nurse out through the door. Seeing the men running off, she rushed to Harry and knelt on the ground beside Micah, who was tending to Harry although his shirt and waistcoat were still soaked with Aiden's blood.

'What can I do?' Judy asked.

'Hold his head and talk to him,' Micah said, recognising Judy's need to help. 'Don't!' Micah shouted as Harry closed his hand on the knife. 'Stay absolutely still and don't touch it. He looked at the wound and applied pressure. It was all he could do out in the open without instruments and it hadn't worked for Aiden. There was no reason for him to think that the most basic of first-aid techniques would work for Harry either. He only knew that he had to try. He was aware of Edyth crouched beside him, talking to Harry, but he couldn't concentrate on anything except Harry's injuries.

Micah was still working on Harry when a doctor joined them, pushing Micah and Judy aside. The police followed and ran out through the gates, five minutes too late.

Edyth watched, mesmerised, as two porters and a

nurse lifted the tall slim body of her brother on to a stretcher and carried him into the hospital.

At midday, Micah walked out of the office where he had been talking to a senior police officer and into the waiting room to see Edyth and Judy sitting bolt upright and blinking hard – he suspected in an effort to stay awake. Aled was sitting across the room from them, flanked by a protective guard of four police officers. Micah couldn't help thinking that all the precautions were too late.

Edyth turned her dry-eyed, anguished face to Micah's. 'Any news?'

'I've just seen a doctor. Harry is out of surgery and out of danger. But they won't let us see him or wait any longer. Apparently we're disrupting the normal routine of the hospital.'

'You most certainly are.' A sister bustled in carrying a brown paper and string carrier stamped with ROYAL INFIRMARY, PATIENTS' PROPERTY. She went to Edyth. 'You are Mr Harry Evans's sister?'

'I am.' Edyth reached for the bag.

'Visiting is every Wednesday evening, from six o'clock until seven, and Saturday afternoon, three until four. Only one telephone call a day permitted to enquire after the patient.' She thawed a little when she saw the pain and exhaustion in Edyth's eyes. 'Mr Evans is doing fine. If you have to get stabbed, he chose the right place to do it, outside a hospital.'

'And David Ellis?' Edyth dreaded the telephone calls she would have to make to her parents and to Mary.

'As well as can be expected and resting comfortably.'

Unable to listen to any more platitudes after the long night and morning, Micah said, 'I'll meet you and Judy outside, Edyth. If you have the keys to Harry's car, I'll drive you home.'

'If you don't, Edyth, you can take my car,' Aled offered.

'Harry had his somewhere.' Edyth rummaged in the carrier bag and pulled them out. She gave them to Micah.

Aled looked to Micah. 'Micah—'

'It's been a long night, I'll see you later, Aled.'

Aled nodded and turned to the police. 'I've heard what I wanted to. I'll go with you to the station to finish making my statement.'

Micah walked out of the front door of the infirmary ahead of Judy and Edyth. A porter was scrubbing blood from the area around the cars. A thin watery sun shone down from a cloudy sky and all the stonework in the yard was glistening and damp from a recent downpour.

'You might not have saved Aiden Collins's life, Micah, but you saved Harry Evans's.' The doctor who had operated on Aiden was leaning against a wall, smoking a cigarette. He offered the packet to Micah, and Micah took one.

'I did what anyone would have done,' Micah said.

'You did what only a doctor could have done. You clamped the left gastric artery. If you hadn't, Harry Evans would have bled to death before he even reached theatre.'

'It's just as well that he was stabbed outside the infirmary.' Micah turned up the collar on his shirt as rain spattered down.

'It's just as well that you were around, Micah. You're wasted as a pastor.'

'Have you been talking to my sister?' Micah bent his head to the match the doctor struck.

'No, why do you ask?'

'No reason.'

Micah saw Edyth and Judy walking out of the door arm in arm. 'Look after the invalids, for their sake.'

The doctor smiled. 'I'll do that, Micah. Bye.'

Micah opened the door of Harry's Crossley. 'Bed for you two and no arguments.'

'After I've spoken to Mary and my mother.' Edyth

closed her hands into fists. 'Damn Aled James and damn the day he stepped off the boat in Tiger Bay.'

'Harry, David and a lot of other people, including Aiden Collins from the other side, would probably damn him with you.' Micah looked at Judy. But she climbed into the back of the car without saying a word.

A week after his operation, Harry was well enough to sit up in a chair at the side of his bed and read through the papers he had asked his solicitor to send him. Aled found him doing just that when he walked into his private room bearing an enormous basket. He dumped it on Harry's locker.

'I brought you some fruit.'

'So I see. On behalf of the entire ward I thank you, because there is no way that I will be able to eat all that.'

'You no longer have a police guard outside.' Aled pulled up a chair and sat beside Harry.

'The sergeant came in yesterday to tell me that they have picked up the two men who killed Aiden and attacked Freddie, David and me. Would you believe that they are called John and Tom Smith?'

'Interesting names, aren't they? What's even more interesting and galling is that the hired killers get caught, go to trial and hopefully a hanging and Charlie Moore and Geoff Arnold who apparently have been working hand in glove and employed them walk free.' Aled sat back in his chair. 'But to look on the bright side, the employers will lie low for a while.'

'You seem very sure of that,' Harry commented.

'I am very sure of that. Neither Arnold nor Moore would be walking around if I could prove anything, and they know it. But despite distributing largesse far and wide I haven't found anyone willing to grass on them. But I took care to let both of them know that I've hired a few more men, every one of them a trained soldier.

Which brings me to one of the reasons why I have come to see you.'

'How did you get in?' Harry looked through the door. There was no sign of the sister or the staff nurses who had no compunction about shooing out his parents, Edyth and Mary if they stayed one minute after the bell had been rung to signal the end of visiting. Or the police when they came with their endless questions about the man who had knifed him – a man who had been clearly identified by Micah, Judy and Edyth on the day of the attack.

Aled rubbed his thumb and forefinger together. 'The usual way.'

'You bribed the sister. I don't believe it,' Harry said.

'The sister cannot be bought, but lesser minions can. The dragon is on lunch break and half an hour will have to suffice for what I want to say you and David.'

'Have you seen David?'

'Not yet. Is he in a private room like you?'

'The general ward where I'll be moved later today. They keep these rooms for the critical patients.'

'And those rich enough to pay for them,' Aled said wryly. 'If I'm going to see David I'd better tell you why I'm here or I'll run out of time. First I want to thank you for taking the knife that was meant for me.'

'What are brothers for?' Harry joked.

'We might have the same father, Harry, but we'll never be brothers.'

There was a serious undercurrent to Aled's voice that Harry didn't dare contradict. 'I also wanted to tell you that in return I am going to give you the present you want most of all in the world.'

'Which is?' Harry asked warily.

'I'm giving David and Judy back to you.'

'Aled . . . '

Aled left his chair and returned it to the corner of the room. 'We live in different worlds, you and I, Harry. It's better that we don't see one another again. Just one favour in return.' He looked towards the window so Harry couldn't see the expression on his face. 'Be good to Judy. She's going to need all the kindness and support she can get for the next few months.'

'Harry is being discharged from here on Saturday and I'll be leaving next week.' David handed the fruit basket that Aled had brought him to one of the trainee nurses. 'I've been thinking about the club and the—'

'I've been thinking too, David.' Aled moved the chair closer to David's bed and lowered his voice so the men in the neighbouring beds couldn't hear what he was saying. 'It isn't that you don't handle yourself well, you do – for a kid.' He knew David would take his last comment as an insult, just as he'd intended. 'But after what happened to Aiden I've decided to employ older, more experienced people. No reflection on you, just the time and the place we live in.' He took an envelope from his inside pocket and handed it to David. 'Keep that safe and give it to Edyth or your sister when they come in to visit you. It's six months' pay. Call it danger money for getting beaten up. The doctors have told me that it won't take anywhere near that long to get you back on your feet. So you can take a holiday.'

'Mr James, please . . . '

Aled left his chair. 'It's for the best, David. I need people I can rely on around me and frankly,' he looked down on him, 'you're just too young and inexperienced.'

Aled turned on his heel and left the ward. He dared not look back. He'd ordered a special dinner to be served in his suite at the Windsor Hotel in a couple of hours but he doubted that he or his guest would eat it. He had one more goodbye to say and it was going to be the hardest of all.

Harry and Edyth's father, Lloyd, wasn't given to anger or rages, but when he and their mother Sali returned with Harry's wife Mary to the rooms above Edyth's shop after visiting Harry and David in the Royal Infirmary on Wednesday evening he was furious. He looked at the supper Edyth had laid out on the table in her upstairs sitting room, walked past it, and sat on the window seat.

'You have to leave Tiger Bay, Edyth,' he said sharply. 'And so does David. The sooner the better.' He looked around the room. 'Times are hard and you may not get as much as you paid for this place, but if you want to buy a comparable business in Pontypridd its price will be just as low.'

'Dad . . . '

'Looking at those two boys lying in their hospital beds was no different to looking at the broken bodies of the soldiers who were stupid enough to sign up to fight the politicians' senseless battles in the Great War. And I saw enough of those when I visited your Uncle Joey when he was convalescing in 1918. Make no mistake about it, Edyth, Harry and David are casualties of war – a stupid crass gang war – and over what? Money.'

Micah, who had been roped in by Edyth to provide moral support in Judy's absence, dared to speak up. 'With all due respect, Mr Evans, what happened to David and Harry could have happened anywhere in Wales or Britain.'

'You think so?' Lloyd's eyes were cold and Edyth silently willed Micah not to continue the argument.

'David could have taken a job as a bookie's runner anywhere. They have them in Cardiff, possibly even Pontypridd, and where there's money to be made, if you'll pardon the very bad pun, there'll be turf wars. As for the men who killed Aiden and attacked Harry and David, the police have them in custody. They'll be tried, sentenced and punished. So, far from being a lawless place where murderers are free to roam the streets, you have to admit that Tiger Bay is better policed than many other areas.'

'Like Cheltenham and Mayfair, for instance,' Lloyd suggested caustically.

'Aled James didn't attract any of the wrong kind of attention until he started making money and moving in on other people's turf, then people saw him as an easy target. They've since discovered how wrong they were. And Harry was only attacked because he was mistaken for Aled.'

'We told you, Dad, the men who attacked Harry called him Aled. They really thought he was Aled James,' Edyth pleaded.

'Edyth has worked hard to build a successful business here, sir.' Micah pressed home the small advantage he felt that he and Edyth had gained for all it was worth.

'So you're telling me that unlike Aled James, Edyth hasn't attracted the wrong kind of attention from the natives of Tiger Bay?'

'Yes, sir.'

Lloyd looked at him. 'Not even from you?'

Edyth crossed her fingers behind her back to no avail.

'I love her with all my heart, sir, and I hope to marry her as soon as she is free. With your permission,' Micah added tactfully.

Lloyd turned to Edyth. 'And what do you have to say about this?'

'That I love Micah too.'

'I see.' Lloyd's grimace turned to a smile. 'Well, he's better than the last one you married, I'll give him that.'

'Lloyd, what a thing to say,' Sali reprimanded. 'Now come to the table and start eating. Mary will want to get back to the children to make sure that our housekeeper has bathed them and put them to bed properly. That's if she got a look in with all the aunts wanting to take over.'

'You will come here for lunch on Saturday before you take Harry back to Pontypridd?' Edyth asked.

'That depends on how Harry feels,' Mary answered. 'It's a pity that David has to stay in hospital another week.' She sat next to Edyth at the table and Edyth blanched when she saw the dark circles beneath her sister-in-law's eyes. 'The turf war', as Micah had christened it, and the worry over Harry and David had taken their toll on all of them but Mary had suffered the most.

'You heard David tonight,' Edyth said. 'He point blank refuses to leave the Bay. But don't worry, he's comfortable living with Micah's sister and I'll find him a job here in my baker's.'

'A made-up job?' Lloyd asked.

'No, Dad.' Edyth stretched the truth. 'My delivery boy Jamie is going to sea.' Edyth knew it was no more than a vague hope on Jamie's part the way shipping was. 'In the meantime, Jamie can train David up to replace him, that way the transition will go smoothly.'

'Where's Judy tonight? Is she in the club?' Sali asked.

'No, Aled closed it for a week out of respect for Aiden, but he intends to reopen it next Tuesday.' Edyth gave Micah a quick conscious look. 'She's gone out for dinner with a friend.'

'This is just like old times,' Judy said when Aled opened the door to her and showed her into the sitting room of his suite.

A table had been laid next to the window, a steaming trolley of hot chafing dishes pulled up alongside it. A waiter was standing in front of a stand holding a bucket of ice. He was uncorking a bottle of wine.

'As soon as you have finished doing that, you can leave,' Aled said abruptly. 'We'll serve ourselves.'

The waiter opened the wine, placed it in the bucket and retreated to the door. 'Enjoy your meal, Mr James, Miss King.'

Aled took Judy's coat and carried it into the bedroom. She looked around and noticed a few small changes.

There was a selection of framed photographs among the litter of invitations on the mantelpiece. One of Freddie, Aled and Aiden that had been taken the night the club opened and another of Aled with a young attractive blonde.

'Who is that?' she asked, when Aled returned from the bedroom.

'Councillor Harvill's daughter. We're going to be married.'

'You're what?'

'Married,' he repeated. 'The councillor is a strong player in the Chamber of Commerce as well a member of various influential committees. Businesswise he can do me a lot of good.'

Judy's legs buckled from under her and she sank down on the sofa.

'Are you all right?' He poured her a glass of wine and handed it to her. It slipped through her fingers and spilled on the carpet. 'Leave it,' he ordered when she stooped to mop it up. 'Housekeeping will see to it.'

'Sorry,' she snapped. 'My maid's training is showing through. When will you marry . . . ?' Judy pointed at the photograph.

'Councillor Harvill's daughter? Her name is Moira, by the way. Probably next spring. Her mother seems to think it's the best time for a society wedding.'

Judy's green eyes blazed as she looked at him. 'I thought . . . I thought . . . ' She fell silent when she recalled her conversation with Edyth. She had admitted that Aled wasn't the type of man to be faithful to any one woman. He had never promised her anything . . . so what right did she have to be angry with him because he was marrying someone else?

'You didn't think that you and I were going to have anything other than a good time together, did you, Judy?' Aled chided. 'Given your grandfather's blood, you know I could never take you to a Chamber of Commerce or

Council function. I need a wife who can help me get on and up in the world.'

'I know what people think of my grandfather's blood,' she said acidly. 'Thanks to your insistence on taking me to a department store in the middle of Cardiff, I know only too well what white people outside Butetown think of coloured people. I believe they place us slightly higher than dogs and considerably lower than human. What I didn't know was that you thought it was fine for us to be employed by you and, like Aiden, even die for you. To use us as bed mates to make love to but never to be seen with in polite circles.'

'Judy, it's the way of the world; I live in it as best I can. We had fun. But it was never going to last, we both knew that . . . ' He tried to touch her and she moved away from him.

'I take it there'll be no romp in the bedroom tonight. I'd better telephone Anna Hughes and ask her to send up Gertie's replacement. I hear she's quite a pretty little redhead.'

'You bastard.' Judy brought her hand back and slapped him with full force across the face.

'If you feel like that about me, Judy, forget your contract and working in the club. I won't hold you to it. I'll send the clothes I bought you to Edyth's shop.'

'Keep your bloody clothes.' Forgetting her coat, Judy wrenched open the door and fled so Aled wouldn't see the tears in her eyes. It was just as well she didn't look back at him or she would have seen the tears in his.

'Leave the chair here, please,' Harry said to the porter who had wheeled him to David's bed.

'Be back for you in two minutes or Sister will have my guts for garters.' There wasn't a trace of humour in the porter's voice.

'This is my brother-in-law,' Harry pleaded, 'give us ten.'

'You can have as long as it takes Sister to get back from her meeting, not a second more,' the porter said on his way out.

'You're going home?' David asked Harry.

'Back to Pontypridd for a couple of weeks until I get back to normal and then home to the farm. Remember we talked about that pub.'

'I have some money saved but it's not enough. Not even with what Aled gave me and I'm not sure I should keep it—'

'Listen, David. I know Edyth means well in offering you a job but you don't want to take it, do you?'

'It smacks of charity.'

'I've thought of a way for you to get that pub right away.'

'I'm not taking anything from you.'

'No gift, David. In fact, I'd be taking something from you. Mary loves the farm. I know she'd live out her life there if she could, but strictly speaking it's not hers.'

'As far as I'm concerned she can have it,' David said carelessly.

'If you sign over your share of the family farm to my trust it will release enough capital to buy you a pub. I've had nothing better to do than write to my solicitors when I was here and they sent me details of some of the properties that are for sale in Butetown. It's a good time to buy now – the slump has forced prices down.' He handed David a pile of estate agents' brochures. 'Take a look at them. I know you'll need help to run it, but there are plenty of good men out of work, including Jed King, and if you're not too proud I'll send the accountant down from Gwilym James once a week to check you're on the right track. But I warn you now, I'll charge you the going rate for his services.'

'I'd expect you to.' David sat up and winced as he moved his back.

'That's the porter coming back for me.' Harry grabbed

David's hand and shook it. 'One more thing before I go, if you're thinking of taking on a resident singer I know someone who might be in the market for a job.'

'It's good of you two to come and see me off.' Harry grasped Edyth and Micah's hands as Lloyd wheeled him to his car.

'I wanted you to come to lunch,' Edyth complained.

'As soon as I'm up to it, we will, won't we, Mary?' Harry smiled at his wife.

'I promise, Edyth.' Mary couldn't stop looking at Harry and smiling.

'Just one thing, sis,' Harry said casually. 'I've had nothing to do this last week except catch up on paperwork. The Gwilym James charity fund has agreed to supply both Butetown's Salvation Army soup kitchen and the Methodist Hall with fifty plain loaves a day. Can you bake that many?'

'Oh no you don't, Harry Evans. That's charity . . . '

'Yes it is,' Harry agreed blithely. 'Gwilym James has always given away five per cent of its profits to the poor. But if you can't handle the contract, sis, we'll have to find someone who can. And that will be a pity, because after tasting it, I've no doubt your bread is superior to everyone else's.'

'Harry . . . '

'A yes or no will do. Take it or leave it. The contract is going begging. You have the capacity?'

'Yes,' Edyth answered, 'of course I do.'

'Then that's settled. I'd hate the unemployed and the children on the Bay to settle for second-rate bread. No, Dad.' He shook off his father's helping hand, closed his hands around the arms of the wheelchair and levered himself upright. 'I will get myself into the car under my own steam, thank you. I'll tell my solicitor to put the contract in the post, Edie. It's worth over fifty pounds a week. I know bread is plain goods and there's not as much profit as pies and pasties but it should take your turnover back up to where it was when the builders were working on the Tiger Ragtime.' Harry fell into the back of the car and sprawled out weakly on the back seat. Edyth reflected that it was just as well her mother had decided not to come to fetch him with her father and Mary. The way Harry was lying, there wouldn't have been room for her.

'Edie.' Lloyd opened his arms.

'Dad.' Edyth hugged and kissed her father, then Mary. 'Look after Harry.'

'And you look after David. You're sure it won't be too much for you having him recuperate with you next week,' Mary asked.

'Not at all, Harry tells me he's so immersed in the pub he's decided to buy, he'll be no trouble at all,' Edyth assured her.

Lloyd shook Micah's hand. 'Look after my most troublesome daughter for me?'

'I will, sir,' Micah assured him.

'It's Lloyd, not sir.'

Micah and Edyth stood in the car park of the Royal Infirmary and waved them off.

'Back to the baker's?' Micah asked as Lloyd's car disappeared from sight.

'Please.' Edyth climbed into the passenger seat of his van.

'It seems to me that your brother has tried to put the whole of Tiger Bay to rights with his plotting while he was in hospital,' Micah commented as he drove out on to the main road.

'He takes after my mother in that respect. You should hear some of the stories my uncles Joey and Victor tell about her. It was my mother who persuaded my grandfather and uncles to sell some of the terrace houses they'd bought when miners' wages were high, to buy my

Uncle Victor his farm. And she persuaded the management of Gwilym James to give Uncle Joey a job when the pit wouldn't take him back after the strike because of his union activities – although Harry has always said that Gwilym James got the best of that bargain. Uncle Joey is a born salesman.'

'So, putting the world to rights is a family hobby.' The traffic slowed and Micah rested his arm around her shoulders. 'I only wish he could put your annulment to rights. I can't wait for us to get married.'

'I need to talk to you about that.'

'Don't tell me that Peter has changed his mind about giving you one?' he said anxiously.

'No.' She took a deep breath and steeled herself for an explosion. 'I received the papers from Peter weeks ago.'

He slammed on the brakes and pulled into the side of the road. 'How many weeks ago?'

'Eight . . . nine . . . '

'And you didn't tell me?' He glared at her.

'Micah, please don't look at me like that. Nothing's changed. I love you—'

'Evidently not enough to marry me,' he said curtly.

'Not enough to subjugate my life to yours the way I did when I was married to Peter. I want to be your wife in every sense of the word, Micah. I want us to have a home and a sitting room where we can shut out the world if we want to, not a public room in the mission where sailors sit and sing and eat waffles and drink beer and aquavit all night. I want us to have children, who we can spend time teaching and watching grow . . . '

He started the engine and she fell silent. He drove directly to her shop and stopped outside.

'Micah?'

He continued to look straight ahead out of the windscreen. She opened the van door and stepped out on to the pavement. He drove away before she had time to close it.

# CHAPTER TWENTY-THREE

'It's not the Ragtime, but it's a nice little local,' David said proudly to Harry. He looked expectantly at Judy and Edyth, obviously hoping that they'd heap more praise on the pub he'd bought.

'It's a very nice little local,' Harry agreed. 'Mary and I are most impressed.'

'Or we will be when the builders have finished,' Mary qualified. It had taken Harry days of coaxing, and several invitations from Edyth, to persuade Mary to make the trip down to the Bay to see David's new home and business.

'You made a wise choice and spent your money well.' Harry lifted up his plate and passed it to Edyth. 'I'll have another slice of chicken pie, please. It's very good. Did you make it or Moody?'

'Neither of us.' Edyth cut into the hot pie. 'Judy did.'

'My congratulations to the chef. This is a very tasty lunch and just what we need on a foul Sunday like this.'

'When I saw the weather this morning I wanted to catch the train down from Pontypridd. Harry wouldn't hear of it. But I'm dreading the drive back. Harry isn't that strong yet—'

'Yes I am, Mary,' Harry contradicted. 'And we will go back later this afternoon and back to the farm tomorrow.'

'It's a long drive to the farm. We could wait another day in Pontypridd,' she said hesitantly.

'Did you all hear that?' Harry looked around the table.

'My wife volunteering to stay in Pontypridd an extra day, rather than go back to the farm.'

'Stop teasing Mary, Harry,' Edyth reprimanded.

'That's right, gang up on me,' Harry grumbled good naturedly, heaping mashed potatoes next to the slice of pie Edyth had given him and smothering the lot with gravy. 'Lennie, David, both of you are far too quiet. I need male support here. Where is Micah by the way, Edyth?'

'He had to go back to Gdansk on family business. Something to do with his father's estate,' Judy answered, hoping to spare Edyth some pain. No one had seen Micah since the day he had brought Edyth back from the hospital. Not even Helga, although he'd sent his sister a note telling her where he was going and ordering her not to worry, 'for the sake of his niece or nephew'. Judy suspected, but she didn't know for certain, that he and Edyth had quarrelled. A temporary pastor had been assigned from Swansea but he wasn't Micah and, on that basis alone, the locals had unanimously decided not to like him.

Harry lifted his glass of water. 'To David's pub, his life as a landlord, to wish him luck in finding good staff to run it and to the singer who's agreed to bring in the customers.'

Edyth, Mary, Judy, Lennie and David all lifted their glasses and drank.

'If you don't bring them pouring through the doors, Judy, nothing will,' Lennie said, serious for once.

'Is the band playing with you, Judy?' Harry returned to his pie.

'The Bute Street Blues is no more,' Judy said. 'Abdul Akbar – he played trumpet – has agreed to play the piano for me and Steve Chan has offered to play the drums. With Micah and two of my uncles away and Jed working behind the bar for David those two are all that's left of the band, except me. But, to look on the positive side, my

Aunt Bessie is behaving like the cat that has the cream. With my uncle in regular work and Jamie and Kristina both working for Edyth, she's never been so well off. It's the first time Uncle Tony and Uncle Ron's families haven't had to go to the tally man for a sub before their ship has come in.'

'Have you thought what your opening song might be tomorrow, Judy?' Harry sprinkled more salt on his potatoes.

'"Dancing With Tears in my Eyes".'

'Good choice,' Lennie concurred.

'Who can that be at this time on a Sunday?' Edyth said at a loud hammering on the door.

'Someone who wants bread,' Harry suggested.

'They'll be lucky. We sold out before midday yesterday.'

'You're still eating, I'll go.' Judy dropped her napkin on to her side plate and left the table.

'Has Judy settled back to working here?' Harry asked when he heard her running down the stairs.

'Not really,' Edyth replied honestly. 'It must be hard serving people in a shop after receiving standing ovations in the New Theatre and starring in the Tiger Ragtime and she still has the radio show to do. She might not realise it but I know her working here is only a stopgap until another impresario snaps her up.'

'It can only be a matter of time.' Lennie went to the window and looked outside.

'I can't understand Aled sacking me and Judy,' David said heatedly. 'It's not as if either of us did anything—'

Voices resounded from downstairs. Judy's high-pitched and furious intermingled with a man's deeper, steadier tones. Edyth left her seat.

'I'll go down,' Lennie volunteered.

'This is my shop—'

'It's someone from the club,' Lennie explained. 'I know him.'

'As I'm the man of the house, I should be going.' David put down his knife and fork.

'You have a back problem. Besides, the fact that Judy is arguing not fighting with whoever it is suggests he hasn't a knife in his hand. That means that even I, a born coward, can see to it.' Lennie left the room and walked down the stairs into the hall.

'I don't care what Mr Aled James said, you are not bringing any of those clothes over this doorstep,' Judy shouted. 'Not one, so you can put them all back in that van right now!'

'Problem, Colin?' Lennie asked.

'I've been asked to deliver these here, Lennie, but the lady won't take them.' The middle-aged van driver looked to Lennie for help.

'I'm not surprised,' Lennie said with a straight face. 'A devout Christian like her wouldn't take delivery of anything except a Bible on a Sunday.'

'Sorry, madam.' The man stepped back. 'I should have thought. Mr James gave me the job as an extra and as I'm busy early on Monday to late on Saturday I thought I'd get the job done now. But I can see it was a mistake. I'll come back tomorrow evening. Say around seven.'

'No, you will not. Not then and not ever.' Judy glared at Lennie. 'What did you tell him that for?' she raged as the driver returned to his van. 'Those are the clothes Aled James bought me, and I don't want them. I'd feel as though—'

'He was paying you off?' As a crowd of children were collecting around the door Lennie closed it.

'Exactly!' She looked at him. 'I'm sorry, I didn't mean to rant and rave at you. It's not your fault that Aled James and . . . that he sacked me—'

'And broke your heart. Just as you broke his.' Lennie sat on the stairs.

'I didn't break Aled James's heart,' she said angrily. 'He's getting married.'

'Who's the lucky woman?'

'Councillor Harvill's daughter – Moira.'

Lennie laughed. 'Councillor Harvill doesn't have a daughter but he does have a wife called Moira, she's forty years younger than him but they are legally married. I know because they recently celebrated their first anniversary at the club.'

'Then Aled's not marrying her.'

'I think her husband might have something to say about it if he did. Not to mention the law. Last I heard it was illegal to have two husbands alive at the same time.'

'Then why did Aled tell me that he was marrying her?'

'Because he wanted to make you angry enough to leave him and never come back.'

'Because he didn't want me hanging around him or his club,' she said bitterly.

'You couldn't be more wrong, Judy. I think letting you go was one of the hardest things Aled James has ever done. Not because you were a draw in the Ragtime, but because he loved – loves – you very much. But he's terrified that if he allows you to stay with him he won't be able to protect you.'

'I don't need protecting.'

'Aled believes that everyone who works for him needs protecting,' Lennie declared. 'He's even given me my very own toy soldier to walk me back and forth to the club. He might have won the battle but the turf war is far from over. And the more successful Aled is, the more enemies he will make – enemies who think they can pocket his profits if they get him out of the way.'

'Then . . .'

'I have to agree with Aled; in this case love isn't enough. You're better off working here and singing in David's pub. There might not be room to put your name in lights over the door but you can still audition in the New Theatre. And who knows,' he raised his eyebrows, 'they may put on *Peter Pan* again.'

'You think Aled loves me?' she whispered.

'Enough to let you go, Judy, and that's a lot. I don't think I could have done the same if I'd been in his shoes ... Judy, where are going?' Lennie shouted as she wrenched open the door and ran down the street.

'To find out if what you said is true.'

Lennie smiled as he stood on the doorstep. He knew lovesick when he saw it and Judy had been singularly miserable that morning. Not at all the chirpy girl he had come to know and love – more than a little – when they had played together in the New Theatre. But for all of his well-intentioned motives he wasn't sure that he'd done Judy any favours.

Ever since he'd heard a rumour via a waiter in the Windsor that Aled James had used and abandoned Judy King because of her West Indian blood, he'd felt that she deserved to know the truth. And, after watching Aled mope around the club ever since he had let Judy go, it hadn't been difficult to work out that his employer was head over heels besotted with Judy.

Aled James loved Judy, possibly even as much as Judy loved him. But, he also knew that Aled's fears for his employees' safety were very real. And neither he nor the rest of the staff of the Ragtime were imagining the people who occasionally followed them home from work in the early hours.

Micah walked up to the front door and dropped the suitcase he was carrying on to the step but he held on to his bag. He looked at Judy's back as she raced down Bute Street. 'Is Judy practising for the 'thirty-two Olympics in Los Angeles or has she just found out she's been given an audition for the West End and she's decided to run all the way to London?'

'Bit of both, I think. You going or coming?' Lennie asked.

'Coming in, if Edyth will see me.'

'Don't tell me that you two have been quarrelling as well.'

'As well? Who else . . . ?'

'It's a long story.' Lennie grinned.

'You can't quarrel with someone who doesn't speak to you.'

'I don't know Edyth that well but she doesn't strike me as the sulky sort,' Lennie observed.

'She isn't, I am.' Micah walked into the hall and closed the door behind him. He heard Harry and David talking upstairs. 'She has visitors?'

'A room full.'

'Is the kitchen in the bakery empty?'

'As far as I know,' Lennie answered.

'Do me a favour – ask Edyth to come down and see me, please.'

'I can but ask.' Lennie ran up the stairs as fast as his short fat legs would carry him.

Unsure of the reception Edyth would give him, Micah left his suitcase in the hall and carried his bag through to the kitchen. Hungry, he'd half hoped to find a pastie, pie or sausage roll, or at the very least a bread roll, but it was spotless, pristine and empty.

He sat on a chair, but he didn't have to wait long. Edyth opened the door so hard it bounced back on its hinges and hit her on the nose.

'Clumsy to the end.'

'If you've come to carp—'

'I came to see if you want a lodger.' He lifted his bag on to a chair. 'I've taken Helga's advice and given up my job in the mission. I went back to Gdansk and collected my papers from the hospital there. It took some wrangling but the Royal Infirmary has agreed that I can finish my doctor's training here in Wales. I won't get much in the way of pay for a year, and the most I can pay you is fifteen shillings a week.' He finally met her steady gaze. 'You did say that you have two spare rooms.'

'One, David's moved in. The builders are working on the pub he's bought and it won't be ready for at least a month.'

'I don't care if it's the smallest box-room.'

'The answer is no, Micah, you cannot have my spare room, I need it for guests. But,' her tawny eyes glinted with mischief, 'if you're prepared to share with me, that's different.'

'Only after we're married.'

'Can't we practise first?'

'That's my Edyth – shameless.'

'And very much in love,' she whispered before kissing him.

Judy reached the club as the van driver was ferrying all her clothes back into her dressing room. She pushed past him and went into the bar. Half a dozen brawny men were lounging around a table drinking pints of beer. Freddie was behind the counter, serving them.

'Boss is in his office,' he said when he saw her.

'Thank you,' she called before charging down the corridor. She thrust open the door. Aled was sitting behind his desk.

'Are you clearing my dressing room to make room for a new singer?' she demanded.

'What if I am?'

'I want to apply for the job.'

'I'm not auditioning previous applicants.'

'I never applied.'

'But I let you go, remember?'

'And I was fool enough to believe what you said. Do you still want a singer?' she repeated.

'I sent you the clothes—'

'And I sent them back.'

'They don't fit anyone else. All the singers I auditioned last week are twice your size.'

'All the more reason to take me back.'

'Just as a singer . . . '

'No.'

'Judy, I don't know how to live any way except the way I have done since I was a child – fighting the world and everyone in it for a living. After meeting Harry, Edyth, you, I know life can be different – but not for me. I'm so used to living on the borders of the law I make enemies on both sides. Gangsters, police, politicians—'

'You love me. Go on, deny it?' she dared.

'I may love you, but I couldn't protect you or David or Harry. When I think that my own brother nearly died for what I did . . . '

'But he didn't.' She sat in front of him on the desk and wrapped her arms around his neck. 'I love you.'

'I should send you away.'

'Even if you arranged to have me shanghaied and put on a slow boat to China I'd find my way back to you, my darling man.'

Freddie crept up to the open office door. He saw Aled and Judy locked in one another's arms and closed the door softly so as not to disturb them.

He was smiling when he returned to the bar. It was his first smile since the doctor had told him that Aiden was dead.